MIRAGE

MIRAGE

Web Shifter's Library #2

Julie E. Czerneda

DAW BOOKS, INC.

DONALD A. WOLLHEIM, FOUNDER

1745 Broadway, New York, NY 10019

ELIZABETH R. WOLLHEIM
SHEILA E. GILBERT
PUBLISHERS

www.dawbooks.com

First Printing, August 2020
1 2 3 4 5 6 7 8 9

To My Beloved Aunts and Uncles

I've a few. They've been important to me all my life, and remain so, which would be why families keep expanding in my stories, and I write aunts and uncles who sometimes have quirks, but always bring love. I'd like to introduce mine.

On my Mom's side, from oldest to youngest, though Mom was the baby: Ruth (we never met, but she was beautiful), Ginny (raised grapes and Great Danes) and her Dennis (gave excellent hugs), and Myrtle (we never met, but I've her symphonies.)

On my Poppa's side? The reason I grew up believing everyone spent summers in Winnipeg, having wonderful parties. From oldest to youngest, though my Dad was the eldest: Stan (worked in a zoo and my brother's namesake) and his wife Doris (ever beautiful), Joyce (braved ice storms for family) and her husband Sam (gentle and kind), Connie (we're not to have favorites, but she's everyone's) and her husband Bob (loving and strong), Douglas (dances and dares all—and lived in our basement), Hazel (our sparkle) and her husband Fred (worldly and wise), Gordon (travelled and created—and lived in our basement) and his wife Edith (made of grace), and last, but not least, Marlene (who couldn't stay).

Thank you, one and all, for enriching my life and connecting us one to the other. And for all my wonderful cousins. (I've a few of those too.) Family does matter.

Acknowledgments

Thanks for the warm welcome to the return of her Blueness in *Search Image*. I thought you'd be happy to see her, dear readers, but your reaction's been simply wonderful. And look. Here's more!

Thank you to my editor, Sheila E. Gilbert. Her keen eye was essential, as always. Amazing to think this wee dynamo of knowledge and heart celebrates her 50th year in publishing as this book is in your hands. (And I've been asking her "but do you *like* it?" for almost half that.)

So many authors, artists, and publishing folks owe their careers to you, Sheila. So very many readers have enjoyed the result. Congratulations, from the bottom of my heart. Here's to the years to come!

I'd like to thank Adam Auerbach for bringing my charcoal heads not only to life, but into a cover that captures the essence of this story. And to Matthew Stawicki, whose perfect rendering of Esen graces the spine. As she does me in the author photo by my talented partner, Roger Czerneda. See how much is in a cover?

My continued love and gratitude to all at DAW, including Betsy Wollheim, Peter Stampfel, Lindsay Ribar, Leah Spann, Katie Hoffman, and the imperturbable Joshua Starr. And to the talented team at Penguin Random House who cheers on each of my books with skill and delight: Alexis Nixon, Jessica Plummer, and welcome, Stephanie Felty.

Sara Megibow is my agent. Ta Da!! Whenever I say that, I feel like tossing glitter and cheering because Sara's also a gem. I learn from her. We celebrate—and hold our breath, crossing fingers—together. (And saw *Endgame* together. Yes, she's that cool.) That's how we look into the future too. It's amazing. This book will be out in time for Sara's first Canadian convention, Can*Con 2020 in Ottawa. Have her sign your copy—she's part of the reason you have it, after all. How fun is that?

My dear Kiwi friends. I'd planned and hoped to put this book in your hands at ConZealand, so imagine I have. Many of your names from *Search Image* reappear here, and I thank you for that trust. A few have expanded roles, and I hope you enjoy those: Malcolm Fletcher (Constable Malcom Lefebvre), Russell Kirkpatrick (Carwyn Sellkirk, Transport and Greetings), Sally McLennan and Norman Cates (Ally Orman, Response Room), and Henri and Steve Reed (Henri Steves, Assessment Counter and Esen friend). Roger and I will be back. In summer. We've promised.

There's an official Tuckerization: John C. Pershing II (Reeve Joncee Pershing) won the bid at the largest, most fun fan-run charity auction I've ever attended, at ConStellation in Lincoln, NB. I mention "the shirt" and will not explain. You'll have to go. Thank you to the concom and attendees for having me as your guest. I'd a wonderful time—and so did Sara. We had our first toast—and panels, and meals, and games—as an author/agent team, along with K.D. Edwards and Dan Allmon. Our thanks to Leslie Huerta of Francie & Finch Bookstore for hosting us! Great big hugs to Jodie Meyer and Patricia Scott. Marjolaire Schlake did such a brilliant detailed cosplay of Aryl Sarc from my Clan Chronicles I couldn't believe it was for me—no, really I didn't. Not till she finally sat beside me and told me. A humbled thank you!

When you've a book out in December, the party spills to the next year. It's a rule. *The Clan Chronicles: Tales from Plexis* was royally feted everywhere we—Roger as cover artist, me as editor, and so many of the authors—went, but I must point to the launch at Ad Astra 2019 as the ultimate. Our thanks and love to the concom, Bakka-Phoenix (Scott, Michelle, Becca!), Chris Szego (cookies!), and especially our authors who assembled, some from afar, to make this a once-in-a-lifetime affair. Thank you: Amanda Sun (Ontario, Canada), Don Montgomery (Ontario, Canada), Elizabeth Farley-Dawson (North Carolina,

USA), Ika Koeck (Selangor, Malaysia) who also helped me start my newsletter, Janet E. Chase (Nevada, USA), Karina Sumner-Smith (Ontario, Canada), Marie Bilodeau (Ontario, Canada), Mark Ladouceur (Ontario, Canada), Nathan Azinger (Washington, USA), Paul H. Baughman (Pennsylvania, USA), and Tanya Huff (Ontario, Canada and GOH). The rest were there in spirit!

My thanks to Brandon Crilly and Evan May for chatting tea and books with me (and Kevin Hearne) on their podcast *Broadcasts from the Wasteland.* And to Kingston's Limestone Expo and Ottawa Comic-con for hosting me.

I ushered in a new fantasy novel in August, *The Gossamer Mage,* and couldn't have done it without the support of bloggers and store staff and—oh, my—you readers. My deepest, most sincere gratitude. I'd list you here but haven't room for more than two. Our dear friend Anne Bishop who invited me to join her for two events. Gab and giggles! And Jeanné Giddens who discovered my work and made extraordinary videos to celebrate it. Thank you both!

In September, Roger and I were guests of FenCon, Dallas, TX, and can attest to the warmth of its hospitality (and climate) and joy of its fans. We'd a fabulous time and special thanks to William Ledbetter, Rhonda Eudaly, Avi DiGioia, Ellen Schlakman, Marianne Dyson, and Willie Siros, among others, for taking care of us. Hi, Kimm!

Can*Con 2019? With its impressive Science/Environment con on top of everything else? Cosmic Gods, people, if you keep upping your game, I'll need to give you your own page. Suffice to say you hosted the most glamorous and enjoyable Prix Aurora Awards I've ever attended, deservedly won yours for Best Fan Organizational (which I'd the honor to present, with an impeccable poker face so No One Guessed, to Marie Bilodeau and Derek Künsken), and the karaoke party? Nice.

Cheers, Bryan and Misty, and thank you, Misty, for introducing me to the expanding fusion of art and science that may well save the planet. Congratulations, Erin, because You Did It and we're so very proud. To all of my family, thank you for the laughs, tears as required, and cuddles.

Last and never least, thank you, Roger, for once more leaping into the breach and doing All The Things so I could write *Mirage.* Time to pop the cork, love!

CONTENTS

Makings

"SHUT the doors!"
 "We can't—"
"Get the nets!"

Pounding footsteps smother the words from their mouths. Alien feet don't appreciate the correct response to alarm is to seek sanctuary. Alien mouths don't know silence is safer.

Humans.

Every Sacrissee knows better. She does, though her ears ring from the deafening concussion that shook the world moments before, filling the air with dust and stink. She struggles to move— suddenly can move as lights go dark, taking with them the strange blanket that had held her flat.

Flat is *wrong*.

Staying here is *wrong*.

When her feet find the floor, she runs.

Nasal bulb rigid with distress, she cowers before the opening of what had been a wide doorway, hiding within piles of still settling debris, coated in dust.

OUT is dangerous, every Sacrissee knows.

But the *IN* behind her offers no safety, only distraught Humans and the too-big, too-bright room where she'd been before the flat and blanket. There'd been Sacrissee in the room with her, too many and all young and all *wrong.*

She isn't sure why she believes that, but it is true.

Too much here is *wrong,* starting with the blue Human symbols where her fur thins over her hand. OOLA-TB333401. She tries—*always tried, they all did*—to rub them off. Her skin has grown red and sore. *Leave it, Oola,* as Humans called her, putting their creams on her skin, unable to say her proper name with their mouths. *Easy, Oola. Lie down, Oola. You're doing well, Oola.*

"Make it quick."

A whisper from outside the once-door. Oola crouches lower, pulls in her tail lest it betray her. Are these more sensible Humans?

Her first impression is favorable. These keep to shadows, are like shadows in their black garb, but keep talking, which isn't sensible. "First corridor left, straight to the fourth door," says one. "That's secure storage."

"And locked. Be ready to blow it too. Carefully."

They hadn't been careful with this door.

One steps too near, flushing Oola into the open. She runs, dashing across the perilous *OUT* with its sunbaked stones. She isn't alone. Others run, too, this way and that, coated in dust and panting with distress. Some are younger, smaller. She pushes them out of her way.

Some are older, much larger. She dodges those, aims for the welcoming shadow cast by the aircar parked across the stone.

Is stopped by a warning "Ssssuppptt!" and tail slam, for the shadow is occupied.

There are three, large and mature enough to feel the rut and be angered by youth, and Oola freezes in place, as she should.

Tails subside at her courtesy. "Come with us, little one. We will take you to a good place. A new *IN.*"

Another: "We just got out ourselves—"

The third: "Would you leave her?"

When she hesitates, a hood is pulled back. The eyes regarding her kindly are yellow.

AND WRONG!

Oola leaps away before she thinks. Others collide with her. She collides with them. She leaps and spins, heart pounding. Moves ever forward, toward the gate. They all are, all but the *wrong* three, clinging to their shadow.

Through the gate is Rattisila, her beautiful city, with its comforting walls and arches, unlike this terrible, Human, place. Her *IN. Sanctuary.*

She is within the gate when a second explosion trembles the ground. She glances back. Smoke rises from the windowless building. They were not more careful. Giant words in Sacrissee and comspeak drop from their place over what had been the door, letters tilted and thus *wrong,* but she can read, and reads them as they fall.

"Molancor Sacriss."

1: Greenhouse Morning

WHEN the first snow stuck to the last leaves of fall, I'd found the effect charming and hauled Paul out to see. Multiple times. However, by this point of winter, snow in trees meant wet frozen lumps landing on my head if I wasn't careful or even if I was.

Oh, I liked snow, under the right circumstances. Thinking of those, I held out a paw as I walked, catching plump snowflakes. My useful *fingers* were covered in warm purple knit, courtesy of Ally Orman who loved a creative challenge. I'd received an embarrassment of such gifts from the staff of the Library, who thought there were two of me.

There were, as far as they were concerned. Esolesy Ki, who oversaw the Garden, cheerfully did vague non-important tasks and was the only Lishcyn on Botharis. My other identity here? Esen-alit-Quar the Lanivarian—also the sole representative of that species on this cheerfully backwater world, not that I'd planned it—and curator of the All Species' Library of Linguistics and Culture. *Which I had.*

With Paul Ragem, who was himself Human, born here, and my first, best friend.

I scuffed my feet along the path, wishing his home planet had more to offer in boots than rubbery sock things meant for sick bovines.

There were far more mes, of course, none of whom I'd shown our staff. I'd particularly not shown them the real me.

The real me? Esen-alit-Quar is my name, as Lanivarian is the form of my birth. Esen for short, Es between friends or in a hurry. My real nature—my species, if you will? Web-being.

Not an informative name, granted, unless you knew more about us, which very few did and if my web-kin, Skalet, had her way, no others would. On that, we'd come to an understanding.

I wouldn't tell anyone else, and Skalet had agreed, as if granting a great favor, that those who already knew of our existence—because of me—could continue to live. She'd even, in unguarded and rare moments, admitted Paul was an exceptional member of his species, which he was, despite being perilously curious.

Along with compassionate, brilliant, stubborn—

Our colleague Lionel Kearn, on the other hand, seemed to have earned Skalet's respect. Something I'd been trying in vain to accomplish the past 554 Commonwealth standard years of my life. I wasn't sure Skalet's improved regard was altogether safe for poor Lionel, but he continued to breathe, so there was that.

What were we? Descendants of Ersh, the first of our kind to leave our natal interstellar home and acquire intelligence. Ersh went from mindlessly gobbling the products of stars to develop an unfortunate taste for living mass, in particular that which could think and scream and pass along cultural nightmares to be a bother later.

After causing more than her share of mass extinctions, Ersh, no longer mindless, developed a conscience. More, she declared a purpose: to remember the accomplishments of those likely to become extinct.

To assist in this purpose, she made us, the members of her Web, each budded from her flesh. *Except for me, but no one expected me.* Among Ersh's rules for us? Respect what lived and thought and, above all, remain hidden from it.

A Web-being has perfect memory, including that of our molecular structure which we manipulate at will. It prevents aging tissues and dispenses with unpleasantries such as poison or disease-causing visitors, so we're essentially immortal. Ish. We share what we've experienced as individuals by biting chunks of flesh out of one another and assimilating the information stored therein.

Precisely balanced chunks, of course. We're conscious of our mass at all times and it wouldn't do to be greedy. Ersh, as Senior

Assimilator, taught us restraint while sorting our new memories through her own body first, deciding which to share. *Rarely the fun ones.*

As a bonus, we can become whatever living shape we, or another of our Web, have assimilated. For a while and with effort; otherwise there's an explosive, though local, release of accumulated energy. *I'm getting much better at that.*

Any living shape capable of thought, that is, because Ersh's personal evolution locked us into that requirement. *It's safer for all that way.*

Our ability is not only ideal for storing information about ephemeral species—for Ersh insisted we collect everything possible, from biology to poor habits—it's essential camouflage. Semi-immortal shapeshifting aliens who ate one another being awkward at best to explain, there was our bothersome lineage. Our kind, through Ersh, was responsible for consuming the life on entire planets, even if it had been ages past. Ersh had made sure I alone learned that troubling history.

There's a downside to being a Web-being, at least for me. When we cycle our flesh into that of another species? We remain ourselves. Who we are. Unique individuals of that species, down to the correct relative age.

Suffice to say my Human-self, Bess, elicits a distressing parental instinct in other Humans that's rarely helpful, a tendency to be dismissed that occasionally is, but, regardless, I avoid being one as much as possible.

Ersh avoided being Human too, unless for my education. As a Human, she was a terrifyingly ancient female missing most of an arm. Sacrificed, she'd remind me endlessly, to keep our existence secret from ephemerals.

A deeply disturbing example that hadn't stopped me rescuing and making friends with a curious Alien First Contact Specialist named Paul Ragem. *Ersh knew I'd some issues with impulse control.*

Ersh was gone, most of her, immured into the rock of her mountain on Picco's Moon. I'd some bits hidden away in a cryofreezer I really should assimilate and be done with, but as I'd already consumed several, her memories rising up to my shock and dismay at the worst times, the appeal was limited.

I'd thought I'd lost the rest of Ersh's Web. Lesy and Mixs to Death, an invading, non-sentient Web-being who gobbled them up, our own flesh the tastiest. Skalet when her favored form, the Humans called Kraal, had failed in their attack against Death. Ansky, my birth-mother, to her formssake at the time, the Articans.

If you see a theme about being careful what *you are, it's true.*

In the end, Paul and I found a way to stop Death. *Because no good deed goes without dire consequence*, as Ersh would say, Lionel Kearn and others pinned what Death had done to other species on me, the Esen Monster. To keep my secret safe, Paul didn't cut off an arm.

He did worse. He pretended to be dead for fifty years, severing himself from his family and friends, the future he'd thought to have. Now he was back, but the wound had yet to heal, if it ever could.

I paused, looked around to be sure no one was watching, then stuck out my tongue to catch a large, lazy snowflake. Unlikely to find anyone else in the Library Garden at this hour—or season, for that matter, most of the plants dormant or dead—but dignity mattered.

I tried for a second snowflake, only to miss. It came to rest on the tip of my nose. I stared cross-eyed down my snout until the flake melted, then licked off the drop.

There'd been snow the night Paul learned I wasn't safe, when I'd seen fear distort his dear face and known it was of me. I'd run from him then, not trusting him or the nascent friendship between us. Run straight to Ersh, as it happened, forced to share what I'd done.

Fortunately for Paul, I'd an ability only Ersh among the others possessed: I, too, could sort the memories in my flesh. What my kin tore away in their jaws to assimilate contained what had happened, but not my friendship with Paul. Later, I became even better at sharing only what I wished.

Unfortunately, with Ersh now so much rock, this ability meant I was, though Youngest and least, now Senior Assimilator for the Web of Esen.

As for my dignity, I wasn't worried about Paul, or Lionel, catching me licking snowflakes, though the former enjoyed throwing balls of snow for me to chase that occasionally connected. *Chasing was fine, but this me wasn't fond of being wet.*

No, since I'd learned Skalet too had faked her own death, recently coming back to life to be part of the tiny Web of Esen, I'd avoided any behavior likely to reinforce her disdain for my callow youth. *Such as snowflake licking.*

Frozen stems and branches rattled in the freshening breeze. The wind heralded a forecasted plummet in temperature, and as clumps of snow began to plop onto the path, I stopped dawdling. *Being on a secret errand.*

The Garden's greenhouse was my destination, as it was every morning. The building was private and mine, not that Web-beings needed or cared for possessions, but we could, I knew from experience, grow fond of inanimate things. My Lishcyn-self had a great fondness for silk as well as fudge. *Which wasn't a great combination of loves unless, like me, you could use a steadily increasing girth as an excuse for more shopping.*

As for the Garden? To be blunt, as a Web-being with a conscience and friends, I needed easy access to living mass. What was encompassed by "plants" was an excellent, didn't-take-it-personally, source to assimilate at need. My Lanivarian-self had assisted Ersh in her greenhouse, but it was my Lishcyn-self who'd come to love growing plants.

To indulge that love, I'd brought in hundreds of species from as many worlds, kept from venturing onto Botharis' own verdant landscape—*itself hardly free of invasives, but I'd promised*—by Skalet's Kraal bio-eliminator field overhead and underground. According to the Library's mission statement, our Garden was for the respite and comfort of visiting scholars. A bit of home, away from home.

It wasn't quite a lie.

The truth was no one had the time. Scholars arrived in a rush to learn if their offering of new information for our databases—*which included the one in my flesh, not that we mentioned that*—had been accepted. If yes, it was another rush to pose their question at one of the many species-specific inputs, conveniently located within their appropriate habitat zones. Receiving their answer—*which I'd verify against my flesh if necessary, not that we mentioned that either*—they'd have to hurry to catch the last train to the spaceport before their ship left.

Their haste was entirely our fault. The Library wasn't designed for overnight guests or even much in the way of a linger. We'd cheerfully expected Botharis to build a proper shipcity, or at least stations in orbit.

But no. Not yet. Admittedly there was a ramshackle village growing between the train station and the field—the reliable profit to be made from gullible aliens coupled with the onset of winter inspiring several local entrepreneurs to dig in and stay put, adding whatever they could carry to shore up walls and roof their marketplace tents—but only Constable Malcolm Lefebvre appeared to notice, being called on occasion for over-festive behavior or theft of what shouldn't be there in the first place.

Meanwhile Botharis, specifically the Hamlet of Hillsview Preservation Committee, was still processing how *we'd* got here, let alone the influx of the non-Human. Paul appeared close to losing even his exceptional patience with their fussing.

If a scholar's offering to the Library wasn't accepted—and there remained a thriving local industry in fake artifacts to up those odds—said scholar wanted to leave as quickly as possible.

Meaning no one bothered to find the Garden, let alone walk outside in it. Other than exobotany students, who only came in summer, and yes, there had been the solitary Anata who'd hidden in the shrubbery—consuming much of it—but Celiavliet Del had left. As far as I knew, and Paul regularly reminded me to check.

There'd been no more unusual pruning.

The Library Garden was, in other words, exactly as I'd hoped from the start: my very own, mostly private, microcosm of the wider universe. True, the organisms hadn't evolved together, having a host of differing adaptations and biologies dumped into the same environment to survive, thrive, or do neither.

I did coddle my fystia bush—what was left of it—with a heated blanket in winter, and there were other plants receiving extra treats. After all, the Leaping Forsber needed fresh poultry every few weeks and you couldn't expect a Nidlerose to bloom, ever, if it didn't burn once a year. Most received no more than the forests and fields surrounding the Library grounds.

It was a glorious muddle, full of smells, tastes, and textures to appeal to a wide variety of mes. On golden spring days, gleefully watching sprouts and buds, I was convinced something remarkable would come of it. In the bitter short days of our second winter, I doubted anything would, but a Web-being, even a young one, was nothing if not patient, and as Paul would point out, my plans typically had unanticipated results.

I chose to take that as a compliment.

Muddle or mess, glorious or doomed, the Garden did one thing marvelously well. It kept a secret. Housed one, in fact, for Lesy, like Skalet, had proved to be not-so-dead after all. She'd left smears of herself on her artwork as her version of a signature. Having created enough art to fill a shrine on Dokeci-Na, I'd been able to glean enough of her to, well, put her back together.

Sort of. New Lesy was, to be blunt, a work in progress, prone to hide in pots and unable, thus far, to cycle or communicate. Pretty much all she'd done to date was eat. Mostly me, with pre-sorted memories I hoped would restore her personality, but being what she was and not yet full-size, Lesy compulsively consumed whatever living mass was in reach.

She couldn't be trusted. *Most certainly not with friends.* Which would be why I'd agreed with Skalet to hide our web-kin in the greenhouse, and why I spent most of my time worrying how to tell Paul.

Unlike the Library, as modern as extruded slurry could be, or the wooden farmhouse that had housed four generations of Ragems, the greenhouse was a monument. Or had been. Duggs Pouncey, our now-permanent general contractor, had found its remains in a dump outside Grandine, the planetary capital. For centuries, the graceful metal arches and glass panes had sheltered imported plants beloved by the Humans who'd first settled this world. While I felt some empathy for their futile attempt to keep home handy, eventually seals leaked, local pests entered, and—frankly—modern Botharans didn't care, having beloved plants of their own.

Arriving at the greenhouse door, I stomped my inadequate boots on the mat to knock off the snow and knocked. Lesy had learned the vibration meant incoming mass. *Admittedly not the ideal association with a knock on a door,* which was why I'd taped a sign saying "DO NOT KNOCK" to this one. I'd fond hopes at some point she'd switch to associating me with the sound, instead of breakfast.

Nothing. I angled my ears, those sensitive organs sticking out through gaps in my hat, but detected none of the usual clatter-smash of a motivated Web-being near fragile objects.

The knit gloves might have muffled my knock. Stripping one off, I curled my fingers into a paw and used the knuckle pads to rap more firmly on the door.

Still nothing. Except the small drift of snow hanging over the door I'd failed to notice in time came loose to land on my neck, sending cold wet fingers through my formerly dry fur.

The night before had been the coldest yet. Lesy could have oozed into the compost, though if she had, there'd soon be no organisms left to generate heat inside.

Time to open the door and find out.

It didn't budge. Locked from the inside, that meant, surely beyond Lesy's present capabilities. She was good with pots; not so much walls, windows, or doors.

Most likely a shovel handle had fallen across the door, as had happened to me more than once.

I wasn't the one inside. I was outside, growing cold as well as damp, and didn't have time for this. Swallowing a peevish growl, I considered my options.

Option.

With a sigh, I stripped out of my warm clothes, doing what I could to keep the inner layers, and me again, dry. Shivers raised the fur along my back and limbs in an instinctive reaction to being naked in the snow, a reflex which served the ancestral form of a Lanivarian if not my modern civilized version, with its neatly shaved snout and thin coat.

In the glass of the door I could see the blurred result. A ball of skimpy fluff. A cold shivery one.

Enough of this . . . I released my hold on this form, the exothermic reaction melting a puddle where I'd stood. Web-form.

I was myself again, part of me thought, the part exulting in the restoration of full senses. Oh, I lost touch, hearing, sight, and couldn't smell—that favored pastime of my Lanivarian-self—but those were nothing to what I gained. As my true self, a teardrop of blue web-flesh, I drowned in rarer exquisite sensations: the complexities of chemistry around me as other life metabolized or decayed, as water shifted from crystal to gas and back; the dizzying spin of stars and atoms; the harmonies of electromagnetism and radiation. The planet beneath me throbbed with gravity, its paired moons beating in soft synchrony; all the while the enticing nearness of another's web-mass filled me.

Don't get caught, the rest and more sensible part of me knew.

I thinned, ready to squeeze myself between the bottom of the door and tiles, sparing a moment to feel rather clever I'd tilted the tiles myself to make an Esen-sized gap.

But there wasn't one.

New Lesy plugged it. Explaining why the door wouldn't open, if not why she was holding it closed with herself.

Ersh.

It wasn't to grab a nibble. Lesy wasn't moving, not even with the temptation of my tasty self in reach.

A self less than useful in this situation, so I oozed over to the bag I'd left with my clothes. In less time than Paul's heart took to beat once, I'd absorbed both bag and contents, assimilating the useful living mass of the duras leaves inside into more of me, shedding the rest as water, and cycled . . .

. . . getting dressed as quickly as my now-shaking paws allowed.

I went on all fours, at a careful out-of-range distance, and whispered, "Lesy, it's Esen." Which she should know, but I wasn't taking anything for granted. "Go to your pot." This being our most reliable communication after *Don't bite that!* Which didn't always work.

The condensed clot of blue under the door didn't budge.

"Stay there," I ordered, ever the optimist. There must be other ways into the greenhouse. *Maybe ways that wouldn't entail breaking any of Duggs' irreplaceable antique windows.*

Alas, the entire structure was made of glass except for the supporting metal bars. A broken pane of irreplaceable antique glass later, I made it inside. The breaking—and my scramble through pots and soil on the workbench below in order not to slide onto the floor—sounded as if the place was falling apart. It wasn't, having stood up to snow and storm as long there'd been people on this planet who'd let it be. Then again, it hadn't had to survive me.

Buildings could be repaired.

"Lesy. I'm here."

Warmer inside than out, except where the wind slipped through my entry point, bringing along thick flakes of snow. Warmer and moist, for I kept replenishing the greenery. Smaller Lesy had ignored those hanging overhead. Now, by the plant-free debris on the floor, slightly larger Lesy had found a way to reach them.

She'd found the mousels, though I trusted the Botharan Bats to evacuate to safety.

My web-kin splashed against the door in a wave of unmoving blue. By the dents in the door, she'd done so violently. By the way her edges blurred deep into the metal, she didn't plan to let go anytime soon.

Only one way to learn why.

For the second time, I shed the garments of my Lanivarian-self, and cycled.

Even as I released the command, *share* . . .

. . . I formed a mouth.

Elements

POLIT Evan Gooseberry, presently assigned to the Human Embassy on Dokeci-Na, stepped from the train onto the platform of the All Species' Library of Linguistics and Culture and felt another pang of guilt.

He could have called first. Should have. Surprising his friends had seemed a brilliant idea back in the office, when he'd opened the generous travel voucher from Great Gran and known beyond doubt the very last place he wanted to spend his vacation was home. Evan sighed, distracted by the thick plume leaving his lips as the moisture from his lungs froze. Not that he didn't love Great Gran and miss his relatives, most of them, but the voucher?

Was a trap. As the most eligible Gooseberry, the one destined to receive The Gooseberry Lore—the official record of their family name traceable back to fabled Earth, with annotations—Great Gran was bound and determined he begin producing more Gooseberrys as soon as possible, by any means available. A visit home, now, would involve her *helping.*

He wasn't ready. Didn't know if or when he would be and most certainly didn't want to be paraded in front of would-be partners, however handsome or accomplished. Or breathing through two nostrils, Great Gran hinting it might be time to adjust his standards.

Bringing Evan across space to Hixtar Station on a quite comfortable starliner with his own stateroom, to switch to a smaller, but clean transport ship with shared accommodation to land on Botharis, then what seemed the longest part of the journey, the train ride here.

Clouds chased one another across a ridiculously blue sky. Beneath was snow—actual frozen crystals of water—blanketing the hills beyond the low sweep of the Library. The building itself wore its layer like a white scarf elegantly draped over its curved roof.

Evan knew the place, though he'd only spent a couple of days— albeit intense, memorable ones—here before. The Library consisted of a single floor above ground, with two basements below, but the building was immense, extending outward in pleasingly organic lines, edged by cleared pathways and cradled by its Garden.

Granted, its construction was an elaboration of a Commonwealth Survey emergency survival shelter, cheap and sturdy, if completely foreign to Botharans who considered the Library an architectural marvel, but to Evan what it was, what it represented, was unique and priceless. A place where knowledge was exchanged to prevent ignorance of one another resulting in catastrophe.

Where he'd friends, good ones. The best people to vacation with— —*unless he'd come at a bad time.*

Having taken an eager step forward, Evan stopped in his tracks, blocking the stampede of scholars of myriad species exiting the train behind him. Hearing the chorus of outraged squeals, growls, and complaints from behind, he tried to get out of their way.

Too late. Hands, or their equivalent, seized him in various places, picked him up, and tossed him aside.

Evan landed upright, thigh-deep in the snow he'd admired. Flailing his arms, he lost his balance and sat, up to his elbows in the soft sticky white stuff. As for who, or what, had put him here?

He caught a fleeting glimpse of a trio of Human-sized beings as they surged ahead of the rest down the path through the waiting Library doors, black cloaks bulging at the back over what might be anatomy or something brought for Assessment. *Esen would handle them,* he assured himself. The Lanivarian had a rare gift for understanding other species.

Meanwhile, he was stuck in snow. *In snow!* His worries vanished. Laughing, the Human grabbed handfuls of it, tossing them in the air, because he was here, wasn't he? Legally, on paid leave this time, entitled to five full days with his friends.

Friends who'd understand why the sight and feel of *snow* was remarkable and well worth enjoying. How he'd missed this experience in his thirty-odd years of life was beyond him. Maybe he could bottle some, to take back and show Trili, his closest friend at the embassy.

Better yet, ship a container to Great Gran Gooseberry—

"Are you done?"

The deep lovely—*familiar*—voice spoke as Evan threw another handful into the air. With a slight motion, the Kraal turned so the glob missed her immaculate uniform. It didn't, he winced, miss the exo-suit of a late passerby, but the being inside didn't appear to notice, navigating the path as if solid ground were a novelty.

"Isn't it wonderful?" Evan blurted.

Skalet—Human of the Kraal persuasion, head of security for the Library, and without doubt the most dangerous individual he'd ever met—gazed down at him, lean features inscrutable. A distort-hood veil blurred her affiliation tattoos, a touch of mystery atop what was menace.

Others might quail under that regard. Evan grinned and patted the snow to either side. "My first."

Brows rose. "I see. And are you aware, Evan Gooseberry, of the risks? Should this first and wonderful snow melt, soaking your garments, you could freeze to death." Offhandedly. "Though you might just lose your toes."

His backside had grown numb, come to think of it. Evan reached out a gloved hand.

She gripped it in her bare one; an effortless tug brought him staggering out of the pile onto the path. "Thank you," he began, hurriedly dusting off the snow, though none appeared to have melted and his toes felt normal in their new boots.

Evan straightened. They were alone on the path, the train silent and empty, its doors still agape. Those into the Library closed behind the straggler, presumably to keep the warmth inside, and he would have headed there at once, but something warned him against it.

"Is there a problem?" he asked, very quietly, for there had been, and danger, when he'd last been here. After their time facing it together, Skalet might consider him an ally.

Or not, given last time he'd surprised her—and himself—with the arrival of a Survey ship and armed troop under his command.

More surprises, Evan told himself, *could be a risk too.* "I meant no harm," he said. "I thought it'd be—fun if Paul and Es and Esolesy didn't know I was coming—" He blinked. "But you did. How?"

The corners of her lips deepened. "The local post office isn't accustomed to receiving sealed diplomatic luggage."

Not brilliant at all. Suddenly his toes tingled and hurt. Much as he feared their loss, Evan couldn't move. "Did you tell them it was me? Of course you did," he went on to himself, unable to stop. "Why wouldn't you? It was a stupid idea. I apologize for causing trouble."

"On the contrary." Now a smile, if one with disconcerting *appetite*. "I'd never interfere in a surprise for Esen-alit-Quar. As for Esolesy Ki? She's gone until this is over." Her gesture dismissed not only the glorious snow but winter itself. "Her nerves can't take the long nights. Not that it matters to you." With cruel perception.

Shamed, Evan couldn't protest. Skalet was right. He did his best not to have favorites, and the Lishcyn was a most pleasant individual, with many exceptional qualities, and he was fond of her.

She just wasn't Esen, who was braver, more charming. Even playful.

Not done embarrassing him, the Kraal nodded toward the Library. "Paul's in his office. You won't surprise him." Said with respect.

An emotion Evan shared, along with a confounding array of others. Paul Ragem was—he wasn't—they weren't—

His stomach lurched, already upset by the challenges of unpredictable travel and company—though there'd been only one moment of pure unadulterated *FEAR* when Evan opened the accommodation door on what appeared a *SPIDER* but was really an Oieta adjusting the tubes on her exo-suit, and he'd recovered well. He was doing better than well, really—hadn't brought his auto-therapist, only the monitor—

Three Urgians burst out of the Library, overts waving in disappointed fury, running this way.

SNAKES!

—but being startled while already upset shattered any preparation or mantra.

SNAKES!!! Helpless, Evan hyperventilated, gorge rising in his throat, every limb shaking, and he couldn't—

Skalet moved to block his sight. Leaned into the clouds of his gasping breath, eyes glittering. "So. This is how it bites." As if satisfying a curiosity.

As if cataloguing a weakness. One he couldn't afford, not with her, and Evan struggled to calm himself. *Tentacles. They were only tentacles. Harmless—*"It's n-nothing," he managed. "I-I'm fine."

"You've failed." Judgment rendered, Skalet stepped away, voice distant as the hills. "Get back on the train."

"No." Anger steadied him. "I don't run from my fear."

A hairless brow lifted in consideration.

He waited, eyes watering. Cold numbed his feet and fingertips, as well as his nose.

At last, "Stay, then."

He sagged with relief.

"But know this, Evan Gooseberry," Skalet told him. "There's more to fear here than you could possibly imagine." A cold smile. "You may wish you'd run."

2: Greenhouse Morning;
Library Morning

*S*KALET.

　　She'd left Lesy to me, or so I'd believed. Whether impatient with our web-kin's progress—likely—or disappointed in mine—doubtless—for whatever reason had crept into her bald head our web-kin had taken it upon herself to offer Lesy an irresistible bite.

With any luck, she'd taken a bite of her own and assimilated New Lesy's memories, which to this point consisted mainly of pots.

　　Maybe there'd be a medley of my memories of Old Lesy, too, but I'd yet to taste any sign those had taken hold. No, it'd be mostly pots.

　　Skalet couldn't sort her memories beyond the dictates of biology: the oldest tended to huddle deeper as if ashamed of themselves, while the newest and most recent clung to the outside, like the skin of an onion.

　　Hence that bite of Skalet meant New Lesy was assimilating what I hadn't planned her to know until she was herself again. *If then.* How we'd detected her web-flesh signature on Evan's prized statue of Ersh as the Dokecian leader, Teganersha-ki; how we'd schemed to go to Dokeci and destroy what we'd thought dangerous scraps; how I'd collected those instead—ignominiously dumped in a cryosac.

　　How I'd brought them here, allowing them to merge into one too-small, fragile Web-being.

　　Skalet's sharing would have provided the layout of the Library and our house, adding escape risk to all the rest. Then there were her latest murders and—oh, yes—her brazen theft of Survey technology for her Kraal affiliates.

Ersh. I'd had to nip Lesy to confirm all of this. In return, I fed her what I hoped would help. I tempered the events—Skalet's skewed perspective on them—with what I'd experienced. Given Lesy the why of things. The who. Shared, though it was hard, the glowing warmth of the symbiont, Pearl, who'd become part of me.

Because it was too late for partial truths or comfort, I'd shared next how I'd had to cycle, ending Pearl's existence. To save the Mareepavlovax. To save Paul Ragem, who wouldn't leave without me.

After our sharing, Lesy had flowed into a pot she'd outgrown, tipping it over as she squeezed as much of herself as possible inside. Seeking what comfort she could.

I understood why Skalet hadn't been able to wait. She wanted our Web to grow, to be more than the two of us. Though she wouldn't admit it to herself, what Skalet wanted most was Lesy back as she'd known her. Their personalities had been as different as any two of us had been, but as Lesy was the very first budded from Ersh?

Skalet craved an Elder. More than that, she craved another Webbeing created as she'd been, formed by the battle of flesh against flesh: what goes fighting for more, what stays grabbing what it can. Becoming separate, yet always part. Moons orbiting the world of Ersh.

Nothing like me.

Understanding didn't mean I wasn't furious. Poor Lesy. She'd blocked the door to keep us out, to protect herself. Assimilation was painful. Demanding. Confusing—that above all. To fit a sudden flood of memories that weren't hers around the careful dribbles I'd fed her since she'd arrived. Around what, if any, she'd kept of her own.

Whatever the sum, would it restore the Lesy we'd known? Loved?

I could hear Ersh now.

Foolish, Esen. You can't bring back the dead.

Lacking sufficient mass to return to my Lanivarian-self, I left my clothes and boots in the greenhouse with Lesy, flowing out the gap under the door. The window I'd broken would need to be covered somehow. Under the circumstances, a work order for maintenance posed undue risk.

Nor could I ask Paul. *He'd have excellent advice, but as it would come with that fond, if exasperated, look and probably a scolding?*

No. Best to approach the subject of the greenhouse and its occupant after I'd resolved matters. And made his favorite sandwich. Maybe Auntie Ruth's Macaroni—

I flowed across the snow to a dormant poplar. Dormant wasn't dead, a useful distinction given my need for mass.

I entered the pores of the tree, sending thin tendrils of me within its woody channels, going down into the roots. Risky, spreading myself through non-sapient mass. Even as I changed tree-mass into more of me, my thoughts grew sluggish, muted, tuned to long seasons and the unending reach for light.

There. Instinct knew when I'd enough and must pull free. I cycled . . . . . . blissfully warm. Larger.

And stuck. I bent at a central segment to confirm that yes, my posterior was underground. No problem for this powerful, elegant form. With a shake and tug, I freed myself, scattering remnants of tree.

Few sentient species inhabited frigid environments. Almost none embraced the cold with the carefree joy of the ShimShree, and I couldn't resist a moment of sliding across the snow, my many flattened legs like oars, my smooth underplates my personal sled.

I stopped when I realized I was carving a trail like some mythic giant serpent throughout the Garden.

Maybe it would snow tonight.

On such uncontrollable events did life revolve, at times. At least now I could fix the windowpane.

Reaching the greenhouse—and ignoring the *NOT ICE WRONG!!!* response of the senses of this form to glass—I lifted my anterior portion, aimed my rostrum at the broken window, and spewed. The act of spewing being remarkably enjoyable, I not only filled the empty pane, I continued to either side until I'd left a beautiful floweret of, well, spew.

Which would harden at this temperature into a clear tough substance. Had I wanted to spend more time as a ShimShree, I could have spewed myself a lovely little home, somewhere with a view. Perhaps up in another tree or on the roof—

Before this form gleefully led me further astray, possibly for the entire winter, I cycled . . .

. . . to stand, shivering and fluffed, but proud.

Careful not to startle Lesy—and risk her still-growing appetite—I slipped into the greenhouse to retrieve my clothes. She'd left her pot, but the lid to the compost had fallen to the floor, implying she'd recovered sufficiently to hunt fungi.

Relieved, I dressed and let myself out.

The day's first train having arrived, it was time to head to the office.

The All Species' Library of Linguistics and Culture consisted of facilities for them and those for us. *Us* being those working here. *Them* being everyone else, though occasionally that seemed to blur.

For them, Paul and I had designed—with me as eager test subject—areas suited to as wide a variety of life-forms as possible. Decorative and practical changes in flooring helped guide our visitors to the habitat zone most ideal for their use. Though occasionally that seemed to blur as well, given the morbid curiosity of those inclined to seek information about a different species in the first place. There were warning signs and staff trained to intercept thrill seekers, but every so often misadventures happened. The worst, to date, was the Heezle who'd lustfully followed an Iftsen into that being's caustic atmosphere, getting second-degree burns and a stern talking to about interspecies' boundaries. Boundaries of more concern to non-Iftsen, if it came to it.

For us, there were discreet accesses into the various zones, in case of besotted Heezles and so forth.

For them, there was the Lobby with its tall windows and convenient racks for outerwear and boots. A convenience for me as well, there being a wealth of biological material left on such articles, simply waiting to be assimilated and remembered.

One must keep up, as Ersh would say.

For us, there was the counter where "gemmies," as the artifacts were called in the Hillsview pubs, were assessed. While we'd thought asking for new information for the Library in return for a question would keep

updating the files on slang, materials, and cultural shifts, what we received all too often was stuff.

Henri and her helpers kept a tally. "Stuff" fit our criteria for "new
information" forty percent of the time.

Sixty percent, therefore, did not.

At first we'd insisted, politely, that visitors take their rejected offerings away with them. It soon became apparent this was wishful thinking on our part. Oh, an Ervickian would offer to consume whatever
they'd brought, but then they'd regurgitate it when no one was looking,
making matters gooey. Those who'd brought actual treasures typically
clung to them, though they were the worst about complaining our staff
didn't know a priceless artifact from a ration wrapper.

The rest? Who were the most?

Left their offerings behind. A trickle landed on the counter of The
Anytime Chow Inc. Food Dispenser. Luckily for interspecies' relations, its surly operator, Lambo Reomattatii, had come to the somewhat
startling conclusion the items were gratuities. Even more puzzling, the
Carasian broke each apart, zealously hoarding the remnants until deciding to dispose of them all to start again.

No one, not even Paul, was inclined to question the personal habits
of a giant shelled being with a temper shorter than a mousel's eyelash.
A being, moreover, who'd become an indiscriminate carnivore, once
"he" became "she" in another molt or two.

Not a concern yet shared with the staff. Nor, more importantly, with
the Hamlet of Hillsview Preservation Committee, its members convinced we'd pulled a trick on them somehow because surely they'd
never agreed to this many aliens traipsing through their beloved countryside on a daily basis.

They had, we'd documents filed at every level of Botharan bureaucracy to prove it, and none of our visitors traipsed, but—as Paul assured
me when I snarled—none of that mattered. They'd seen who and what
came down the starship ramps.

Frankly, the first Heezle might have done it.

Those visitors with manners, or who read the signs, used the recycle
canisters by the main doors. The rest were more, shall we say, creative.
Or vindictive. After a few months, the Hamlet of Hillsview Preservation Committee met on this particular issue, producing with laudable

unanimity a directive to the Library to retrieve and deal with the litter, complete with a map attached to indicate where offworlders dumped their trash.

We couldn't keep all of it. The forty percent we accepted as new information was filling the first basement level and would soon encroach on the second since it turned out successful visitors to the Library wouldn't take back what they'd carried here either.

I'd amended the brochure given on Hixtar Station to any who planned to come to the Library. It now stated, in warning colors appropriate to the widest selection of prospective visitors, that any object brought to Botharis must leave the planet with the individual who'd brought it.

Paul had laughed at me, then arranged for a disposal company.

Them. Us. In reality, the Library was for everyone, our small effort to protect the known universe from potentially deadly ignorance. *Conflict vanished*, according to Ersh—and she would know, having been around when humanity stepped off its home planet—*when both sides demonstrated mutual respect and decent manners*.

The tricky part?

Ensuring both sides knew what those were.

We were ready. While we didn't advertise our underlying purpose was to avert disastrous misunderstandings, the Library was designed to alert Paul and me of any questions implying the possibility. Thus far, only one had. Evan Gooseberry's.

Together, we'd stopped the Dokeci from exterminating the last of a species by mistake. Not a bad "spot of work," as a Botharan would say. *Now.* A generation ago they'd have said "spot a'sweat" going to prove the Library earned its keep even for Paul.

Who, yes, didn't use slang, being a linguist and well aware of its pitfalls, but Web-beings had a different perspective on vernacular. Ersh had taught us such fleeting terms used correctly—in species-specific manner of course—would convince those around us we belonged more than any recitation of facts. *The opposite being true, we knew better than to guess.*

I entered the Library for this day's spot of work using the nearest gate from the Garden. It wasn't a pretty gate, being a field portal fitted with biosensors, but in winter I appreciated how the grate in the floor whisked away any deplorable melting snow. I was somewhat disheveled and damp, but on time. For some "on time" might be in place and ready to help Henri at the Assessment Counter, or Ally Orman in the Response Room; for me, since Lesy, it had evolved more into "Esen's said hello to someone in the building, so she *is* here, but no one knows where, exactly."

Skalet would. We'd *negotiated*—there'd been raised voices and drool—which of the snoops she'd hidden in every nook and cranny during the Library's construction must be deactivated. Paul remained unconvinced we'd any privacy.

Fortunately, my web-kin considered it beneath her to inform mere ephemerals where I was.

At the moment, damp and disheveled me was in the Chow for a bracing hot drink before being "on time." Once Lambo cooperated.

Soon didn't appear likely. The back of a shiny black carapace remained presented to me, marred by permanently embedded footprints. Evan Gooseberry's, as it happened, not that any of us had the nerve to tell the Carasian his last molt hadn't been perfect.

"I know you can do it. You made Esolesy hot fudge tea."

"You stink."

My damp fur might have a slight musty tang. "Once I've the drink, I'll leave and take the stink with me."

"No." A stalked eye appeared over the carapace to glower at me. "You are not Esolesy."

I kept my ears lifted in a pleasant expression. Though sorely tempted to remind the creature I was in charge here, along with Paul, pulling rank wouldn't budge Lambo. "She told me you made the very best she'd ever had."

If the only. While my Lishcyn-self found fudge irresistible however it was consumed, Lambo's version of fudge tea was a first.

A second eyestalk joined the first. "Esolesy has good taste. When she's back, you can try hers." A third. "She is coming back, isn't she?"

Lambo was rude to everyone—except Paul—so it was possible I'd missed the development of a fondness for my otherself.

More likely this Carasian didn't like change. "She'll return in spring." Once the ground thawed sufficiently for planting to resume and, more importantly, the sun came back. While the Library Garden was my Lishcyn-self's particular delight, the lengthening dark of each winter night—especially after facing the Great Dark of the Mareepav-lovax Harvester—invoked a primal terror.

It had been Paul who'd urged me, being kindness itself, to avoid the form for the rest of this winter. I'd agreed for his sake, my friend having to walk beside my quivering self with a large lantern, when he could get me to leave the house at all.

Lionel had come up with the where and how. Esolesy Ki, staff and friends waving farewell, left Botharis on the *Largas Pride*, to do some offsite work for the Library. Rudy Lefebvre, ship's captain, Paul's cousin, and one of the few to know exactly what I was, arranged for "Esolesy" to be seen boarding his ship, after a very pleasant going away party at the Library which I attended.

The figure going up the ramp hadn't been me, of course, but Rudy, swaddled in blankets. I planned to have words with him later about the quantity of blankets, let alone the clumsy gait he'd affected.

"Lambo. Please. I've been outside and I'm chilled. I'll take any hot beverage you'll make for me."

The Carasian rattled around to face me, great claws down, handling claws up. In one was a cup full of steaming liquid. The clever scoundrel had known what I'd order the instant I walked into the Chow. "Here."

I took the cup. "Thank you." *At last.* But—it wasn't fudge tea. It couldn't be.

It was *green!*

I looked up in dismay. "What's this?"

"Your hot beverage," with an unsettlingly coy tilt to every eyestalk.

"You can't poison me before I've started work," I objected, refusing to be intimidated. "Paul won't be happy."

A claw snapped. "Fudge."

I curled a disdainful lip and lifted the cup. "This isn't fudge."

"Then you aren't being poisoned, are you."

Oh.

I'd possibly spent too much time as a Lishcyn. I looked down at the cup again and lapped up a little of the froth with my long tongue, which wasn't done by proper modern Lanivarians. Being the only one around had its advantages.

Mint. Creamy, hot, mint. While my preference would have been to roll in it, which was in fact proper behavior if done with friends, this would definitely do. I took a good swallow, enjoying the warmth filling my insides.

"My thanks," I said, this time sincerely.

Lambo's head carapace tilted from side to side. A dismissive shrug.

About to leave, I hesitated. The big Carasian wasn't our grudgingly helpful food dispenser operator. Well, he was, but the role had started as Lambo's disguise to gain access to the Library and become permanent. Since, we'd learned the Carasian was a drive engineer, an exceptionally gifted one, educated at the famed university on Senecort XX with practical experience at the great Dresnet Shipyards, doubtless with his choice of research postings. *Until he became she and ate her fellows.* It tended to limit opportunities.

Instead, Lambo had followed rumors of a revolutionary new star drive linked to Paul's mother, Veya Ragem; they'd brought him here.

Where Veya wasn't. Before learning her son still lived, Veya had died in space. We'd believed by accident. *Much,* I reminded myself grimly, *of what we'd believed had been a lie.*

"Any new leads?" I waggled my ears. "On the *other* project."

I'd thought the question safely vague, but Lambo reared up in alarm, newly sharp clawtips snapping a little too close to my snout for comfort. I took a step back, protecting my cup. "If you don't want to talk—"

"To you?" His voice dropped to a whisper like rumble. "Are you Lionel, the authorized individual? Is he here to vouch for you?"

This was ridiculous. *No, this was more of Skalet's meddling.* She'd brought Lionel into the mix without my consent or knowledge, and had I known, I'd never have agreed. Explaining why she hadn't asked me first. *Usually my tactic.* I narrowed my eyes at Lambo. "I—"

A bellow cut off anything I could say: "GET OUT!"

I retreated to the hall with my cup of nonpoisonous mint, exchanging nods of camaraderie with those passing by. *Who hadn't Lambo shouted out of the Chow?*

That said, now I really wanted to know the status of their search for answers. Especially as I'd engaged Skalet in it without Paul's knowledge. *It was that, or watch her find out on her own and berate me for keeping dangerous secrets.*

For this was dangerous. Veya had been the navigator on a secret Survey ship, the *Sidereal Pathfinder*. The ship had been testing either Lambo's star drive and/or a breakthrough navigation system when something had gone wrong. *Pathfinder* had been abandoned by all hands. Veya had been accused of stealing its secrets and driven out of Survey. No one alive knew the truth, for the ship herself was lost.

Until an image resurfaced of a derelict, adrift in a far reach of space. An image I hadn't shown Paul. He'd barely begun recovering the family he'd lost. His birth-father, Stefan, was here now, on Botharis. He'd reconciled with his beloved Uncle Sam and several of his extended family. Including a remarkable number of great-aunts.

Most wonderful of all, Stefan had brought Paul a message left for him by his mother. *"What we believed is lost simply waits for better eyes to find it."* Veya hadn't believed her son was dead for an instant. She'd hidden a special toy of his where she'd known he'd find it, a message through time letting him know she'd understood. That she'd hoped they'd be together again.

For a short-lived species, Humans had such abundant hope.

Had I known before setting Skalet loose, I'd have destroyed the image of the *Sidereal Pathfinder* and buried the mystery in Veya's past. Paul Ragem, my first and dearest friend, was happy. Happier than I'd ever seen him.

It wasn't a good feeling, to hold a secret that might change that.

Suddenly, I lifted my snout to sniff what changed my mood for the better. Much better. A delightful, friendly scent.

Evan Gooseberry.

Fresh Evan Gooseberry!

Makings

LOCKS are serious business in Rattisila, as they are across Sacriss VII, and throughout the worlds of Sacriss System.

Locks and hinges. Bars, too, and anything to keep the *OUT* where it can be observed with caution and care, where reasoned judgment can consider consequences. For what isn't of the *IN* poses the greatest danger to the whole. So says instinct. So says law.

Thus it is after caution, care, and gravely reasoned judgment the breeding group *IN* this humble Sacrissee home agree the one lingering *OUT* for the past three solars, snuffling at doors and vents, is indeed their offspring, she who had been taken for treatment.

Agree joyfully that this lock could open, this bar lift, and this door ease open sufficient to permit the half-grown pup to enter, then close, lock snapping shut just shy of her tail. The bar goes down behind the pup's supine, panting form as those already *IN* retreat to individual secure cubbies, there to observe from safety before offering more.

The offspring should be grateful. Should remain prone and submissive until the will of those already *IN* is revealed, understanding acceptance is not to be done in haste. Any Sacrissee would.

This one is different. This one rises to stare into peepholes meant to protect those *IN.*

And when those *IN* see her *wrong* yellow eyes, they agree, in sorrow, what they must do. What Sacrissee had always done.

Cull the different.

[⟨•⟨|||⟩•⟩]

Oola is thrust *OUT,* locks and bars thumping in place behind her.

She staggers away, across the cobblestones. Stops to stare at the blood streaked blue over her hands and throat. Knows it's *wrong* to fight the will of the *IN.*

As she'd fought. There are those in pain behind the locks and bars. The authorities will be called.

There is one dead. The authorities will hunt her.

She stands, *OUT* and desperately alone. Unfair. Unjust. She belongs *IN!* She is not *WRONG,* to be culled.

Her nasal bulb swells, ready to voice her agony. But when she does, as she does, what comes from her isn't an anguished, eloquent "Ssssuppptt!"

What comes is a deep, shuddering *HOWL!*

Oola cringes. The sound is *wrong.*

Witnesses retreat and close their peepholes, the tiny pops as each are locked like rain hitting sand.

All abandon her. Her kin. Their neighbors. All. How could *IN—* the most basic right—be forbidden?

Defiantly, Oola *howls* again. She whips her tail, leaving the scar of her outrage on the wall of what had been home. *HOWLS!*

A distant echo. Another *HOWL.*

She leaps from shadow to shadow, to find what answers her grief.

3: Lobby Morning

THE Lobby was jammed with incoming scholars. We'd started off calling them clients, and not everyone who sought answers at the All Species' Library of Linguistics and Culture was an academic, but the new name, unlike the old, hadn't offended anyone yet and pleased the staff. With the exception of Lionel who—in what he fondly believed a secret but even maintenance knew—considered the seething mass to be noble pilgrims after knowledge. *He'd a sentimental streak.*

I kept to the wall as I tracked the scent of freshly arrived Evan, in case there were clusters of Rands hidden in the crowd. Ersh's exhortation *Trust me, one mind is sufficient, Youngest* had made the younger me eager to give the colonial form a try. How bad could it be?

Having found out for myself, her warning made perfect sense.

I'd have dropped to all fours to add speed, but I was now among those who'd find that shocking in a civilized being. Which was prejudice of a sort because there *were* civilized beings with four on the floor, but being curator, I'd an image to uphold and excellent bipedal posture.

Besides, I didn't want to lose the scent.

I slowed further, catching another scent woven into Evan's, and managed not to growl. *Skalet.* My having called her—*for convenience only, one time*—our head of security? She'd given herself the job. Not that she was in charge of anyone but herself. Our need was for Botharans—for we hired from the Hamlet of Hillsview—willing and able to assist an onslaught of overly-focused aliens to find their way. *Usually to the nearest appropriate accommodation, there being none on the train.* Our greet staff enlarged over the winter as farmers were happy to find secondary employment; we were happy to have anyone accustomed to large oblivious mammals and quarrelsome little birds.

On his previous visit, Skalet had developed an *interest* in Evan Gooseberry which wasn't safe or healthy for the young, naive Human. *If she'd taken it on herself to be his escort?*

My low growl startled the Ervickian nearest me into regurgitating its breakfast. Before anyone from the Library noticed, meaning I'd be the one tasked with the cleanup, I slipped behind a trio of cloaked figures.

Turning my head as I was drawn to a faint *Evan* scent here, on a cloak, as well as a stronger trace going toward the admin corridor, doubtless to Paul's office.

I paused to lick my nostrils then tested the air with more care.

Aha! Beneath the *Evan* and the clouds of scents from those around us—including the rank contents of the Ervickian's stomach—was what only this me could have detected.

Something else. *Something impossible.*

We'd a new species in the Library, one known never, ever to leave its home system. Not in any Human record, nor, more impressively, in Ersh memory.

Yet here they were. Disguised by thick heavy cloaks, but not hidden from my nose.

Sacrissee.

My heart pounded and had I not cycled recently, thanks to Lesy, I might have had trouble holding this form. Sacrissee, here? Having been one, I knew the power of its protective instincts: to remain in the family group, to avoid—or rebuff—strangers, above all, to stay *IN* safe territory. The wonder, according to Ersh, wasn't that the Sacrissee had evolved from cautious solitary herbivores into an intelligent, technological species.

It was how much of their ancestral nature they'd retained. The thorn bush walls they'd thrown up around their homes and fields, opened only for the rut or to rebuff would-be trespassers with their whiplike tails, were today cities constructed as a maze of thickened walls, pierced with elaborate peepholes for the shy creatures to survey their surroundings from safety before venturing *out*. Arches within the walls connected buildings to roadways, each opening aligned to prevent line of sight between any two dwellings.

Openings streaked with oily fluid, for Sacrissee retained the urge to scent mark their territory and possessed convenient glands beneath their forearms to do just that. Non-Sacrissee learned to carry solvent.

An implausible society to embrace space flight, but the Sacrissee had, viewing the light of their star as celestial walls and thus a comfort. *Proving intelligence could justify almost anything.* They spread throughout their solar system to settle all fifteen habitable worlds, doing their best to make each, other than topography, a reassuring copy of their biological home, Sacriss VII.

When the Commonwealth arrived, the Sacrissee had, it was re-ported, peeked at them through their holes for over two planet months before allowing themselves to be seen. It had taken another month and a half before they'd permitted the first contact team to exit their ship.

Now each world in the Sacriss System boasted at least one shipcity, with its associated local Port City and All Sapients' District. Trade and commerce were things the Sacrissee valued, as well as the sharing of knowledge. Lionel Kearn spoke highly of his colleagues there.

None of whom would have gone outside their group nor left the light of their home star.

As these had done. *Why?* My temperature soared, and I panted to dump heat as I followed them. They moved in a straight line for the Assessment Counter and appeared not to notice those around them. I knew better. There were no streetlights in a Sacrissee city. These were beings who emerged at dusk or later, when they could flit from shadow to shadow, hiding in archways unless choosing to be seen. Moreover, these would be acutely, painfully aware of being surrounded by strang-ers, defined as any *out* of their kin group.

I eyed the lumps protruding from the backs of their cloaks. Tails, tucked under the fabric—long thin tails, reinforced with bone at their tips. Lashing out was a skill; scoring walls a means to leave a firm statement. Let alone what that tail could do to flesh, if a Sacrissee were truly frightened.

Not in our Lobby, I vowed to myself.

I tensed when a suit-encased Oieta cut across the path of the Sacrissee. The Soft Companion, a Human, tugged her vulnerable charge out of the way. Just as well; my current-self, however civil, well-dressed, and upright? A fanged predator.

Not the me to comfort our visitors.

Overall, Humans got along best with Sacrissee, patient with their idiosyncrasies and attracted by their fur and large gentle-seeming eyes. Plus I'd noticed Humans tended to react protectively to whatever scampered into holes when disturbed. *A species' flaw.* I could list thousands of life-forms who'd turn teeth, venom, or other personal weaponry on whomever followed them into their burrows, something I told my Human friends as often as they'd let me.

Best I leave the Sacrissee to a Human. I let a few beings get between us but kept our unusual visitors in sight. Easy enough. They were heading for the Assessment Counter.

The queue was shorter than usual, meaning most of those off the first train hadn't brought objects and thus could go directly to one of the Library's many interactive stations. The process there was similar: before asking a question, a new item of information must be offered and accepted. To no one's surprise, the Hamlet of Hillsview Preservation Committee didn't care to know what aliens did *inside* the Library.

Perhaps it was time to offer a tour.

After I'd discovered why the Sacrissee were here.

I caught Skalet-scent again, meaning she'd been prowling around the Lobby. As for her ill-thought visit to the greenhouse? *A conversation for later and alone.* She'd be of help here if I could convince her to cycle into Sacrissee.

Given my relative age in the form, our visitors would either offer a friendly nipple or hide me in a bush. *Life was rarely fair.*

Nor did Skalet willingly exist as anything but her Kraal-self.

A stronger whiff of *Evan.* Who'd be, I thought happily, a superb choice to interact with skittish aliens, other than Paul who'd a gift for putting the most demanding guest at ease.

And who, no matter how busy, could read this or any me with a glance. *And was as quick as Ersh to notice I was hiding something.*

Or if I was upset, as I would be until Skalet and I *talked. There would*, I decided, *be biting.*

Best I avoid my perceptive friend—for now.

I sniffed deeply, hoping for more directionality on Evan, only to intercept the potent cloud of *disappointment* emerging from the Seitsiet who'd been turned away from the counter. Nasal passages stinging, eyes watering, I bolted in the opposite direction.

Straight into Duggs Pouncey, our general contractor, chief of maintenance, and the person who—by being the most competent in the Library and arguably this continent—kept everything working.

Duggs, not expecting a chestful of panicked Lanivarian to start her day, staggered, dropping her tools to steady me.

A plunger, plus wrenches, rang on the floor—implying a plumbing disaster. As those most commonly occurred in one of the multispecies' accommodations and, this early, had likely happened late yesterday and been ignored by the night cleaning staff, the torrent of swear words burning my flattened ears might have other cause than me.

Maybe.

I risked a quick grateful lick of her chin, rewarded by the taste of toast and butter.

She set me down at once. Was that a growl?

Silly Human. I began picking up her tools.

Duggs raised one hand. Stop, that meant.

Plunger in hand, I pricked up my ears and cocked my head in what Paul considered a shameless, if irresistible imitation of the local canid. "May I help?" I offered. *If there was one thing I was good at, it was cleaning alien goop from an accommodation. Or any surface.* Ersh had made sure of that.

Her brown weathered skin reddened over cheekbones and forehead. "Can you get my life back?" she snapped, eyes fierce. "Because anything short of that, Esen-alit-Quar, is not going to improve my day. Give me the damn thing." She reached for the plunger.

I tilted my head the other way, trying to puzzle this out. Duggs had owned a successful construction and restoration company in Lowesland. She'd agreed to build the Library because the project intrigued her, and I'd thought stayed for the same reason. After all, Paul and I had plans for the spring—plans needing Duggs.

Plumbing repairs, it occurred to me belatedly, *might not be the ideal use of her skills.*

I refused to relinquish the plunger. "Leave this with me." I used my firm, if higher-pitched, *I'm the boss* voice. It made Paul laugh, but you worked with what you had.

Sure enough, Duggs' mouth twitched. She handed me the tool bag with its wrenches. "Iftsen Habitat Zone."

Of course it was. I kept my ears up with an effort. "Good. We'll talk later."

She nodded. As she turned away, I could see her shoulders shaking. A much better resolution than Duggs walking out the door, *if slightly humiliating.*

Even if it meant I wasn't going to see Evan Gooseberry anytime soon.

Elements

LIBRARY Administrator Lionel Kearn leaned back in the armchair to gaze through the restored window wall in Paul's office. Snowy fields. Snow-topped fences and hedgerows. The farmhouse and barn on a not-too-distant hill. A peaceful scene and he sipped his tea, letting the calm settle into his bones before he returned his attention to his companion. "How bad is it?"

"Nothing to worry about." Yet Paul Ragem continued to frown at the sheets on the desk between them.

"But—?"

"The Preservation Committee wants more assurances the Library's keeping its side of the agreements. It's within their rights. Except this." His finger stabbed the topmost. "Suddenly they want real-time access to visitor travel itineraries and ship logs. Ours too."

"They can't have them," Lionel replied evenly. Their privacy was paramount to protecting Esen and Skalet; no need to state what the other knew full well. "We guarantee anonymity to the scholars, from their presence here to their queries. That's not a promise we can break." Not if they were to help those in trouble.

"And won't." The finger pushed the sheets to the side, only to draw them slowly back. Paul's frown deepened. "The request itself bothers me. I can't think of anyone on the committee who'd come up with it. You?"

Lionel sipped his tea, considering the question. The Hamlet of

Hillsview Preservation Committee had, before the Library, consisted of local residents who weren't so much Against Progress as determined to make it Slow Down and pay attention to the past. They'd two notable projects to date. One was their annual fundraiser to restore the historic fountain in the village square. According to Paul, the fountain hadn't worked in his lifetime, spouting a green liquid in summer and clogged with debris, weeds, and, most recently, a sizable colony of mousels. The mousels were quite safe; the repair estimate grew with each year of neglect, thus far outpacing the committee's attempts.

The committee also, after intense deliberation and research, had created a list of Historically Significant, if dull, paint colors to be used on buildings fronting the main street. With typical Botharan resistance to regulation—a trait Lionel observed was exaggerated in those living on the other side of the world from the seat of planetary government and doing fine on their own, thank you—local businesses had elected to use variations of pink and purple and bright yellow instead, those not being on The List.

The eclectic result proved charming, attracting a small but significant influx of tourists in summer and again in fall, to the delight of the Hamlet of Hillsview's Chamber of Commerce.

Frustrated but determined to Make a Difference, most recently, the Preservation Committee voted to add the Ragem farmhouse and barn to Hillsview's "Acclaimed and Untouchable Historical Sites," apparently preferring nature to rot the empty wooden buildings over yet another annual fundraiser to preserve them, but failed to put that before the village council for its vote before the Ragem property, along with several adjoining farms, were sold to a dead man.

Who wasn't dead after all.

Lionel studied his friend fondly. Fifty years on Minas XII. Raising a family while running a business—with a Web-being for a partner—had matured the brilliant so-eager young specialist with whom he'd served into the impressive person sitting here. Slim build. Quiet confidence. The thick black hair, forever tumbling over forehead and eyes, had a touch of gray. *Living with Esen could do that.*

Paul's face? At first, Lionel hadn't recognized the subtle change in it, then did. Years living a secret, of protecting Esen while they guarded against the arrival of another feral Web-being, had dropped an impenetrable shield over what had been a face full of expression. Only when alone with those he trusted did Paul's self-control and awareness relax.

Regardless, it had become a good, strong face. A leader's. Whose gray eyes still brimmed with eager curiosity and daunting intelligence, and whose capacity for compassion and understanding surpassed anyone's Lionel knew. *An excellent match for the dear little Blob.*

He took another sip of tea, focusing on the problem at hand. Who on the committee would ask for starship logs? Lionel ran the names through his mind. Change came reluctantly, if allowed at all, to the hamlet. The Library had been the biggest local upheaval since the third Kraal invasion—arguably with greater impact—and even that hadn't budged those serving. He ticked off in quick order the two from the village's elected council, both part-time politicians more concerned with local farms and businesses than preservation, then Hillsview's reeve, Joncee Pershing. Joncee was listed on every committee but, according to Henri, notorious for never attending their meetings. To be fair, Joncee wasn't only the reeve. He ran the postal service, land claims office, and volunteered at the fire hall.

Was the request from one of the citizen appointees, then? The trio were the heart and soul of the committee. Retired schoolteacher Ruth Vaccaro, architect Lenan Ragem, and Art Firkser, an author of historical romances as well as publisher of the *Hamlet Times*. People who cared deeply for the tangible memories around them, especially buildings.

Unlikely. No one on the committee or council had ever been off-world, let alone dealt with alien cultures—Kraal didn't count.

"You're right," Lionel said at last. "None of them have the mindset or expertise to ask for or comprehend travel data." They had supplied site plans to the County—no, Provincial Preservation Board. "Another level of government?"

"Hard to believe they'd cooperate. The only thing the committee dislikes more than us is interference from above." Paul folded the sheets and tucked them in a drawer. He came around his desk to sit in the chair beside Lionel's. After pouring himself tea, he raised the pot. "More?"

"I've enough, thank you." Lionel pointed to the now-clear desk. "Whoever started it, we need a response. I'm happy to draft one." He waggled his eyebrows. "Courteous. Conciliatory. Suitably vague on compliance."

Paul snorted. "Or Esen could go to their next meeting. As a Ganthor."

Surely a joke. "That'd get their attention," he replied cautiously because it might not be. Paul was capable of losing patience, particularly with xenophobic fools.

"They don't deserve her time." With, to Lionel's relief, a fond chuckle.

They sat and drank tea in a moment of mutual contemplation of the marvel that was Esen-alit-Quar; Lionel, for his part, with a deep gratitude he'd been permitted to know her secret—more, been accepted by the remarkable being as a friend.

As for Paul?

Lionel smiled to himself. Paul and Esen were more than friends. They were the best kind of family to one another, sharing an unbreakable bond of love and trust.

His smile faded. Not how he'd describe his relationship with Esen's web-kin. Skalet was, in her way, remarkable. Exceptional, in fact. Their bond, should he dare imagine one more than his admiration and her finding him *useful*, lay in fraught, uneasy territory, the earned mutual respect between those once enemies. Not between equals. How could he, a being whose entire life span was but a blink to her vast time, possibly compare to her?

Not *friends*. That, he'd never dare think.

Though Skalet chose to rely upon him, to ask his help in solving the mystery surrounding Paul's mother and the *Sidereal Pathfinder*. In turn, he'd enlisted Lambo, hoping to learn whatever the brilliant creature found. Thus far, his own extremely cautious inquiries within Survey—tapping a network he'd created to hunt Esen—had been fruitless. Not even the redoubtable Mesa Timri, now of the *Resolute*, had information to share.

Of itself, telling. How long it took didn't matter. Patience was his strength; he'd persevere a lifetime if necessary.

Lionel'd agreed to keep what they learned—if they learned anything—between the two of them, Lambo knowing only what was necessary to continue searching, until Skalet declared it time to share. He believed his silence protected Paul and Esen from needless anguish.

Then came a moment like this, when Paul spoke of Esen, when

Lionel realized anew the boundless affection between them. How could he not feel his silence betrayed their trust, regardless of the reason, and hadn't he betrayed them before—

"Don't say it, Lionel," said Paul, as if reading his mind. "I know that look, my friend. The past is behind us." He put his hand on Lionel's shoulder, gripped hard. "What matters is here and now."

Because Paul believed they were done with secrets. That what difficulties remained could be dealt with by dealing fairly with those around them and determination.

If only that were true. Nodding, Lionel coughed to clear his throat. Managed a firm, "What matters is the Library's purpose. Our purpose."

He didn't deserve the smile that lit Paul's eyes and took those years from his face. Hadn't earned it.

He would, Lionel Kearn swore to himself. *He would.*

"Now," Paul said briskly, "before the day gets busy. How do we keep Duggs Pouncey? Esen and I've been talking about it, but you mentioned you'd an idea?"

With a relief he didn't mind the other seeing, Lionel lifted his cup. "Two, in fact. First, I take over immediately as maintenance supervisor—a task we know she hates. I'll need help," he went on, anticipating Paul's concern, "but we've room in the budget for an assistant."

"Who's a plumber," Paul suggested.

"Just so." Lionel let himself smile. "My second thought? We put Duggs to work right away. The sort of work she came here to do."

"We can't renovate the house or barn." With a grimace. "They'd be after us before the first hammer."

"Yes, but didn't Esen say she'd like an addition to her greenhouse? Something complicated—" Lionel moved his cup in a spiral "—involving varied interior environments. Oh, and a tunnel into the basement for rainy days."

"Doubtless with a slide." Paul laughed, his eyes bright. "Perfect. I'll have the Old Blob draw up her wish list. The plans alone will take weeks. Anything," more seriously, "to keep Duggs. We couldn't function without her."

Lionel nodded. "I'm sure that's why Duggs has stayed this long."

"Then let's make her glad she has. Esen's greenhouse it is."

4: Habitat Zone Noon

UNTIL becoming Iftsen, I fretted about Lesy, worried about the Sacrissee, and longed to dash after Evan. *Who'd probably come to play in the snow.* I was also more than a little hungry, the green stuff of Lambo's more warming than filling.

On cycling in the dense smog within the habitat air lock, all of that melted away. Being Iftsen was, well, blissful.

If messy. I rocked forward over crinkly yellow flakes of my Iftsenself's skin, shedding among the ways this form protected itself from its corrosive environment. The air lock had filled with a delicious—to Iftsen, as I could attest, sucking the stuff into my bladder—mix of what most oxy breathers would find noxious. Sulfur added its tang. Technically, Iftsen were, as Humans, theta-class, taking in oxygen and exhaling carbon dioxide; they'd simply evolved within a more challenging atmosphere.

I liked the form. It was sturdy, refreshingly absent of significant age markers, and being dorso-ventrally flattened made it easy to squeeze between narrow spaces. Or other Iftsen. My current mood and gender was signaled by the irregular lumps around my other edges. Ersh considered them the ugliest form to achieve sentience, which was arguably true; an Iftsen resembled a lump of goo solidified after being spattered against a wall.

Adept goo. Extruding a handling arm—a talent this form shared with Quebits, who were much less fun to be—I grabbed the plunger and entered the zone.

Would New Lesy remember her fondness for the species? It wasn't— as our other web-kin assumed—that they'd hosted her first art exhibit. *Not only.* When she'd brought me there with her, Lesy'd told me what she loved was their openness. Iftsen welcomed anyone and everyone, without question. As they were prone to celebrations, drunk or other- wise, most of the time, it made joining a party as easy as opening the door.

Which I did.

The two scholars who'd entered the habitat before me had extruded sex organs and were cheerfully stacked atop one another in front of the Library terminal, sex a typical recourse during vigorous debate. Three, I corrected, spotting the First Citizen to the side. He—*no, currently it*—would be the individual delegated to be responsible while the others were not.

The stack burst apart, pseudolimbs being reabsorbed or reformed. There'd been four in the combination, not two, raising my Iftsen count to five. Not counting me. Iftsen Secundus was home to several good- naturedly coexisting subspecies. Two of these were Nabredan, by the protrusions above their single eyes. The rest, Moberan with frills.

As, today, was I.

Forgetting, or postponing, whatever urgent question had brought them across space to the Library, all five began rocking toward me, waving various fresh body bits in joyful invitation.

I raised the plunger.

At once, the Iftsen rotated and went back to the terminal, three landing close to it.

Some things were universal.

My job, having avoided entanglement, was to find out what these or previous guests had done to the accommodation between this habitat zone and its neighbors. *Or left jammed in it.*

Brandishing my plunger, I rocked steadily off in search of adventure.

Elements

WARNING delivered, Skalet stalked away. Her rigid posture and long strides spoke louder than words. *Done with you.*

The train stood waiting. Steps away. He could join the others who'd failed in their quest. Leave before anyone knew he'd arrived.

Instead, Evan Gooseberry took a steadying breath and followed the Kraal into the Library, though he stayed well back.

Inside was better. Warmer. Full of life. Skalet vanished into the crowd. Feeling safely anonymous again, Evan went to the nearest rack for such things and shed his outer layers of protective clothing—two coats, a vest, a scarf, two pairs of gloves, and hat—finding it much easier to move when finished.

Seeing others remove their boots, he sat on the bench to do the same, newly grateful to Aunt Melan Gooseberry for her many and detailed exhortations regarding the perils of space travel. She carried extra footwear at all times, citing The Lore in which it was recorded that Sedemny Gooseberry died after a hostel carpet proved to be the previous guest and hungry for bare Human toes.

Evan had tucked a pair of slippers in the pocket inside his innermost jacket. Along with a hairnet to prevent clingers, that hazard of lesser-quality starships. And a quantity of emergency rations. *You never knew.*

Not his statue of Teganersha-ki. He'd left it at home, where it wouldn't elicit further strange and alarming reactions from Skalet. Or Esen, for that matter. He did, however, have his holocube. Great Gran knew he was on vacation and would expect messages. Doubtless she'd sent a few already.

The slippers were knitted, the wool a mottled pink and blue; gifts from close family tended to a theme. Putting them on cheered Evan immensely. He clung to that feeling as he stood and headed for the hall to the administrative offices, including Paul's.

The hall was behind the Assessment Counter, accessed by walking alongside the queue of scholars waiting with their objects clutched in species-appropriate ways. You lifted the end of the counter and went through. The door behind stood open.

Evan's journey started well. As a career diplomat, he knew better than to make eye to ocular contact with any of those waiting as he passed. Nor did he react, beyond an inner wince, to the comments of those believing he was pushing ahead. Head up, focus to the front. *Nothing to see here,* he did his utmost to convey.

And it would have worked, because he reached the counter without incident, Henri recognizing him with a big friendly grin and wave through—

—when something whipped around his legs and hauled him to the floor. Evan found himself flat on his back, staring up into the shadowed faces of three Sacrissee.

Upset ones.

During his studies in diplomacy and interspecies' relations, Evan Gooseberry had read about the Sacrissee and been captivated. He'd done a report on their nonverbal, non-fluid communication, namely tail-slapping—grateful, if bewildered, vids of their whiplike tails hadn't brought *SNAKES* to mind. He'd discussed how they'd exhale into their closed nasal cavities, causing the balloon-like bulb on the front of their face to swell, the air released in an emphatic "Ssssuppptt." The behavior was assumed to be part of posturing during the rut by both sexes, but Evan earned high marks for pointing out instances of "Ssssuppptt" observed in trade negotiations with non-Sacrissee, making this an important signal not fully understood. He'd finished by speculating the rumored communal nursing, if it existed, could be to tighten kinship bonds, but as Sacrissee rightly refused to share information on such a sensitive topic, Evan had concluded more study would be needed.

Flat on his back, being stared at, Evan wished he'd done more himself on the species, for if he'd ever needed to communicate effectively and quickly, it was at this moment. He recognized their cloaks. They'd tossed him in the snow, too. Having been in their way twice, he could hardly take it personally.

Henri leaned over the counter. "You all right there, Evan?"

Other than being flat on his back—"I'm fine, Henri," he replied, surprised his mouth worked. "Nice to see you."

"You, too."

A Sacrissee let out an anxious little "huffft, hufffts." The others echoed the sound, the combination like a tiny engine trying to go up a hill.

They were more worried than he was.

Evan raised himself on an elbow. "My apologies," he said in a carefully gentle tone, though the scholars in the queue behind the Sacrissee were growing restive and loud about it. "I wasn't pushing ahead. I'm going to the office." He pointed to the hall. "That way."

"Come on through." Henri helpfully raised the side of the counter. "I've let Paul know you're here."

He didn't dare smile and show teeth, not with the hood-shadowed faces aimed at him nor with the tail that had brought him down still snug around his calves. "May I rise, please?" he asked, suggestively wiggling his slippered toes.

The Sacrissee ducked with a muffled chorus of "huffft, hufffts, hufffts." The tail remained.

"Honored visitors," proclaimed a new, most welcome voice, "on my authority I invite you *IN*. It is safe to disengage."

The tail slipped itself from around Evan's legs. The Sacrissee peeked from under their hoods, as if assessing their direction, then bolted through the open counter to huddle together in the hall.

Paul Ragem reached down to help Evan to his feet, then drew him close. "Welcome back," he greeted warmly. As the two stepped apart,

Evan for his part unable to stop grinning like a fool, the other added, "Nice slippers."

The Sacrissee darted a few steps ahead, in Evan's estimation dismayed by the lack of hiding places in the wide hallway, then stopped to look back before darting another few. Suddenly, they rushed in the third open door with an explosion of delighted-sounding "huffft, hufffts!"

"When Henri called, I dimmed the lights," Paul explained as he walked beside Evan. "They should find it more comfortable there. As for you—" with a shake of his head and a glad look, "Joncee's bringing up your bag. This is a wonderful treat, Evan." The glad faded, caution replacing it, and he lowered his voice. "Or have you come with a question?"

One already answered, Evan thought happily. "Not at all. I'm here on vacation. I wanted to surprise you and Esen."

The smile that did things to his heart. "And we couldn't ask for a nicer one. First, though. Do you mind coming with me—to talk to our anxious guests? I've sent Lionel to find Esen."

"Hom Kearn's stayed, then?" He hadn't expected that.

"He has indeed. Lionel did such a great job as temporary administrator, we made it permanent. He'll be pleased to see you too. So, want to meet the Sacrissee again?"

A chance to watch Esen and Paul in action? He'd learn more than a month at the embassy. "Lead the way, my friend." Evan rested his hand on Paul's back, confident the gesture would be welcome, relishing the permission he had to be close to this amazing Human. *Not as close as he'd longed to be.*

Close enough. More than anything, Evan wanted Paul to be happy. Once they'd time alone, he'd ask him about the love his friend had left behind on this world, the one Paul hoped to find again.

Evan could hear Great Gran now. *You're a romantic. Always will be.*

Guilty, he thought happily.

5: Accommodation Afternoon; Office Afternoon

*W*HAT hadn't *been wrong with the accommodation.*

I couldn't entirely blame the Iftsen, though among the items I'd pulled from the drain had been enough skin flakes to re-leaf a tree. There'd been several large hard pits, at a guess the remnants of breakfast had by the four Ganthor before arriving yesterday. *The timing was about right.* The worst culprit?

Whomever the body part belonged to, I wasn't willing to nibble to find out. I put the wizened roundish, longish, purplish *thing* into the disposal and listened to the device *crunch* for several minutes before a burp of methane pronounced it was done.

Having acquired any still-living mass, I set the room sanitizer for extreme prejudice—in other words, several cycles of acidic steam with soap between just in case, followed by a rinse of NoMoreBio™ and blow dry—then locked the door behind me and activated the "Please use next available accommodation" sign. The message displayed in multiple formats. My personal favorite was a narrow tactile tray that slid out around waist-height for a Human, though we'd installed it after the sole Ket came and went.

There would be more. I hoped. Not that I could be one and interact. I'd need a hoobit around my neck. As the precious item was gifted to a Ket at birth and I was disinclined to pay a grave robber—again—for one buried with its owner, being Ket was, sadly, out.

I'd fed Duggs' plunger to the disposal unit as well. *She wouldn't want it back.* It hadn't been as useful as the five arms with their gripping tips of my Dokeci-self, though I'd washed those thoroughly before cycling. *It wasn't as if anything would stick.* Might have been the thought.

I recovered the clothes my Lanivarian-self didn't seem able to keep on for more than a few minutes today, dressing in one of the convenient closets we'd had built throughout the Library. Convenient for me; I'd seen no evidence Skalet ever used them, implying she'd her own arrangements. *It wasn't as if she cycled as often.* Each of my closets contained extra outfits and sacks of dormant, but alive vegetables for mass should I need it.

During the interior work, Duggs had questioned the need for so many in the blueprints. I'd been ready with an unlikely *at the time* tale of having extra plungers nearby, but Paul stepped in smoothly to explain the "closets" were to help staff avoid interacting with a scholar, if necessary. Having met Lambo for the first time, Duggs agreed.

Not entirely false. I'd complimented Paul later on keeping a perfectly straight face while telling it.

Although I'd cycled twice, dismembering any remnant molecules from the accommodation, once a Lanivarian I couldn't help but spritz my fur with dry shampoo, followed by a good shake. Leaving dry shampoo and fur throughout the closet, I spared a moment to hope Skalet would be the next to use it.

Not a proper grooming and my clothes itched over the result, but I felt renewed—as well as reasonably sure I looked like I'd been dragged backward through thorn bushes. *Nothing new.* My efforts at dignity and executive comportment were often doomed to early failure.

Not, I reminded myself, *what mattered now.*

We'd Sacrissee in the Library. By now, Paul would have them in his office—probably with Evan, Paul as aware as I of the young diplomat's stellar qualities—and they'd be waiting for me. At least I hoped they'd be waiting.

Being already rumpled, I saw no reason not to drop to all fours and run.

Paul must have put the word out. Each and every staff member I passed waved at me, then pointed to where I was already going.

I accepted their urges with my ears up. They were being helpful and I, to this point, hadn't been; taking over Duggs' task not being among my understood duties and helping Paul interpret inscrutable species my most crucial responsibility.

Though I could argue he didn't need me this time. Though shy and retiring, Sacrissee were fluent in comspeak and dealt with Humans regularly. While their journey here was notable and unusual, surely they wouldn't have made it without knowing exactly what they wanted from the All Species' Library of Linguistics and Culture.

I'd remember that thought later.

I dropped to all fours again to bolt under the counter, making Henri jump, and was almost intercepted in the hall by a red-faced Lionel who looked to have been running, too. I dodged around him with an apologetic tuck of my tail, it being abundantly clear I'd been summoned, and ran the rest of the way to Paul's closed office door.

Where I rose to my feet, ran a paw from snout to forehead to settle any loose hairs, then knocked lightly, twice.

Lionel caught up to me. I gave him a toothy grin and he shook his head ruefully. "I looked for you everywhere—"

Just not in the Lishcyn habitat zone or accommodation. "I'm here now," I pointed out cheerfully as the door opened.

"Good," Paul said, inviting us inside with a gesture. "Thanks for finding her," to Lionel.

If the Human blushed, I couldn't tell. I gave Lionel a consoling pat on the forearm. *This me wasn't good about being caught.*

As we entered, the smell of anxious Sacrissee filled my nostrils. The scent came close to that of a non-sentient deerlike animal of the plains of southern Lanivar fondly referred to as "Little Yums."

I swallowed a flood of drool and hoped no one, especially our guests, would notice. *Don't be controlled by another form's instincts,* being one of Ersh's warnings. Usually shouted at me. *Not that it helped.*

The intensity of the office lights had been lowered to dusk-like conditions, the window opaqued. The Sacrissee, still shrouded in what had to be too-warm cloaks, over fur no less, stood shoulder to shoulder in the corner farthest from the door.

Closer was— "Evan Gooseberry!" I greeted happily, my tail giving a most undignified wag as nose and vision identified the shape ahead. Beside me, Lionel gave a little start. Hadn't known our wandering diplomat had arrived, then.

"Hello, Esen. Administrator." Evan was, as my eyes adjusted, sitting not in one of Paul's comfortable chairs, but on the floor. Cross-legged.

With, I squinted, these eyes unable to make out color in this light, motley slippers on his feet.

Lionel, aware of something I wasn't, sat down beside Evan, both remaining perfectly still.

Paul closed the door. Ah, I thought. Putting us *in,* a comfort to our guests. "Let me introduce you," he said in his *to work, Esen* voice.

Promising myself a good sniff of Evan's slippers, not to mention a lick to taste the person who'd become one of my favorite Humans, I gave Paul my full attention, looking for my cues.

Clothes didn't help. Like Lionel and me, Paul wore the staff outfit we'd picked as alarming the fewest number of species, namely a neutral brown tunic—with smock, if required—over a light yellow shirt, with brown pants; all fabrics resistant to bodily fluids. *The most likely ones.* A name tag readable by coms and other devices sat above his left breast; doubtless his access key was in one of the discreet pockets, as was mine. *Plus I'd a snack.*

Beneath the clothes, the pendant I'd given him to mark our fiftieth year in business as Cameron & Ki Imports; our fiftieth year of a partnership beyond anything in web-memory. Within the pendant, a cryo containing web-flesh. Mine. I felt a surge of affection for the little bit, having so recently been web-flesh again myself. Then an unexpected wariness. I'd meant it as an introduction to any other Web-being Paul might encounter, to keep him safe long enough to escape or become friends.

Now, without Paul's knowledge, it contained the secret Ersh had given me, Skalet had wanted, and I dared not keep in my flesh. A Web-being's ability to move through space—at an unacceptable cost in other lives.

What if New Lesy found it?

An eyebrow lifted. *Hurry up, Es.* I searched his face and Paul let me see his delight at contact with this species, then concern. About why they'd come, but that eye flick downward? Oh. That was me, like this.

Excellent point. I pursed my lips to hide my fangs and adopted as harmless a posture as possible, keeping slightly behind Paul as he led me to the middle of the room and stopped. "This is Esen-alit-Quar, the Library's curator. Together we offer our assistance in your query."

A hand appeared from beneath a cloak, three blunt-tipped fingers and a longer, opposable digit holding one of our brochures. "Contingent upon our bringing information the Library does not yet contain. Is that correct?"

The Sacrissee's voice didn't match those in my memory, a difference subtle, if puzzling. Putting that aside, for now, I focused on what he'd— for the voice was the deep tenor of an adult male—said. "We could waive that," I offered, knowing Paul would agree, "in consideration of the great distance from Sacriss and the comfort of your home star."

The three exhaled together, giving their "huffft, hufffts." As the sound was the equivalent of Lionel's cough, namely either a call for attention, polite disagreement, or possibly a dry throat, it wasn't helpful. I rephrased the offer. "We allow you to make your query without new information."

"There is no need," the speaker assured me. "We are the information."

With that, all three pulled off their cloaks.

The voice hadn't matched because the body didn't.

These weren't Sacrissee at all.

"Lights, up ten percent," Paul ordered.

As with the voice, Ersh-memory jarred with what I could see for myself, confounding my first impression. The attractive cream fur of the front, the dappling camouflage on the back and limbs was on these a black as rich as Evan's skin. Instead of lithe graceful torsos and limbs, theirs were stockier, more heavily muscled. I recalled wide handsome heads, fronted by that generous nasal bulb between large soft brown eyes; slim mobile ears and callused buttons to mark vestigial horns. Below, strong thickened lips and chin, borne on an elegant neck.

The faces looking at me were narrower, exaggerating eyes that weren't brown or soft, but pale yellow, shockingly bright against their darkened hides. The ears were larger, the horns no longer vestigial but curved upright and pointed. The lips had thickened, as had the neck; only the nasal bulb remained unaltered.

That and the hands.

I'd been wrong, these were Sacrissee; but I wasn't wrong, for they weren't, not the ones I'd assimilated and *knew* as no other here could.

Paul glanced at me. I answered the question in his eyes out loud. "You are not an unrecorded subspecies."

Ersh had watched the Sacrissee cull themselves before leaving their homeworld. To this day, they rejected those who were different during the rut and would put "tainted" offspring *out* to die. *It worked for them.* I didn't like it any more than I had Tumblers sorting the children to live. *I didn't have to.*

"We are new," claimed one of the two females. "This satisfies your criterion."

From the other, "We have come with a query."

"No more delay." The male exhaled noisily, inflating his nasal bulb, the tissue thinning to reveal the bright blue of blood coursing through vessels beneath. "Give us access to the Library at once!"

The *or else* was as plain as that nose. I watched Paul tense; Lionel and Evan rise quickly to their feet, no longer showing themselves submissive and harmless but ready to defend.

Sacrissee negotiations were infamous for the patience they demanded from alien participants, being a peaceful slow spiral of almosts and not yets and maybe in a while.

Not these. Another, more profound difference from the Sacrissee of before. These were aggressively direct, even courageous.

Or foolhardy. I reserved judgment on that one.

I curled a lip over a fang, unsurprised when none of these *new* Sacrissee flinched or when Paul asked the right question. "Who's in danger?"

Bulbs enlarged. I spared a heartbeat to note the tracery of blue was unique to each, before all three made a sound not in Ersh-memory.

They *howled.*

Together, not overly loud, and with a pleasing harmony, but the fur on my neck rose and I'd actually drawn breath to join in when I remembered my manners. Howling was not done outside immediate family.

If you were Lanivarian. What rules applied to these beings I didn't know and couldn't guess, though I longed to pull some hair and find my own answers.

They stopped, releasing the air from their nasal bulbs with simultaneous soft blubbery sighs.

"All. We are all in danger," the smaller female announced. "They would cull us."

"We claim sanctuary!" the others said firmly.

Paul turned to stare at me. As did Lionel. Evan, too, when I snuck a look at him.

One quiet little Anata in the shrubs. One!

Some things you didn't live down.

Elements

UNLIKE the Youngest's foolish closets, this space didn't exist on any plan, nor had it been made by the Pouncey-Human or her crew. The bubble had been inserted while the walls and floors of the building had been poured, undetected. Secret.

The technology lining it had come after. Translight com and other communication tools. She did not sully this form with needless Kraal implants, despite the urgings of her affiliates. Unlike the tattoos, re-membered by her flesh, devices would have to be reinserted each cycle. Foolish, to rely on machines so quickly redundant. Useful once, if that.

Displays surrounded her. Standing bathed in their flickering light, eyes shifting from one to the other, Skalet could surveil most of the Library, inside and out.

If not the places the Youngest insisted be private.

Inefficient.

The side of a bargain that permitted the rest of this essential equipment—let *her*—watch for danger. The Library must be protected.

Until the Youngest tired of it. The time would come. Her Human, Paul Ragem, age and die. *Inevitable.*

Without meaning to, Skalet's gaze found the screen showing Lionel Kearn, his image captured while chasing after Esen.

With the sweep of a finger, she could erase it.

Why had she'd kept it?

Knowing herself, searching for hidden weakness, was how she'd survived as a Kraal, how she'd continued to reenter and thrive in their society through generations.

What was Lionel to her?

An ally. An individual of tenacity and impressive scholarship. *Admirable.*

There. A sense of *warmth.* Of *attachment.*

Skalet inhaled slowly, welcoming the cold—this space wasn't served by the Library's environmental systems, keeping it from detection—as it moved into her lungs. Sought *clarity.*

Found *CHAOS!*

Images. Voices. Moments and *feelings* that weren't hers, had never been hers, mustn't be—

Lesy-taste.

She'd gone to the greenhouse because she couldn't find Lesy on the displays. To—it was true—check for herself Esen's boasts of progress. She'd not gone intending to share, but the scraps of Lesy had remembered old tricks. Hiding in ambush. Spying. Attacking!

She'd barely managed to cycle before teeth had seized her flesh, tearing loose great strips, going for more. It hadn't been sharing or permitted. It was *theft!*

A threat to life.

To fight back—but she hadn't thought of fighting, had she, she'd been too horrified, too—*afraid*—all she'd wanted was escape—to flee the greenhouse—

She'd had to form a mouth of her own to reclaim the necessary mass. *BIT!*

Assimilating annoying memories of Esen. Esen the pretty. Esen the tasty. Esen the kind. She'd staggered from the greenhouse as Kraal, dropped naked into the snow, knowing only that she'd failed. They'd failed. This wasn't Lesy—or Ersh had protected them—

More welled up! *Lesy-taste. Lesy-TAINT!* Corrupted by what wasn't real, had never been real, weren't memories but *FANTASIES*—

A *giggle* vomited from her lips as Skalet collapsed to the floor, crushed by weight she couldn't bear and didn't know how to shed. She

gasped as her body temperature soared to fever levels, then beyond.
Fought for control.

Losing . . . losing . . . drowning.

A thought welled up; offered a lifeline. Skalet grabbed for it, held it,
pulled herself to safety with it. Esen was Senior Assimilator.

This was her fault.

6: Office Afternoon

*H*OW *could this be my fault?*

As even I wondered, bathed in the suspicious gaze of three Humans obviously wondering the same, I hurriedly recalled every word of the latest brochure I'd sent to Hixtar Station for distribution to all who were coming here.

Nothing stated the Library would offer sanctuary to those in danger.

Well, there was that bit of fine print. About protecting visitor privacy as our top priority and our promise of a secure, safe place for inquiry, added after the unfortunate events last summer. There'd been an alarm—*false*—as well as a bomb threat—*real*—plus the destruction of Paul's office wall when he and Lionel were kidnapped.

Then there'd been the corpses outside our barn—

None of which were my fault, I reminded myself, having been a plot by the late Victory Johnsson, also known as Janet Chase, to steal secrets which we didn't have about Veya's rumored star drive. Not that we knew who she'd worked for, but Skalet was *looking into it* and not a single legitimate patron had been harmed.

In case the news dissuaded future scholars, Lionel had suggested we offer reassurance. I'd taken it upon myself to do so.

My wording might have been too *reassuring.* Meeting Paul's look, I let my ears droop an infinitesimal amount.

His lips tightened, meaning *I was in so much trouble,* then came the slight nod I'd hoped to see. *We'd resolve this together.*

After we did, then would come scolding. Which was fine by me; having been scolded for centuries by Ersh, Paul's version, with his *this is how you do better from now on,* was more apt survival coaching than anger. With, depending on what I'd done, some good-humored teasing and snacks.

"Is this where we shall live and be protected?" one of the Sacrissee asked, tail whooshing through the air, but not contacting anything. Yet. "Inadequate."

Might not be snacks.

Lionel's cough came out a little like "huffft," and I remembered his time with the species. Sure enough, three pairs of ears tilted his way. "My name is Lionel Kearn, honored guests. Library Administrator. Allow us to go *out* as we research all necessary—parameters. In the interim, food and drink will be delivered here. Polit Evan Gooseberry will remain *in* with you."

Evan gave a smart half bow. "Mine is the honor," he acknowledged, proper and sincere, if a tad breathless.

Here on business, then, not for fun with us.

I'd no right to feel hurt. The indicators had been there. I'd smelled *Evan* on one of their cloaks. I sniffed, discreetly, detecting *Sacrissee* on Evan. Though what connection the Human Embassy on Dokeci-Na could have with the Sacrissee, who hosted several Human embassies of its own, was beyond me to guess. Not to mention their systems lay in opposite directions from the Library though all travel to the Library converged at Hixtar Station, and I supposed, by the timing, they'd could have traveled here on the same train and probably on the same starship.

Besides, who didn't deserve Evan's help? The Human had every right to champion another species' cause, and an admirable predilection to do just that without asking. Even if it would have made me happier if he'd come to see us.

Being less mature than I should be, I sulked until I noticed Evan's slippers.

They engulfed his feet, revealed in the raised lighting to be a quaint mottled pink and blue. Handmade slippers, like my knitted gloves; almost a certainty, a gift from another Gooseberry. Undignified, warm, and fun. *Not footwear for any sort of crisis.*

Making it more likely Evan had met the Sacrissee by accident on the way here. *Which did happen.* The next time he glanced my way, I let my tail drift happily from side to side in welcome.

The corners of Evan's green eyes crinkled in what would have been a smile had we not been in what Skalet would call a *situation.*

Wherever she was, I knew she'd be aware of this one. And wouldn't care, unless these "new" Sacrissee posed a threat.

I winced inwardly. *Skalet might consider giving sanctuary exactly that.*

Paul tipped his head at the door. With a last, wistful look at Evan, I left the office.

Once the door closed, Paul turned to Lionel. "Well?"

Who was the expert on the non-Human here? I felt affronted. I felt diminished. I—

My friend glanced at me. "We need somewhere private."

—I was vitally important and we'd secrets to discuss in private. My ears shot back up. Paul, reading all this, snorted, but gently.

Meanwhile Lionel considered the problem. "Not my office." An embarrassed shrug admitted that he left his door open, and staff tended to use his office as a quieter break room than their own. Which was, I thought, a testament to how good an administrator he was.

"The Response Room?" I suggested. "Ally could take her break or work with Henri."

"That'll do." Paul turned to go. The Response Room was at the far end of the admin hall, on the same side as his office. The distance from our scholars was deliberate. We'd an automated system of servo tubes enabling us to remotely deliver the collection's response to a question, be it datacrystal or physical interpretation. Scholars notified the Library where they'd wait for their answer, patiently or otherwise, and we prided ourselves on speedy delivery. Not one missed their return train.

Especially since I'd stopped trying to present each response in person.

But before I followed Paul, I paused to look at his closed door. The faintest whine bubbled up.

"It was my idea," Lionel said apologetically. "Was I wrong? Should we leave Evan alone with them?"

Paul crooked a finger. "It won't be for long," he assured us. "Besides, our Evan's a trained diplomat."

Elements

LEFT to their own devices, any Sacrissee he'd read about would have hastened to mark every reachable surface—including him—with *tartt*, the fluid released from glands along their arms. These didn't, lacking either the compulsion or the glands. Instead, the three stood motionless, staring at Evan Gooseberry with their unusual yellow eyes.

It was all they'd done since the door closed behind Esen's lovely tail, and he hadn't dared move. *Which was ridiculous,* he told himself, duty stirring. His first job as a diplomat-in-training had been to arrange seating for whomever—whatever—came to the Human Embassy on Urgia Prime. From there, he'd worked up to beverage service— knowing what wouldn't upset stomachs or sensibilities a crucial skill— and by the second time his path crossed with Esen and Paul? He'd sat the desk where Humans came to complain about Dokeci, not typically a huge responsibility, but the role included soothing ragged nerves.

It came down to comfort. In general terms, upset visitors tended to be less upset when they realized someone cared.

Most of them. There were those who considered attention to their physical, highly personal needs to be the worst kind of alien intrusion. The embassy'd a list he'd memorized.

Sacrissee weren't on it, meaning he could, if he dared move, be constructive. Evan cleared his throat. "Honored guests. Is there anything I can do for your comfort while we wait?"

The male's nasal bulb inflated. Evan waited for the "Ssssuppptt!"—the emphatic probably less than pleased—but instead what came out was a low sound, like a *howl*. It wasn't in the literature. What could it signify?

The females did the same an instant later, suggested they used the sound to communicate with one another, not him; Evan waited.

At last, a female spoke to him. "We presented new information. By the terms, we are permitted to submit our query to the All Species' Library of Linguistics and Culture. This is what we want you to do. Now." With a snap of her tail.

A reasonable request. The director's office would have the facility. Evan looked for something less intrusive than inviting the Sacrissee to use Paul's desk interface. There. A com panel on the wall identical to the one Esen and he had used to access the collection on his previous visit.

Feigning confidence, Evan strode to the panel and boldly keyed in the code he'd seen her enter; he'd a talent for remembering such things. *If not for asking permission first.*

The black of the panel flashed red, the interface to the Library's collection appearing next. Evan blew a soundless whistle of triumph before turning to the waiting Sacrissee. "Ask your question," he told them, skipping past the part where he'd no idea if they needed some technical authorization to confirm having brought something new.

Which they had, so, "It should work," he added hopefully.

Exhibiting a welcome trust, or he wasn't as scary as Esen, they huddled with their backs to him to confer with one another in their own language. To Human ears, it resembled bubbles popping through mud, interspersed with squeaks, whistles, and that odd little howl.

Evan went to take a seat, Sacrissee known for the time they devoted to discourse, only to bounce upright as they whirled around, tails lashing the air. "We're ready," the female announced briskly. "How is it done?"

He knew how he'd done it. *Should work.* "You speak your query to the interface in whatever language you prefer. The answer—" His hadn't come right away, most arriving from other sources, come to think of it, though the collection had produced a very useful etymology of the Dokeci usage of "elves." He did know the Library somehow vetted answers through the Response Room, to prevent any possible confusion.

Best err on the side of caution. "The answer will be delivered to you when it's ready. To your *IN*."

Pleased "huffft, hufffts." Then, from the same female. "I will present our query."

Evan indicated where she should stand, then bowed. "I'll return when—"

Now an alarmed "Ssssuppptt!"

"No one goes *OUT!*"

"Then I'll stay." Happily so, Evan's curiosity thoroughly aroused. Would theirs be a question about some critical trade negotiation? A linguistic quandary offering new insight into the Sacrissee themselves— or even about their yellow eyes? Why a diplomat could go through an entire career without such firsthand discovery.

Evan blushed to himself, having made more than his share already, to the chagrin of some of his seniors and flattering, if humbling, attention of others. He hadn't tried to find aliens in crisis—content to do his everyday work at the embassy and avoid conflict—but they seemed to find him. If Great Gran had taught him anything at all, it was you helped those in need. She couldn't have imagined that would be a desperate Popeakan or the last remnants of a dying civilization. He certainly hadn't.

Though Great Gran had been so impressed, she'd added those stories, tactfully free of sensitive information but slanted to impress, to his entry in The Gooseberry Lore.

To be read at the next family gathering. *Another reason not to go home.*

Now, with Sacrissee doing the unthinkable, leaving their home system, demanding sanctuary from strangers, was it happening again?

Of course not. Evan shook off a shiver of apprehension. He was on vacation and this merely an excellent chance to learn.

Finally convinced he wasn't bolting for the door, exposing them to the dreaded *OUT*, the female approached the interface, speaking in comspeak what must have been planned and rehearsed.

"I request a list of theta-class worlds, sorted by culture and species, open to refugees fleeing persecution and where an individual's genomic privacy is guaranteed under the law. Give added weight to those of greater distance from the Sacriss System, and/or lessened contact with Sacrissee."

Evan nodded to himself. Her request answered a question of his own: why they hadn't sought sanctuary closer to home by walking into a Commonwealth Embassy. Every species whose awareness encompassed such concepts knew the Human Commonwealth welcomed refugees; a willingness to succor the desperate, be they Human or not, part of the requirements for admission.

Compassion, with a dose of self-interest. Humanity was late into space, playing catchup with those civilizations already there, and, as a species evolved to form relationships? The best way to fit in was to learn entirely new ones. Luckily, adapting to the new and outright weird proved a Human skill.

There'd been some growing pains with the program. Occasional confusion between snack foods and pets—or worse, offspring; early developmental stages being difficult to convey or secretive. Misunderstandings over what constituted "desperate" and "refugee" continued, as evidenced by young Ervickians of low status within their birth crèche who, on hearing of free food in embassy waiting rooms, would clog those rooms on their respective worlds until someone thought to notify the Ervickian equivalent of their nanny to haul the freeloaders out.

At which point the nanny would berate the ambassador, the sorting within crèches being natural, socially significant, and not to be circumvented by lewd Humans offering disgusting scraps, and demand so-called hush credits to prevent scandal.

Sacrissee were prone neither to petty theft nor extortion. The Commonwealth had an embassy on every world of the Sacriss System; all these individuals had to do was walk into the local one and plead their case to someone like Evan.

Ah, but the next step in the bureaucratic chain would be a request for proof of identity and that?

Meant a genome scan. Returned to the owner and wiped from records, but given the number of obligate predators and incompatible biologies—let alone the vanishingly rare but still dangerous pathogens able to leap planetary biologies—the Commonwealth was adamant, the rule firm. Compassion was not to endanger those already in its care.

Granted the three were outside the norm for their kind, but they were still Sacrissee. *Weren't they?*

Request made, the female sagged as if spent. Her companions bounded to her side. The male groomed her left ear vigorously; the second female gave a shoulder for support; but it was to the Human she looked for reassurance. "Was it clear, what I said? Did you understand our request? What we want and why?"

"My understanding would be a Human one," he cautioned.

An amused "huffft," then, "Speak it anyway."

Evan chose his words with care. "From your request, I understand that there are Sacrissee—" *don't accuse; don't make it personal* "—in need of a new *IN,* beyond their sun, without barriers to those who are different."

"We didn't ask to be as we are," the other female replied.

"Ssssuppptt!"

She ignored the male's rebuke. "This Human knows we're the ones with doors closed against us. We're the ones threatened. Forced *OUT—*"

"You're exhausted."

"We all are." With a tail slap. "The truth, Human? We need more than sanctuary. We seek a true home, where our kind will be welcomed *IN* forever."

Heartfelt, that plea, cutting to his core; Evan trembled with his earnest desire to answer it. *To help them.* Saying, "I hope the Library finds you one," was worse than useless.

He fell back on his training. *Assist with the basics.* "While you wait, would you care to rest?"

The smaller female's "huffft, hufffts" held doubt.

True, none of the furniture in the room suited their anatomy but that, Evan thought, scrutinizing what was here, could change. "Give me a moment."

He moved the homely teapot and cups to Paul's desk, wishing he'd had tea—but then he'd need an accommodation and no telling how long he'd need to stay *IN.*

Next he moved the table from between the armchairs to one side. It appeared an antique, real wood, and possibly of the Ragems, so he picked it up again and tucked it in a safe corner.

Unblinking yellow eyes tracked his every move. Nasal bulbs filled and emptied with soft shudders. *Stay calm,* Evan told himself, trying not to notice, but their attention pressed against him. Unsettled, weary attention.

Hoping Paul's chairs weren't heirlooms, Evan took the first and tipped it forward, then the second.

A shame there weren't three. He'd make do. Evan grabbed Paul's desk chair and upended it, detaching its base. He pushed the chair between the armchairs.

Eliciting now-puzzled "Huffft, hufffts."

Lifting an edge of the new, handsome carpet, Evan pulled it up, wincing as edges tore free of whatever tacked it down, but didn't stop until it was free. He heaved the carpet over three tilted chairs with a final effort.

Making a wide, gently sloped hill.

Puffing, he turned to explain, but the Sacrissee were hurrying forward.

"Delightful," the male exclaimed.

"Gratitude," from the taller female.

The smaller said nothing, too busy lowering the front half of her body onto the waiting comfort of what was, Evan thought proudly, a functional replica of a Sacrissee resting mound.

The others followed, draping themselves over, laying thick chins on the carpet. With sighs that crossed species' lines, they became limp. He smiled as their tails curled together.

A knock on the door made them all start. "It's probably the food Lionel promised," Evan said, glad they settled again at his word, though probably too exhausted to do anything else.

He opened the door with care, nonetheless, to find Quin Spivey, one of the Library's Botharan greeters, with a large bag over one shoulder and a series of bottles dangling from a string. "Hi, Evan," he began, then his eyes widened as he took in the state of Paul's office.

"I'll put it back," Evan promised in a whisper.

"Seen worse," Quin replied with a grin. "Henri tucked a sandwich in there for you."

"Most appreciated." To his embarrassment, his stomach growled as he took the bag and string.

Quin gave him a more serious look, nodding to the room's other occupants. "Use the com if you need anything, Evan."

"I promise."

He closed the door, feeling less abandoned.

Not that Paul, Esen, and Lionel had abandoned him. He'd wanted to meet the Sacrissee.

He just hadn't expected to be responsible for them.

Nor, at the moment, had the aliens any other recourse than him. With a rush of empathy, Evan put the bottles on Paul's desk, pulling out fist-sized, presumably edible, sacks of fragrant green stuff from the bag. The Carasian had outdone himself—not herself yet, not that he'd tell anyone and start a panic. *Lambo's next and possibly definitive molt shouldn't be for a while.* He hoped not to be around.

Sacks in hand, Evan turned to the Sacrissee. "May I bring you your portions?" he asked kindly, seeing they hadn't budged from their sag into the carpet.

A chorus of soft "huffft, hufffts" confirmed his guess.

This wasn't so bad, Evan told himself happily. He'd helped Paul and Esen, and Lionel—and seen to the comfort of those in need.

Not a bad start to his vacation.

7: Response Room Afternoon

PAUL led us into the Response Room. Ally Norman raised both eyebrows as we entered, not pausing her work. "Good morning, Paul. Lionel. Esen." This with eyebrows down—*I might be late for mine.*

Ally's part of our shared task was using the fabricator, in this case, or any of the materials lining the shelves of the room to create an object that would convey an answer from the Library. Most of our scholars were satisfied to toddle home with a datacrystal stamped with the Library's authorization and guarantee, but we'd those reliant on tactile or physical information. For them, an object—or scent pouch, for we could do those, too—was a trustworthy format; provided by the Library, it ensured they'd properly understand and process the answer.

Paul and I shared a dread someone who'd come to the Library to clear up a misunderstanding might leave with a new one. *Not on our watch.*

Ally was creative and truly excellent at her job. As she could be only Human, however, I worked alongside her, testing and giving final approval for anything less than straightforward. *Occasionally, there were cookies.*

When I was Esolesy Ki. I really should find a reward for my Lanivarian-self. One that wouldn't fluster Ally, who'd yet to forgive herself for first mistaking my fine, civilized self for a scruff, the local canid pet. *Ear scritches were definitely out.*

"May we have the room for a few minutes, Ally?" Paul asked.

"Sure. I'll see if Henri needs a break." She shrugged off her smock, hanging it on a hook next to the lab coat I should be wearing. "Wind's picking up." Ally nodded to the horizontal slit of window near the ceiling. I felt she'd understated the situation. Snow was going sideways in a white moving wall.

"That it is," Paul acknowledged. "Thanks." He closed, then locked the door behind her. "Lionel, if you'd order food for our guests?"

The other Human nodded, going to the com.

Lambo would resist, loudly and with colorful profanity, any suggestion he put together food trays for strangers, defined as anyone who hadn't had the dubious pleasure of begging for food in person from the Carasian. I angled my ears to get the full benefit.

I'd underestimated the guile of our administrator. "Lambo, I may be going to the Sacriss System shortly and wish to reacquaint myself with their palate and preferences. Please prepare me a sample of food items suitable for Sacrissee and have them delivered to Paul's office immediately. If you can do it."

"At last, a worthy challenge," came the answering joyful bellow. "You neglected beverages. I will include those too."

When Lionel turned off the com, Paul said what I was thinking. "Nicely done." Then a sharp, "What's wrong?"

For Lionel was staring at the panel. "There's an alert. A request to the collection from your office. How—"

They looked at me.

Conceivably my fault. "Evan might have seen me enter my code," I confessed, tail sliding between my legs. "In the Chow last summer." If so, he'd an excellent memory for his kind.

Paul—who'd an exceptional one, particularly for my missteps and their consequences—merely chuckled as he stepped up to tap the interface controls. "I've authorized the request. Shunting it and the response here."

We listened to the collection's recording of the Sacrissee's request.

Paul gestured us to the stools around the worktable. Seeing how serious he'd become, I didn't take my first choice, with its intriguing for-Esen basket of feathers, sitting instead where the table was free of distraction.

Lionel used the back of his hand to ease the basket aside; feathers made him sneeze. "They can't stay here," he began rather confusingly, but I knew what—who—he meant. "To start with, we've nowhere to house them—"

"Not in the Library," I interrupted. "Our house has room."

Paul gave me a quelling *oh no you don't* look.

I pretended not to see it. "You and I could move upstairs," I continued, having wanted to shift our sleeping accommodations anyway. Paul's once-secret third floor, disguised as the original roof to anyone who looked up, was far more comfortable than the rest of the old building. And had a view of the Garden. And—

"And we'd break a significant clause in our agreement with the Preservation Committee, among others," Paul reminded me, aware I'd an ulterior motive. "Our alien visitors are restricted to their starships, the train, and to conduct their business at the Library in timely fashion."

"Unless they're tourists. Or houseguests. Or," with a determined lift of my jaw, *being in the right,* "work here."

"Ordinarily, any of those options would do." Lionel's creased brow meant something I didn't know and he wasn't about to tell me.

Ears lowering, I looked to Paul, who would. "What's not ordinary?"

"I'm not sure, Old Blob. Let's say it wouldn't be wise to draw the committee's attention right now."

My ears sank further. "They've another bake sale soon," I offered. "I'll buy all the cookies this time."

"They could close the Library," Paul said, flat and sure.

I stared at him in disbelief. As a Web-being, I approved—most of the time—of the Preservation Committee. They did important work, keeping alive the memory of the past, and it wasn't their fault we'd intruded. To consider them a threat?

My friend knew his world and these people. I swallowed a whine of protest. "We've done everything they wanted. They haven't—" I added, "done anything *we've* asked."

His impulse was to ask me for patience; seeing it in his face, I wrinkled my snout in denial. *They were fools.*

Paul gave a slow nod. "A response is underway, trust me. That our scholars continue to come such distances under conditions primitive by any interstellar standard and, significantly, a growing embarrassment to our friends in the planetary government—speaks to the importance of what we have to offer. Our proposal for a space station and shipcity is still winding its way through the bureaucrats in Grandine."

Inspiring an immediate image of an Oieta trying to squeeze through a line of angry Nummeries without setting one off, the species currently at diplomatic odds over water rights. *Not helpful.* "Then they haven't said no," I replied, ever-hopeful.

"The committee could give them a reason to," Lionel said, ever the worrier. "If they found out we were letting the Sacrissee stay indefinitely—"

"We keep it quiet." Paul tapped the table, eyes flashing with determination. "We don't turn away anyone in danger—not without first testing their claim."

"Very well." Lionel didn't like it—*too much time with Skalet*—but came forward in his seat, producing a noteplas with an expressive sigh. "Es? What can you tell us about them?"

I could say anything—and had—to Paul Ragem, my first and best friend. Doing so to another Human, even Lionel?

Ersh—

I pushed the feeling aside. "They aren't in web-memory." I uncurled my fingers and pretended to pluck a hair from my arm. "Until I've a sample to assimilate, I won't know what they are, beyond some version of Sacrissee."

"'We are new,'" Paul quoted thoughtfully. "Precludes a remnant population that avoided the major cull—ah. The Library's finished." He set the response field so the list hung in the air over the feathers, each entry a tiny orb above its name, species, and culture.

There weren't many. The Sacrissee's stipulation of complete genomic privacy eliminated the majority of advanced civilizations, theta-class or sucking methane, knowledge of one's fundamental plumbing crucial to planetary efforts to eradicate plagues and so forth.

I waited, watching in silence as Paul and Lionel pinned orbs with their fingertips, tossing them aside, or vocalized other constraints, planets winking out.

The worlds of the Kraal Confederacy shouldn't, in my opinion, have made the list in the first place. They abhorred other kinds of Humans; while they worked in the Sacriss System, they'd never welcome non-Humans dirtside.

Away went those technically theta-class, but otherwise inimical to the species. *Who'd want to live confined to a dome or suit?* Paul grabbed a cluster of Fringe worlds in his fist and flung them aside.

Lionel looked a question. I answered, flattening my ears. "The Gnarl Collective. We suspect they traffic in the living." Paul's Group, now mine, had flagged those planets. The Group's original mandate had been to gather data for me while protecting my secret, scouring communications and data streams to forestall links being made that could lead to the existence of Web-beings.

· *Or bother Paul:* my added instruction.

Some having met me in person, they'd expanded their work to, as far as I could tell, stop me having fun. In their terms, keep me from preventable hazards. Hence flagging slave worlds. And worlds with cataclysmic geology. The Ycl homeworld went without saying and—

"Colonies about to be recalled. Economy near collapse. Disputed territorial claim." Paul's fingers flew, erasing world after world until one floated serenely before us.

"Minas XII." He sat back as if stunned.

"We liked it," I ventured. I'd chosen it not only for being located along Death's path, but because it welcomed those wanting to disappear. Paul had found me there, to my everlasting joy, and it had become our home for fifty years. A home containing friends and family. Enemies, too; not all the memories were good ones. Most were, and I leaned forward. The climate and terrain were challenging, but no more so than areas successfully settled by Sacrissee in their own system. Best of all, we'd still ties to Cameron & Ki, our import business, with its excellent resource. "Largas Freight. We—"

Paul lowered his head, giving me *that* look.

I might have had a brief vision of leading a herd of bounding, happy Sacrissee down a ramp to their new home—"We can recommend a reliable transport option," I finished brightly.

"For whom?" my friend countered, ever-sensible. "We don't know if we're talking about these three, or some unknown number. Nor have we determined why these Sacrissee left Sacriss in the first place."

"And it could a ploy," Lionel suggested.

"By Sacrissee? To what, inhabit our Library?" I flicked my ears. "They're afraid. I could smell it. They've a reason to be."

Paul nodded, half-smiling at me; my tail might have drifted sideways a smidge. "Say we take their request as it stands. A place free of genetic scrutiny," he mused aloud, no longer smiling. "For someone 'new.' Collection: director's priority query, verbal response." The interface blossomed into life, pulsing blue as it waited. Paul's eyes met mine. "Is Sacriss signatory to the Machin Protocol?"

"It is not, Director."

Lionel looked sick to his stomach.

Had I been Lishcyn, I would have been too—in all five.

Those signing the Machin Protocol included the Human Commonwealth and most, if obviously not all, aligned worlds. My birth-mother Ansky had obtained and read the document for Ersh and our Web; a proposal swiftly adopted by so many species clearly of interest to ours. Also, anything dealing with sexual reproduction, *as I could attest by existing,* intrigued her. I ran through the memories Ersh had sorted for me.

Machin was a planet that had been close to ecological and environmental collapse, a stage many ephemeral species achieved in their rush to become civilized only to pause on that brink to seriously reconsider their lifestyle choices. *The survivors,* according to Ersh, *preferred change over extinction.*

The Machinii had taken a different approach. Instead of healing their damaged planet, they tried to remake themselves, to become what could survive on what would be left. The sole life-form, perfect in every way.

Nothing lived alone. Well, we did, but we'd evolved in vacuum, not on a rich, juicy-with-neighbors' rock. When we assimilated any other form, what we remembered and could recreate wasn't a solitary thing, but the genetic stew of organisms who'd become obligate partners at the cellular level.

Biology being deliciously messy, as Ersh would say.

The Machinii's effort to save themselves had been doomed before it started, not that they'd invited comment or scrutiny before it was too late. They'd collected the eggs of their next generation; their sole future, as every adult had but one cycle of reproduction, synchronized across the species, dying once their offspring hatched. They'd subjected the embryo within each egg to genetic modification, of itself a common, well-regarded medical technique for saving lives.

That wasn't what the Machinii did with it. They intended to evolve, within a single generation, into what could live in their warm, rising oceans. They threw away everything they were and had accomplished, discarded and disregarded every other form of life on their world, all to create a future that couldn't exist.

Nothing lived alone.

Today, Machin wasn't a dead planet. Far from it. Nature, left on its own, had healed itself. Evolved. Ansky'd slipped through the quarantine to explore, her final memory of the place of standing in a richly complex forest in that remembered form. The last Machinii.

They'd killed their children, trying to save them when they should have—could have—saved it all. When the first Humans arrived and interpreted the records left behind, saw the mounds of broken shell and huddled bone, they'd left in haste, as if such a horrendous mistake were contagious.

They usually were, I agreed, having a longer perspective than most.

The Machin Protocol was an attempt to prevent any more. Those signing it agreed individuals would remain free to modify themselves or accept modification prescribed for those in their care. Governments would not. Those contacted by the Human Commonwealth committed in their species-appropriate way, each vowing never to engage in wholesale inheritable modification of their own kind without informed unanimous consent.

I'd questioned why, when tampering with their own evolution was dangerous—not to mention inconvenient for us—ephemerals had left in the loophole of doing so anyway.

Ersh had been amused. *Biology's messy, Youngest,* she'd said again. *But it's all they have. You can't stop life trying to survive.*

"—seen three individuals," Paul was saying. I pulled out of memory to pay attention. "Hardly an indication the Sacrissee have begun wholesale tampering with their population—anything less won't matter to the Commonwealth."

"And Humans modify all the time," I pointed out. It came out something of a complaint, but then these beings didn't have to assimilate as broad a variety as possible of something in order to become an inconspicuous and normal something.

Whimsical choices like gills did not help.

"This could be more of the same," Paul agreed. "But collectively, Sacrissee are intolerant of difference."

"These individuals could be escaping prejudice."

By coming here? I didn't voice my doubts. Paul would have them too.

"I'll find out." As a Web-being, I'd no qualms about violating anyone's genomic privacy. *And ached with curiosity.* "There'll be hairs on their cloaks," I said, licking my lips. And skin flakes. Then there was footwear, for they'd worn winter-suited boots. *The genetic bounty from sweaty enclosed toes alone—*

Lionel closed his noteplas. "I can make some quiet inquiries of my own. If they must stay the night?" We nodded together; he sighed. "Very well. Duggs could run heat to the greenhouse."

"No. No. Bad idea." Paul's eyebrows began moving together, the way they did when he detected I was up to something. *Which I was, but he wasn't to know. Yet.* "The greenhouse isn't available," I went on in a hopefully less desperate tone. "I've been renovating." My arms milled in space. "Dirt everywhere. Mold. Unhygienic. Totally unsuitable. How about the basement?"

Meaning Lionel's bedroom. To his credit, he didn't object as I had. "I'm willing to sleep in my office—for the night," lest we take this as permission for a long-term arrangement. "But there's not much room when you add Evan."

"'Evan?'" I echoed, my voice squeaking.

Paul frowned. "It's his vacation."

"We made him part of a Sacrissee group," Lionel told us, shaking his head. "They'll expect him to stay *in*."

Not my fault. I was not going to explain this to Evan.

Paul reached up, cupping Minas XII in his hand. "Before we give them their answer," he said grimly, "let's be sure we should."

Which was not "speedy delivery." We'd had responses briefly delayed for any of several reasons. The scholar was asleep in the accommodation. The format was tricky to make. I'd wanted a snack. Rarely, we'd needed more information to answer fully.

Never had we considered holding one back; I didn't like the feel of it. "Why?"

His gray eyes were troubled. "It's not just the Sacrissee, here and within their system. We can't pull Minas XII and the people there into a situation before we have more answers. And certainly not without their informed consent."

"We need Joel," I said, grasping something of what Paul meant. Joel Largas, head of his extended family, grandfather to Paul's offspring, and our trusted friend.

I loved it when Paul's face lit up. *I loved it more when I'd a clue why.* Not having one, I glowered my puzzlement as he leapt to his feet, leaving Minas XII hanging.

"Fangface, you're brilliant," he praised, rubbing his knuckles on my head affectionately.

Reading my confusion, he laughed. "What Joel Largas doesn't know about Minas XII isn't worth knowing. We'll bring him here!"

The third member of our little group gave his little cough, but his eyes gleamed in agreement. "And just where are we to put Joel?"

Nowhere near my greenhouse, I vowed.

Elements

THE room on the lower basement level had been his haven; now it would serve the same purpose for their nervous guests. It wasn't much. The addition of a standard Survey cot and crates acting as a table couldn't disguise a space meant for storage, but Lionel liked it. *Liked what it meant.* A home, with a roof overhead, after a lifetime spent in space.

He wasn't the first to sleep here. The cot had been Paul's, allowing the director to snatch a few moments of rest during the Library's frantic first months. Lionel hadn't peeked, but he wouldn't be surprised to find a variety of Esen-suited bedding tucked inside one or more of the crates.

There was a com on the wall and, thanks to Duggs, that other essential: a portable but most adequate fresher with accommodation tucked in a corner behind a screen. Homier touches, too. Lionel'd spotted a beautiful rug of braided fabric in the village market and been drawn by its blues, greens, and browns—not the sort of item he'd ever thought to afford, being made by hand. When he lingered to admire it, the rugmaker had barked at him to pay her a shockingly low sum for it or move along.

He'd bought it, then splurged on a large blue and green ceramic pot, also handmade. It sat on the crates and Lionel used it as a substitute for a drawer, filling it with socks.

The rug's texture underfoot felt delightfully irregular and complicated. The pot had a small lump on one side, near the bottom. Glorious imperfections, making each utterly unique and his. Lionel had the names of both artisans, not that he'd be greedy, but another rug, to hang above the cot; perhaps a second pot in a complementary shade—

Not what mattered now. He started rolling up the rug. They were in the thick of it. Things would get messy and if only—

"Joel? Or Esen."

For the second time today, Lionel squinted suspiciously at Paul, who gave back an innocent look he didn't believe for an instant. "I refuse to believe I'm that transparent."

"You're not." A small smile. "But you haven't moved for a full minute."

Feeling a little foolish, Lionel hurriedly finished rolling the rug and got to his feet. "Since you ask? Both. You may trust Largas—I don't. And how can we let Esen—?" he waved a hand in the air. "The Sacrissee claimed sanctuary from precisely this type of intrusion." He clamped his lips tight. *Paul had asked.*

The other Human leaned against the wall, gaze steady. "Why didn't you speak up?"

"Get between the two of you?" Lionel shook his head.

"Ah." Paul looked down. When he looked up again, his eyes glinted with resolve. "The three of us," he corrected. "You know as well as I do how impulsive Esen can be and however laudable her intent? It's up to us to keep her out of trouble."

"What about those around her? What about the Sacrissee?"

Paul pursed his lips. Nodded. "Fair question. Wrong moral compass. We designed the Library to give Esen, and Skalet, regular contact with as many sentient life-forms as possible. Don't fool yourself they only acquire biological data to support the work we do. They must have it, or risk discovery. To be around Web-beings, Lionel, means accepting them for what they truly are. Not just their form of the moment." With a snap.

He deserved that. Needed the reminder Esen wasn't the adorable young Lanivarian—wasn't only that. *And Skalet*—Lionel coughed. "You're right. I'm sorry, Paul. I should know better."

"How?" A generous smile invited his own. "Es and I've been working at this for half a century and I still slip up. Please don't tell her I said so."

"I promise."

Paul straightened, moving away from the wall. "Now, your concerns about Joel."

Distressing, what he had to say; that didn't make it less important. "He's not as he was." They'd the news from Rudy. Joel Largas had been powerful and vigorous, but age and a hard life took their toll. That, and a more recent debilitating stroke. "I told you about his health."

"Joel would never betray Esen."

"No, not deliberately. But, Paul, in his present condition, the stress of the journey here and the Library itself, full of curious strangers. An inadvertent word—"

Paul flinched.

Lionel softened his tone. "You could consult him over secure coms."

"Esen wants him here. I do." A deep breath. "Minas XII is Joel Largas. We can't send the Sacrissee there without his approval and I guarantee he won't give it unless and until he meets them face-to-face."

"Then, if he comes, we take precautions," Lionel insisted. "Joel isn't left alone. He's monitored at all times. And we limit his time on Botharis—keep it as brief as possible."

"Agreed." A flicker of grief crossed Paul's face, disappearing behind something grim. "Skalet mustn't know you doubt him, Lionel."

He'd counted on her help. "But—"

Grim became dark. "Remember what they are. Skalet accepts us; she won't extend that tolerance to Joel Largas. If she thinks he poses a threat—she will kill him."

He wanted to protest, defend her. *That he couldn't meant he believed it too.* "Understood. I'll contact Joel at once. Make the arrangements."

"Thank you. The Sacrissee need their new *IN*. Unless there's something else?"

Lionel, numb, shook his head.

Paul picked up his blue-green pot. "Best we take out anything breakable." He glanced inside and chuckled. "Lionel, I've told you. You don't have to live like this. You can have furniture."

Arms around his rug, Lionel hesitated before admitting, "I wouldn't know what to buy. Or where."

"Once the Sacrissee leave, ask Ally to help you with that." A thoughtful look, then Paul gave a quick nod. "I think it's time we told you. You won't be staying down here much longer. Come spring, we'll have Duggs work on rooms for you attached to the Library—unless you'd prefer housing in the village?"

He mustn't be the cause of expensive renovations, but live some- where else? Feeling oddly unsteady, Lionel clutched the rug. "The room is fine," he heard himself say, when what he wanted, what he should say was *I love it here. I've purpose. A home. Don't make me leave.*

He should have remembered to whom he spoke.

"Thought as much." Paul's eyes warmed and he smiled. "Esen said to assure you a proper apartment was already in the budget and that yes, we want you here." With emphasis. "We need you, Lionel. As our friend and the Library's guiding hand."

Lionel struggled for words, the right words. Before he could, Paul nodded toward the cot. "Remember how to collapse it?"

"I remember teaching you," he replied, finding his voice again.

Feeling at home.

8: Library Afternoon; Office Afternoon

WHILE overjoyed at the prospect of seeing Joel again, I was far less happy with my current assignment, having learned how Paul and Lionel planned to break the news to Evan about where his vacation would take him next.

Me.

Yes, I wanted to get my paws on the Sacrissees' cloaks—and hopefully their boots—which Paul knew well. Something else he knew was that I cared about Evan, and the young diplomat had a soft spot for this me. Outwardly why I'd the job, while Paul and Lionel hurried, with Carwyn's help, to prepare the latter's quarters to become a Sacrissee plus Human *IN*.

If I didn't know Paul equally well. He counted on me to cushion the blow by gazing at Evan with what Humans considered my soulful "puppy" eyes.

Shallow beings. My eyes were normal for a Lanivarian and I was not—*by that species' generous standards*—in any sense a pup. Still, I'd take any advantage, however embarrassing.

It wasn't helping me knock on the office door. I stood outside and smiled at Ally, heading back to her now-vacant workshop. Nodded at Quin, going the other way to start his shift greeting scholars. The next train would be arriving, if not already here, the Library full of intent, hopefully ordinary aliens with easily answered questions.

We'd sufficient strange for one day already.

Our staff being a cohesive, chatty group, the next person to amble by and see me loitering outside Paul's office would fuel rumors I was reluctant to face the director, thus likely in trouble again. Or about to be, the parameters on Esen's anxious loitering being loose.

While I'd receive sympathy along with those hastily hidden grins? *Best not.*

I knocked once, lightly, then went in without waiting.

The illumination had been reduced to minimal again, but this me had excellent night vision. I saw Evan sitting on Paul's desk, eating a sandwich. He waved me inside.

I closed the door as I entered because our three Sacrissee, eyes closed, were asleep on what looked like a rubbish heap. No, that was Paul's new carpet overtop of—yes, every chair in the room.

Clever Evan. Maybe he'd like to stay with them for the foreseeable future—

I dismissed the thought. The Evan I knew would want to go outside. See snow. Visit us. Gaze longingly at Paul when he thought the other wasn't looking. Play games with me. All things I enjoyed.

Could we get the Sacrissee out on a return train by tonight?

Ersh! I should be ashamed of myself. And was. What was best for the Sacrissee had to come first. I'd take what I could of my new friend.

Making sure Evan was looking at me, I touched the not-so-hidden after all access panel, giving him a smile of approval. *Not all plans went awry.* I jumped lightly on the desk beside him, something this form did well, and sat beside him, which it didn't unless my tail was out of the way first, a constraint I forgot when distracted. *Like now.*

Once I'd squirmed to arrange myself in comfort, he bumped shoulders with me, then tore his sandwich in half to offer me a share.

Such excellent manners.

I hoped he wouldn't think less of mine when I started licking inside a Sacrissee boot.

In hindsight—rarely the view I started with in most forms—letting the Sacrissee feel too much at home wasn't going to end well.

Proof arrived as I'd my snout deep in my third alien boot. *Something* grabbed my tail and pulled, hard.

Indignant—*and hurting*—I curved my spine as my head popped free of the boot, ready to bite whatever my teeth encountered first. As that was a highly unsatisfactory mouthful of cloak, I gave myself credit for diplomacy under extreme circumstances as I spat it out with a growl.

"Esen. It's all right."

Tell that to my tail. But the anxiety in poor Evan's voice acted like cold drips of water. I finished calming myself with a shudder from nose to rump, letting my tail be.

The Sacrissee weren't asleep. The three of them stood in a defensive half-circle facing me, cloaks held out in front as if that would save them. *Which it had.*

"Did we pull your tails?" I demanded. "Did we?"

"Why were you snorting in my boot?" countered the male Sacrissee.

Because the inside had been delectably ripe and a little snort moistened my nostrils to gather more. I'd need to cycle in order to assimilate the information caught in my mucus and waiting in my gut—this me conveniently unable to digest hair—

They didn't need to know.

"Esen saw a mousel," Evan claimed, coming to stand by me. "Running into your boot. Esen caught it."

Evan didn't need to know either.

I ran my tongue over my teeth as though enjoying the aftertaste. "It's gone," I assured our guests.

"Protecting our *IN*," murmured the small female with approval and the cloaks lowered. "Our apologies, Curator. Hom Gooseberry."

Another worrying tinge of territoriality, though I'd have expected scent-marking first. Come to think of it, the air was free of any tartt tang—still, names for the first time, complete with Commonwealth honorifics, was an improvement I'd have ascribed to rest and food, along with our diplomat's skill with furniture, if not for the request as yet unanswered within the Library's collection.

Evan, meanwhile, led the way in courtesy. "May we now know your names, honored guests?"

Yellow eyes exchanged looks, then the smaller female spoke again. "I am Saxel Sah. With me is Acklan Seh," the male "and Maston Sah," the other female. "Together we are of the *IN* who refer to their collective selves as The Emboldened."

"Or The Cursed," Acklan said, giving that strange *howl* with the words. This time I caught the vibration of his collapsed nasal sac.

"Emboldened," insisted Maston, tail swiping across the back of his legs.

I didn't like the implications of either; hopefully, the terms helped Lionel and Paul search whatever databases they accessed, legally or otherwise.

"Do you bring the answer to our request, Curator? Is that why you've come?"

Though tempted by the truth, that I'd come to snort in his boot, I behaved. *I'd moments of maturity.* "Your request continues to be processed," I replied, implying progress without promising anything.

A dissatisfied tail swipe cracked the corner of Paul's desk.

"I've news," Evan said hastily, prompting me to tilt a curious ear at him. "Your proper *IN* is ready for you." The message must have arrived while I was occupied in boots. "If you'll come with us?"

As one, the Sacrissee drew themselves close, tails lifted in threat, and shouted "HERE IS THE *IN!*"

I eyed them a moment, then, rather than waste my breath arguing, went to Paul's window wall and dialed it back to transparent.

Sunlight dazzled across snowy fields, flooding the office with light.

The Sacrissee hid themselves inside their cloaks, crying a communal "Ssssuppptt!" of alarm before bolting as one for the door.

Evan glared at me.

I returned my most innocent look.

Had my tail not throbbed, I'd have wagged it.

Elements

*U*NACCEPTABLE.

Rejecting weakness did not dispel it.

Skalet stepped into the training harness, turning everything else off within her bubble. Isolated, *insulated,* freed from distraction, she keyed the harness setting to its midrange. Hairlike needles penetrated muscle groups and joints.

Her body arched involuntarily with the first jolt, blood filling her mouth. Three generations ago, the Kraal Confederacy, House Bract to be precise, had perfected the technique to keep a body battle ready within a confined space. An advantage carrying that House to victory times without count.

Newer Kraal, weaker Kraal, eschewed its hard discipline, installing facilities and tracks to bloat their ships. Avoided the bright, needful pain.

She, who remembered for them, did not. Another jolt, and Skalet reveled. This was feeling *alive.* This was *real.* This pushed aside the stains in her mind, the Lesy-taint, returning *focus.*

These Sacrissee. She'd dismissed them. No longer. She'd tapped into the Library access from the director's office as well as several possible choices, but she'd known—oh, yes—between the *children,* Evan and Esen, they'd go to the closest. *Paul's.*

Another jolt racked her from fingertip to toe. The harness sucked away sweat, collected urine and fecal matter, ran electrolytes directly into her bloodstream.

Fugitives meant pursuers. Pursuers implied the three had value: either in their continued existence, something they carried or knew, or in their deaths.

She'd no preference. Any valued commodity attracted attention. Attention was what their Web did not need, especially with Lesy—

—a giggle bubbled in her mouth. Strange wild thoughts welled up, shapes and images that weren't real—

Skalet reached a desperate hand. Keyed the setting to maximum.

As searing pain ripped through this form, *AGAIN* and *AGAIN*, she refused to cycle and save herself. This was who and what she was. *Discipline. Purity.*

Lesy wouldn't steal them from her—

9: Lift Afternoon

WE emerged triumphant—
Well, I did.

Evan stayed close to the Sacrissee, offering a string of unnecessary apologies for *someone's* rude behavior, along with promises their new *IN* had no giant openings to the *OUT,* and would they keep moving to the lift—

The word was like magic. The Sacrissee abandoned Evan and their shuffling anxious pace to spring forward, cloaks billowing like wings as they bounded down the hall.

This me, being faster, arrived first. I interposed myself in front of the lift and pointed to an invisible line on the floor. "Wait right there."

Any unsuspecting member of our staff already in the lift didn't deserve to be crushed by stampeding—they weren't scholars. That much was plain. Stampeding, overly aggressive Sacrissee. Who didn't fully stop until I showed teeth.

Herbivores.

Evan ran up from behind, but his slippers offered less than no traction when it came to stopping. He slid toward me in slow motion, waving his arms as if it would help. *Or asking for it.*

I grabbed his left wrist and shoulder, managing to keep him on his feet as I heard the lift open behind me.

The mix of dismay and embarrassment on Evan's face as he saw who was inside the lift told me who it was. Only one individual in-spired that reaction in us both.

Skalet.

I turned and there she was, immaculate in her black Kraal uniform, fasteners glinting like eyes. *Not that Skalet couldn't intimidate naked.* No masking veils or hood here, where she controlled surveillance; her affiliation tattoos stood stark beneath her pale skin. Blood-red on her right cheek for House Bryll. Black over an eye for Arzul; from ear along her jawline to neck for Bract. Others, dulled by time but no less potent. She wasn't armed—*not obviously.* Paul had managed that feat, determined not to provoke the Botharans any more than we had.

Her presence shouldn't provoke the Sacrissee. Kraal were common in the Sacriss System, conducting normal Kraal activities such as weapon manufacture, weapon dealing, and the exchange of clandestine information concerning, of course, weapons. Sacrissee tolerance, ac-cording to my web-kin, hinged on a hefty transaction tax and a treaty to protect Sacriss from other Humans, namely the Commonwealth.

The Sacrissee had a similar treaty with the Commonwealth—and every other species who fared through their skies—making it impos-sible for hostilities to start against them without dragging along the civilized universe.

Anything to protect the *IN.*

Skalet's gaze lowered to impale me. "Visiting scholars are not per-mitted to use the lift or enter the basements."

"These are honored *guests*," I told her, keeping my ears up though she looked grumpier than usual. I'd be pleasant as long as possible. Namely until Skalet found out these Sacrissee had claimed sanctuary from an as-yet-undetermined danger, potentially luring that danger to the All Species' Library of Linguistics and Culture. Therefore, as head of security, she should have been briefed first and why hadn't I done so—making it my fault.

Maybe she wouldn't find out about the brochure.

"Nor are 'guests' permitted to stay in the Library."

Ersh. She had.

My ears tried to flatten. I twitched them back up. "Paul and Lionel are waiting for us below. The administrator's generously offered his room to our honored guests. Please escort us there." *Meaning we'd a plan underway, it wasn't mine, and just this once would she go along without arguing.*

"Surely unnecessary, Esen," Evan said worriedly, completely missing the subtext.

Before I had to be blunt, Skalet, who missed nothing, wordlessly stepped deeper in the lift.

The lift could hold three Humans and one of the bigger Library carts. I put myself beside my web-kin as a kindness to the young Human; although Evan and Skalet had forged an alliance of sorts, they were in no sense *friends*. I couldn't imagine her having any, given her opinion of mine. It made me sad.

Not a reaction she'd appreciate. Nor was I ready to forgive her for Lesy. If we'd a minute alone—

The Sacrissee darted *in,* their instinct to seek the smallest confined space somewhat at odds with courtesy. Evan avoided being trampled by pressing against me as the lift doors shut.

Which was how, when the lift doors reopened seconds later on the second basement's bright main corridor, I felt him turn to stone.

Elements

HE'D no fear of places. None. Not a trace of claustrophobia or its opposite according to every therapist and expert who'd tested Evan's brain, meaning there was no reason he couldn't move.

Except he couldn't. When the lift door opened *FEAR* had gripped him and he didn't know why or of what, an absence of understanding adding *PANIC* to fuel the *FEAR* and he couldn't move even to gasp for air—

Fingers clamped on his neck. He hadn't seen the Kraal move and now she pulled him near, kept hold. "If you wish to ever be of use, Human," breathed that rich chilling voice, "hear me now. Memory must be sorted. Selected. Controlled. Here we were threatened with death. Remember what matters. We did not die because you wouldn't stop. Do not be stopped now." With a shake, Skalet released him.

All in the time it took the others to leave the lift, Skalet after Esen who herded the Sacrissee into the hall. *Where he'd walked on burnt feet, and such was the power of memory he could smell his dissolving boots.*

The Kraal might have the mental discipline to pick and choose what she remembered. He couldn't. *Going into the hall was impossible.*

Esen looked back, sudden concern angling her ears. She made to return to him and he shook his head.

"Run, then." Skalet reached back into the lift and touched the control.

The door shut on Esen's shocked face.

He could walk out of the lift on the main floor. *Of course he could,* Evan railed to himself. *Nothing had happened to him here.*

Ambushed by his own mind. Again. As always.

Shame made him numb. Skalet had been right. He was useless to his friends. Unworthy of being here. *What had he been thinking?*

Sick and empty, Evan walked away from voices, trying to leave behind his own as well. He walked until he was alone and lost in a maze of corridors.

It was then he found the door.

Not to one of the habitat zones, those were in other wings of the Library. This would lead out to the Library Garden and Esen's greenhouse.

Away from anyone.

He wasn't thinking clearly. Wasn't making good decisions or even reasonable ones. He was, as Skalet had predicted, running from what he couldn't escape, his own inner weakness.

Wasn't the first time.

Evan entered the door and sealed it behind him, feeling a relief he knew was a lie.

His first flight, the dozens after, had been at home, where he could run to the little cottage Great Gran had built for him near the beach, its interior free of any of his triggers. She'd leave him to work his way through whatever fear had sent him there, activating the cottage's linked therapist if he needed help. *Back then, it had been always.*

The last time he'd fled like this had been during his first week at the Diplomatic Service Academy. There'd been no cottage to shield him, but he'd found a cupboard, somewhere. Managed to activate the link to his auto-therapist, but the signal wouldn't go. Later, he'd learn it was because the cupboard was in the "sensitive" portion of the archives, blocked from unregistered personal devices—

Evan ran his trembling fingers along the nearest white wall. Curled them into a tight fist and waited for his hand to stop shaking.

—Unable to summon help, the cupboard turned from haven to prison. One in which he locked himself. He'd be rescued, no doubt. Have to explain why he was hiding in a cupboard instead of attending the class taught by a *SNAKE-FEAR-SNAKE,* when prejudice wouldn't be tolerated, couldn't be, not in a diplomat, and the truth relegate him to Human-only worlds forever.

If he wanted to live, not only live but have the life he'd come to the academy to earn, he had to find his own key—

Evan's hand steadied; the crippling spin of *wrong thoughts* eased. He'd done it then. He'd do it now.

The starting point was ever the same. *Forgive himself.*

Easier in a cupboard.

He almost chuckled. Clearer-headed, if heartsore, he began to notice his surroundings. Anyone who'd been to space would recognize the hall-like space with its consecutive doors as an air lock, the control panel and mechanisms standardized across species' lines for reasons owing as much to safety and commerce as physics. There was even the usual grate underfoot to remove moisture.

Most didn't smell like wet canid. Evan spotted the cause hanging on hooks near the exit door. Esen's outerwear, the hem and collar still damp from melting snow.

Evan regarded the exit with new interest. After self-forgiveness— *not even close, but after*—he'd need a serene place where he could reflect upon the cause of his bolt from the basement.

Or could distract himself from the humiliation for a while.

Where better than the Garden?

Evan couldn't get his arms into the narrow, low-set sleeves of Esen's coat, but it made a decent cloak if he ignored the ample tail slit. Her charming knitted hat fit nicely over his dense curls, though the earholes meant drafts at the top. The fingers of her gloves drooped past the tips of his, waving like little flags.

The boots, though. After Skalet's horrifying caution about wet, then frozen toes, Evan didn't want to risk going outside in his slippers, but Esen's boots were peculiar to say the least. The round sole was wider than the spread of his hand and the upper portion formed a thick-walled cup, topped by a rubbery membrane with a strap to hold it snug around a leg.

Nothing ventured— Evan took off the gloves and his slippers, sitting on the floor with one of the boots.

Before trying to squeeze in his foot, he pressed his finger into the ball, then heel, finishing by wiggling all his toes inside his socks. No pain. Not so much as a scar. He frowned, thinking of what Skalet had said about memories. He hadn't thought about the scalded soles of his feet since they'd healed months ago.

If not of this, or the threat to their lives, then—

The answer snicked into place, as if he'd known all along.

He hadn't feared the basement because of what had happened to him.

It was what hadn't.

Evan shuddered. The last time, there'd been an explosive device meant to kill Esen and Paul. Skalet had disarmed and removed it, but in his nightmares afterward—many and vivid—she'd failed. *They'd* failed. Everyone in the Library had died.

The last time, he assured himself, there'd been criminals. Skalet wouldn't be surprised twice. He wasn't entirely sure she'd been surprised then, come to think of it.

He didn't need an auto-therapist to tell him to return to the Library, trusting the perfectly competent people here to have checked every corner of the basement levels for more explosives—*FEAR!*

Reasonable apprehension, he corrected himself, *informed by past events and prudent.* All he had to do was dial it down to mild scream. Better yet, a whimper.

A nice calm walk outside should do it.

If Esen's boots fit.

10: Basement Afternoon

ON the positive side, the signs of my fury—hackles up, snarling from the depths of my Lanivarian soul, flipping drool strings— were such that the Sacrissee erupted in panicked "Ssssuppptt! Ssssuppptt!" and leapt by Paul to plunge into the safety of their waiting *IN*. Followed by Lionel, presumably to reassure them I was harmless.

On any other side, failure. Skalet might have been stone, eyes staring down as if the floor was of overwhelming interest—or watching for drool. Refusing to engage until I calmed myself.

I knew the approach. *Smug, overbearing, know-it-all Elder.* After all, I'd had five of them most of my long life, each and every one—with the exception of Lesy—intent on my learning to behave. *Calm yourself, Youngest,* would be the start, then scolding, one or more lectures, and more scolding. There'd be a quiz later. Sometimes years later, my Elders having perfect memories and my getting into trouble something of a repetitive theme.

Lesy, when I searched my memories, didn't participate. Not because she was on my side, oh no. Our tender web-kin avoided scenes, as she called them, at all costs. Scenes were disruptive to her creativity.

They'd been disruptive to whatever ears I'd had at the time, my other Elders, including Ersh, convinced volume would speed my reformation.

I retrieved the drool strings with my tongue before they reached my clothes or Skalet's boots, swallowing the snarl with them. The worst of it? This time my Elder was right; I had to calm myself. Temper wouldn't help, even though Evan had done more than any of us to help the Sacrissee. And shared his sandwich, which was more than a certain web-kin would have done, meaning he hadn't deserved— I growled at her. "What did you say to Evan?"

Skalet lifted her head to rake me with an assessing look I tolerated because I'd no choice, probably deserved, and Paul was approaching, his face like thunder. A shaved eyebrow rose, distorting a tattoo. "With those ears? You heard."

Yes, but I wanted her to admit it in front of Paul, the Human having stopped to watch us with a new and quite unnecessary caution. Just because Skalet and I—*once*—had almost cycled and consumed Evan Gooseberry—

Who hadn't known what to fear. Who still didn't.

I focused on my web-kin. "You scared Evan."

A stern flash from those eyes. "It doesn't take much. He's full of fear."

Paul called Evan Gooseberry the bravest person he knew and wasn't wrong. "You reminded Evan what happened here," I countered, somehow keeping down the snarl and refusing to look to Paul for moral support. "You were cruel."

"I was not. I offered him assistance, Youngest. A reconsideration based on our shared memories. He failed to accept."

Web-thinking. Tinged with *disappointment*. Skalet had, in her terms, done Evan a great favor.

I could almost wrap my head around it, if not why.

"Where did Evan go?" Paul demanded, no longer at a safe distance.

Skalet gave a tiny shrug. "He didn't say. The Sacrissee don't belong here. Give them their response and let them leave."

Answering any doubt regarding her ability to snoop inside the collection.

"You aren't in charge here." The two were of a height, formidable in their own way and all too aware of each other as potential threat. Whenever they faced off, as now, this me wanted to snarl while curling my tail between my legs. *Confusing to say the least.*

Except for the part where I'd defend my friend against any danger, including any posed by my disagreeable web-kin, and she knew it. She'd push, amused. Or scornful. *Amused scorn being the default.*

Paul wouldn't. He valued my Web as a Human valued family, despite my fervent explanations to the contrary. *I supposed he couldn't help it.* Sure enough, he glanced at me, his stance easing, but I didn't expect what he said to my web-kin next. "What's wrong?"

I certainly didn't expect Skalet to stiffen then snap, "You've endangered the Library, Director. Taking in strays—ignoring basic security protocol. I've warned you repeatedly."

But my friend had that look, the one meaning he heard something in her voice I didn't. A reminder he understood this version of my web-kin in a way I couldn't; one I doubted Skalet would appreciate. His head tilted. "You've been hurt."

My turn to do a quick assessment. Skalet, catching me, scowled. "I'm fine."

I took the tiniest sniff. My marvelous nose couldn't detect emotion; it could detect a sudden sweat. Despite her aloof cold expression, the perfect posture, Skalet was agitated. Enough to dump heat. I twitched an ear at Paul. *Careful.*

He acknowledged with a slightest hesitation before he spoke, hopefully choosing different, safer words. "Let us help you."

Or not.

She moved before either of us could react, seizing Paul's arm to spin him against her. The gleam of a pin, doubtless poisoned, hovered over the beating pulse in his throat. "I need nothing from a *Human,*" whispered into his ear with the disdain of eons. "I need nothing from *her.*"

Not true. I'd no clue what had set Skalet off and no time to guess, busy fighting the urge to cycle and *remove this threat.* Whatever instinct was trying to bully me into action would have a messy, regrettable, and likely permanent result. Paul might survive the pin—he wouldn't survive us battling nearby, demanding mass—*Ersh!* I held form with an effort even she might have complimented. *Or not.*

Paul's gaze never left me; his expression remarkably composed. He trusted me as no one ever had and I found I could speak. "Calm down," I ordered. "We've a situation underway." Which was very mature and I impressed myself, then couldn't help but add, "Getting emotional won't help."

Skalet's glare should have impaled me on the wall. My tail wanted to slide between my legs. Instead, I raised my ears halfway and wrinkled the snout she'd broken once before. *Behave,* that meant.

A flicker of—*could that be gratitude?*—crossed her face. Before I could be sure, Skalet gave a short hard laugh and shoved Paul away from her. The pin vanished. "Let me escort the Sacrissee back to their transport," she said, as if nothing had happened.

While I felt like shedding. *Definitely having a conversation, and soon.*

Proving himself equally able to dismiss life-endangering events, Paul shook his head at her. "They've requested sanctuary. The Sacrissee don't leave our protection until I'm satisfied it's safe for them to do so," he stated. "Join us. It's time we found out what they're afraid of."

No missing the pleasure that gave her. Skalet's fingers twitched as if she'd the Kraal impulse to touch her tattoos in respect. "Of course, Director."

I'd missed something profound between the two. *It wasn't the first time.* But this, I thought uneasily, might be harder than usual to understand.

The day wasn't going well at all.

I hoped the Emboldened Sacrissee—or Cursed, depending which of our guests you asked—appreciated the swift efforts of Carwyn, Paul, and Lionel to turn a room in the Library into a Sacrissee dwelling, complete with an impromptu curtain trailing warning bells where the door should be. Someone had cut a tiny peephole at Sacrissee eye-height.

They wouldn't feel guilty, as I did facing that curtain. Poor Lionel was on the other side. He hadn't much before, now had less, and I could only hope Paul had convinced our friend and colleague this was temporary. We'd the plans for a new residential wing, albeit a modest one, ready to implement. Lionel needed a proper residence.

The project should keep Duggs Pouncey happily employed. *I wasn't entirely confident of my ability to judge Human reactions at the moment.*

As Paul touched the curtain to signal our intention to enter, I kept my thoughts firmly in the future, distraction the best way to recover my balance after the whole pin at neck incident. Evan needed a place to stay too and we'd Joel arriving with Rudy. Why, we should double— triple the planned space!

Or, warming to the concept of company who weren't frenzied scholars, *what if Paul's offspring accepted his invitation?*

The twins would stay on their ship, the *Largas Legend*. Not for lack of desire to see their father again or to meet the plethora of relatives they hadn't known existed until very recently—Paul hadn't let me listen into that conversation, but he'd come away misty-eyed and smiling to himself so I had to assume it had gone well—but Luara was a pilot and Tomas, like their grandmother, a talented navigator. They set foot dirtside as little as possible, following their mother's course since old enough to leave home. Char Largas captained the venerable flagship *Largas Loyal* for Largas Freight and, last Paul had heard, settled happily in a life-contract with her ship's comtech.

Connections rippling across space to include me, at least the Esolesy Ki version. *We could have a party—*

Bells tinkled in cheery agreement as I pushed through the curtain behind Paul.

In hindsight, I should have stayed in the hall.

The instant I appeared on their side, the Sacrissee reacted, loudly expressing their displeasure, each lash of their bone-reinforced tail tips leaving significant holes in the wall plaster.

I could appreciate their viewpoint. After all, they'd fled my snarling presence only to have me follow them *IN*.

Too late now.

Skalet looked bored, Lionel perturbed—these remained, if temporarily, his walls—and I sneezed, dust reaching my sensitive nostrils.

Taking a step farther into the room, Paul clapped his hands together, gaining our guests' attention. *And mine,* curious how he'd tackle what was, to Sacrissee, impassioned commentary. Like the Iftsen and the accommodation, some guests naturally had more impact on structures than others.

"Do you wish your response or not?" Paul asked in the firm, no-

nonsense voice that tended to stiffen this particular spine because it meant *someone* was in trouble, usually me.

This wasn't me, I thought, abruptly confused. *Was it?*

Tails lowered. Stilled. There was a chorus of anxious "huffft hufffts." Followed by a *howl* directed at me.

That being clear, if offensive and unreasonable, I stepped behind Paul and kept my lips lowered over my fangs. *Maybe they'd forget I was there.*

"The Lanivarian isn't welcome," Saxel Sah announced.

Or not.

Paul stiffened. "That's not your—"

I put a gentle paw on his back. "If you can manage without me, I've other duties." With a tongue-lolling grin at the smaller female that held no humor at all and showed all of my shiny teeth.

My friend turned to look at me, his face suffused with rare anger. "This is not negotiable." He spun around to glare at the Sacrissee. "Esen stays. Or you can leave the Library. Now."

Confronted, any Sacrissee I'd known—or been—would have backed down at once. Or fled. Groveled, if they'd no exit, but the Emboldened did nothing of the sort. Giving their annoying and strange little *howl,* they refused to be cowed and Saxel all but shouted, "We will not leave without our answer!"

Gaining Skalet's abrupt focus and probable threat assessment, which would have been gratifying except the Library's purpose—our purpose—was to help prevent misunderstanding.

To cause one was unacceptable. *I knew better.* I relented, hiding my teeth once more, and patted Paul's rigid arm. "I'm not offended, and I must go. I regret making our honored guests—who came in distress for our aid—" *that for Skalet* "—less comfortable." I resisted the temptation to assure the Sacrissee they were probably too tough to eat anyway.

"You've nothing to apologize for, Esen," Lionel said, his tone no happier than Paul's.

Ersh. I'd caused a Human revolt.

Which was when the Cosmic Gods intervened.

The belled curtain jingled. Carwyn Sellkirk, the Botharan responsible for coordinating interstellar travel as needed when she wasn't greeting new arrivals or hanging curtains, pushed her way into the room. "You have—to come—at once!" she exclaimed, as breathless as if she run from the train platform, which seemed silly as the room had a com link and we each carried one. Her arms waved to herd us out the door. "At once!"

"This isn't a good time, Carwyn," Paul said, not moving. He couldn't help but look at me. I flattened my ears at the insinuation, having been Right Here. "Can it wait?"

Carwyn's face remained uncharacteristically pale, but Paul's tone steadied her. That, and her own good sense once she noticed the Sacrissee, clustered shoulder-to-shoulder in alarm; *never panic alien guests* being one of the Library's founding principles, not that we always knew what would. She took a deep breath. "It's Constable Lefebvre, Director. He's waiting in the administration office. There's an L.I. involved."

Short for Lamentable Incident, our code for a problem beyond excess slime in the wrong accommodation or an irate scholar. Our code for risk to the Library, or to life—

Or both. I swallowed a cowardly whimper. *Lesy?*

Paul, blissfully unaware I'd installed a barely sentient Web-being in our greenhouse, gave Carwyn a brisk nod. "An administrative matter, then," he declared smoothly, having written the no-panic principle in the first place. "Please remain *IN* and comfortable," he told the Sacrissee, not that they'd budge willingly from their claimed refuge—*we'd probably need to sedate them for a move*—but the courtesy was reassuring. "Your response will be provided as soon as possible."

Yellow eyes widened above furiously expanding nasal bulbs. Tails lifted.

"Lock the door behind us," Skalet told them in her best Kraal obey-me-or-suffer voice. She pushed the curtain aside to demonstrate closing the door, then tapped the control to activate privacy mode—something Lionel had deemed essential after Lambo rumbled into his room in the middle of the night. "Open it only to those you have met face-to-face and authorize."

Eliciting disturbingly gleeful "huffft, hufffts."

Invigorated by the potential for disaster or sharing my own fear of its cause, my surprising web-kin led the way out, striding toward the lift. Lionel and Carwyn followed as if compelled. The door closed behind us, presumably locked. *Quick learners.*

A hand pressed gently on my shoulder; Paul, delaying us a moment in the hall. I looked a question.

He bent to whisper in my large and lovely ear. "Something's shaken her."

Skalet? If I'd been Lishcyn, my jaw would have unhinged and dropped right there.

A shrug to acknowledge the unlikelihood, but Paul's expression remained serious. No, determined. "It must have happened today, or last night. Anything I should know, Fangface?"

He knew there was; there wasn't a me he couldn't read. Fortunately, before I had to respond, meaning either a lengthy confession with scolding, or attempting to lie—*which wouldn't work, so it'd be a confession*—Lionel called anxiously. "The lift's here."

Paul's little frown said *not done with you.*

I managed a credible ears-up and alert *let's go.* After all, we'd a Lamentable Incident.

Both of us forgetting poor Evan.

Elements

THE path to the greenhouse led off to his right, recognizable despite the dramatic change from the Garden Evan remembered. Leaves were missing, turning shrubs, hedges, and the occasional tree into sticks. On those trees still with leaves, branches bent under clumps of sparkling snow, and Evan paused, enchanted once again. He drew a breath in through his nostrils and let it spill out between his lips, enjoying the fog in front of his face.

Then coughed, because the air had grown colder.

He held his borrowed coat tighter and took a step, pleased when Esen's unusual boots didn't flop around his feet. Stuffing a folded slipper in each had helped. The straps were snug around his calves and the contraptions should stay on, if he didn't run.

Run . . . Skalet had used the word like a weapon.

No, Evan corrected, determined to phrase the moment properly, she'd recognized his reaction to the basement. Understood it before he had. Offered him options to deal with it and it wasn't the Kraal's fault he'd picked the wrong one.

Fault. Guilt. Wrong. Blame. Unhelpful words, potentially harmful ones. Pushing them aside, Evan crunched along the snowy path in Esen's strange round boots, concentrating on what had gone well. The Sacrissee. Esen—and presumably Paul—approving his use of her code on their behalf.

So when he stepped into the first sinuous track, he didn't notice until he had to lift his right foot to climb out of it.

Only one sort of being left such traces in snow. A ShimShree. There was a ShimShree at the Library!

Evan couldn't believe his good fortune.

He'd wanted to meet one since learning they existed, but the creatures required temperatures well below the freezing point of water—explaining why a ShimShree scholar would choose winter for its trip to the All Species' Library of Linguistics and Culture.

Some called them Giant Snakes, explaining why Evan's cousin Wenn Gable Gooseberry had sent him a vid of a writhing bundle of the things. According to Great Gran, who refused to invite her to family gatherings, his cousin started as a cruel child and had grown to a vindictive adult.

The vid hadn't been the only time Wenn tried to trigger one of Evan's phobias. This, however, had done the opposite. Evan had been mesmerized. ShimShree were nothing like *SNAKES*. They were enormous graceful beings, their handsome chitinous body segments topped with regal tufts of brilliant hair, each segment after the head bearing paired paddle-like limbs. The heads themselves were complex, a significant portion of their structure involved with the production of an exudate used for everything from literature to building homes like spun glass.

A technology based on spit couldn't help but charm the child he'd been. Learning more as a diplomat-in-training of the ShimShree's intricate, cold-adapted culture, from their Grand Dance of Parliament—debates literally carved through ice—to their passionate blizzard-triggered courtships, cemented his interest as an adult.

Without an instant's hesitation—or sober second thought about encountering a strange being who might be after its own privacy; not to mention one of the largest known sentients who could crush him with a paddle stroke before noticing his presence; nor the crucial point of how he'd communicate without expert translation via a Petani, the only other species able to appreciate a ShimShree's linguistic blend of paddle-slap and water-based chemistry—Evan enthusiastically followed the wide curved track, lurching side to side in Esen's boots with all possible speed.

Despite the cold and his inadequate clothing, the young Human was sweating by the time he concluded the ShimShree must have been, well, playing in the snow. There were only two apparent stopping points, neither with a giant serpentine alien waiting to exchange philosophy: a deep jagged hole through the snow into the ground below, and a patch of hardened spew over a window on the nearby greenhouse. The two made no sense.

To a Human, Evan reminded himself. They did to the ShimShree.

Going to the nearest pane, he pressed his gloved hands to the glass, then his nose, trying to see through the frost if the alien was inside.

There. A glimpse of blue, *moving.*

ShimShree were white with black markings, but their hair tufts came in various colors. He'd never heard of a blue one—

Regardless, Evan rushed to the greenhouse door, coming to a puzzled halt. He mouthed the words on the crooked, handwritten sign. "'Do not knock.'"

Clear enough.

Without knocking, Evan Gooseberry opened the door and went inside.

11: Admin Office Afternoon

NEWS of the Lamentable Incident stood waiting for us in the Administrator's Office, next door to Paul's. Lionel's domain, having accepted the title and duties from us, and doing a much better job. Ordinarily, he'd have been here to greet the constable and learn about the problem.

Instead, we piled through the door—all but Carwyn, who'd received instructions from Paul when I wasn't paying attention.

Constable Malcolm Lefebvre appeared unfazed by our sudden arrival. Not surprising; Mal, as we called him, possessed an unshakable calm, developed during his years as a patroller in the tumultuous fringes of Commonwealth space; a calm easily maintained in what was, he'd confided to his nephew Rudy Lefebvre after a few beverages, a relaxing retirement as shepherd to the peaceful inhabitants of Hamlet of Hillsview.

There was no crime to speak of in the village, other than the occasional discovery of a Kraal weapon in a field or a cache of the things in the foothills. Both featured lethal traps for the unwary; reminders of the Kraal Confederacy's annoying interest in Botharis. An interest presently of the *don't bother us/won't bother you* sort, though Skalet assured us certain Kraal Houses remained hopeful of a repeat invasion.

In my estimation, the Botharans would deal with them as they did everyone else, including the Commonwealth, by waving a numbingly long list of municipal funding requests related to local infrastructure and would they like tea?

It hadn't always been that easy. I'd Skalet-memory of blood spilled and grudges held. Part of the constable's duties was to maintain the call-up list of those willing—and able—to form a local militia at need. But Botharis was a relatively poor planet, of next to no strategic importance, while Botharans, as a rule, were unusually stubborn even for Humans and difficult to budge. *I could attest to both traits.* The Kraal might have claimed to add Botharis to their Confederacy five times in the past sixty years, but they'd left almost as quickly as they'd come.

The latest attempt had been missed by the local population, preoccupied with the cornish harvest; a fatal embarrassment to the House responsible.

There being no war at the moment—and Skalet's efforts as S'kal-ru, the trusted highly placed Kraal Courier, to ensure there wouldn't be, or we'd at least have warning—our constable kept himself pleasantly occupied. Mal stretched his long legs to walk the village laneways each day, chatting with passersby and, yes, taking cups of tea. He'd escort those who'd enjoyed more than a few non-tea beverages at a local pub, to be sure they made it home without sleeping in a ditch. Until we'd arrived, the greatest challenge of Mal's posting had come in the shape of Bertie, an amorous stag from Rhonda Bozak's herd who'd escaped to wander the village, bellowing lustfully at the moons.

The All Species' Library of Linguistics and Culture changed all that, having invited the known universe to visit without security clearance. *Skalet remained displeased.* They arrived only via our landing field, located as far as feasible from the village to satisfy the Preservation Committee.

A field firmly within—as it turned out—the jurisdiction of the Hamlet of Hillsview constabulary. Meaning Malcolm Lefebvre.

Unpredictable aliens. Rowdy starship crews. With no shipcity yet, thanks to the Preservation Committee, we'd no patrol presence or port authority, though an unofficial Port Village had sprung up; those entrepreneurs in tents adding wooden sides and roofs come winter. As for crime? There'd been two as yet unsolved murders (Skalet's fault), a kidnapping (not her fault) that revealed the Kraal warship hovering behind a moon (that was), and a still-thriving market in fraudulent artifacts conducted mostly by Paul's cousins.

There'd been a third murder. I'd consumed the evidence, shedding the mass once comprising Victory Johnsson as a puddle of water I'd mopped from our kitchen floor. At the time, I'd hadn't been able to bear the thought of Paul finding her corpse in our home.

Since? I didn't like having a secret, but this one I was glad to keep. Mal had concluded Johnsson, his most likely murder suspect, fled off-planet, an explanation Paul preferred to his own theory, that Skalet had disposed of the body somewhere on the grounds. I didn't remind him Skalet would have consumed the body, it being extremely likely he'd read the real truth in whatever face I used and the secret be out.

Through it all, our constable had remained unperturbed. According to Rudy, his uncle appreciated the importance of the Library's purpose and the jobs it provided the community. According to Paul? Apparently, I wasn't to believe Mal's melodramatic sighs whenever the word "retirement" came up. The former patroller relished tougher puzzles to solve than a rutting elk.

He didn't relish whatever puzzle had brought him here today. His strong features were set in harsh lines and his eyes were stone-cold, piercing me where I stood beside Lionel before moving on. This wasn't a friend's kindly uncle or cheerful neighbor. This was the patroller who'd received a commendation for single-handedly bringing down a ring of saboteurs, leaving none alive.

My tail stopped wagging.

"Constable Lefebvre," Paul greeted, abruptly formal. "Carwyn used the L.I. code. What's happened?"

"And how can we help?" I jumped in, ears perked at their most innocent. *Whatever "this" was couldn't possibly be about me.*

Drawing Mal's disconcerting stare. "I've received an alert of a possible biohazard at the Library."

Then again . . . Lesy qualified as a hazard to life, but she wouldn't reveal herself to strangers. *Shouldn't,* if her still-assimilating memories held enough Ersh, who'd given us strict Laws about such things. *Not that I'd paid attention.* An attitude I'd kept from Esen-mouthfuls.

My second was to worry what I'd ordered for the Garden—to my shame, it was only then I remembered Evan. *Where was he?*

"Specifics," Skalet demanded.

Don't panic without them, I told myself.

"There's a ship with a dead crew on your landing field," the constable said, each word crisp and defined as if he gave a report. "I've ordered the ship sealed until someone can tell me what killed them. What we do know is the *Stellar Trumpet*'s passengers disembarked and took the train to the Library. I've closed the field and ordered your operators home on my authority." Mal looked to Paul.

Who nodded absently. "Contain the situation."

"That's the plan," Mal replied. "I've spread it about there's an undisclosed problem with the system. Your visitors stay put and out of harm's way."

The excuse would work for a while. Our trains occasionally ran late, the operators tending to livestock or relatives, or taking a birthday pint at the pub; staff and repeat visitors wouldn't think it odd. As for the rest—I focused on not looking at Paul. *And not whining,* this me being a little too expressive. The Sacrissee. *Evan!* Had they come on that ill-fated ship?

"We appreciate your quick action," Paul replied, directing a sharp look to Lionel who all but saluted.

"I'll tell the staff—"

"That can wait," Mal countered, freezing Lionel in his tracks.

Skalet's lips twisted. "You've contacted other authority."

Lucky guess or intercepted communication?

The constable looked as if he'd like to know too, but didn't ask. "I've sent a call out for the nearest Commonwealth medship. One's diverting here."

Paul had gone pale. "You think the crew died of a transmissible disease."

"I think we don't take chances." Mal gestured at our surroundings. "You've invited the universe to pop in for a quick visit. Who knows what's come along?"

I bristled. There were medchecks at Hixtar Station, let alone those when individuals boarded their transports. "That's more than improbable, Constable Lefebvre," I said icily. "It's—"

"Impossible? There's always a first time," he assured me, a new edge to his voice. "It won't be here."

Skalet gave a tiny move, regaining Mal's attention. "Has the medship sent any requests?"

"Everything we know, or can learn, about the *Trumpet*'s passengers. Their point of origin. Previous stops. Medical histories."

The slight lift of Paul's hand held authority. Having not whined, *yet,* I wasn't sure whose reaction he wanted to silence until I saw Lionel's face, flushed with outrage. My friend spoke, pleasantly enough. "Mal, you know we don't collect such information."

"I suggest you start. Now."

"I concur," Skalet said, being less helpful than usual. I lifted a lip to show a fang. Ignoring the hint, she continued, "A necessary compromise, given the potential consequences, is to obtain those facts and swiftly. Before stopped trains becomes a panic."

"On Botharis?" Paul's tone was deliberately incredulous. I started to relax.

"Even here—" Her strong lean hand swept through the air. "—planetary plague is a terrifying prospect."

So much for relaxing. "The ship's crew were Human," I concluded, staring at the constable. We might not collect "facts," but I'd no doubt my paranoid web-kin's Kraal associates sent her updates on ship arrivals and departures.

"Not all, but yes, some were Human." Mal looked at Paul. "Meaning if this is a pathogen, people here could be at risk."

"They're *all* people."

The words, and Paul's emphasis, warmed my Lanivarian heart. I aimed my ears at the constable, waiting.

Meeting my look, Mal gave an acknowledging nod. "That they are. My apologies, Esen." He ran a hand over his face. "While I'm hoping for a mechanical problem on the *Trumpet,* the medship says we can't take any chances. None of my people are to approach. I need the passenger information, Paul. I assume it's too late to isolate them."

Skalet looked amused.

"Then till we figure this out, ships stay in orbit and everyone here stays put."

"You're imposing a quarantine," Lionel deduced. He didn't look happy. I shared the feeling, as would Paul. We were about to be stuck with a hundred and forty plus scholars—depending on how you counted the communals—who, once the afternoon train failed to arrive, would demand an explanation or alternate transit we didn't have.

They'd all want lunch. Lambo would have fits.

"That's up to the team from the medship. I'm taking precautions. Answer me this. Where are your visitors better off? Here, or roaming the village?"

"If they'd let us build a multi-species' hotel at the landing field—"

Paul gave me his *not now* look, then turned back to Mal. "Here. We'll do what we can to identify and question those who came on that ship—discreetly and without revealing why—" This with a meaningful look at Skalet. She tipped her head in gracious acknowledgment.

Smug, that was. Nothing pleased my web-kin more than a stealthy inquiry. Unless it was being the only one who knew a secret.

We'd additional resources. "Evan will have noticed who came on his train. I'll ask him," I offered. *High time I found our wanderer anyway.*

"Polit Gooseberry's back?" Mal sounded newly alarmed, which really wasn't fair. Yes, the murders and other nastiness had taken place during Evan's last visit, but they'd had nothing to do with him. Except for the troops off the *Mistral*—

"On holiday," Lionel explained, quickly changing the subject. "We've staff with medtech training. Shall I advise them?"

Mal and Paul exchanged glances, sharing an instant of species'-specific mutual comprehension that utterly escaped me.

Paul spoke. "I think Mal would agree we should keep this to those here," he said. "Until we know what we're dealing with," he added, correctly interpreting the flattening of my ears.

I didn't like it. I didn't like any of it.

At least it wasn't about Lesy.

Elements

THE greenhouse was empty of ShimShree, if not of frost and icicles. Evan's footsteps crunched over hardened lumps of soil, and, despite the lack of wind, he shivered. The place no longer held any life—hard to imagine it ever had.

Then what had he seen?

Something blue. Something moving. Curiosity piqued, Evan continued deeper into the building, checking under benches and atop them.

A pot shattered!

He stopped moving; stopped breathing, truth be told, because suddenly he remembered mousels among other startling and scary aspects of being outdoors, which this felt, despite having a roof and walls. Because those were clear, other than the frost, offering no protection at all—

"Human."

At the voice, Evan squeaked and jumped, unable to help himself. "Who—who's there?" He frowned, looking around. There was no one in sight. A com link? "Show yourself!"

The most beautiful Human he'd ever seen in his life rose from behind a workbench. "Evan Gooseberry."

She knew his name. *How could she know his name?* He'd never seen her before.

And he was seeing all there was of her, for the person who came around the bench, walking gracefully toward him on long slender legs, was completely naked. Unless he counted the thick white hair streaming down her back and shoulders.

Her head tilted to one side, large blue eyes studying him. "Can't you talk?"

"Aren't you cold?" Evan blurted. He could see for himself she was and tried not to stare at her stiff nippled breasts which was, as Great Gran had taught him, rude. It didn't help that her flawless skin, blue veins showing through, had tiny bumps over it, but his gaze finally locked on her face.

And was lost. He'd never seen a face like it, meant to be immortalized in works of art. To inspire song and poetry. The bones beneath the skin, the soft lines etched by eye and lip, were perfect. More than that, they spoke of perfection within, of laughter and kindness, of bright joy and—

"I am cold, now." She shivered convulsively and the spell—wasn't broken, he thought, but whatever held him enthralled faded.

Hastily, Evan pulled off Esen's hat and gloves, holding them out. "Take these. And this." He shook off Esen's coat.

The woman came forward, her steps small, almost timid, then stopped.

He gentled his tone. "You're right. My name is Evan."

Another flash of those remarkable eyes. "I recognize your face. Evan Gooseberry. Esen likes you."

He smiled, delighted to know Esen had shared his name and image with what must be a friend. Her smile echoed his; a smile more brilliant, more alive, than any he'd seen. *That's it,* Evan thought. She was more alive than anyone he'd met.

Unless it was Esen. "Please, put these on."

She donned the cap, putting the gloves aside to take the coat. Instead of laying it across her shoulders as he had, she tied the arms together and slipped her head through, the coat hanging in front. Reaching behind, she snicked the fastenings of the coat so it wrapped snugly around her.

"Wish I'd thought of that," he admitted.

"I've had more practice." She seemed to lose all concern over him, walking around, fingers trailing along the edge of the bench. She lingered in front of a pot with a strangely tender smile.

At that moment, it dawned on Evan who this must be and why she'd be here, naked. He blushed fiercely. "You were expecting Paul—Paul

Ragem—weren't you?" Here, in the flesh, was the love Paul had left behind on Botharis, let believe he was dead, over fifty years ago. The one Paul had confessed he hoped to find again—a secret told to him and him alone. *Not even Esen knew.*

Her face lit up. "Paul."

The warmth in her voice filled Evan with joy for his friend, even as it ended a fantasy of his own. *A selfish one*, he reminded himself. "I can go find him, if you like. He's probably been held up in the Library." By Sacrissee in the basement—

"Don't, please." Her eyes clouded and she took a step back. "I'm not ready, Evan Gooseberry. I'm—" Lips quivered, losing the next word, and he didn't understand.

Or did he? "You're afraid, aren't you," he guessed, and she stopped her retreat. "It's been a long time."

A whispered, "Yes."

"Everything's—everything's changed, hasn't it. It's different, now. You're different."

"Yes." She studied his face. "You're very wise, for one so young."

His face warmed again. "Not according to my Great Gran. She thinks I've a great deal to learn. Which I do," he added quickly.

A small smile. "Wise indeed. Would you visit me again, Evan Gooseberry? I should like that."

"I would like that, too, very much. Where?" he asked.

Her smile grew. "Here. I will be here. Or I may, now that I've clothes, walk in Esen's garden."

He'd never, ever, met anyone like her. "But—you really should have boots first. Proper ones," Evan qualified. "And more clothes."

"Will you bring those for me?" The smile turned mischievous. "It'll be our little secret. You mustn't tell anyone, not Esen or Paul, we've met. Not until I'm—ready."

Later, Evan would remember this moment and know his romantic side had taken over, thrilled to be part of a scheme to surprise Paul, missing all the clues this was something else entirely.

But that was later.

"I'd be honored." He winked. "What may I call you?"

She held up her hand, examined the back of it, then looked at him from between her fingers. "Lesley."

12: Portal Afternoon;
Admin Office Afternoon

A third train had arrived and disgorged its scholars before Mal ini-
tiated the shutdown, but as the first train bound for the landing
field wasn't scheduled to leave until after noon, it seemed a normal
morning. At least until our guests were notified they were stuck here. I
wasn't sure Mal appreciated the enormity of the task facing us.

Our staff were prepared as best we could. Paul had informed them
of the upcoming train stoppage and the only grumble had been the
postponement of the lunch hour three-on-three pond hockey game,
held every day on Ragem Creek. *Which I'd looked forward to showing
Evan, it being among the odder things I'd seen Humans do for fun.*

As for our basement guests? I'd waited for Paul to tell Mal about
them, but he'd left the topic alone. I supposed, having barely settled the
Sacrissee *IN*, they weren't going anywhere, but I didn't envy Paul Mal's
reaction to such delayed information. *There could be scolding.*

Meanwhile, I was busy. I'd detected Evan-scent when we'd left the
lift and had no difficulty finding it again, despite the number of others
who'd donated their molecules to the corridor in the meantime. Given
the number continuing to do so, dropping to all fours to bring my sensitive nose closer to the floor wasn't an option.

It didn't matter. Evan had been upset and sweating. I could almost
see him hurrying along, taking turn after turn. His choices led away

from the busier portions of the Library, improving the clarity of his trail, and I've have found him—

—had he stayed in the Library.

Oh dear.

I stood inside the portal to the Garden I'd used this morning, registering the lack of my winter garb with some pride. Resourceful, our Evan. If impulsive. I hadn't thought to meet anyone more prone to that particular character flaw than myself, not that Humans took the same dim view of personal improvisation Ersh drilled into me over our centuries together.

Then again, Humans didn't explode when stressed.

They were, however, desperately fragile, especially outdoors in winter weather. To top it off, Evan hadn't had supper, had shared his small lunch with me, and I'd no idea if he'd had breakfast on his ship.

A ship I urgently needed to talk to him about, wanting reassurance it hadn't been the *Stellar Trumpet.*

He wouldn't have gone far, I told myself, eyeing the outer door control. Certainly not as far as the greenhouse—

The only certainty was Evan Gooseberry was not predictable. I sighed, debating the time it would take me to collect another set of outdoor clothing for this me versus the unpleasantness of running through the snow in my staff clothes. *Cycling into something snow-capable wouldn't work at all.*

Before I could come to a decision, the outer door control light came on, indicating someone coming in. The door behind me, to the warmth and security of the Library, closed automatically, sealing me in to wait for whomever it was.

An instant later, the outer door cycled open, letting in a whoosh of frigid air, a swirl of snow, and, to my relief, a shivering hunched Evan Gooseberry. *In my boots!* Who looked remarkably happy for someone with icicles in his hair and bounded forward to trap me in a most unwelcome cold and snowy hug. "Esss-sen!" he greeted through chattering teeth. "Www-hat arre y-yyou do-ing heee-re?"

Resisting the urge to nip, I endured for the eternity of a second before squirming free. I closed the outer door, about to shiver myself. "This is not appropriate behavior," I scolded, chagrined to recognize the Ersh in my tone. *Still, I'd reason.* "You scared us! And where's the rest of my winter gear?"

"G-got w-et," he explained, which was no reason to discard what would have kept some of him warm—and the snow off his head—and now I'd have to hunt in the snow for my knit gloves—"S-orry, Esen." His teeth stopped chattering as the small blizzard he'd brought with him was replaced by warm air from the Library. At least the snow melt went through the grate in the floor. Evan sat abruptly on the bench to remove my boots, his knit slippers popping out. He put those on and stood.

"What were you doing out there?"

"Following the ShimShree." Evan grinned at whatever showed on this me's face. "I found its tracks and went looking for it. No luck. Do you know where it is? I'd love to meet one."

Ersh. Was every mistake I'd made today going to bite me? "SeneShimlee left this morning," I said glibly.

He looked charmingly disappointed. "'SeneShimlee'? That's a beautiful name."

Which it was, being mine in that form, but irrelevant at the moment. I opened my mouth to ask about his ship—

"How did SeneShimlee leave? For that matter, how did it get here?" Evan kept going, peppering me with pointless questions. "Did it come on a Petani ship? I didn't think a freighter with a large enough hold could land on your field. How did it manage the train—"

The door into the Library cycled opened. Seizing the opportunity and his damp chilly sleeve, I tugged Evan through it. "We'll talk about the ShimShree later. Come with me. Now."

He came willingly into the corridor, only to gently free his arm. "I've something to do. I'll be back soon," he promised, then walked away without me.

When had I lost control of the situation? I hurried to catch up, snarling under my breath. "Now where're you going?"

The perplexing Human, sounding cheerful and quite mad, announced: "To get my things. I must go outside again. It's incredible, Esen. The snow. The sparkles. Don't worry. I won't be long."

I bolted to get in front of him before we reached the part of the Library with other, hopefully less mad, beings. "Evan. Stop!"

He obliged, looking less cheerful. "I have to do this, Es."

"And I have to talk to you, right now." I collected myself. "Did you come to Botharis on the *Stellar Trumpet?*"

Evan hesitated, biting his lower lip. "I wasn't lying, Esen," he said, making no sense. "I'm here on vacation—to see you and Paul. It was just coincidence I traveled with the Sacrissee."

That would be yes. The hair rose between my shoulders, an instinct beyond my control. "It's all right. You aren't in trouble," I told him, though he was. *We might all be.* "But you must come with me, Evan. Right now."

The dear fool cast a longing look back at the door to the Garden. "Can't I—"

This time, I snarled.

Constable Lefebvre had set up in Lionel's office, though courteously refused his desk. He'd asked for and received a simple table and chair, along with a pad of actual paper—not an expensive rarity on this world—and a translight com to keep the inbound medship updated—which was.

I dragged poor Evan straight to him. It was either that, or risk being overheard in the halls. Plus the fool kept insisting he'd somewhere else to be and wouldn't explain. Had I been not been focused on the entire *was he about to die from plague* worry, I might have been suspicious.

Hindsight being perfect, I should have been.

In the here and now, having whispered a warning not to mention the Sacrissee—that being Paul's duty as well as the resulting scolding—I pushed Evan through the door ahead of me and closed it behind us, announcing a little too forcefully, "He was on the ship."

Mal took one look at Evan and waved him to a chair. "Polit Gooseberry, isn't it? I'm Constable Malcolm Lefebvre—Mal. We met in the fall."

"Evan, please." Evan remained standing, concern on his face. "What's this about? Am I in trouble?"

Clearly, I hadn't been convincing. *Humans.*

"The *Stellar Trumpet* failed to lift after her passengers disembarked. Including you, I take it?"

"Yes." Evan sank into the chair; settled himself, too, for the anxious creases on his face vanished, replaced by a sober intensity. "A problem with the ship?"

"A problem with her crew." Mal paused, gauging who sat in front of him, then gave a slight nod as if to himself. "I'm sorry to say they're dead."

"And you suspect a contagion," Evan deduced, his voice rock steady. I supposed working at an embassy on an alien planet gave one an immediate grasp of the worst-case scenario. "I witnessed no sign of illness among the crew while I was on board, nor has my monitor detected any symptoms in me." He reached into the hair behind his ear and pulled out a silver disk. "I wear it at all times. Primarily for my mental health, but it has full diagnostics." He gave a self-deprecating shrug. "My Great Gran worries."

"Thank her for it," Mal advised, his own face easing.

"I will."

I pulled up another chair to join them, careful of my tail and ignoring the constable's raised eyebrow. *Ersh had had a far more intimidating* why are you still here? *look in any of her forms.* "We need to find whomever *else* was on the ship, Evan." I hoped he'd grasp the stress on "else."

He did, though he gave me a woeful look. Our Evan being honorable and honest, he wanted me to let him be both.

In answer, I flicked my ears into a guile-free angle that wouldn't have fooled Paul, hopefully fooled the constable, and signaled Evan, who knew Lanivarians, to lie.

With a *you owe me* roll of his eyes, the diplomat turned back to Mal. "There were non-oxy breathers on board; I've no knowledge what kind. At least one Oieta. I didn't get a name. Marcy—" He paused to clear his throat. "One of the crew said the Oieta's Soft Companion was a female Human, if that helps."

"I'm sure it will, thank you." The constable wrote on his notepad, something Evan, fond of writing himself, might have appreciated under better circumstances. "Anything else?"

"I kept to myself," Evan admitted. "When I left the ship, two other starships were unloading as well, and you know how the field is. Everyone mixes together going through the—" He searched for a polite term for the conglomeration of unsanctioned and unregulated pubs, restaurants, and fake artifact dealers in the Port Village. "—the market. By the time I reached the train platform, I'd lost track of who'd come from where."

"Would you recognize the Oieta?"

"Yes. I mean, I'd recognize the exo-suit," Evan qualified.

"Excellent, Evan." The constable's smile was more official than reassuring. "Please come with me. I'm going to walk around a bit. Let's see if we can find your traveling companions. Esen? I believe Paul's looking for you. Something about the Iftsen zone?"

At this, Evan and I exchanged matching looks of dismay.

If not for the same reasons.

Elements

THE unprecedented and unwelcome request to invade the pilgrims' privacy from the Hamlet of Hillsview Preservation Committee was now a command from much higher authority. Lionel Kearn desperately wanted to believe in coincidence.

Nothing in his experience made that easy.

"Here." Skalet indicated one of several displayed images. Each had been recorded by a different snoop, hidden around the Library.

By the angle and view, he'd gained a good sense of where to find them. Sharing the locations could be a mark of trust—or test of it. In this instance, Lionel felt no urge to tell Paul or Esen what they likely already knew. He'd sent an initial carefully worded inquiry to his contact on Sacriss VII. Contacted Joel Largas, who hadn't asked questions, agreeing to come at once. Five full days translight, if they pushed the ship, and they would.

As for his other secretive line of inquiry? Lionel's most promising lead about the *Sidereal Pathfinder* was also the most disturbing. He'd teased out patterns of starship disappearances, Commonwealth and others, some beyond Sacriss, in fact, but faint, nothing definitive. Still, enough to cost him sleep at night. *Death had left a similar trail—*

Right now, this hunt was the priority. He studied the image. It showed the Sacrissee in front of the Assessment Counter, Evan at their feet. "We've placed them in the Library and arriving on the train. What makes you think the Sacrissee came on the *Trumpet*?"

"Neither of us accept coincidence." At his slight start, Skalet turned to regard him, a brow lifting. "Correct?"

"Uncannily so," the Human admitted, winning a tiny smile. He blew out a breath, then gave a grim nod. "It's possible they claimed sanctuary because they knew what had happened—or would happen—to those left on the ship."

"Exactly. I could wish our leaders less compassionate and more willing to conduct a needful and thorough interrogation."

Lionel went to speak, then thought better of it.

She noticed, of course. "Ask."

This could go badly. But he needed to know. "When I visited the university on Sacriss XIII, I observed the academics responded more readily—and in greater depth—to queries from other Sacrissee." A frustration among so many at that time. "Understandable. The ultimate *IN,* after all, is being of their kind."

Skalet didn't appear offended. "You want me to cycle into the form in order to question them."

"It's not what I want," he replied at once, aghast she'd think so. "It's what's best for you. What's feasible. In no way can I appreciate the difficulty—the effort and risk—involved."

"Nor can I explain it." Did a hint of something vulnerable—almost fear—cross her face?

Impossible. Nonetheless, Lionel's heart thudded in his chest. "Forgive me. Please forget I mentioned it."

"No need. Your suggestion has merit." Skalet reached up, tracing the tattoo from her ear along her jaw and down to her throat as if seeing it in a mirror. "I prefer to be thus, Lionel. I am my best," she continued, in her low, rich-timbred voice, "thus."

She'd every right to be what she chose; he'd been wrong to disturb her sensibilities. *Too used to Esen,* with her slipping in and out of shapes at whim. "Then if it's necessary to have a Sacrissee interrogator, we'll ask Esen."

Her laugh startled him. "Oh, that wouldn't go well, believe me." The finger that had traced the tattoo came down to touch the back of his hand. "Such consideration. Gratifying."

Pinned by her curious regard as much as by her fingertip, Lionel felt short of breath. He searched for deflection and found it on the screen. "Evan Gooseberry. Who else arrived on the same train as the Sacrissee?"

"Help me look."

He shifted his stool closer. They pored over the images together, Lionel doing his best to keep up with Skalet's lightning-quick searches through the multitudes in the Library.

An abrupt break in the feed turned the screen blank. "What was that?"

"Of no concern," Skalet replied in her low rich voice. "I blanked the input for a few moments to check a setting."

The images resumed.

He became aware of the now-feverish warmth of the body next to his. Dumping heat was a Web-being's reaction to stress, necessary in order to maintain their form. It happened to Esen regularly.

It shouldn't happen to her Elder, the formidable Skalet.

Was it his fault? Because he'd suggested she cycle? Or because she'd had to explain to a mere ephemeral Human why she wouldn't?

Regardless, he'd crossed the line, Lionel decided gloomily.

It didn't occur to him Skalet's distress might have another source or to offer to help.

He cleared his throat. "There's an Urgian," he noted. "A delegation," he corrected.

"I see them." She didn't appear to notice anything odd in his tone. "There were several non-oxy breathers on the train as well. Regrettably, I had to remove the snoops from the habitat zones. The Youngest objected."

"So we can't identify them."

"Not reliably. The suits tend to a sameness." Skalet waved her hand and the big screen went blank. "We've a starting point."

The "we" reassured him. "What's our next step?"

"Locate and isolate our suspected passengers." Another wave, and the entire screen filled with a live view of the Lobby, jammed to the walls with now-unhappy scholars, the word out about the trains. They'd be even less happy when they learned they couldn't leave the building.

"I don't suppose Paul will let us use gas," Skalet mused. "They'd be easier to sort unconscious."

Lionel stared at her.

Skalet gave him a sidelong look, then stood with a chuckle. "Your face, Lionel. I wouldn't use gas." Her eyes glinted with amusement as he rose to his feet. "Too imprecise."

That he believed. "We'll start a queue at the Assessment Counter," he said. "A customary process that allows us to pull aside those of interest with minimal disruption." He glanced down at the screen with an inner shudder. "If this lasts, I don't know where we'll house them all."

"I do."

He regarded her with a worried frown. "Without resorting to stasis or body bags."

Skalet pretended to be shocked. "Lionel!"

He kept frowning.

She grew serious. "A subordinate made a valuable suggestion. We've access to what will serve in the short-term. No need to worry about longer, is there."

Understanding, Lionel grew cold.

Longer would mean the constable had been right to take precautions against a plague. Those inside the Library would have to be evacuated to the medship. Botharis would close their unruly little landing field and shut down the Library; trivial concerns amid one far greater.

Longer meant the disease, if it was disease, had spread.

13: Closet Afternoon

WE were hiding peculiar Sacrissee in Lionel's bedroom; Evan had stolen—and lost—my new hat and gloves; a deadly *something* was on the loose that wasn't Lesy—who was on the loose and deadly; I'd yet to chastise Skalet for her behavior or have lunch; and Paul sent me hurrying to unplug the accommodation next to the Iftsen Habitat Zone.

Again.

None of which remotely equivalent in importance, but I sang the list to myself as I tottered through the smog, it being very Iftsen to reduce everything to an even footing before establishing priorities. *Plugged pipes won.*

My companions, Mobera and Nabreda, sang a harmony of sorts with me. They were happy to remain in their habitat indefinitely, assuming we could supply wine, though in no personal danger from a pathogen. Their skin, including the lining of those internal organs subjected to what entered from without, was an environment too hostile for most microorganisms.

Well, except Tripdolee Lichen. The tough tiny conglomerate of fungus and friends willingly took hold in the acidic damp of an older Iftsen's body folds, producing a greenish glow in the dark considered—depending on subspecies—an indicator of maturity, sexually alluring, or, commonly, both.

Suffice to say, no Commonwealth medteam would consider the Iftsen at risk or probable vectors of anything but a Good Time.

Singing my vow to send wine, I left my cheery companions and their once-more working accommodation—whatever they kept doing to it I didn't want to know and didn't ask—and returned to the closet to cycle once more.

The moment I did, I reconsidered my priorities from a Lanivarian perspective, then curled into a morose ball on the floor, covering my snout with the plume of my tail.

As a means of hiding from unpleasantness, curling in the closet wouldn't work for long. Paul needed me. Everyone did. The potential of any confusion in translating "sorry, you can't leave and don't eat that," let alone the pending trickiness of conveying to beings of over a hundred different biologies—some adverse to admitting they'd a biology at all—that they must "be examined by a Human expert to be sure they weren't contaminated?" No one came away happy and I wanted no part of that.

I puffed little breaths through the hairs of my tail. *Staying in the closet.*

As for our Sacrissee? I'd discovered what they hadn't wished known. Their hair tips had been Sacrissee. What I'd snuffed up from their boots was not, complicating everyone's life.

Definitely staying in the closet.

The gentle knock a short time later was not entirely a surprise.

I flattened my ears and pretended not to hear.

The next, firmer knock expressed the conviction I Was Inside, ears flat and pretending.

Good thing I'd locked the door.

"Esen," a low earnest whisper. "I know you're in there."

Paul. I puffed more air through the long hairs of my tail. Doubtless he'd been trying to do all the translating by himself, with some help from the Library and hopefully Evan but probably not Skalet—who despised repetition—and I'd have felt guilty, but I knew what was outside the door with my friend.

Chaos. Unhappy, unresolvable chaos.

The door opened, spilling light inside. Meaning Paul cheated and unlocked it using his all-Library access I hadn't thought worked on my closet, but should have realized would. I refused to budge, peering rebelliously from under my tail.

He squeezed inside and closed the door. The light went out.

This was new.

Even as a morose ball, my Lanivarian-self took up most of the available floor. *Good thing we hadn't stored a sweeper in here.*

Paul eased himself down with a grunt, sliding me over to make room. From the soft thud that came next, he'd leaned his head against the wall. *Exasperated, no doubt.*

After a long moment, he said, with no exasperation at all and—if I wasn't mistaken—a smile in his voice. "We need more of this, Fang-face."

More what? "Closets?"

Fingers found my neck, then the soft spot below an ear. "You know what I mean."

There was a funny undertone to his voice. *Exhaustion,* I decided. Wriggling, I rested my head on Paul's shin. "More resting?"

"Time together. Alone." He found the other ear. "More of that."

Confusion clouded my pleasure in the caress. "We live together," I pointed out warily. In some disarray, the wood of the staircase destroyed by Lambo yet to be stained and a temp shield securing where Paul's bedroom wall also had been ripped apart by the Carasian—who'd had a traumatic molt, so wasn't to blame—but overall, our farmhouse was cozy. "And we work together every day."

His fingers paused. "What do you think of that work?"

I didn't think about it; I just did it. *Not the right answer,* I guessed. My Human was like Ersh. The simpler-seeming the question, the larger yawned the pit of mistake and consequence.

"What do you think I think about it?" I countered, feeling clever.

"That working here's become routine. Tedious. That you're late every day now because you're bored and don't want to tell me."

No, I was late every day because I had to look after the Web-being hiding in the greenhouse or she'd eat someone. *Definitely not the right answer.*

I opened my jaws and pretended to chew on his shoe. Which was surprisingly tasty, so I stopped before drooling on his sock. "I'm never bored," I assured him. "You know that."

"Then there's something else going on. Something you want to tell me about, but haven't figured out how." With that note of fond exasperation. "Why is it so hard, Old Blob? Skalet I understand, but you and me? We're friends. Partners. Family."

"The best of my Web," I responded, touched. Paul was right, as usual. I was not, as usual. *Time for honesty.* "There is something. I've been waiting to talk to you—waiting for us to be alone and together when you aren't being called away because everyone else needs you and their problems matter more than me—" I snapped my jaw shut. *Where had* that *come from?*

"Idiot." He pressed his face into my fur. "Nothing matters more than you."

Muffled, driven by warm breath into my skin, the words held such power I didn't trust myself to answer.

Paul sat up again. "If you ever want my undivided attention, Fang-face," he promised, a smile in his voice, "you've only to say so."

"What if it's a crisis? What if the Chow breaks down?" I lowered my voice. "What if your aunt calls?" Paul having several, all of whom were formidable, demanding sorts. Then there were the uncles—

He began to shake—I realized belatedly with laughter. "Oh, you mean what if we're trapped in the Library with anxious scholars and staff, under threat of possible disease and quarantine, not to mention poor Evan caught in the thick of it?" Paul stopped laughing. "In case you hadn't noticed, Esen-alit Quar, there is a crisis and despite it, here I am, with you. I always will be."

"Always" wasn't a reasonable word for an ephemeral to use. *Nothing*, I thought happily, *was reasonable about Paul and me.* Accepting the notion made me feel not so much older as bigger. Braver.

A smidge more responsible. "I'm sorry. I shouldn't have stayed in the closet when you needed me."

He rapped the wall with a careless knuckle. "Taking time to care for yourself is never wrong. Feel better?"

"I will." Once I told him about Lesy, I would. Which logically meant telling him what had happened this morning to bring on whatever it was I hadn't seen in Skalet's Human-self that had drawn his compassion, much as I doubted she'd the capacity to feel trauma.

Drama, yes, and scorn; maybe I should leave out Skalet for now. But not Lesy—

Although there'd doubtless be scolding. Feeling rather dizzy, I braced myself. "Paul, I brought something back from Dokeci-Na—"

The door opened. Skalet loomed over us, her shadowed face expressionless, meaning she couldn't decide whether to be appalled or amused. *Appalled, most likely.* No accident, this interruption; in her opinion, Paul Ragem had no place in our Web or right to any of its secrets.

As Senior Assimilator, I'd every right to glower at her and did. "Go away. We're busy. Having a meeting," that being a wee bit plausible.

Paul, the responsible one and as yet blissfully unaware of our greenhouse conspiracy, got to his feet—without stepping on me, which couldn't have been easy—to join Skalet in the hall. "What's wrong?"

"The guest accommodations have arrived. That Pouncey female refuses to let them be deployed." Her lovely smooth voice could drip acid. "Order her to comply."

I scrambled to my feet, Skalet turning sideways to let me out of the closet. "What accommodations?" I demanded, closing the door in case she thought she was welcome. *It had been ever so much nicer inside.*

"You didn't . . ." Paul's voice trailed away. His eyes narrowed in accusation. "You did."

"I solved a problem."

From the look on my friend's face, whatever Skalet had done had created a new one.

At least she was acting more like herself again.

Makings

THERE are hunters. Sacrissee know there are always hunters in the *OUT*.

Oola knows. Wearing dried blood not her own, she keeps to the deepest shadows, clings to edges and safer—*never safe, never* IN—places. She hears the hunters coming. If they have her trail, surely they have every trail, for others must have escaped with her.

She can't be the only one left. But she no longer dares *howl* to find more.

The hunters move in the light as if they've no fear. As if they own it.

Sacrissee peek *OUT* from safety, flinch back with quiet "huffft hufffts." Smug and satisfied to be *IN*.

Oola's tail lashes the wall.

At the sound, peepholes slam shut.

At the sound, footsteps pick up speed.

Oola backs into a corner and licks her lips.

Let them come.

Servocleaners move through the streets in the revealing light of midday, crisscross the cobbles, and brush along the walls. To reassure those *IN,* they give forth a delicate hum reminiscent of the fuzzy blue and black pollinating insects found in fields and courtyard gardens, stingless and friendly.

Peepholes remain closed.

Servocleaners are programmed to surround exceptional messes, to use their bodies to hide the disgusting sight while a visual goes to a living supervisor requesting instruction. With Rattisila's shipcity nearby and alien crews wandering about, let alone the inhabitants of the All Sapients' District, this protocol prevents those visitors *sleeping it off* from being incinerated, then vacuumed for disposal. Most of them.

Encountering another such mess, servos gather from other streets and alleys. To hide this will take more than the usual number of them. So many come, they block the street entirely.

The visual they send, of body parts and torn flesh and clots of red blood mixed with blue, has one response by law: immediate on-site incineration. Hide the evidence.

A cloaked Sacrissee watches from a rooftop, recorder in hand and aimed down.

Then *HOWLS.*

14: Lobby Afternoon

WHAT Skalet had done was use her authority as S'kal-ru the Courier to order her warship, the *Trium Pa,* to send down Kraal-issue *sous*—noncombatant—settlement tents for our guests.

I allowed myself an infinitesimal bit of glee, it being my Elder who'd come up with a plan even I knew was reckless. *Petty, but enjoyable.*

When Paul wanted to move, as now, I had to roll my fingers into my paws and drop to all fours to keep up. Skalet, with her longer legs, matched his strides without effort as they discussed the situation en route. I concentrated on not panting and not nipping my web-kin, however much she deserved it, it being less discussion than verbal battle.

"Why in the hells is your ship still here?"

Fair question. We'd believed—wrongly—the *Trium Pa* had left Botharan space months ago, ordered to do so by the planetary government who'd been perturbed—to put it mildly—to discover a Kraal warship lurking behind their larger moon.

"It remains to provide critical options," Skalet replied coolly. "As now."

"Undermining any credibility we'd left on this planet." Paul could snarl almost as well as this me. "Those options better not include troops—not again."

I snarled with him.

"No one's landed. Control yourself, Youngest." Skalet might not be amused by Paul's fury; she was by mine. "*Septos Ank* dropped the tents in the adjacent field."

As if an armed Kraal scout doing a strafing run over the Library grounds, followed by the release of unknown heavy objects from above, was better.

Shaking his head in disgust, Paul moved even faster.

No living thing, sentient or otherwise, had been under the crated tents when they struck the ground. Had there been, I greatly feared Paul would have ordered Skalet to leave the Library and Botharis. A confrontation he couldn't win.

I wasn't sure I could.

Fortunately, we didn't have to test the boundaries of coexistence with my web-kin today. Skalet wasn't wrong. The Hamlet of Hillsview, however hospitable the majority of its inhabitants were, couldn't absorb over a hundred aliens; the school was the only structure able to hold more than a handful at once—and only those able to use a Human-centric accommodation.

The Library had the space and biological facilities, but no other comforts to offer, other than for those few willing to stay in their unique habitat zones. *We'd best not run out of wine.* To house our scholars while the trains were stopped, we'd need the tents. If the Commonwealth medship found a pathogen and we were put under quarantine, we'd have to house our staff as well.

And if that sickness was already here, or struck? I cringed at the thought.

No matter what happened, from the muscle jumping in Paul's jaw we'd be making changes in future—assuming the All Species' Library of Linguistics and Culture had one after this. Emergency shelters and supplies topping the list.

Here and now, we'd a neatly stacked set of Kraal-issue crates containing the former outside the main entrance, gathering snow.

Crates staff hadn't opened after retrieving them because a grim Duggs Pouncey stood in front of the stack, holding a large hammer I couldn't tell if she'd forgotten she held or had brought to use on the crates. She wasn't alone. Three other Botharan staff members were with her; without hammers but looking equally grim. They weren't, I knew, against sheltering our guests.

They were vehemently opposed to Kraal settlement tents reappearing on their planet.

Skalet should have known better. *She had*, I realized, a sour taste in my mouth. My web-kin expected Paul Ragem to deal with what she'd consider a spot of inconvenient local resistance.

Mal and Lionel stood with backs to the doors and Duggs, their attention on the crowd waiting for the train service to be restored. The Assessment Counter was closed on the premise those here had already shown Henri their stuff and we didn't want to tempt them into repeats. We'd a few scholars still at interfaces, but the rest?

Were here, in the Lobby, waiting for a train that might not come. Those whose anatomy fit Human furnishings or could fold onto a bench looked somewhat comfortable. The rest did not.

Well, there were the few making themselves right at home, like the Nerpuls who'd burrowed into one of my large decorative planters, tossing the plants to the floor. The plants, in turn, were being used as bedding—and possibly supper—by a trio of Anatae. A pair of Urgians hung by their overts from coat hooks, either sleeping through the racket or composing their complaint into pithy limericks.

Because everyone else was talking. After all, everyone had come to the Library in search of information and that was exactly what they were doing now. Asking one another. Trying, loudly, to ask members of other species. Loudest of all were the ones demanding answers from our poor staff about the trains, what sort of world didn't have other modes of transport available, and what were they to do in the meantime?

Plus one request to eat a neighbor, a conversation I caught in time to wave Envall Ragem, our most physically imposing greeter, to help Carwyn. *Size occasionally mattered.*

Thinking of food led me to fond thoughts of our Carasian. Lambo could distract the gathering; looming overhead from the upper level walkway would do it. *Those newly enlarged claws.* I sincerely hoped his absence didn't mean Lambo had barricaded the Chow against the masses because then we'd have nothing to feed them but each other.

It didn't occur to me to worry about the basement; *later, I'd remember that.*

The scholars weren't, for the most part, interested in a purely Human argument outside in the frigid cold, given the icy air pouring through partly open doors, though a couple of still agile Prumbins were bumping one another and looked prepared to rush outside presumably to see if we'd lied about the train, which was why our constable and Lionel blocked the exit.

While Paul talked to Duggs.

I'd confidence. No one was more persuasive than my friend, and he'd the advantage of Duggs' respect—unless Skalet had lost that for him.

Wisely, my web-kin kept her Kraal-self out of Duggs' sight.

Spotting me, Lionel beckoned urgently. I went over to him, angling my ears his way in case he thought to convey something audible over the din. Sure enough, when I reached his side, he leaned down and shouted, "Skalet didn't mean any harm." At the incredulous wrinkle of my snout, he flushed but went on stubbornly, "These are improved models, with controllable internal environments and flexible bio-accommodations."

Just like Skalet to give me more to clean. Still, none of this was Lionel's fault and, however mystifying, I appreciated his continued loyalty to my annoying web-kin. I worked my snout and ears into a more conciliatory expression. "Where's Evan?"

The noise level rose, possibly in response to the next rumor train service had been restored—we'd an Ervickian with a sense of humor—so all I caught was "—Garden—"

I could see through the doors that the winds had picked up even more. In open areas it'd be close to the condition locally known as a "blizz-out," when at times you couldn't find your hand in front of your face, let alone a path back to safety.

The rest could deal with the Lobby filled with upset—and to be honest, somewhat ripe—aliens and the standoff at the door.

I had a potentially lost and frozen Human to scold. *Once I found him.*

Elements

GREAT Gran called them "Putrid Gripes," people like Wenn who treated others like playthings, especially those weaker or unable to defend themselves. Or who were embarrassingly naïve, as Evan Gooseberry had been when Lucius Whelan had sent him, uninvited, message after message with vids of—of things he didn't want to see or do, not with Lucius.

Maybe with Paul . . .

He shook his head to clear it. Paul Ragem was his friend, a very good friend, and in love with someone else. Lesley. Lesley and Paul. Paul and Lesley. Evan felt a rush of joy, being big-hearted and a very good friend himself. He couldn't have timed his vacation any better. To be here to see Paul's hope come true at last.

Not that he'd watch, he told himself, suddenly flustered.

Lesley was why Evan had slipped away from the constable once they'd found the Oieta from the *Stellar Trumpet* and her Soft Companion. He'd tried to find Paul, to tell him about Lesley and, given the seriousness of the situation, to offer to take care of her. But no one knew where Paul had gone, or Esen, so Evan—knowing it was sensible—had left word with Lionel he was going to the Garden for a walk to clear his head.

He hadn't dared tell the truth. What if this wasn't a mutual romantic assignation gone awry? What if Lesley was a Putrid Gripe and hiding naked in the greenhouse some sick joke? Thanks to Lucius, Evan Gooseberry had a new sense of what people were capable of doing. Tricking someone into feelings was among them.

Not Paul. *Never Paul.*

His luggage remained wherever it had gone and he'd needed his own outerwear. Thinking of Lesley's height, Evan had found Ally and asked to borrow her coat and boots. After assuring him his request wasn't the strangest of her day, Ally'd complimented him on finding a way to avoid the racket until the trains ran again.

Embarrassed, Evan couldn't tell her he loved the "racket," if not the reason for it. To be surrounded by interesting individuals of such varied species? It was like a dream come true. He'd have stayed and gladly.

But Lesley was still out in the cold. She could be hungry, so Evan went to the Chow next. He found it deserted, the sullen lights on the massive food dispenser behind the counter as intimidating as Lambo; in no way a device to attempt on his own. He still had the emerg rations in the pocket of his inner coat.

Encountering a cart loaded with supplies in the hall, Evan'd helped himself to a blanket and a bulb of water. Wasn't Lesley trapped at the Library as surely as those indoors?

And indoors, where it was warm, was where she belonged—not in the freezing greenhouse, with night coming.

Preparations made, all Evan had to do was get outside.

To his dismay, it was no longer as easy. The staff corridors were now locked and the Lobby jammed with aliens. Almost at once Evan found himself too close to a Heezle, who batted eyelids at him and leaned encouragingly. The bundles in his hand made it impossible to wave the appropriate gesture of disinterest.

Finding a gap, Evan evaded the Heezle and dashed behind the long coat rack, with its hanging Urgians. He counted to twenty, giving time for the Heezle to fixate on someone else, then slipped back out again, walking close behind a cluster of Rands.

He couldn't see the Heezle. Relieved, Evan headed for the admin corridor.

The Assessment Counter might be closed, but the area in front of it was clogged with a sputtering group of Odarians, trunks waving as they voiced their complaint. Something about a persistent Heezle.

Evan would have felt some guilt in the matter, but Henri nodded and took notes, carefully out of reach of the sputter. Spotting Evan, she waved him through, eyes twinkling.

Knowing the way, Evan retraced his steps through the hallways to the Garden portal, his plans firming with each step. Whatever Lesley's motives, he was determined to see her to a safe, discreet location. That plainly wasn't the Library.

Making Paul and Esen's farmhouse the best choice. If the sun hadn't set yet. And if he could find it. Evan nodded to himself and straightened his shoulders, sweating a little in his coats. How hard could it be?

He'd been there before.

Once in the portal, Evan activated the door controls, then put on his gloves, gathering his bundle. This time, he was properly dressed and prepared.

The exterior door opened, and a blast of wind shoved him back a step before he could brace himself against it. *A blizzard on top of everything else?* He'd checked the local weather forecast, always of interest if not always comprehensible in a meaningful "wear this" way. There hadn't, he was sure, been mention of a blizzard or storm or even more snow.

Forecasting on a world like Botharis, where the weather wasn't scheduled and told how to behave, might not be the exact science he'd known.

The more reason to get Lesley into these clothes and indoors.

Five standard minutes later—which could have been fifteen or ten because it wasn't night but wasn't day and he wasn't baring skin to consult his chrono—Evan Gooseberry came to the conclusion he'd made a potentially fatal mistake. More than one, really, the first being underestimating the danger posed by frozen precipitation and rapidly moving air. The second?

Expecting the deep imprint left by the ShimShree to guide him to the greenhouse, as it had before. Most had filled with windblown snow. He resorted to kicking at the loose stuff, guessing what felt raised and hard underfoot were the edges of the trail.

Or patio stones. Or logs. Maybe a bench.

It had to be the trail. He kept going, kept guessing, because mistake number three gave him no choice. He'd lost the Library. Maybe if he'd goggles or a light, he could penetrate the walls of white—

How much worse it must be for Lesley, alone out here with only Esen's coat, gloves, and hat. *She must be terrified.* That thought kept him going most of all.

Fifteen minutes, or an hour later, Evan walked into a tree. His bundle and arm cushioned the blow, but a low branch snapped across his forehead, stealing his hat and sending hot blood trickling down the side of his face.

He pushed away with a growl, squinting into the wind. It had shifted to push from behind, toying with him, but he'd been going in the right direction, he was sure of it, and wasn't about to be fooled. This time, though, he walked with a hand out in front, the bundle under the other arm.

It would have helped if the snow were an even blanket, but far from it. Sometimes the track was scoured clear.

Others, like now, snow reared up waist-high, forcing him to go around or climb over.

Evan paused to gather his strength. The wind paused as if to gather its, and that's when he heard the singing.

His head snapped around.

Lesley, it had to be. Refusing to be wrong, or to wonder why anyone would be *singing* in this, Evan worked his way across what wasn't a path but snow-wrapped clusters of little bushes toward the sound, mentally apologizing to Esolesy as those bushes cracked and snapped underfoot.

A dark mass loomed in his path, by the feel, a hedge, thick enough to block the wind. For that reason alone, he'd have stayed by it gladly, but the singing hadn't stopped and the singer was beyond the hedge. Evan sidestepped, keeping a gloved hand on the prickly stuff. There must be a hole in it somewhere. A way through—

The hedge fell away from his touch, though it still blocked the wind.

Evan stepped forward to discover a second hedge behind the first. Between them was room to walk.

Between, the air was still. It gave the illusion of warmth and peace; as if in argument, his bare ears began to throb and his nose drip. He shivered.

A few steps more and Evan found himself outside again, the hedge behind him.

The wind swirled around this place, as if it didn't dare enter. A narrow path led between rows of dry frozen stalks taller than he was; distracted, Evan tripped on the first step down, catching himself in time.

Three steps, then the stalks were gone and Evan found himself in the open, an open more like an outdoor room for branches arched high overhead to form a totally inadequate ceiling this time of year. *Pretty and private in summer,* he thought, bemused. Rough-hewn rocks made a wall of sorts around a circular patio, clear of snow.

At the center of that was the singer.

No, dancer.

Singer-dancer. Who sang without words, the melody flowing with her every move, inspired by movement, the artistry of each dependent on the other in a way he'd never seen before.

It was Lesley, wearing only Esen's hat and knit gloves, and he would have called out to stop her, should, for surely her toes—at the very least—were freezing, but this?

This was the goddess of winter, skin pale as ice, white hair drifting back and forth like snow on the wind, and he couldn't bring himself to interrupt anything so beautiful.

The song ended of its own accord, her body paused in an achingly graceful curve, her head up as though listening to the wind. Then, with unnatural speed, Lesley disappeared into the gloom and snow.

Had he glimpsed a flash of blue?

"Evan?"

He whirled around, so startled he tripped. Esen reached out a gloved paw to steady him. "Easy there," she said kindly. "Glad I found you."

Had she seen Lesley?

It didn't matter. He'd Ally's coat and boots in his hands, the blanket, and Evan tried to think of a reasonable explanation or how to confess but his brain felt frozen and his mouth wouldn't work.

A snowflake settled on Esen's slender snout. She licked it off, then stuck out her tongue to catch the next. "I hid in a closet," she informed him cheerfully. "This is prettier."

He wasn't—well, he had, the first time he'd run outside, but not now. "I wasn't hiding," he protested, then realized he'd ruined a good excuse. As for pretty, it was getting darker as the sun set, blurring the difference between hedge, tree, and stone, and the air hurt to breathe. With a convulsive shiver, Evan came to a decision. "I met someone here."

Esen became a statue.

He hurried on, despite the improbable words. "She hadn't any clothes, so I gave her your coat and went back for these." He lifted the bundle. "She'll be in the greenhouse. I hope. Her name's—"

"Lesley."

Esen knew! Evan smiled as he shivered, relieved to his chilly core. "You know her."

"And you do." Esen's ears were pinned beneath her cap so he couldn't read an expression beyond the incredulity in her voice. "Why am I not surprised," she muttered. Louder and with reassuring warmth, "Thank you—more than I can say, Evan—for your kindness to Lesley. You get inside." She reached for what he held. "I'll look after her now."

Evan clutched his bundle. "The greenhouse isn't shelter. There's ice inside. I'm sure Paul would want Lesley to wait for him in the farmhouse."

"Paul?"

If she'd been incredulous before, this seemed shock. Evan hesitated, unsure, then rushed on, "I'm sorry you didn't know, Es. Paul—he cares for Lesley. He always has. Deeply. I wasn't to tell you—or Esolesy."

Esen shook her head in a very Human denial. Or disbelief. "I said I'll look after her, Evan. You need to get back inside." The Lanivarian made a grab for the bundle.

"No." He held it out of her reach. "I'm coming with you."

"Evan—" with a snarl of pure, deserved, exasperation.

"I have to," he confessed in a small voice. "I'm lost."

15: Greenhouse Sunset

THIS, I decided, would be how Paul felt when I came to him midway through a plan that wasn't going exactly as expected. As the next step would be my friend helping me fix things—*a friend who'd apparently been keeping a secret of his own lately and wasn't here anyway*—I'd no choice now but hope I could.

I'd no clue what about Evan had inspired our web-kin to cycle at last and reveal herself to him. *And couldn't ask.* Meaning the only way to know if Lesy could be trusted around him again was to dangle the young Human in front of her.

Ersh save the fool. I wasn't sure which of us I meant.

Evan, following behind me and warned, firmly, not to so much as think about grabbing my tail for a guide, wasn't one, not really. Kindhearted, curious, brave, yes. If he believed Paul had feelings for someone—*whatever that was about*—Evan would care too and take action. Our young diplomat was inclined to rush ahead without checking for cliffs. He might grow out of that.

Or not. As someone prone to similar missteps, I'd have sympathized except for the size of this one.

If Lesy had reacted otherwise and consumed Evan's mass?

While I'd have grieved his loss—Ersh having taught us to regret the premature end of any ephemeral life and he was that rarity in mine, a friend—the tragedy wouldn't have ended there. Lesy would have had to be removed as a threat to others. I could do it.

I would have, I realized with a dark cold surety new to my existence, and not to save others. Oh, no. I'd have acted out of self-interest. Explaining Lesy's presence to Paul would have become impossible. Even if he could forgive Lesy for her instincts, he'd never forgive me. Our friendship would have ended, forever.

Better Lesy die, than that.

Efficient. Skalet-voice, not Ersh's, and, Cosmic Gods, when had I become her?

When I'd ignored the danger of bringing insensate bits of web-flesh to a place full of vulnerable, ephemeral beings. When I hadn't told my best, first friend what I'd done and why before Lesy grew to a perilous size. When I hadn't *asked* before bringing her bits onto the ship home if it was a good idea—and been willing to be told *no, Old Blob, it's not.*

I whined under my breath, pushing through the snow.

"Are you all right?" the instigator of my inner turmoil asked considerately.

Not in any sense, I wanted to snap, but that wasn't true. However upset I felt at what might have happened? The reality was Evan hadn't been eaten. Perhaps, thanks to him, our web-kin had just proved herself restored to us, sane and whole.

After all, Lesley was her choice of Human name, a form she didn't use near Ersh. Or Skalet. She'd shown me, on one of our excursions; being a callow few centuries myself, I thought it made her look old.

Which she was. I took Evan's free hand before he walked into my mummified fystia bush and helped him around the obstacle. *Older than any but Ersh.*

Walking through blinding snow, something this me did by closing my eyes most of the way and relying on web-memory for the path, I found myself thinking about Lesy. More precisely, the weird little *taste* now part of me.

I'd never shared directly with Lesy before, receiving her memories presorted through Ersh. When I'd absorbed Lesy-bits from the shrine on Dokeci-Na, I'd been careful to shunt them aside, safely isolated from my web-flesh.

This morning I'd been too focused on my outrage at Skalet, deter-mined to know what damaging memories she'd forced on Lesy, to hes-itate, let alone pay attention to what else I'd assimilated. Now I did, urgently hunting any sign she was a risk to those in my care.

Finding tiny, odd feelings. Wee, peculiar urgings dashing about that weren't appetite, but were hungers nonetheless. Larger, and growing, a dissatisfaction with what was—

"Esen? Why h-have we s-stopped?"

I returned to myself with a start, hearing Evan's teeth chattering. "Sorry. We're almost there."

With Lesy.

By the time the greenhouse rose from the shadows to block the wind, I hadn't thought of anything I could do about the situation—other than be web-flesh as soon as possible to excise the *strange* from Lesy. And hope she didn't assimilate Evan. And that Evan didn't succumb to the cold before she could.

My Lanivarian-self panted with stress.

Evan had grown oblivious, no longer replying when I spoke to him. By the time I thought to give him my hat, his curls were frozen and I feared for his ears. *If the tips of mine were nipped, I deserved it.* He moved stiffly, icicles adorning eyelashes and nostrils. He was panting too, unwisely; I doubted he had inner warmth to spare. *Or time.*

There were prints, Human sized and shaped, before the door, imply-ing Lesley had come home, not Lesy, adding the new worry she'd dam-aged her Human-self and wind up remembering it as missing toes.

Not my fault.

What was? Evan being in desperate need of shelter. My "DO NOT KNOCK" sign mocked me as I went to open the door. I'd listened to his urgings and hurried the pair of us after my essentially invulnerable web-kin when I should have marched the Human to the Library, a destination he wouldn't have expected and one where I'd help to tie him up if necessary.

Where he'd be safe.

Instead, he was in danger of frostbite and near comatose, granted

Lesy didn't assimilate his mass. There was a small heater in the greenhouse—Lesy hadn't needed it, but it could save Evan—

Skalet pulled the door from my paw, opening it wide. "Get in, Youngest."

Her hand shot past my head. I turned in slow motion as she tossed a black powder into Evan's face, then caught his collapsing body in her arms. "Let's get him warm, shall we?"

I'd missed a memo.

Struggling to catch up, I followed Skalet into the greenhouse, closing the door and shutting out the wind-driven snow. There was a glow ahead.

My eyes adapted to the dimmer light and the glow resolved into the opening of a Kraal emergency shelter. She'd set one up *inside* the greenhouse. "How—"

"Always you dismiss technology." Smug, that was. "I put a tracker in Evan's coat when I first encountered him." She bent to enter the shelter, still carrying the Human.

"Why?"

She laid him on the waiting pallet with what sounded suspiciously like a chuckle. "Our diplomat is like you, Youngest. Full of knowledge without practice. Perilously attracted to what isn't your business." With impersonal efficiency—Evan might as well been a corpse—she stripped off his snow-crusted outer clothing, tossing that aside. "When the tracker showed him heading here, I activated my preparations. Remove his boots and socks. I trust you're grateful, Youngest."

Skalet didn't know about Lesley. Didn't know Evan had met Lesy's Human-self.

The realization silenced whatever I might otherwise have said.

I took off Evan's footwear, moving aside to watch Skalet check his toes one by one. She produced a tube of cream, rubbing the substance over his feet, then any other exposed skin, including his nose. She finished by wrapping the unconscious Human in a self-warming blanket, and I was still no closer to understanding her care for him.

Or what I was supposed to do now.

As Senior Assimilator, I could bury the memory of the last hour or so deep in my flesh and keep it from her. *How was that fair?* Based on this morning, Skalet had grown desperate waiting for any sign of Lesy's recovery. She deserved to know our web-kin had cycled successfully—and been sane enough to talk to another being without assimilating his mass or revealing our nature. *Ersh would have been proud.*

No, I corrected myself. Ersh would have expected no less of my Elders. Only I'd succeeded in true disobedience. *And look where that had got me.* Not that I regretted a moment. Well, I regretted several, maybe many, but what mattered was the sum of my life till now, with Paul in it? I wouldn't change if I could.

As for what I'd do to protect our future? Unsettled—*afraid*—I felt the tip of my ear. Chill flesh and damp fur, that was all. I pushed it upright despite its attempt to sag in distress. I had to talk to Paul as soon as possible. Tell him about the newest—by far the oldest, but Humans wouldn't think like that—member of our Web. Find the right words to explain her unique nature. For Lesy was his future, too.

A talk over cups of Lambo's hot mint drink. While wrapped in a warm dry towel. Two towels. Maybe a talk that could wait until everyone was safe and the Library back to normal—

Probably not.

Skalet ran a medscanner over Evan, nodding to herself. "I estimated his mass; he'll be under another 40 minutes. Given the cold and his species, I'd no option but to use *Tilenex*; his memory of more recent events will be confused or missing."

An option she'd prefer and depending what was in those memories? Skalet might have done us all a favor. *Not that I'd admit it.*

"Once his core's warm," she continued, "we'll take him to the Library where I trust you'll keep better watch on him."

Skalet's presumption of authority, especially when it came to how to treat one of my friends, should have raised my hackles. Would have any other time, but all at once I remembered Paul's puzzling concern about her. "How was your sharing with Lesy?"

Skalet couldn't help a dismayed flick of her eyes to Evan's unconscious face, covering her reaction with a furious, "That's not what she is—not anymore." She spat to the side.

She'd tasted it too. The *strange.* Been upset by it—badly enough Paul had noticed, even if I hadn't. "You'd never shared with Lesy before," I guessed out loud. "Only through Ersh."

Skalet flinched. *At the name, or the truth?* Both, I thought. Her nostrils flared, then she answered, low and grim, "The Senior Assimilator for our Web feeds first, then shares what is needful, no more. No less."

"Then why share—"

"It wasn't my idea. She took me by surprise. Are you happy, Youngest? She attacked this me! What else was I to do?"

Run? She couldn't. I never had. The thought of Skalet freezing in horror then cycling in self-defense was painfully familiar. Ersh's tactic—*Share, Youngest*—when I was to learn what I wouldn't enjoy, didn't want to know, and couldn't refuse.

Skalet had been shaken to her core, either by what she'd assimilated from Lesy, or by the experience itself. *Both.* Now my web-kin waited, arms tight around her middle and lips pressed into a white line, for my answer. Pleading, in her own way, for help.

I thought of Paul. Of how he knew what would comfort me, even when I didn't, but what Skalet needed—who she needed—wasn't Paul. Or me. "Where's Lesy?"

"I don't know." With a sneer and most un-Skalet-like *I don't care* undertone. "I assume she's hiding in a pot, as usual. She was always a sneak."

An Elder, displaying weakness and poor manners? Ersh knows I should have been appalled; instead, I felt a wave of pity, some for myself as I glimpsed the eons ahead. *And here I'd wanted to be the mature one.*

"Stay with Evan," I ordered my troubled web-kin. "I won't be long."

Makings

HUNTERS are everywhere, in the Vast *Out*. Sacrissee know this to be true.

Not all have learned this lesson.

The first-floor basement of the All Species' Library of Linguistics and Culture, with its overcluttered shelves and bins of visitor-brought items, isn't an easy place to navigate quietly. Not when your body is the size of a small groundcar and comes equipped with great crushing claws as well as smaller handling ones, appendages that, while powerful and useful, tend to knock over things.

Things such as an assortment of poles—more rightly varied objects categorized as pole-shaped by virtue of possessing a length allowing them to lean precariously against one another in a long line.

The Carasian, Lambo Reomattatii, pauses to admire the inexorable tumble, clatter, and crash. He'd—for thinking in the other pronoun, the one to come, *perfection,* might hurry the transformation and *he* isn't ready—barely brushed one of the things, yet the entropy made inevitable by the laws of physics knocks pole after pole to the floor until the last, at the far end of the storeroom, succumbs.

There being no one else down here to notice, once the show is over, he continues his search. For what, now, that's the true and vexing question—although he acquires a set of strong hooks to bolt to his glorious new carapace and what could be a new apron—but Lambo will not overlook any possibility. Did not Lionel Kearn, learned and interesting for a Human, challenge him with uncovering secrets concerning Veya Ragem, her lost ship, the *Sidereal Pathfinder,* and its rumored advanced star drive and nav systems? They could be here.

And hadn't he come to Botharis to just that purpose? At times, the universe could offer a pleasing congruence. As tonight, when his purpose allows him to avoid the masses stuck in the lobby since morning and continually demanding food service.

Bah! Fasting is good for the metabolism. And delays molts.

A soft quick rattle gives the Carasian pause again, coming as it does at a distance and from a direction impossible for an errant claw or carapace edge to be the cause.

He activates the remote to turn off the lights, then sinks into a silent, hunter's crouch. Delicious, to be mistaken for a shadow, deeper than any, then pounce. Though not yet at the magnificent stage of life where the next step would be tear apart and eat, there is nothing wrong with practice.

When nothing happens, the Carasian gives a disgruntled rattle of his own and orders up the lights, resuming his search. A mousel, most likely.

Never seeing the hunters who, having made their entry through a newly created hole in the wall, disappear into shadows of their own.

16: Greenhouse Night

L ESY wasn't in a pot. She wasn't Lesy either; her Human-self huddled under my missing coat, my gloves on her fingers, and my hat on her head.

This wasn't about me, I reminded myself.

She'd gone to ground, hiding, as Skalet accused, behind the compost bins at the rear of the greenhouse. As I approached, her head lifted. "You. It is you."

We'd been family—*were family,* I insisted to myself, despite shivering at something in her voice. I knew what it was. I'd become accustomed to Human voices, their tones, their cadence. Lesley spoke like someone who'd forgotten how.

"Lesy—"

She drew handfuls of long white hair over her face, looking out through the locks. "Call me Lesley. You should be—Bess!" with a sudden smile, as though the memory pleased her. "That's the rule," almost sternly.

Which didn't please me. Ersh's rule, to match shape, was more a guideline even she'd only followed when it suited her; it'd be inconvenient in the extreme to start following Lesy's choices. *My rules now.*

I settled for, "It's too cold, Lesley."

"Evan's bringing me clothes. Where is he?" Her face thrust through her hair, eyes darting around.

"Who is Evan?" I asked, testing her.

"Your friend. He's pretty," with a giggle. "Where's Paul? I want to meet him too. We can all be friends, Esen. Human friends." Another giggle.

My hackles tried to rise under my coat. While a pleasant-sounding outcome, *an improvement over any I'd imagined,* Lesy's giggles had a higher than normal pitch.

Itchy. I focused. "Do you know where you are? Do you—" *Remember wasn't a word to use, not yet.* "—feel well?"

Lesy put a gloved finger under my chin, tilting her head to study me. If she was confused by the new-to-her dapples marring my snout, I'd no intention of explaining.

"I feel many things, Esen," she said at last. "What you want to know is if you've put me together *well,* as if I'm some puzzle with parts having a single way to fit, with all others wrong." She leaned forward to touch her nose to mine, whispering, "I've no idea."

I responded with a quick lick before she pulled away, feeling many things too, chief among them an upwelling joy I didn't dare trust, not yet. For instead of licking back, as Old Lesy would have found a way to do in any form, New Lesy wiped her chin with my glove and looked confused.

Patience, I told myself, moving on to practical concerns. Her Human-self showed signs of hypothermia, as had Evan. While he'd brought her warmer clothes than mine, clothes with a smell I knew, Lesy didn't need them—and Ally would in order to go home. Surely soon.

"It's time you became yourself again," I told my web-kin. "I'll come back in the morn—"

"No." She curled into a tight huddle again, peering up at me. "Human is the right shape. The safe shape."

Instinct, to blend in and hide web-form; no doubt why Evan had met this form of Lesy. Ersh's training too, overcoming our baser one, *to consume,* and I was beyond grateful. But now? "You're safe here—"

"Am I? Evan came. Others could."

Complicating matters. I could do as she'd done to Skalet: force her into web-form by cycling myself. I would if pressed, and could, thanks to Skalet's "preparations" including sacks of duras leaves—but that wasn't a conversation. *Wasn't kind or welcome,* as I'd learned the last time I'd forced Skalet to cycle and share for her own good.

Let alone Skalet's opinion now.

"I like Evan. He's pretty. I'm pretty too," Lesy told me, spreading out her arms.

She was beautiful as a Human, as she was in any of her forms, and the Lesy I'd known enjoyed embellishing that beauty with whatever a species provided, from dresses to sticky bits of fluorescent mucus.

Not the point. "You can't stay Human," I insisted. "Not now."

"Skalet does." Lesy looked beyond me. "Don't you."

I'd felt Skalet's silent presence at my back. Much as I wanted to know what she thought of this version of our web-kin, now wasn't the time. "Skalet isn't living here. You'll damage this form if you keep it before we find a more suitable place for you. Somewhere warm."

She pouted, the first true "Lesy" look I'd seen on this face. "I must stay Human."

"Fool. As am I," Skalet said, her voice bleak and without hope. I wanted to whine in response. "What you feel is my compulsion, assimilated from me. Ersh kept my shame secret." Her hand gripped my shoulder, fingers biting through coat and jacket. "Show her. I know Ersh shared with you, Esen-alit-Quar, why I find myself compelled to this shape above all others."

It hadn't been a pleasant sharing. "But Evan—" I began.

"Remains unconscious and unaware." Her fingers eased their punishing tightness, but stayed on my shoulder. "Don't rush. We'll need these clothes."

I didn't always forget that. Well, I did often enough to warrant Skalet's reminder. I shed the outer trappings of being Lanivarian, Skalet doing the same.

Lesy shook her head, refusing.

Meaning my nice new knit gloves and hat would soon be reduced to their molecular components and shed as water, to freeze on the floor. Along with my coat. All of which Evan had taken in the first place.

At least I'd still my boots.

Time for the memory Skalet considered her "shame."

As if it wasn't cold enough already.

17: Picco's Moon, Two Hundred Years Ago

LIKE many young beings, it came as something of a revelation to me that my Elders had been young once themselves. Or at least younger, with all that implied about having made choices—or mistakes.

It was the latter which intrigued me most. Or formed the single defining aspect of my early own life—whichever way you preferred to look at it—though during my first few centuries of life?

I was almost always: "Esen-alit-Quar! Where's that little troublemaker?!"

Not that I ever intended to cause trouble. In truth, I went to great lengths to avoid causing anything at all, understanding that anything which attracted the attention of my Elders was not going to end well.

Unfortunately, I possess a curiosity equal to any hunger of my flesh. Half answers, hints, suggestions of "you'll know when you're as old as we" only fanned that curiosity, particularly as I found it hard to believe I'd ever be as old as any of my Web. The Web of Ersh. Ersh herself was unimaginably ancient.

And the most likely individual to find fault with me at any given moment.

Or the second-most. Skalet took my occasional missteps as her duty to announce—or even better, cause.

Mistakes aside, *Why?* was my preferred conversation starter, perhaps because it made my Elders flinch. Now when Ersh deigned to offer the answer to a question, one had no choice but to live with the consequences. But my curiosity was so vast—or, more accurately, my ability at that age to imagine such consequences so limited—that I would continue to push Ersh for answers long after any other of my kin would wisely back away. It didn't help that those answers were most often doled out to me, in typical Ersh fashion, not when I first asked, but rather when she felt knowing them would educate me even more than in their substance.

So it was with war.

War wasn't a new concept to me. I'd assimilated the cultures, histories, and biologies of thousands of intelligent species from Ersh. I was familiar, if never comfortable, with war as a fact of life for some, the inevitable end of life for others.

What was new was the warfare lately shared by Skalet. Even filtered through Ersh, her memories of the Kraal's battle for Arendi Prime and its aftermath were like a stain, affecting my every thought. How had a Web-being, sworn to preserve ephemeral culture, become so very good at waging its wars?

Not that I thought the question through in quite those terms. With what Ersh would doubtless consider a selfish fixation on my own life, I wanted to avoid learning any more than I had to about war and destruction. In particular, I didn't want any more lessons on the subject from Skalet.

Skalet probably felt the same. Certainly, she made it abundantly clear our sessions together were a waste of her talents in tactics and strategy. When Ersh wasn't in range, that is. Otherwise, as well argue with the orbit of Picco's Moon as one of Ersh's decisions about my education.

Still, there had to be a way. Rather than grumble to myself, I decided to go to Ansky. However, it is the way of our kind that we literally have no secrets from Ersh. Something which hadn't actually occurred to me when I decided it was safer to approach my birth-mother than the center of our six-person universe.

My chance came during Ansky's turn to make supper, a tradition at those times when our odd family gathered in the same place, in this case, Picco's Moon.

Carved, like the rest of Ersh's home, from rock almost as old as she, the kitchen was a sparse, practical room, able to accommodate a variety of cooking skills while safely housing a maturing Web-being prone to explode without notice. When it was just Ersh and me, food came out of the replicator and the counters became cluttered with what had her attention at the time, from greenhouse cuttings to bits of machinery. When Lesy played chef, gleaming porcelain of unusual shapes appeared, and woe betide any who disturbed her delicate—and often unidentifiable—concoctions. I was definitely forbidden entrance.

Ansky, being more competent and Esen-tolerant, greeted my arrival with a friendly, if absentminded, wave of welcome.

"I can help," I offered, grabbing the largest knife available and curling lip over fang in mock threat. Assorted vegetables were already cowering on the countertop.

For some reason, Ansky rescued the knife from my paw with a deft slip of an upper tentacle. She liked to cook as a Dokecian, the five-limbed form possessing sufficient coordination to stir the contents of pots, dice vegetables, and carve meat all at once. I watched her wistfully—my own ability with the form still limited to pulling myself around and under furniture, at constant risk of forgetting which handhold to release before tugging at the next. A regrettable incident involving a tableful of crystals and a coat rack had led Ersh to forbid me this form indoors.

"I'd ask you to do the dishes, but . . ." her voice trailed away meaningfully.

My current self, my Lanivarian birth-form, abhorred water, something Ansky knew from experience. "I've gloves," I assured her, my tongue slopping free between my half-gaping jaws. I resisted my tail's urge to swing from side to side. Smiling was fine, but Ansky wouldn't approve a lapse of good manners.

We settled in, shoulder to shoulders, working in companionable silence. If my washing technique lacked finesse, at least the clean dishes arrived intact on the counter. I wasn't the only one who measured my growth by such things.

But I hadn't come to Ersh's steamy, fragrant kitchen—which had perfectly functional servos, so the physical effort to produce both steam and fragrance was unnecessary, but no one asked me—to be helpful. I'd come with a problem.

Of course, Ansky knew it as well. "So. What is it this time, Esen?" she asked after a few moments.

I almost lost my grip on one of Ersh's favorite platters. "It?" I repeated, keeping my ears up. All innocence.

My birth-mother wasn't fooled. "Let me guess. Skalet's latest enterprise."

My tail slid between my legs as I scrubbed a nonexistent spot. Confronted by the very subject I'd hoped to discuss, I found myself unable to say another word.

"She's become such a nasty morsel."

I couldn't help but stare up at her. Each of her three eyes were the size of my clenched paws. Two looked down at me, their darkness glistening with emotion. "Did you think this sharing was welcomed by any of us? The taste of her memories, even first assimilated by Ersh, were—unpleasant."

I remembered Ersh-taste exploding in my mouth, the exhilarating flood of new memories filling my body. Remembered too much. Skalet hadn't merely observed the Kraal's latest war—she'd helped orchestrate it.

That conflict and her cleverness would be my next lesson. There would be lists and details beyond what Ersh had filtered for me during assimilation. Worst of all, there would be Skalet's unconcealed pride in her work. *How could she?*

I wouldn't put up with it. I'd hide until she left again. I'd—I'd undoubtably be found, reprimanded, and have my lesson anyway.

To hide the shaking of my gloved paws, I shoved them deep in the suds-filled sink to rescue drowning utensils. "I don't understand her," I said finally, unable to keep a hint of a growl from the words. "She acts as they do. Why?" With great daring, I clarified: "Why does Ersh permit it?"

"You'll have to ask Ersh."

The noise I made wasn't polite, but Ansky refrained from comment. "When she's ready, I'm sure you'll find out." Then she said something strange, something I would come to understand only later. "The forms we take are ourselves, Esen-alit-Quar. We are no more immune to our individual pasts than any civilization is immune to its history. Never fall into the trap of believing yourself other than the flesh you wear, no matter its structure. Skalet—" A tentacle nudged the pot I was holding in the air. "Enough gossip. I need that one next."

Much later, having done Ansky's cooking justice, I was doing my utmost to appear attentive and awake, my posture as impeccably straight as a form evolved from four-on-the-floor could manage. My involuntary yawns, however stifled, likely ruined the effect. "Was there anything else, Ersh?" I asked, before I could yawn again. It had been a longer day than most, given my now-departed web-kin had left disarray and laundry sprawled over their rooms. Being least and latest made any mess my responsibility.

The tall mound of crystal that was Ersh in her preferred form gave an ominous chime. "Should I not ask you, Youngest?"

One of those "examine your soul for spots'"questions. I was suddenly alert, if incapable of figuring out a safe answer.

Before I needed to do so, Ersh continued. "You would know more about Skalet's fascination with war."

How? I didn't quite gnash my teeth. I should have realized Ersh would have shared with each before they left her again. I couldn't blame Ansky. All Ersh had to do was take a nibble and she'd know all we'd done and experienced.

On the bright side, while I couldn't deny my question, she might answer it. "Yes, Ersh," I said hopefully.

Ersh leaned forward and I eased back, careful of my toes should she decide to tumble. A graceful and powerful mode of locomotion, but one I judged safer observed from a distance. "You wonder why I tolerate it?"

This being a far less comfortable question, I did my best to shrink in place without appearing defensive. It was a posture I'd yet to master, but the effort sometimes mollified Ersh. At least it made me feel a smaller target. Then, as usual, my inconvenient curiosity overwhelmed my sense of self-preservation. "You let her do terrible things," I whispered. "Why?"

"I let her be her form's self, Youngest," a correction, but mild. "The consequences are as they are."

"Beings suffer and die."

"Skalet engages in war, Youngest." As if this was an answer.

I tilted my head, wary but wanting more. "What of the Prime Laws? She ends sentience before its time."

"The Kraal are a violent species."

"Their species is Human," I corrected automatically.

Ersh's chime grew a shade testy. "A technicality. The Kraal refuse to mingle their genetic material with others of that heritage. It will not be long—as we measure time—before this is a matter of inability, not social preference. You would be wise to pay attention to this process. It is not uncommon among ephemeral cultures."

The ploy was familiar. Distract the youngest and she'll follow along. "Why—" I said stubbornly, "—do you let Skalet participate so fully in this culture?"

Ersh settled herself with a slide of crystal over crystal. Reflected light ran over the floor, walls, and ceiling, making me squint. "You know the beginnings of that answer, Youngest." There was no doubt in her voice. "You were there, when Ansky and I discussed Skalet's first mission with the Kraal. From that, everything else has followed."

I'd been there? Before I could open my mouth to dispute this, however poor a decision that might have been, memory *rearranged* itself. To be more exact, memory reared up and shook me in sickening fashion from head to paw, recollections of that time before I had words of my own to use abruptly gaining coherence. With the perfect memory of my kind, it seemed I had recorded much I knew Skalet herself would have wished to know—

Or not.

Pressure mattered. Little else. Time. I knew the passage of days, marked them by movement conveyed by waves pressing against me.

Me. Me. Me. I knew *me*, that I existed, if then I had had no language in which to express that knowledge.

But the memory of a Web-being is perfect in every detail. So it was that when Ersh challenged me to consider such things as beginnings, I recalled my own—and by so doing, I applied what I'd learned since to the experiences so precisely recalled. The result was—interesting.

The waves of pressure which so entertained my proto-self had been generated by three sources. The inner workings of Ansky's body—the pulse of heart and lungs, the rush of blood through arteries, the gurgling of her digestive tract—all of these transferred through the amniotic fluid in which I rested as a symphony of pressures against the cells of my exquisitely sensitive skin. I'd hum along.

Then, there was the impact of large muscle movement. Oh, be sure I noticed when Ansky dropped to all fours, or stood on two legs, or bent over, or laughed.

Last, and most intriguing to recall, sound. I'd registered everything I'd heard through the walls and fluid of my living cradle through ears disposed to greater range than most sentient beings possessed.

Especially when those around me were, well, shouting.

I ignored innumerable heated "discussions"about Ansky's lamentable condition, cueing my memories to one word: Skalet. Sure enough, they'd argued about her as well.

"—Skalet? She's incapable! A coward! I tell you I'll be fine. Send me. You know I'm better at learning culture, at blending in with other species. Let our web-kin skulk somewhere else."

Skalet? Even as I tried to wrap my brain around what Ansky was saying, very loudly and with enough passion to shake my surroundings, Ersh replied, "Thanks to your blending, you can't travel until this latest creation of yours is uncorked and given to its father. I intend to monitor this emerging kind of Human closely. Skalet will go, and she will learn them for us." The unspoken *or else* penetrated Ansky's abdomen; either that, or I was influenced by my subsequent wealth of experience with that tone.

My world shifted and jiggled, then a tidal wave hinted that Ansky had moved to another chair and dropped in it without care for me. Parental she wasn't. "It won't be long." This with certainty. Warmth implied a paw pressed over me. I kicked at it. "She's impatient."

Really, I wasn't. Especially in hindsight.

"She?" Ersh's chime was nicely ominous. "Don't become attached."

Perhaps my presence—or her preoccupation with its inconvenience—gave Ansky a little more spine than usual. "Becoming attached is my skill, Ersh. Who else brings back the interpersonal details we need about a sentient species? Who learns what it is to *be* that form? Skalet?" The growl under the word brought an instinctive echo from me, albeit consisting of a pathetic, soundless tensing of a breathing system that had no air in it yet. "Skalet spends her time in other forms—which is as little as possible—hiding in bushes. She uses gadgets to record from a distance, then presumes to tell us she's gathered information first-hand. But she'll have no convenient hiding places at this Kraal outpost. As befits a culture almost constantly in conflict, they're more paranoid than she is about surveillance. Her devices will be useless."

"Yes." Ersh somehow made the word smug.

I blinked free of memory, for an instant finding it odd to have air against my eyes. "You threw Skalet off a cliff," I concluded, doing my best to restrain a likely regrettable amount of triumph at the thought. Ersh had tossed me from her mountain to encourage my first cycle into web-form. Skalet's plunge had been no less perilous for lack of rock at the bottom. For I knew the Kraal.

Not personally, being too young in Ersh's estimation to leave her moon, but the assimilated memories of my web-kin were clear enough. Kraal society had evolved an elaborate structure in which every individual had an allegiance to one or more of the ruling Houses through birth or action. Moreover, those allegiances, called affiliations, were permanently tattooed on each adult Kraal's face. While they allowed no images of themselves until death, to ensure only final affiliations were recorded for posterity, their gates were guarded by those who remembered faces exceedingly well. Only those who had been introduced by a known and trusted individual would be admitted, given that advancement through Kraal nobility typically involved assassination of rivals by as clever a means as possible.

Not a group to overlook a stranger.

"Why?" My favorite question. I stared at Ersh, a mountain of crystal shaped in hardness and edge.

Her voice could be as warm and soft as any flesh. "Why did I put her at risk? Because Skalet resisted being other than herself. The idea of a different form influencing who she was terrified her. She would be crippled by that fear, useless to our Web, unless forced to live it."

"Why the Kraal?" I whispered.

"An act of charity, Youngest." I must have looked confused because Ersh clicked her digits together with an impatient ring. "Like Skalet, Kraal do not welcome physical contact, unless in practice drills. Like Skalet, they do not welcome personal questions. They share an obsession with intellect and games. And respect authority."

I ignored the last, most likely aimed at me. "What happened?"

As Ersh winked into the blue teardrop of her web-form, I realized my curiosity was once more taking me where I'd doubtless regret going.

Not that fear could stop instinct. I released my hold on this form, cycling into my true self, and formed a mouth for Ersh's offering of the past.

Gloves froze and stiffened; coat fabric froze and crinkled. The slight whoof of air that escaped the face mask with each breath added its moisture to the rim of ice searing both cheeks and chin, that flesh rapidly losing all feeling anyway. Another being might have feared the cold, the darkness, and the howl of a wind that ripped unchallenged across this plain of floating ice from an empty ocean 600 km away.

Then again, another being wouldn't have preferred chipping frost from the antenna array, a duty that entailed far more than finding and climbing a ladder in the dark, over company and warmth. But Skalet craved these moments of solitude, no matter how punishing to her Human-self.

For the Kraal outpost was as close to a hell as any Human legend remembered by the Web. At the southern pole of an uninhabited world known only by a number, those assigned to it faced two seasons: a summer of sharp blinding ice crystals, in air that struggled up to -20°C under an unsetting sun; or a winter of utter darkness, where ceaselessly drifting snow erased the tracks of any who dared move outside at temperatures that solidified oil, let alone flesh.

Not that either season made hiding easier. In the summer, movement could only be concealed within tunnels through the snow, joining each of the domes. In the winter, radiation leaked by suit or building would betray them. For this was an outpost of that deadly kind: a spy set in place for a war that might come their way, at best an expendable asset, at worst, a prized target.

Skalet, to her surprise and growing dismay, fit in too well.

The eighteen stationed at the outpost were, to put it plainly, disposable. The arrival of another such was occasion for no more than a shifting of bunk assignments. Skalet's calm acceptance of a lowermost bed had nothing to do with stoicism, although it impressed the Kraal. Dumping heat was essential for a Web-being forced to hold another form and the temperature at floor level in all the buried domes was close to the freezing point. A cold bed was thus, as Skalet would say, *convenient.*

But her behavior set a pattern. Ersh's orders and her situation notwithstanding, our reluctant web-kin wanted as little to do with Kraal as possible. She took the worst shifts. She'd seek out the most dangerous, dirty tasks and do them alone. She'd eat first or last and clean up every trace of her existence. Unfortunately for Skalet, everything she did to avoid the other eighteen at the outpost only served to enhance her reputation. The others admired her fortitude, nicknamed her "Icicle," and whispered of rapid promotion. Several went so far as to broach offers of support, gambling, with the single-mindedness of true Kraal, her inevitable rise in rank would similarly increase that of her allies.

Skalet had no idea how to stop any of it, short of disobeying Ersh and fleeing this world.

Case in point, this afternoon's trip out to the antenna array. Skalet would have let someone else take the dangerous duty—and praise— but such excursions were her only escape from the populated tunnels and tiny rooms of the outpost.

And there was, she admitted, a peculiar satisfaction in pushing this form to its limits. There could be no radiation released outside the protection of the walls and snow cover—a snow cover that had to be routinely reduced or they'd be buried permanently. Such radiation would not only risk discovery of what was to be a secret from all Kraal but House Bryll but would also ruin the observations being made by the sensitive equipment—the reason for being here in the first place.

This meant no light or beacons to guide her from the safety of the outpost to the array. Instead, Skalet reached for and found the guideline leading from the dome entrance to the distant equipment. If she let go, it was a step in any direction to be completely lost. If she was in truth what she seemed, it would be a long while before her frozen body would be recovered.

They'd lost two techs this winter, before her arrival, a distressing tally even for the Kraal.

Skalet knew every step of this journey, the ramp-like rise to the surface from the dome entrance, the hit of wind, the emptiness to every side.

But even she kept her glove, stiff and frozen, on the line there and back.

It took as long to peel off the rock-hard layers of frozen cold weather gear as it had to stagger out to the array, dig free the ladder's base, climb the ladder, dig free the chipping tools, and hammer clear the tracks, wires, and supports. All the while the wind. All the while the knowledge that nothing else stood above ground. Hopefully.

Skalet fought her numb fingers and toes, hanging her coats by their hoods on the hooks lining the corridor walls. No space was wasted. Her gloves went into mesh hanging from the ceiling, taking advantage of the warmer air to dry. Boot liners joined the gloves. Drops of sweat melted from her hair and she swept the loose strands impatiently beneath their strapping. She'd shave the stuff, but to be inconspicuous among the fashion-obsessed Kraal of this era meant shoulder-length locks confined by annoying leather bands. *Inefficient.*

A similarly-banded head popped out from one of the small round doors. "Good timing, Icicle."

Skalet raised one eyebrow. "How so, Lieutenant?"

Lieutenant Maven-ro, a capable sparring partner when not exhibiting a curiosity the equal of a certain web-kin's, and as little welcome, flicked her fingers against the bright red tattoo curled on her right cheek. House Bryll held her affiliation, that promise of unquestioned obedience, if not the return vow of unwavering protection. Front-line Kraal soldiers understood their worth. Skalet's own cheek bore a twin mark, though applied in paint rather than embedded ink. "We've guests."

Guests? How had she missed an arriving transport? Alarmed, Skalet reached for the knives in her belt. The energy weapons the Kraal favored were forbidden within the domes. Fire was the enemy; extinguishers hung at intervals on every wall and drills woke them just as regularly. Were these guests a new threat?

"An unexpected visit, but by one who is entitled to do so." Mavenro's eyes gleamed approval. "Come. A meeting's called. Your presence is commanded, Icicle. If you've sufficiently thawed, that is."

Humor. The Kraal, like other Humans, were prone to its use in stressful situations. Skalet saw no purpose to it.

It didn't help her feel any better at the thought of some Kraal authority interested in her.

Meetings were held in the one room large enough to hold everyone, the dining hall. Not by accident, it was the only portion of the outpost to benefit from the Kraal aesthetic—at least to the extent that the wall without kitchen equipment was crusted with gilded metal plaques commemorating the achievements of House Bryll in battle. A small and central spot was reserved for accomplishments from this obscure little outpost. The Kraal were also afflicted with Human optimism.

In Skalet's judgment, the expected future of the place was more accurately seen in the lack of ornamentation anywhere else. The poorest Kraal House indulged in ostentatious display everywhere possible; even warships boasted wood carving and lush upholstery. Here was ice, frost-covered metal, and bags of supplies.

Reluctantly accepting her tiny glass of serpitay, the ceremonial drink no Kraal gathering of import could start without, Skalet eased behind others. She couldn't disappear from view completely; her Human-self was taller than most of the Kraal assigned here. Every set of shoulders was braced, as if ready for anything.

A querulous voice demanded "This is all?"

"The full complement, Your Eminence." The outpost's commander, Dal-ru, touched the backs of his hands to his tattooed cheeks and bowed, a gesture echoed by everyone in the room. "We await your pleasure."

The pleasure they awaited belonged to the oldest Kraal Skalet had ever seen for herself. Ersh-memory held older, but not by much. In a culture like the Kraal's, such age meant extraordinary value to a House, toughness, or, most likely, both. The female's maze of tattoos warred with wrinkles; her face might have been heartwood, ringed by the passing of countless seasons, a record of survival and success, for they were the same among Kraal.

Impressive.

"What's the status of the fleet?"

"Fleet, Your Eminence?" Skalet was amused by the immediate tensing of everyone in the room. She knew, as well as they, there'd been nothing on their scans for months. Which put the obedient Kraal likely to offend this noble no matter what. Dal-ru took the braver course. "We haven't detected any ship movements."

Her Eminence had not come alone, although her entourage was peculiarly small for a noble away from flagship or homeworld. Undoubtedly, Skalet thought, others waited outside the domes, perhaps within the connecting tunnels. A courier, for such the noble must be, traveled with sufficient force to affect the actions desired by her House. Here and now, she was flanked by only two black-garbed guards, taller than Skalet, more muscular than the most fit crew of the outpost, girded with every weapon possible, including several that would be fatal to all if used in this room. Now, one stooped to whisper something urgent in the courier's ear. She shooed him away impatiently. "Then that's the status, isn't it?" she snapped. "I trust you have eyes on all scans for when that changes?"

Seven Kraal bowed hurriedly and dashed from the room. Two had been in front of Skalet. Thus exposed, she found herself caught by the curious regard of the old noblewoman's milky eyes. "Who are you?"

Skalet's bow was impeccable, the brush of knuckles to fake tattoo exquisite. Inwardly, she trembled. "S'kal-ru, Your Eminence. Tech Class—"

"Ah. The Dauntless Icicle. Attend me." The noblewoman rose to her feet without assistance, a smooth efficient motion that lifted Skalet's eyebrow in involuntary appreciation. *Admirable.*

I knew Ersh filtered my web-kin's reactions to their own experiences before sharing them with me, probably viewing most as nonessential to my learning. Oh, I assimilated physical sensations, such as taste, and useful emotions such as fear, but, to this point in my life, the latter came to me so dimmed the memories could have belonged to any of us. This sharing was different. The intensity of Skalet's fascination with the old Kraal came through as clearly as the remembered chill from the outpost. I fluffed out my fur and shivered. "I thought Skalet didn't want to be noticed."

"What have I told you about asking questions before you've finished assimilating?"

"Wasn't a question," I mumbled, hastily dipping back into memory.

Ersh, as usual, was right. I now owned this part of Skalet's past— whether I wanted to or not.

"They tell me you don't feel the cold, S'kal-ru. Is this true?"

Skalet, granted the unthinkable privilege of being allowed to sit in the presence of such high rank, hesitated.

"Come now. I didn't invite you here to be a statue. If you won't converse, let me hear that lovely voice of yours. Your commander didn't exaggerate. Surely you sing."

Banter, from someone like this, was even more unthinkable. Skalet felt her skin warming as her stressed form dumped heat. Luckily, this intimate setting was, as befitted the outpost, barely above freezing. Their breath mingled and twisted in the air like the fumes of forgotten dragons. "I don't sing, Your Eminence," Skalet said with a hidden shudder, then added honestly. "I don't mind the cold."

"You don't let yourself mind it. That is good. Very good. So few learn to control the flesh, to put aside the instincts that would keep us cowering by the fire."

As this didn't seem to require a response, Skalet merely looked attentive. Her Eminence had taken Dal-ru's office, a room hardly used since its location in a poorly insulated storage dome made it impossible to heat properly. Cases of beer lined the wall behind the ancient Kraal. She'd ignored them, more intent on this strange conversation.

"So, tell me, Icicle, of the state of affairs among the Houses of Bract, Noitci, and Ordin."

On familiar ground again, Skalet took care to answer as any Kraal here could. "The Bract and Noitci share fourth-, possibly fifth-level historical affiliations; both hold ninth-level affiliation with House Bryll. Ordin is a newer House, also affiliated to House Bryll." She flicked her fingers over her tattoo. "Through us, Ordin gains third-level affiliation with both Bract and Noitci."

The wrinkles and tattoos reshaped into a look of pure satisfaction. "The nexus being ours. The position of strength."

Skalet frowned slightly in thought but didn't dare speak.

She didn't have to. The Kraal was terrifyingly good at reading faces. "You see some flaw," she guessed softly. "Interesting. Tell me. I grant you leave to criticize your own House."

"As you wish." Challenged, Skalet drew upon memory. "House Arzul, powerful yet inherently unstable, recently lost reputation and ships to Noitci, itself a fairly weak House but, thanks to a high-status alliance, temporarily enjoying a tenth-level affiliation with Bract, one of the strongest and noblest." She found herself warming to her topic. Her own kin had no appreciation for the subtlety of this culture. "Arzul will rally to reclaim those losses. The nobles of Ordin are too impatient for power and lineage to let this opportunity slip by, or worse, be taken by a rival. They will attack Arzul, acquire affiliation with Noitci through blood debt, and thus gain ties to Bract. Unless House Bryll acts, it will be forced from the nexus to the outside of a new, powerful set of alliances, losing a great deal of status. Perhaps more than a House can afford to lose." A disgraced Kraal House was like a fresh corpse to scavengers. Something to dismember.

"Acts how?" softer still. The Kraal noble leaned forward, creased chin on one palm, sunken eyes intent on Skalet. "Go on."

Skalet could see it so clearly, like pieces on a board before a skilled hand swept them aside. "A preemptive move against Bract. Remove its alliance with Noitci by assassinating the First Daughter before her union, then remove the five who remain in the Bract Inner Circle."

The wrinkles mapped nothing worse than curiosity. "You'd sacrifice a powerful ally and two former lovers of mine to what gain, S'kal-ru?"

"The audacity of the strike would enhance our affiliation with Ordin, a House of significant future promise should Bryll help it survive its own impetuousness. At the same time, Arzul would lose its patron, removing it as a threat to Noitci. Noitci, its alliance cut, would in turn be diminished, as would any affiliations outside of House Bryll held by Noitci and Arzul, drawing both closer to Bryll. Finally, and most importantly, existing alliances would mean the Inner Circle of Bryll would dominate that of Bract in the next generation. The closest affiliations between Houses of true power. All Kraal would benefit."

"This presumes success."

Skalet let herself smile, nothing more.

"Few think in generations. They want gains now, in their lifetimes."

"'What are lifetimes but strokes on a canvas?'"

"You quote N'kar-ro. Not easy reading, S'kal-ru. Again, you impress." The noble paused, wrinkles deepening. "How has Bryll overlooked such quality as yours?"

Not a safe question. "I should return to duty, Your Eminence."

"Your duty is to keep me company while we wait."

"Wait for what?" Skalet's own audacity shocked her.

The courier merely nodded, as if she'd expected the question. "For fools, S'kal-ru, who lack your grasp of tactics. Oh, they see the same patterns, but rather than the prick of a pin in the hollow of a neck, the certainty of poison built for one, they prefer the sound of trumpets and mountains of rubble."

"A planetary assault force?" Skalet's eyes widened. All she'd learned of Kraal pointed to a growing control and finesse of conflict, not a return to the devastating attacks that had almost ended this race in its infancy. "Against what target?"

The other woman's mouth twisted and she turned her head to spit decorously over her own shoulder. "Farmland. Factories. The uninvolved. The *sous*."

Sous. Noncombatants. The quiet majority of Kraal, who served their affiliations through a lifetime of peace and accomplishment, fueling the vast economy that afforded the great Houses their wealth—by convention and utter common sense, untouchable.

Until now. "You must stop them!" Skalet blanched at the ring of command in her own voice. "Forgive me, Your Eminence. I meant no disrespect."

"I heard none. Conflict as a challenge to advance a House tempers our society. Strip challenge from conflict and we become no better than Ganthor, squabbling for the day's profit. Yet even that shame can be forgiven, with time." Her fingers formed a gnarled fist, punching down through the air between them. "To attack those who provide for all? That, S'kal-ru, is to court our own extinction. Which is why I need you, Icicle."

Perhaps some part of Skalet remembered Ersh and the Prime Law. If so, she made a choice to disregard both for the first time in her life.

"What do you want me to do, Your Eminence?"

Circles within circles, folded back on each other until the overall pattern of Kraal society appeared more an orgy of snakes than an organization of Humans—or those whose ancestry traced back to the same trees. Despite the perception of the non-Kraal, war had never been a game to those who created the Great Houses and defended them. They waged their power struggles without losing sight of the future or their desire to make it as they wished. There was much to admire in a culture that took charge of its own evolution.

Until those who believed they had the right chose the short path, the one that wasted the lives and resources on which the future depended.

Skalet fastened the strap of her goggles around her neck, then methodically checked the laces and zips of her clothing. One opening and this form could suffer frostbite and impairment. She could risk neither tonight.

Her role was deceptively simple, elegant in Kraal terms. The Bryll assault fleet would pass in range of this outpost on its way to attack the Bract home system, to take advantage of their scans to detect and warn of any Bract ships in the area. Their fleet would remain unseen until it was too late to mount a defense. Except that Her Eminence, as Courier to Bryll's Inner Circle, specifically those within that Circle in opposition to those mounting the assault, had sent a coded message to the Bract, recommending this system as the ideal place for an ambush.

Bryll would sacrifice her own, Skalet the pin to prick the unsuspecting throat.

Maven-ro, always alert to comings and goings, appeared in her doorway. "Didn't you just come in, Icicle?"

"Hours back." Skalet shrugged her fur-cased shoulders. "Weather's worsening. We can't risk anything impeding reception." She flicked two fingers against her pseudo-tattooed cheek. They'd all been briefed by Dal-ru on the importance of protecting the fleet.

Maven-ro's look wasn't as approving as usual. In fact, she began to frown. "It's bad enough out there even Her Eminence's guard has come inside. There's no indication of ice buildup yet. Stay."

Skalet lifted a brow. "If I wait until there's a problem, it could be too late. You know that."

The Kraal shook her head. "There's attention to duty and there's being a fool, S'kal-ru. The winds have doubled. You won't be able to stay on your feet, let alone hold to the guideline."

Skalet rattled the clip and safety cable around her waist. "I'm prepared."

Maven-ro threw up her hands. "Fine. Go freeze stiff. If we find you this spring, we'll stand you up as a flagpole."

It didn't seem humor. Puzzled, Skalet watched as the other walked away, slamming a door unnecessarily behind her, then returned to her own preparations.

It was worse. Unimaginably worse. The moment the outer door retracted, the wind howled inside the tunnel, blowing Skalet off her feet, rolling her along the icy floor until she hit the yielding edge of a fuel bag. The rubbery material gave her a grip as she pulled herself to her feet.

At least it was a steady wind, to start. She could force her way against it and did, reaching first the door frame, then the outer wall, and, after groping in the dark, the guideline. She clipped herself to it and pressed out into the night.

Lean, drag a foot free, move it up and forward, push it into yielding softness to the knee, to the thigh. Skalet couldn't predict her footing. Drifts were curling and reforming like living things. All she could do was drag the other foot free, up and forward, push it down, and progress in lurches and semi-falls.

She'd run out of choices. There was no living mass except that behind her. Without a source, she could not release her hold on this form and chose another, more suited to surviving these conditions. Not and return to the outpost as Skalet. Only living matter could be assimilated into more web-flesh, and she'd need to replace what she used.

There was escape. She almost considered it as the wind lifted her for an instant, her grip torn from the guideline, one outer glove sailing free and only the cable jerking snug around her waist keeping her in place. She could cycle into a form that flew on this wind, pick one able to hide beneath ice for however many decades it would take for Ersh to notice her absence and send one of her kin to retrieve her. *Disgraced.*

Skalet dropped to the ground as the wind caught its breath, then drove herself to her feet. If she failed for whatever reason, Her Eminence had another option. She could destroy the outpost and all the talented, complicated beings in it, including herself. *Wasteful.*

It was only a question of one step after another. This form would obey her will. It would endure. Skalet pulled her right hand, now clad only in the liner, within the sleeve of her innermost coat, shoving the cuff through her belt as tightly as possible. She would need those fingers able to function once at the ladder.

Her goggles were coated with snow, despite the fur-trim around her hood. No matter. What use were eyes without light? She leaned into the wind again, trusting to the cable. One step after another, a movement that grew only more difficult as she lost feeling below her knees. No matter. She could not control time or the movement of starships, but she could control this body. It would succeed.

At some point, the howl dimmed to a whine and the force pushing her back lessened. Skalet smiled, lips cracking, blood burning her chin. She had reached the array.

The clip had frozen shut. Rather than waste energy fighting it, Skalet drew her knife and cut the cable around her waist. She staggered and caught herself with a grip on the ladder as the wind tried to peel her away again. The climb was a nightmare. Not only were the lower rungs half-buried in a rising drift, but she could no longer judge where her feet would land. Three times Skalet neared the top, only to lose her grip and slip back down.

Once on the platform, she didn't bother looking for the ice-breaking tools. Skalet felt her way down the nearest strut to its linkage with the rest, found the fastener. She drew her knife once more, then shook her head. No traces. Even if House Bryll was as devastated as the courier implied, there would be an investigation. Like other Humans, the Kraal were curious, tenacious beings. Unlike other Humans, the Kraal took the assignment of fault to extremes. For the crew of this outpost to outlive their doomed fleet, this had to appear an accident.

Skalet put away her knife and pulled off the outer glove on her left hand, securing it in her belt. Her fingers numbed almost immediately, but she managed to grip the fastener and twist. It was meant to be mobile to -70°C, so the antenna could be replaced at need. It wouldn't budge.

Cursing substandard equipment, Skalet stripped off her inner gloves, restraining a cry as the wind seemed to flay her skin. She pressed both palms around the fastener, warming it with her own, slightly greater than Human, heat. The core of her body seemed to chill at the same time, a dangerous theft. Skalet fought to hold form as much as she fought to keep her hands where they had to stay.

Another twist. Nothing. She screamed in fury and drove her fist into the metal, feeling a knuckle break, but something else give as well. *Satisfaction.* Another twist and the fastener came free.

By now, Skalet's hands were shaking so violently she could barely get them back into the gloves. She couldn't feel any difference with the protection on, but knew it was necessary. Form-memory was perfect. If she lost fingers to frostbite, she'd remember herself that way forever. She refused to believe it might be too late.

Meanwhile, the wind, now her ally, was busy at work. The strut creaked and groaned, succumbing to the force hammering it. Skalet touched the support, feeling irregular shudders. Good. It would take only the slightest of bends to make the antenna uncontrollable. As if hearing her thoughts, the strut snapped and the array began to tilt.

The outpost—and the fleet—were blind.

Time to leave. Skalet made her way back down the ladder, groping in the dark with her left hand for the guideline. The right she'd drawn inside her coat completely, cradling it next to her heart, a source of searing pain as the flesh thawed and the abused knuckle complained of ill treatment. *Reassuring.*

She'd anticipated an easier return journey, the wind shoving from behind and her trail already broken through the drifts. Instead, with a perversity she should have expected, the wind was a wall in her face and her footsteps had filled with snow. There was only the guideline and the strength of her grip on it.

Her progress became a series of forward stumbles, never quite on her knees, never quite stopping. At any moment, Skalet expected to collide with a Kraal hurrying from the outpost to see what had gone wrong, to try a futile repair. Ephemeral and fragile, yet they readily risked their fleeting lives. *Exceptional.*

Then the line came alive in her hand, yanking her backward into the snow before becoming limp. Skalet stood and gave a sharp pull in the direction of the outpost. The line came toward her with no more tension than its weight dragging through the snow.

The entire array must have become unstable, the bent antenna a sail catching too much wind. Whether the structure had toppled to the ground or merely leaned didn't matter. It had moved enough to pluck the uncuttable guideline from the outpost dome.

So much for meeting a Kraal.

So much for finding her way back.

I whined and curled in a ball, my tail covering nose and eyes with a plume of warm fine hair. Despite this, and despite being perfectly safe and warm, I shook miserably. I'd assimilated nothing like this before. I'd never felt what it was like to truly risk one's form-self. My other web-kin, being far more sensible, would have cycled long before this point. I would have. Skalet's resolve was as horrifying as the Kraal themselves.

If I could have stopped remembering, I would have. But Ersh had given me all of it and I whirled through Skalet's memories as haplessly as a snowflake—or the Kraal fleet.

This form reacted to fear with a rush of blood to the ears, a sickness in the stomach. Skalet ignored biology, intent on her problem. She couldn't see, feel, or hear her way to safety. The broken line in her hand, however, would give her the distance from the array to the outpost. The wind in her face would give her direction. A risk, given that same wind had already swung 180 degrees, but an acceptable one. If she reached the end of the guideline and found nothing, she could walk in an arc bounded by the line—if she could move it—and have a fifty percent chance of being right. Or have to abandon this form when it reached its physiological limit.

But not before.

The guideline proved harder to combat than the wind. Though light, its length gave it considerable mass and weight. Exposed portions flailed with every gust, the rest being buried by the snow of a continent. Skalet barely managed to hang on to the piece by her side and keep moving. Her best estimate put her near or within the outer ring of domes, but they were difficult to detect under good conditions, let alone in the dark. Her goal was the ramp down to the central dome.

Her feet started fighting a drift larger and more compact than most she'd encountered. Gasping with effort, Skalet nonetheless felt a thrill of hope. There were always drifts curving around the slight rise of each dome. She began to step down the other side and suddenly lost her footing as well as her grip on the line. Before she could recapture it, it was gone.

Skalet sat on the slope of the drift and replayed memory. She knew this area, had walked its winter night a hundred times. Yes. She should be able to see the dome from here.

Skalet pulled her hand from inside her coat, using both to remove her goggles. Instantly the cold hit her eyes and lashes, freezing them shut. She rubbed away the beads of ice to peer into the darkness, flinching at needles of hard, dry snow.

There. Skalet threw herself at that dimmest of glows, refusing to believe it was anything but the rim of the door she'd left hours earlier. Seconds later, she was moving down the ramp, waist-deep in new snow but out of the wind at last. The door. Her fingers wouldn't work any-more. Sobbing with fury, tears freezing to her cheeks, Skalet fought this betrayal as she tried to open the latches.

They opened of their own accord, a figure mummified in fur block-ing the light from within. With an incoherent cry, the figure caught Skalet in gloved hands and drew her inside.

The warmth, near the freezing point, was an exquisite agony. Skalet shuddered on the iced floor, gulping air that didn't burn her lungs. The figure pulled off hood and goggles, becoming Maven-ro.

She crouched beside Skalet. "So the Icicle can freeze after all," she shook her head. "Give your report, then get to medical. Scan's gone down at the worst possible time. I'm off to see what I can do about it."

"No . . . no point," Skalet wasn't vain about her voice as a Human, but even she was shocked by its reed-thin sound. She got to her knees, wheezing: "The array . . . it's collapsed . . . the storm. Guideline's ripped loose . . ."

Maven-ro's face paled beneath its tattoo, but her mouth formed a firm line. "It is our privilege to serve. The fleet relies on us, S'kal-ru." She stood, replacing her goggles and hood. "I must see what can be done."

With her better hand, Skalet found and held the other's sleeve, used it to pull herself to her feet. What she hoped were feet—she couldn't feel them. She didn't understand why she felt compelled to stop the Kraal, a flaw in this form, perhaps. "There's duty and there's being a fool. You told me that, Maven-ro." She staggered and Maven-ro was forced to steady her. "Dare you think I would give up and return if there was any hope of restoring the array?"

Maven-ro lowered her head. She dragged off her goggles with one hand, keeping the other firm on Skalet's belt. "Forgive me, S'kal-ru. There are none braver—" Her fingers flattened protectively over the tattoo on her cheek; her eyes, haunted, lifted to meet Skalet's. "But now I fear the worst."

Hands and feet bandaged with dermal regenerators, which with typical Kraal sensibility did nothing to relieve pain, Skalet was in no mood for company. But her visitor that outpost night wasn't one she could refuse, however dangerous.

The courier waved the medtech from the tiny clinic. "Have you heard, S'kal-ru?"

The surprise attack, the ragged desperate signals, and incoming casualty lists had silenced the domes. Kraal walked in a daze, huddled in anguished groups, worried about their future, their affiliations. Except this one. "You brought down your own House," Skalet observed, curious. Under the blanket, her bandaged fingers gripped a knife.

The courier smiled. Her age-spotted fingers lifted to the mask of tattoos on her face, selected one. "With you as my poison, I have cleansed it of those who would have destroyed it. Bryll will rise to prominence once more."

"I don't doubt it."

"But you doubt your own future."

Skalet smiled thinly. "I'm a realist. With what I know, I should prepare to disappear." Which, given transport and a moment unobserved with some living mass, S'kal-ru the Kraal would do.

The old woman's eyes narrowed to slits. "Let go the knife. You are of more value than risk to me."

A figure of speech? Then again, a noble who aged in this society would be no fool at all. Skalet brought her empty hand above the blanket.

"Good. I have another future for you to consider, S'kal-ru. I warn you. It means none of the comforts of homeworld or hearth. No lineages sprung from your flesh."

"I don't seek such things."

"No. No, I believe you don't. Yet you embody all that Kraal aspires to be, which is why I won't see you wasted." As Skalet twitched, the tattoos around the other's lips writhed. A smile, perhaps. "Hear me out."

"I'm at your command, Your Eminence."

"The Noble Houses must communicate, one to the other, even in times of distrust and blood debt. To this end exist such as I, individuals of such clear honor we are given extraordinary latitude without hesitation. There are no watches on our comings and goings. No impediments to our actions; no constraint beyond affiliation. We are few, but we are crucial to the survival of our civilization, as you have seen. I would have you train as my successor, S'kal-ru." The old Kraal moved her hand slowly, carefully, toward Skalet's cheek. Involuntarily, Skalet reared her head back and away. Then, for no reason save self-preservation, she froze to permit the touch. Cold, dry fingers traced the fake tattoo once, lightly. "This might pass muster here, but never on a Kraal world. If you permit me, I will make it real. A ninth-level affiliation through me to House Bract, today's power. What do you say, Icicle?"

To be secretive yet a decision maker, to be needed for her abilities, not just as another collector of dry facts and genetic information.

Skalet found a way to bow gracefully, even lying down.

"I take it you finished." Ersh tumbled to where I stood staring out the window. Picco's orange reflection cast shadows the color of drying blood. I found it singularly appropriate.

"Yes," I said quietly. "It's called seduction, isn't it. When you are brought to desire something until it's impossible to refuse it."

"Apt enough." A chime that might have been pleasure. Or impatience. The tones were regrettably similar. "Skalet might not have grown so—attached—to this culture, had she not been taught to thrive in it."

"Thrive?" I growled. "She's responsible for the deaths of thousands."

"That's what war is, Youngest," Ersh agreed. "A uniquely ephemeral conceit, to settle disputes by ending life."

"Then why? Why do you let Skalet continue? Why not send Ansky or the others?"

"Why tolerate insolence?" I acknowledged the rebuke by lifting my ears, which had plastered themselves to my skull in threat when I wasn't paying attention. Ersh touched a fingertip to the stone sill of the window and the bell-like sound echoed from the corners of the room. *Apology accepted.* "Skalet's mission to the Kraal outpost was her first successful interaction with another species. It has been her only success. She can spy on any species, glean information from a host of cultures, but fails every time to get closer. Except with the Kraal. So you see, Youngling, it is not always simple to decide which of your web-kin goes where. It matters where they feel they can belong."

I had to assume Ersh was telling me something important, but it made no sense. "Skalet wants to belong to the Kraal?"

Ersh didn't often laugh as a Tumbler. The species was prone to a more taciturn outlook. But now she tinkled like a rush of wind through icicles. "Esen-alit-Quar. You have so much to learn. Skalet may be obsessed with the Kraal and this form, but she is one of us above all else. She would never forge true bonds outside our Web."

I shuddered at the thought, heretical and yet attractive, in the way sharp edges attract fingertips. There was a trap I would avoid at all costs. Along with war.

Like many young beings, I would have to wait for the future to prove me wrong.

18: Greenhouse Night, The Present

"**Y**OU could hear what we said? From inside Ansky?"

A little late to worry about your privacy in front of a pregnant Lanivarian. I made a noise Skalet could take as affirmative or not, the rest of my lungs preoccupied with the grueling effort to hold up my end of Evan Gooseberry. Which would have been easier had I been able to return to the Library as anything other than my Lanivarian-self, woefully ill-adapted as a beast of burden, but no.

Time to follow the rules.

As a result, we wore our clothes instead of figuring out how to carry them along with Evan. Her memories of how much worse cold weather could be didn't make my current struggle through the snow easier, although Skalet breaking trail at the front of Evan did. *Efficient.*

I growled to myself, my head stuffed with Kraal thinking.

She mistook my growl, or maybe didn't. "I behaved appropriately for what I was—what I am, Youngest. I do not apologize for the past."

It didn't help that my web-kin, a fit and athletic Kraal herself at the moment, wasn't breathing heavily at all. I was, however, impressed by her near-approach to conciliatory. How long it would last was anyone's guess. In my experience, Skalet rebounded from upsetting situations by becoming less, not more, pleasant.

I'd done what I could: spared Skalet and Lesy a second round with each other. As Senior Assimilator for the Web of Esen, I'd sorted the memories where I wanted them and for whom, extended those within thin pseudopods I thrust upon my web-kin, and endured the eager tear of their jaws with satisfaction as well as pain.

For my first time sharing in multiples—and with a non-Web-being present, admittedly unconscious, but we'd all been aware of Evan—I felt it went well.

It helped I'd enjoyed taking my own chunks of flesh from each in return; assimilating their contents less so, but I'd matured enough to know the *taste* of other lives would settle and not disturb what was me. Mostly. Lesy's *taste* continued to be strange. She did consider Evan "pretty," but the term came roiled up with paint colors and the feel of clay until I wasn't entirely clear what they'd said to one another, only that Lesy longed to commit art on his face. Or his face to her art. That hadn't been clear either.

As for Skalet, I ignored her impressions of what we'd experienced together over the past day, more interested in what she'd been up to without me. Her latest meeting with Lionel, for instance. Skalet remained oblivious to how deeply she'd come to trust the Human; I certainly wasn't about to mention it, trusting Lionel myself.

Her contact with the *Trium Pa* to arrange the tents hadn't gone as well. There'd been a change, one Skalet noted and marked for later action. Captain Haden-ru had shown a new and disturbing willingness to dispute Skalet's direct order, not once, but twice—citing her displeasure the courier would reveal their continued presence in the Botharan System for something so trivial. She'd capitulated with ill grace, as if doing Skalet a personal favor.

Kraal games. I could almost feel sorry for Haden-ru, who'd no way to know she played against the greatest expert of them all. *Almost.* If we had to have a Kraal ship in orbit, I preferred its crew be totally subservient to my web-kin.

Who I could bite.

I'd no inclination to bite Skalet at the moment. If anything, this me felt an unprecedented urge to give her a comforting lick, despite being aware she'd smack my tender nose. Given our history, I shouldn't plan any comforting gestures whatsoever, and avoid close contact at any cost.

Caution notwithstanding, Skalet's sharing had held something else unprecedented. *Fear.* Whatever she'd assimilated from Lesy, Skalet believed it corrupted her from within, stealing her composure and making her weak. She'd fought it. Thought herself recovered.

Far from it. Upwellings of those Lesy-memories would plague Skalet as long as she lived, it not remotely in my power to remove them.

As if to prove the point, Ersh-memory chose that moment to rise up and seize me. I lost all sense of now and snow, whirling back in time . . .

. . . there is no Web. There is but one, *solitary.*

One hidden. Safe, web-mass self-protecting, but . . .

Mere existence has become *insufficient.* Ersh/me is afflicted by a new appetite to satisfy, a longing born of *thought,* a thirst for *more.*

Call it curiosity. Name it conscience. Of the ephemeral civilizations Ersh/me destroyed with once-mindless hunger, of those she's watched fail for whatever reason and vanish, all that remains are echoes in her/my flesh. Their biological essence, yes, assimilated by instinct and part of us forever, but what of their creations? For it is the unique ability of thinking ephemeral life, to make what did not exist before.

Of their built things, within her flesh are only the fragments left in her wake. Of their languages, only screams. Nothing of art, science, or music . . .

Purpose arises, becomes imperative. To acquire knowledge of what is created by what lives, to be preserved . . .

To remember more than causing death and guilt.

A millennium comes and goes. Ersh/my purpose continues. She finds gratification in knowledge acquired, but ephemeral civilizations are just that, flickers in time. Even should she live forever, she'll miss most.

There is but one way to do more. To save more.

Become more.

Ersh/I gathers living mass, assimilates it into more of her own. More. More. Grows without stopping until her body shrieks with agony, signaling the ultimate choice. Divide or become solid, thoughtless, a rock: death by density as web-mass collapses permanently into itself.

The flurry of selection takes place at a microscopic scale, at first following the tenets of survival: save what assists; discard what does not. The process becomes easier, more fluid—then urgent as her personality schisms.

In the final throes, as one splits into two, what MUST remain Ersh/me clutches the guilt, keeps the past and everything that means *identity.*

Because she has, because she remains Ersh/me, in time she remembers her purpose and why she must be more. Resists the urge to consume the tempting morsel, quivering nearby . . .

. . . and names it Lesy.

. . . I snapped out of Ersh-memory to find myself being dragged forward by my grip on Evan's legs, a grip I hastily readjusted so as to not pull off his boots. I kept walking through snow, finding it harder to move from the past—*her past*—to the present. The struggle didn't upset my current stomach, luckily for Evan's boots; it upset *me.*

I'd suspected, perhaps we all had, that Lesy's differences from Ersh's subsequent offspring wasn't anything as simple as *improves with practice.* Ersh had torn herself apart, a sorting into two without logic or forethought. She'd yet to share memories or assimilate another's. Lesy's birth had forced Ersh to invent a way to sort her flesh, to protect what had to remain hers alone.

Like me, learning to be Web, struggling to stay myself. Ersh had understood me before I'd understood myself. She'd known what I could do. Would do.

It wasn't a warm, fuzzy realization. Much—most—of my admittedly short life would have been far less frustrating if she'd sat me down—or whatever—to say: *Esen, it will be all right. You're like me—*

Then again, I'd taken two centuries to learn how to hold form without exploding. *Most of the time.* Maybe I hadn't been the only one frustrated.

The wind faltered, blocked at last by the welcome rise of walls before us. We stumbled together into the Library, for my part overjoyed to set Evan down on the floor. I did my best not to drop him, but an unconscious Human sags in the middle so there might have been a bump as he landed.

He groaned. *Definitely a bump.* I looked to Skalet for an explanation.

"I gave him a rouse shot partway here," she told me. "Unless you'd prefer to keep carrying him through the Library."

"No, no. Good—what is it?"

Skalet had angled her head as if listening.

Her face twisted into a rictus of fury. She pulled out a weapon she'd promised Paul not to carry, waving me to the wall with the business end. Moving with ominous precision, she stood to one side of the door, ready to key it open, only then sparing me a glance to mouth one word.

"Betrayal."

Elements

"SKALET knows," Lionel whispered, putting away his com link. Paul acknowledged with a tightening of his lips. He'd questions—they were drowning in them, suddenly—with only one answer so far.

The Library hadn't been a sanctuary.

The Sacrissee were dead. Murdered when they'd been *IN* and should have been safe. Their bodies—Lionel swallowed gorge, tried to be the dispassionate observer, but this? Their bodies were puddles of swirling blue and black and green—and the smell—

He closed his eyes, then forced them open.

The Hamlet of Hillsview, however unforeseeable the reason, had hired the right Human to guard their peace. Mal stepped over the gore, paper notepad in hand, eyes intent. On arriving at the scene, he'd kept everyone out and sent for Duggs Pouncey. Why became obvious when the contractor arrived in smock and gloves, a cobbled-together forensics kit in her hands.

Duggs worked with the concise efficiency of practice—gained from where or how Lionel had no idea and refused to speculate—silent except to confirm procedure with the constable. She imaged, measured, and mapped each of the remains, scraping samples of gore into labeled jars from the Response Room. Once finished, she sealed the puddle beneath layers of food wrap and went to the next. Every so often she'd look toward Paul, who stood to the side watching the constable, his face inscrutable.

Lionel didn't know what had passed between the two earlier to end the standoff at the entrance, only that the crates had been opened and their contents brought inside the Library, Duggs a dour-faced witness no one dared approach. By the time he'd been sent to check on the Sacrissee, the first tents had begun to inflate like giant brown mushrooms along the walkway over the Lobby, to the noisy delight of Queebs who took them for portable saunas and a most welcome addition to the Library.

He'd discovered what wasn't. When the Sacrissee hadn't responded to his knock, Lionel had risked their tempers by using his access key to override the privacy lock. Stepping in—his stomach lurched and he swallowed bile.

No mystery how the killers had entered and presumably left—presumably, because Mal's first snapped order had been to verify that very important point. So far, no strangers had been spotted, but with the crowds and disruption, no one could be sure. For now, what they had was means: a neat round hole had been carved into the ceiling from the level above, raining gemmies on the floor. Another such hole in a wall of the room above opened to a tunnel leading to the surface beyond the building.

Wind-blown snow smothered any hint of how or when they'd arrived.

An arrival circumventing Skalet's security system, but how? Lionel'd seen enough of it to appreciate the level of technology—and skilled paranoia—she'd invested. The state-of-the-art sensors were hidden and protected. Esen may have requested some areas be private, including what had been his bedroom, but the rest of the basement levels were monitored, as was most of the Library above them.

With redundancies, some of which she hadn't shared. *Reasonable precaution.*

Lionel had quickly checked what he could from the interface in the room, using codes Skalet had given him. Paul had done the same. Everything normal, no unexpected life signs detected by door sensors, no alerts of any kind recorded as the Library was being violated and their guests murdered.

Duggs covered the third and final corpse puddle with food wrap, then stretched. "Where do you want the samples, Mal?"

"Leave them with me, Duggs. Thank you."

"Thank me by calling someone else next time." She grimaced. "I'm off to the nearest shower." Duggs moved toward the door, only to stop and turn to Paul, her eyes narrowed. "I am done, Director. You promised."

Paul let out a breath. Lionel caught the regret in his eyes. "We'll go over the details tomorrow."

They'd lost her, then.

"I'd like you to stay till we get the all clear," Mal said. "The Commonwealth medteam wants to treat this as an unrelated incident, not affecting the lockdown—"

"Make me. Damn Woolies." She glared at the constable. "And damn you, too. You know who did this as well as I do, Mal. There's no bloody contagion. And no bed here I'd sleep in." The glare transferred to Paul.

Who spread his hands in mute apology.

With a muttered curse, Duggs spun around and walked out the door, finding a way to close it emphatically, if not slam it.

The room felt smaller.

"Are all the crates the Kraal dropped accounted for?" Mal asked quietly.

Lionel felt the words like a blow. Duggs had seen it—how had he not? He'd lost detachment, failed in focus, the very qualities Skalet valued in him and Paul needed. "Skalet arranged the delivery," he answered. "She'll be able to tell us if any are missing."

"Your head of security." The naming held doubt. "Where is she?"

"Notified and on her way," Paul said. "This isn't her fault, Mal."

"Then she's incompetent."

Paul quelled Lionel's protest with a tiny shake of his head. "You know better," his friend told the constable.

A scowl. "What I know? In this weather, the Kraal ship could have landed in the next field over. Waited."

"The *Septos Ank* returned to her berth immediately." Lionel sighed inwardly, turning with the others at the deep lovely voice; his relief vanished when he saw the fury in Skalet's eyes. "Or so I was told." Her gaze raked the room, returning to the constable. "We both know this was Kraal work." A glance at the hole. "Beam cutter." A nod to the puddled remains. "Chemical dissolution to prevent identification. Characteristic of House Bract." A disdainful flick of fingertips against the tattoo along her jaw. "I am betrayed."

The constable considered her for a long moment. Skalet waited. Finally he asked, "The dead on the *Stellar Trumpet?*"

"Check the bodies for poison. I'll provide a list of the most likely."

By so doing she broke her affiliation to a formidable House. Risked immediate and deadly retribution and Lionel made an unhappy sound in his throat. Skalet looked at him and smiled. It wasn't in any sense a pleasant expression. "I do not fear them."

He'd fear them for her. The Library's collection held a restricted dataset: Skalet's contribution. Gleaned over an enormous span of time, it contained, among other information, the greatest secrets held by the Houses of the Kraal Confederacy, some so old as to be forgotten, others as recent as yesterday. All to stay secret, for if they were exposed, affiliations would shatter, destroying the Confederacy from within. The resulting bloodbath would spread across space—

If the Kraal learned of its existence, S'kal-ru the Courier would be finished. Skalet, possibly Esen, exposed for what they were. This planet and any who'd been here become targets and there were remote copies putting more at risk—

A cool fingertip traced the back of his hand. Chastised, Lionel exhaled. "Sorry. It's this—" he waved at the puddles, as if three dead Sacrissee came close to the scale of carnage he imagined.

The fingertip tapped, then left. *Reassurance.* He tried to believe it; he did believe in Skalet. Hadn't she lived longer than the Kraal themselves?

Esen had told him of their lost sisters. Web-beings weren't invulnerable.

"I'll pass your information to the medship," Mal was saying. "I imagine they'll want some confirmation before aborting their approach, but I have to agree with Duggs. This was a coordinated assault, not some outbreak. Kraal." The venom in the name made it clear he'd have preferred a plague.

Lionel appreciated his point. They'd gone from a mystery on a single ship—deftly handled by isolating those at risk and summoning help—to facing a foreign power implicated in multiple murders. One, moreover, with a battle-ready ship in orbit, which was more than Botharis had.

"If these three arrived on the *Trumpet*—" Mal continued, frowning. "And we'll discuss what withholding information from authority means later—what's the motive? Who were they? Were they after intel dangerous to Bract or a competing House?"

"They came for sanctuary." Harsh lines bracketed Paul's mouth; he wasted no words on regret or explanation. "Sacrissee, away from their home system, who'd concealed themselves until meeting with us." His gesture included Lionel and Skalet.

Leaving Esen and Evan out. A deliberate omission, Lionel decided, taking the cue. Was Paul trying to shield the pair from questions?

No. He wanted to tell Esen himself. *A duty he didn't envy.*

"They identified themselves," Paul went on, "as Saxel Sah, Acklan Seh, and Maston Sah."

"Likely false, given this—" Mal waved at the food-wrapped puddles "—stops us checking idents."

Skalet opened her mouth, then closed it. When Paul raised his eyebrow, she shrugged. "Other aspects of a person are destroyed by such treatment."

Esen had planned to sample those "aspects" on her own, information Lionel wasn't about to volunteer, not in front of the constable.

Something was going on here. Something more than Kraal infighting, however deadly that could prove to be.

He only hoped the answers hadn't been lost with the Sacrissee.

19: Portal Night; Chow Night

"**Y**OU sure you can walk?"

Evan gave me *that* look and pushed away from the wall. "There's trouble. We need to get there. Oh, my—"

I caught him as he fell forward, the pair of us weaving back and forth before our centers of gravity stabilized. "I'll call for help."

The green eye next to mine closed in mute agreement, lashes pale against his skin; skin I wasn't tempted to lick until he'd washed his face clean of any trace of Skalet's knockout powder.

True to Skalet's prediction—and a tribute to her pharmacological skill—the young diplomat retained only the vaguest recollection of events after leaving the Library the second time. When I'd shaken him vigorously, he'd awakened, babbling about following a siren song into a tree.

There was that gash on his forehead; we'd need a bit of medplas. To get some and, more urgently, deal with whatever had sent Skalet into battle-mode, we needed to get moving. *Small steps.* "Let's get you on the bench," I told my groggy Human.

My Lishcyn-self could have carried him. This me waltzed him clumsily to where Evan could lunge for the bench, hit the wall, and slide down into what was, with my help, sitting. "There was singing," he insisted forlornly. "Such a beautiful voice."

"The wind in the trees," I assured him, slightly jealous. I'd never heard Lesy's Human-self sing.

As this was no time to be caught up in Ersh-memory, I braced myself, panting. *Nothing.* Feeling as if I'd had a narrow escape, I started for the com panel.

Evan grabbed my arm. "You saved me! Thank you. Thank you. And my Great Gran will want to thank you too. I'm the last bestest Gooseberry, you know. But I haven't—" he hiccupped, "—haven't done my duty and made more. Yet. But thanks to you, Es, I will." With a grand wave of his hand to suggest staggering amounts of procreation, with little Gooseberrys everywhere in the known universe and beyond.

The wave freed my arm, but I didn't go to the panel. Instead, I stared down at Evan, noting dilated pupils and a truly goofy grin. Had Skalet expected this and abandoned him to me?

Of course she had. It was almost a relief to have her back to normal. "Evan, you're drunk."

He gave me an owlish blink. "That's what my auto—my auto—this says, too." With a tap to the side of his head. His expression changed to woe, as if flipped by a switch. "Lesley!" The dear idiot tried to stand. I wasn't fast enough and he landed face-first on the grate again. He hiccupped, apparently none the worse for the fall, and rolled his head to look up at me. "Did you save Lesley too?"

"She's fine." How much of this would he remember? I decided to be convincing. "Skalet took Lesley to her home in the village."

An invention I'd need to tell my web-kin before she encountered Evan again. *Lying like an ephemeral, I was.* Ersh would be disgusted.

The Human heaved himself to a sit, legs splayed, his expression flipping back to Good Cheer. He'd fit right in with the Iftsen. "Hi, Esen! What brings you—" hiccup, "—here?"

Cosmic Gods. He was getting worse.

Was that normal? *Nothing today,* I thought desperately, *was.*

"Stay there," I ordered, not that he looked remotely capable of flight. Or reason, so I locked the outside exit. "I'll be right back."

After Skalet, who'd not be amused by my failure to cope with one inebriated Human—even if it was her fault and we'd crises multiplying like Gooseberrys—there was only one person in the Library I could think of who might know how to quickly cure Evan.

And might not blame me for his condition.

I locked the hall door behind me with my code, hoping Evan was too befuddled to remember and key it open from the other side. Though if he did, odds were other Humans would realize what was wrong and help him—but they'd blame me. *And tell Paul—*

I headed for the Chow.

The overhead lights were off, turning the wall-sized auto dispenser—which couldn't be turned off, according to its operator, or the contents would spoil before becoming edible, a term Lambo used a little too loosely—into a malignant work of art.

No, I thought, standing in the doorway, *more like a feisty gathering of Regillian firebeetles up a tree.* With a smattering of fluorescent fungi.

A subdued rattle hinted at another life-form entirely. I took a step inside.

"CLOSED!"

Being prepared for the roar made it no less startling. I shook my fur back down and swallowed the snarl. "Lambo, I know you're in here."

A menacing silence.

Which might have been my imagination but was experience. The Carasian who'd attached him/herself to the Library like an angry barnacle was nothing like others I'd met. Granted, I'd spent as little time as possible near females of the species, including Ersh, Ansky, and Mixs when they'd held *discussions* in the form. Having no male in their pool, those didn't last long before they cycled out of frustration but, while wet, they'd incessantly bellow for more this and more that and would I scrub their carapaces?

Not if I could hide, I wouldn't. Lesy, who loved hiding more than discussions, would help if she was home. We'd crouch behind rocks and she'd tell me bawdy jokes about Carasian sex I was too young to appreciate but found hilarious because she did.

Skalet hadn't participated in either activity. At the time, I'd put it down to her pride and utter disinterest in anything fun. Being too young to understand.

We were of Ersh's flesh. We were in no sense the same and Skalet had been Youngest once, hard as that was to contemplate today. Had her way to survive, unlike mine, been self-isolation?

"CLOSED!"

Another who demanded privacy. "You don't have to open," I said quickly. "I need something to stop Evan being drunk."

Claws snapping hungrily, the Carasian leapt over the counter from his hiding place, landing with a crash and sliding in my direction with all the implacable terrifying threat of a female of that species.

"WHAT HAVE YOU DONE TO MY EVAN?!"

Blamed after all.

Elements

EVAN'S brain was stuffed with socks. Fluffy yellow socks that chirped like Aunt Melan after she'd had beers with Great Gran.

His brain hadn't, he was quite quite sure, been stuffed with socks before Esen left him in this—

Curious what "this" was, Evan opened his eyes. His nose, reassuringly between his eyes, was inside a grate. If he blinked—which he managed after a moment's serious concentration—his eyelashes brushed over the metal. Gazing down, he could see clear pipes with bubbles inside and a puddle of water with teeny waves in it.

Growing tired of watching the bubble pipes and puddle, Evan pulled his nose out of the grate. He rolled his head to the side and saw a foot. In a sock. It wasn't yellow, which confused him for a while.

Growing tired of the confusing sock, he rolled his head the other way and saw another sock. Not yellow. Unless he saw the same sock, head rolling not having an effect.

He wiggled the toes of his right foot to check. The toes in the sock he could see didn't wiggle. He'd company! "Hello!" he greeted. The sound hurt. "Ssshhh," he scolded himself, then hiccupped.

No one answered. If he was alone, Evan concluded, feeling very clever, those were his feet. And if both were his feet, and his face was between them, he was folded in half. That didn't sound comfortable.

Come to think of it, he wasn't. Not at all, especially below his middle. "I have to pee!" he exclaimed. Too loud. He sssssh'd himself again.

If Esen had left him here, and he had to pee, this must be the accommodation; Esen being the most thoughtful, sweetest still-almost-a-puppy person he knew.

"I am going to pee," he informed the grate solemnly.

To do so, first he had to unfold, an act proving easier than expected as his body really didn't like being folded under the circumstances.

Winding up on hands and knees, Evan chose to stay that way, the world having a tendency to sway.

Besides, before he could pee, he had to lift the grate.

The Human stared down at the grate for a while, trying to think with yellow chirping socks for a brain. Eventually, he noticed all his fingers and all his thumbs were holding onto the grate.

He also noticed his stomach had filled with angry little crabs. The sensation was worse than having to pee. Or about the same. Both were a bother, and Evan pondered Protocol. Did one vomit and pee into the grate at the same time, or did one eruption take Precedence?

"Pre-ce-dence," he said out loud, enjoying the word, then "Sshhhh."

Evan Gooseberry grabbed the grate with both hands and pulled up as hard as he could.

What happened next took even a yellow chirping sock brain by surprise.

The grate came up, which he had sort of expected, maybe.

But with it came other things. Bubble pipe things and wire things and long pieces of what he didn't recognize but that sparked. Water, or maybe what wasn't, erupted in a fine mist coating his face that made him want to pee more than ever.

So that's what Evan did.

Then he took a nap.

Someone pulled his eyelid up. Someone pulled it down.

Someone said Very Bad Words.

Someone smacked him on the cheek.

Someone shook him.

Growing annoyed with that "Someone," Evan tried to say a Very Bad Word too. It came out as "Freedles."

Someone patted him on the head.

Evan drifted back into the peace of nothing at all—

Someone stabbed him in the arm!

And from the stab flowed something hot and itchy under his skin and through all his body and even into his stomach and when it reached his head, it pulled apart all the yellow chirping socks until—"FREEDLES!" Evan shouted and sat up.

He was sitting. On the bench. The world didn't move. His brain was—

His stomach insisted on Precedence. Evan threw up.

Into a bucket. Thankfully, there was a bucket. And a hand, cool and callused, supporting his head.

Someone asked, "Feel better?"

And he knew the voice, knew the hand, knew and remembered—if not everything, then enough.

Evan closed his eyes, thoroughly mortified. "Hi, Duggs."

20: Chow Night

"**L**OST something?"

Lambo froze with a great claw poised over my cringing head. Equally immobile, I stared, speechless, as Duggs burst into the Chow supporting Evan with an arm under his shoulder. He looked miserable; she looked—

More than angry. Duggs Pouncey looked ready to tear someone's head from their body with her bare hands and I didn't doubt she could. Hopefully, not Evan's. "What did he do?" I asked cautiously.

Evan gave me a woeful look. Lambo lowered the claw and clanked away the precise distance to keep me in range while withdrawing imminent threat. *I appreciated the distinction.*

"Found him ripping apart the environmental controls in the northeast portal. Blissed out of his gourd." The last with an approving slap on Evan's chest. "Gave him a broad spectrum anti-intoxicant. Keep one in my locker for the crew."

He groaned in response. "I—I'll pay for the damages."

Lambo snapped a handling claw at me. "What have you done to my Evan?"

"You did this?" Duggs scowled. "Esen-alit-Quar."

I was impressed. Just my name, and Duggs achieved a level of scathing scorn worthy of Ersh herself. I'd have felt significant, *if completely undeserved,* shame if I hadn't already seen her anger. It wasn't about me or Evan. At a guess?

Duggs knew what had made my web-kin draw her weapon and dash away.

It was never anything good.

"Lights full." I walked to the door and closed it, then turned. "Evan went outside and hit his head on a tree. We found him unconscious and brought him in. We—" *to say "Skalet" in front of Duggs would be like waving an enemy battle flag in front of a Ganthor* "—administered a mild stimulant, but he'd an adverse reaction." I didn't look at Evan while I spoke. "I came to Lambo for something to help. Thanks for yours, Duggs." Now I looked at him. "Are you all right?"

"My Evan needs fluids." Ignoring the Human's horrified expression— I could smell vomit and sympathized—Lambo went through the opening in the counter this time, humming peacefully to himself as if he'd never slid at me or thrown a tantrum. He began tapping controls.

"Evan. Are you all right?" I repeated gently.

He moved his head, as if experimenting with gravity, then licked his lips. "Yes, I think so," he said. Duggs let him stand on his own and Evan smiled at her, but his smile faded at the grim look on her face. Back to me. "I remember being in the portal. What you said about—" With a tiny nod of gratitude meaning Lesley. "What's happened?" with a troubled glance at Duggs.

Not slow, our Evan.

"What do you think happened?" Duggs snapped. "You broke the damn equipment, set off alarms in maintenance—while I was taking my shower, thank you for that—and there was no one but me to respond because everyone else is too busy setting up piles of Kraal dung in the Lobby!"

An eyestalk on Duggs, Lambo rumbled back, holding out a cup. "Drink."

Evan had to take it, though he looked decidedly queasy at the notion of putting anything in his stomach. Every eyestalk riveted on him, a regard which could be taken as compassionate or ominous. Admittedly, even I had difficulty telling the difference with Lambo.

"Poison's my guess," Duggs said abruptly.

Hastily, Evan lowered the cup, spilling some of its contents. Three eyestalks stayed with it, the rest switching to Duggs. "Isn't."

"Is," she snapped. "Those Commonwealth wool-for-brains—not you, Evan—"

"I've socks," he confessed mournfully.

"—stirring up things. Claiming we've a plague risk from that ship," Duggs continued, her voice hard and flat. "Load of hot steaming dung, that's what it is. Mark me—that crew was done for by the same scums who dipped your guests in the basement. The bloody Kraal!"

I didn't explode.

Given the consequences of losing form now, in front of these three, I celebrated the small victory, however shallow it made me. *As for the rest—*

"What do you mean, 'dipped our guests'?" Evan asked. With understandable confusion as I doubted he thought of the Sacrissee as sheep or knew farm protocols.

"The local Human euphemism for murder," Lambo supplied. "Wait." His voice dropped and every eyestalk glowered at me. "You put guests in the basement?!" As if this transgression of Library regulations was worse than the crime.

"I have to go," I said numbly, easing toward the door. When nothing made sense, I'd one imperative. *Find Paul.* Who'd be upset, who'd need me too—

Duggs stepped in my way. "I made this place for you. I believed what you said it was for." Her mouth twisted, and she stepped up to me, into me, glaring down the difference in our height. "Swallowed the bait like a starved trout, didn't I."

I pretended her fingers hadn't curled into a hard knotted fist. Pretended she wasn't every bit as fierce and physical as Skalet, even if she was. *At least there weren't hammers.* "We've never lied to you. The Library—"

"Is a front for the Kraal. I should have known when I saw *her*," in a tone that raised the hair between my shoulders. Her eyes held something fractured. "If not, then you've put something here they want and they're coming for it, to the hells with the rest of the planet. Are the Woolies on their side? Are they throwing us away like a bone?"

This wasn't the calm, competent Duggs I knew. This—this was the Duggs she'd kept from us all, perhaps even from herself. Her hot breaths dried my eyes and filled my nostrils; her washed-Human scent with its underlay of stress sweat and tinge of *Evan* all there was. I didn't know what to do.

Except give her the truth. "What's here is information," I replied evenly, "Anyone can ask the Library for it. Kraal. You. The combatants on either side of a conflict. Those who believe they're friends but can't grasp the concept. Those who need to communicate and those who only thought they were. The curious." I lowered my ears. "And those afraid. The guests you say have been killed in our basement came to ask for a world where they'd be welcome. The Library found their answer."

"Too late," she ground out.

"For them." I lifted my ears slightly. "Not for those they represent." For among the truths uncovered within my snorts and nibbles was this: the Emboldened possessed a genetic diversity suggestive of a population. Her breathing eased, if not Evan's. "If Kraal have committed violence against the Library and its scholars, Duggs, we will find out who and why."

Her head reared back. "You trust *her.*"

Under no circumstances, but we were family. "In this, I do," I said firmly. "And so should you."

"Gratifying."

Skalet had the worst timing.

Or the best. Being nose-to-nose, almost, with Duggs, I watched her expression as she stared past me go from loathing—of Skalet—to resentment—that for me—to dark curiosity. "I see you agree with me."

I moved aside and turned to grant my web-kin space, only then seeing what she'd done and Duggs meant.

Skalet's affiliation with House Bract was now an intricate line of oozing subcutaneous tissue from ear to throat. Modern Kraal went to a medtech for a mostly painless removal; affiliation, after all, could be re-established. You'd need the skin intact.

This was the old way, a knife wielded on their own flesh by one who wished not only to sever their ties to a House, but to etch into their skin proof of that repudiation.

It hurt. Others wouldn't see, as I could, the clenched fine lines beside her eyes and mouth, the rigidity of her posture. The only reason my tail wasn't between my legs was my total inability to move any body part.

Knowing Skalet, the greater pain would be a betrayal she hadn't seen coming or orchestrated for her own purpose. I could almost feel sorry for her.

A triumphant claw snap. "Good. Bract isn't worthy of you." Having pronounced judgment, Lambo settled into a relaxed crouch. "How do we retaliate?"

"Not on our world, you don't," Duggs warned, stare locked on Skalet. "Not in our space. Keep your war to yourselves."

War. Because of our Library. Potentially consuming it.

"We don't," I said firmly, for some strange reason no longer in danger of exploding, my ears stiff. "We use our resources to help Constable Lefebvre find and bring the killers to justice." I looked to my web-kin. "No matter where we have to go."

Her eyes lit with terrifying joy. "Acceptable."

I faced Duggs next. She showed no expression at all, her eyes calm again; a volcano gone quiet, but in no sense less dangerous. "I'm done here."

Maybe if I'd said the right thing, as Paul would. Appealed to her for help—mentioned our trapped guests and the accommodations—but I said the wrong thing. "The lockdown—"

"Never the truth, is it?" Duggs Pouncey wheeled on a heel and walked out the door.

The Carasian rose to his spongy feet, the clatter of annoyed body parts deafening as he retreated behind the counter. Having expressed his dissatisfaction with my unwillingness to leap into battle, he ducked down and vanished.

Hiding with his broken gemmie collection wasn't as impressive as Lambo probably thought, but all I said, loudly, was, "The Chow opens for breakfast."

Might work. Probably wouldn't.

Evan gave me a somber nod, clearly recovered and doubtless planning how to help. I opened my mouth to urge him to follow Duggs. To leave with her, so I didn't have to worry about him too.

Before I could—perhaps aware I would—Evan strode to the door.

He looked back at me, determination plain. "I want to see them. The bodies."

"They were dissolved," Skalet informed him.

Evan clenched his jaw. "I spent the most time with the Sacrissee since they arrived. I might have insights the constable needs." *So much for protecting him.*

I'd my own pressing concern. "Paul will be there."

Skalet's exasperated shrug at what she considered my "dependency" made her wince.

Served her right.

"Let's go, Evan."

Makings

OOLA lifts a trembling hand before her eyes. It should be hers, coming at the end of her arm, but it cannot be. They are *wrong.* No Sacrissee has claws tipping each finger, like short stiffened hairs.

She tries scraping them off on stone, but they are truly part of her.

They'd appeared when the hunters laid their hands on her.

Alone now, hiding behind crates and canisters, Oola watches the claws withdraw into the thick skin of her fingertips, leaving tiny orange drops behind. The drops kill.

She'd seen, heard the screaming, witnessed the agonizing deaths as the hunters—scratched by these claws, only that—tore themselves apart as if their skin was the enemy.

Frantically, Oola digs her fingertips in the litter and dirt of the ground, wipes them back and forth until certain they're dry and the drops gone. Even then she's afraid to be touched by her own hands.

What is *she?*

Or is the real question: *how is she this?*

She wasn't always. Before her kingroup took her to Molancor, to the Humans, she wasn't this. Oola remembers the prick of pins. She remembers soothing voices and sometime pain.

What have they made of her?

Another *howl,* no longer so distant.

Does it offer kinship? Are there others like her, escaped and safe?

How could there be?

But the sound is all she has left of hope.

Oola rises to her feet.

21: Basement Night

SOME things were true no matter what I was, or where. The greater my need to be with my friend, the harder he was to be with—alone, that is.

Not that I counted Evan a crowd, but there were things I couldn't say to Paul in front of him or anyone else. Urgent things. *Get-myself-in-trouble* things, and the fastest way out of that trouble, I'd learned, was with my friend's help.

Plus, Paul would want to tell me himself about the Sacrissee. Would want to mourn with me, however briefly, before telling me how we'd fix it.

Not that I thought dead guests could be fixed, other than dealing with those responsible and making sure it didn't happen a third time— which probably meant letting Skalet put her snoops back in every room and those horrid persona-scans she'd always wanted—

And Duggs was gone—

Paul would make everything better. That's what mattered.

Evan walked with me to the lift, growing reassuringly steadier with each step. We took the staff corridor to the admin area, not that I wasn't curious what the latest model sous tent looked like and how our guests were taking to them, but to avoid being discovered ourselves. The moment Henri or Ally or any of our overworked staff set eyes on me, it'd be Esen this and Esen that and I'd never escape.

Paul first.

I paused at the com panel. "I'll confirm Paul's still there."

Evan pressed the lift control. "I'm ready now, Es. I can't promise to be later."

Oh. I'd forgotten why Evan had gone outside in the first place. I tucked my arm inside his when the lift door opened. "Together," I said, pulling him inside.

He retrieved his arm, giving me a hurt look, then sent the lift down. "I said I was ready. I know my own head. Now. There were—" he paused, eyebrows meeting, "—yellow chirping socks in it for a while."

That didn't sound at all healthy. I'd discuss appropriate medication for Humans the next time Skalet and I had our own privacy.

"Good, because we're here," I announced unnecessarily, the door having opened on the lower level.

A stranger stood waiting. I blinked, and the tall stern figure regarding me morphed back into Tuggles Cameron, one of Paul's innumerable cousins and someone who did not work at the Library. She'd a weapon holstered on her belt and a hand on it until she blinked too and saw me. "Curator," she greeted. "And Hom?" Her stare at Evan vowed a full interrogation.

Did she smell the tinge of vomit too? It tended to make other Humans suspicious. He really should have had some of Lambo's—

"Polit Evan Gooseberry," Evan said confidently. Had I known an armed guard would have put him at ease in the basement, I'd have arranged one. Or a facsimile. "Assigned to Constable Lefebvre."

Clever Evan.

I kept my ears up and let the tip of my tongue show, signifying agreement and utter trustworthiness, which was cheating as I knew perfectly well Tuggles lived with several scruffs, of varying shape and size. I wasn't surprised when she couldn't help but smile at me, then stepped out of our way and pointed down the corridor.

Not worth telling Paul.

Without Tuggles watching from behind, Evan walking beside, and hazard tape—in happier times the reflective yellow stuff kept aerial scholars from landing where they shouldn't, the concept of barriers difficult for them—ahead marking a square before what had been the door with curtain protecting the *IN*, I'd have bolted straight to my friend as quickly as a Lanivarian could.

Faced with these constraints and the imperative of dignity, I did the next best thing, it being impossible to completely restrain this form or myself. While it was true rapid little hop-steps covered ground no faster and made me look, according to Rudy, as if I walked on hot pavement, it was hop-step or bolt.

Tuggles must have called ahead because Mal and Lionel appeared in the doorway, going to stand on either side. When Evan made to go through, Lionel took his arm gently. "Give them a moment."

Perversely, that made me come to a full stop. Why would Paul want a private moment with me? I knew why I wanted a private moment with him, but this was—

"Esen?"

—*I might be overthinking.*

I bolted through the door into what had been a sanctuary and closed the door behind me.

An acrid burning stench attacked my poor nose. I coughed and sneezed, trying not to breathe.

"Here." Paul handed me a snout mask. He wore the transparent Human version, allowing me to see his dear face. A face carved into new and sorrowful lines and I whined. He reached out and gently took hold of my ear, rubbing it as he said, "I'm all right, Old Blob. You're here," with an effort to smile.

"Here I am," I assured him. Unable to lick through the mask, I bumped my friend with my shoulder, conveying the same message. "Duggs told us. Evan's waiting outside to see."

I'd already taken a quick look. Dead ephemerals returned their constituent molecules to their environment over time, with some help, unless prevented from decay by social preference or being frozen or dried.

These were long gone.

"He can wait," Paul said, then took hold of my head again, this time to search my face. "Was this our fault?" he whispered, his voice breaking. "Did we do this?"

Not the time to take him literally. "Yes," I replied sadly. "Instead of protecting the Sacrissee, we made them comfortable. We disregarded why they asked for sanctuary because we saw no danger. And we saw no danger because we didn't look for it. This is our fault." I watched his eyelids squeeze tight, regretting the tears tracing his cheekbones almost as much as the stupid masks that stopped me licking them away. When Paul's eyes opened, glistening and full of grief, I said the rest. "We made a mistake and they died of it. We won't make that mistake again." *Though there'd be new ones.*

"'We won't make it again,'" he repeated, sealing our promise, sighing after the words. His fingers dug into my neck ruff as if seeking strength.

Far superior to hugging.

Paul pressed his forehead to mine, then stepped back. "We start now," he said, sounding like himself again and ready to fix things.

Making me feel better. "You've an idea?"

He indicated the hole in the ceiling above our heads. "There's a tunnel leading from the storeroom above." His finger tapped the mask over my nose. "Thought you could take a sniff." He bent at the waist, hands on his thighs, and looked over his shoulder at me. "Ready, Fang-face?"

Our game! One we played regularly, if Skalet wasn't around.

Giving myself more room, I curled my fingers into paws, dropped to all fours, then bounded toward the target Paul provided. The Lanivarian term for an assisted leap translated as "soars gracefully on the wings of another."

When my feet hit Paul's back, he was on the rise, giving my next leap a boost that, while not resulting in quite a graceful soar, propelled me through the hole in the ceiling. I landed, sprawling, upstairs.

I stripped off the mask.

The storeroom shelves were intact, though items I remembered lining up in a neat row were now scattered. I put my nose to the floor, to reduce the impact of the stench wafting up from the room below, and half-closed my eyes, savoring this release of instinct—

"Anything?"

—*probably not the time to indulge.* I began sniffing.

Stopped.

Sniffed again, because this couldn't be right.

But it had to be. *This nose was infallible.*

I hurried along the floor, dribbling mucus and slobber, excitedly following multiple scents as they combined into *now and then* and *who and where*. Scrambled into the very cold and damp tunnel cut through our wounded wall. Went on two legs to run up its slope because the scents were focused here and I needed hands to grab the sides and not slip anyway.

I popped my head into the open air, startling Teri Terworth, who must have lost the draw to be stuck outside and guard the hole for the night. Teri wasn't, Paul had tried to explain, earnestly and with flow charts, a close relative of Jan Terworth. Jan having stunned my friend three times in a row despite being a cousin and thus Paul's close relative, I maintained a certain reticence around any and all Terworths, just in case.

Unaware of causing turmoil, Teri waved at me cheerfully, then sat back down by the heatbox, shrugging a blanket over his head.

Back I went, shaking snow from mine. I slid more than ran through the tunnel, bursting out into the storeroom to find Paul waiting. "What did you find?"

Much as I wanted to ask if he'd climbed on furniture or taken the lift—tactics of consequence to future games—I chose to get to the point. "They aren't dead. Not the ones we thought were dead. Others are dead." I paused to lick a dribble from my nose. No need to add Lambo had been here, too, roaming around the room. The Carasian trundled through the storerooms every night.

It was a wonder more wasn't broken.

"Slow down," Paul told me, though I could see by the light in his eyes he'd grasped the essentials. "Who's dead and who's not?"

"Humans came in." I pointed to the tunnel. "Sacrissee went out."

Elements

"YOUR Eminence." The display showed Cieter-ro standing at attention, though protocol permitted a captain to remain seated on their own ship. "How may I serve?"

The vid was one-way. Long fingers toyed with a knife, let light play along the blade. The channel should be secure. *Trust was a liability.*

Risk had to be accepted.

"Report."

"It's as you suspected, Your Eminence. Without your consent, Captain Haden-ru ordered the *Trium Pa* to launch a remote and uses it to mimic communications from an inbound Commonwealth medship."

"Her purpose. Speculate."

Shoulders drew back with pride. "The ruse allows the captain to restrict movement on the landing field and around the Library, while controlling information flow and gaining access to current situation reports by the local authorities."

An intelligent asset, Cieter-ro. "To what end?" Motivation was ever the more challenging to envision.

His eyes glinted with pleasure. "To delay discovery of her affiliates' covert actions on the *Stellar Trumpet,* Your Eminence."

The murdered crew. Feed a plausible suggestion of plague to the constable to leave them—and their ship—sealed and untouchable. "The Botharans won't be fooled much longer."

"Perhaps the delay has been sufficient for Haden-ru's purpose."

"Perhaps." *Interesting.* "Have you identified the inbound ships? Their source?" Another fault to note against the crew of *Trium Pa*, this lack of vital news. They sought to isolate her or, rather, one did.

A liability.

"Both are out of Sacriss System. One is a private vessel registered to Molancor Genomics. The other is the *Tesseer Ra*, of House Virul, an escort-for-hire bringing diplomatic personnel from Sacriss VII to Botharis. What is your command?"

One of the Great Houses, Virul, and potent. The claim of playing escort was a lie. Not even a good one, implying they were expected on Botharis, for to her certain knowledge, if not widely revealed, the *Tesseer Ra* was Virul's current flagship. On board would be a courier, with rank and discretionary power matching her own—*possibly greater.* Able to speak or act for that House; conceivably for others.

Why would the political might of the Kraal Confederacy come here? *Why now?*

Despite Virul's daunting presence, her loyal Kraal could stop the private ship and board it under pretext. Destroy it unboarded. Take any combination of informative actions at her command—none of which Esen would approve.

Inconvenient.

"The moment will come when I require immediate transport. Without question or record."

Cieter-ro pressed the back of his hands to his cheeks. "The *Septos Ank* is yours."

The tip of the knife pointed at the display. "I will require more."

Cieter-ro knew what she asked. She watched for hesitation.

Saw none. *Gratifying.*

"Then more you shall have, Your Eminence." The stroke of a finger along the curl of a red tattoo. Their shared affiliation to Conell, one outside of Bract, Bryll, or Arzul. A vow.

She wasn't the only one to accept risk.

"Satisfactory. As for the rest—continue the pretense of a medship. When the moment comes, accept secure contact with the *Tesseer Ra* and transfer to me."

"Your Glory!" Cieter-ro touched his tattoos and bowed, affected by her belief.

Infected by it, as the actions she'd ordered could only be taken by the captain—the new captain—of the *Trium Pa*.

Skalet ended the link. Considered her knife, with its twin deadly edges and needle-sharp tip, the poison within the handle. Such a Kraal object, with its predictable deceit.

Cieter-ro had suggested the tents. His ship, *Septos Ank*, had made the run to Botharis. A favored ally—

Would be the first to betray for advantage. Affiliation was earned. Whose might he desire, if not hers?

Verification. A coded message-within-a-message activated another resource, unknown to the rest. If her caution was misplaced, Cieter-ro could save himself with an extraordinary act of loyalty. If not—

What would be, would be. Having set the *Trium Pa* on her needful path to redemption or cataclysm—the latter undoubtedly alarming the Botharan government who'd be a nuisance—Skalet returned her attention to her surroundings.

The room was as secure as the channel. Was as newly vulnerable, particularly with unknown Kraal entering the scenario; just as well she'd begun the needful adjustments.

When Paul Ragem offered her this secret place inside the Ragem barn, next to his own, surely he'd known she'd protect both.

If she put a hand to the nearest wall, she'd be close to the Library's heart, the collection itself. Not the sole copy. *Prudent.*

As Esen was not.

This place allowed her to rest this form and care for it. To bathe it and dress. It contained her armory and little else. An exit Paul did not know about, but would expect.

Impressive.

She flipped and threw the knife. Half the blade penetrated the wall by the com panel, the rest sang its eager hum to her, and Skalet felt—

—felt strange. Felt—

Before the rising Lesy-taint could take hold, she snapped a vial and inhaled its contents, then stretched out on her cot.

Remembering what the courier sent by House Bryll to bring down its own had taught her:

Those who do not seize control, relinquish it.

22: Admin Office Night

THE Hamlet of Hillsview's seniormost politician and community leader was waiting for us outside Lionel's closed door, broad shoulders against the wall, the top half of faded coveralls draped around his waist, a loud flowered shirt beneath. A knit cap bulged a shirt pocket and enormous mitts were clipped to his coveralls; by the puddles around his boots, Henri'd let him through without sweeping off the snow. *She didn't let me.*

Few argued with Joncee Pershing. He was a big, friendly, competent Human, with a smile to inspire confidence and a vigorous handshake I knew to avoid, however well intended. Now in his third term as reeve, he oversaw the Hamlet of Hillsview council with a wry sense of humor as well as dedication. According to Henri, Joncee would be reelected as long as he breathed, barring catastrophe. Botharans tended to stick with what—and who—worked.

Three lost Sacrissee might not qualify as a catastrophe.

The day wasn't over.

"Hi, Paul. Esen. Came to deliver this." Nodding to Lionel and Evan, Joncee held up a travel bag plastered in red-and-white Commonwealth diplomatic privilege stickers. "Polit Gooseberry?"

"Thank you," Evan said faintly, taking the bag. Why he'd shipped it like this I'd no idea. The Library had normal deliveries. *Had he brought treats not to be trusted through regular customs?*

Not a curiosity for the moment. The reeve was here as the Hamlet's representative, to see for himself what was happening at the Library. Once we'd suspected Kraal involvement, Mal would have stayed off coms also, but he'd only to send a messenger.

As had Paul, because we'd aliens traipsing after all.

When I'd complained we were in enough trouble, he'd reminded me the agreements we'd signed included one stating the Hamlet of Hillsview Council and its Preservation Committee must be notified if any aliens leave the grounds unescorted, for whatever reason.

I'd blithely assumed the reason would be to use the discount coupons Henri and Ally handed out last year for the Hillsview pub, starting a beneficial local tourism trend. So far, no takers, though some of the coupons, sealed in protective cases, had turned up for sale at auction on Hixtar Station; paper being more valuable offworld than extra fried chips.

Hearing me snarling under my breath in the lift, Lionel had pointed out only the reeve could authorize deputy constables, such as Tuggles downstairs, so the Word Was Out already.

I'd have been impressed by his grasp of the minutiae of Botharan bureaucracy if I wasn't more worried about consequences.

"Not here just for the delivery," Joncee confirmed, losing his smile. I tensed, seeing Paul do the same. "We've a new and serious problem," the reeve informed us. "Rhonda's Elk."

"'Elk?'" Lionel echoed blankly.

By his expression, Paul was equally baffled. *Not reassuring.*

And not "Elk." I didn't correct their use of the term, although there must have been an involuntary twitch of *intending to*, because Paul shook his head at me. But what Rhonda raised in her fields, sometimes grazed in ours, and milked for the benefit of the Hamlet of Hillsview weren't deer at all, but a native Botharan animal who'd happened to evolve along similar lines. Tall, had horns and a temper, and bellowed in rut, so let's call it an Elk, even if biologically it was closer to a weasling.

Ersh had pointed out the tendency among ephemerals, in particular Humans, to name whatever wonderfully novel creature they found after what they fondly remembered—or had seen in a vid and fantasized over. Case in point, Botharis did have dragons. Who weren't, but getting into such arguments rarely went well.

While I mused over nomenclature and the stubbornness of Humans, Joncee kept speaking, his deep voice projecting nicely down the hall, so staff stopped to listen. "Entire herd's gone. After Bertie got out the second time, Mal had Rhonda raise the height of her fences. Whoever took them had to unlock and open two gates."

I hadn't known there'd been a repeat escapade, but the stag was a determined creature, if a tad short-sighted. Poor Mal.

"Surely there's someone else to handle the, ah, case," Lionel ventured, obviously trying to respect a local issue, though it was plain he considered strayed livestock as important as a missing sock. *Wait till we ran out of cheese.*

Joncee shrugged. "Mal's our constable." He came off the wall and nodded to the door. "Shall we?"

Mal had set up an easel with a huge sheet of paper in Lionel's office—his notebook presumably inadequate to the emergency—and was busy writing on it as we entered. "Have a seat. Joncee," with a nod to the reeve. "Thanks for coming."

On the sheet was the word "Sacrissee" with an ominous arrow leading to a circle containing "Unknown Humans, Possibly Kraal." The "X" through the circle indicated Mal hadn't started writing until after we'd clarified who'd died in our basement. *Or had extra sheets of paper.*

Joncee grabbed a chair and put it at the head of the table. After three terms, I thought it likely a habit. "You won't thank me when you hear Rhonda's herd's been stolen," he announced.

"Or were set free." I felt obliged to point out the alternative. Sitting, careful of my tail, I waved at the window wall. "They are native to this region."

The Botharans, Paul too, gave me appalled looks and shook their heads.

"Who'd do that? It's a dairy herd. There are Tigers," Joncee objected.

Just because the local carnivore had stripes—and hadn't been seen in these hills since Paul was a child—and—

Possibly irrelevant facts, I told myself, trusting Paul appreciated my restraint.

"I'll have Terworth check it out," Mal promised. He tapped the board. "Right now, here's my priority."

Joncee ran a hand over his close-cropped hair, feigning a look of relief. "So long as you tell Rhonda." He eyed the board, then pointed at it. "How'd you sort that out? Your message said the bodies couldn't be identified."

While I'd have preferred to bask in well-earned praise for this me's outstanding olfactory ability, I knew better than encourage any thoughts of this me being similar to a scruff. *Unless helpful.* My morals were oddly flexible today.

Paul answered for me. "We found traces in the escape tunnel."

From Mal's brief, thoughtful look at me, the former patroller was aware of a Lanivarian's sensitivity in the *sniff-you* department, but chose not to mention it in front of his boss. I gave a grateful dip of my ears.

"Thanks for that," Mal said, directing the words at Paul. *I still basked.* Then he tapped the word "Sacrissee." "I've put the word out for our people to lock their doors."

Joncee nodded. "What about search parties?"

"We're to stand down."

The reeve's voice deepened into thunder. "Who told you that?"

Mal stepped to the table, leaning on his fists. His expression was deceptively mild. "Order's from the Commonwealth. The medship's due in orbit midday local. Until they're dirtside and can complete autopsies on the *Trumpet*'s crew, no one goes out and the landing field's closed."

"They still fear a contagion?" Lionel's eyebrows rose. "Why?"

"My question exactly," Mal replied. "The Woolies now claim the *Stellar Trumpet* stopped at a port where it might have been contaminated. Not that they'd say where or by what." His lips thinned. "You'd think the mighty Commonwealth doesn't have a high opinion of my ability as an investigator."

Evan looked unhappy but didn't argue.

Joncee growled in his throat. "This is our problem. We can't have killers on the loose."

"We don't know the Sacrissee killed anyone," Paul objected.

Sometimes he was the optimist. I lowered my ears. "If they did," I said very quietly, Evan stirring beside me, "it was self-defense."

"Even so, Esen, they're dangerous. To defeat Kraal? Unarmed?" Mal and Joncee exchanged grim looks. "We've no witnesses," the constable continued, his tone a little too reasonable. "Given the destruction of the bodies—their flight—we can't say this wasn't premeditated."

I stiffened. "The Sacrissee were—maybe still are—being hunted. They're out in the cold—and dark!" Not a dread of this me—nor to Sacrissee—but having been Lishcyn for fifty years, I put a significant amount of dismay into the phrase.

"Joncee's right. The Sacrissee need to be found, for everyone's safety, including theirs." Paul took control of the meeting as simply as those quiet words. No matter the times I'd seen him accomplish the feat—and not always with his own species—I'd still no idea how. "How can we help?"

"The Elk!" Evan erupted, half rising from his seat.

We stared at him.

"Don't you see?" As he sank back down, he looked from one to the other of us. "It's possible to direct the movements of animals, if you know what you're doing." Seeing the startled angle of my ears—this not being an area in which I'd expected expertise from our diplomat—he gave a modest little shrug. "There's a Gooseberry in The Lore who herds Nolish Goats. He and his canids bring them in from the hills and guide them all the way home."

Paul's face lit with comprehension. "You think the Sacrissee released the herd and are using them to hide their trail."

"I think we should consider the possibility."

Mal looked to Joncee, who shrugged. "All right, then," the constable decided. "When I brief the search teams, I'll include finding Rhonda's Elk."

Everyone turned to me. *Sheer form prejudice, that was.*

"I do not," I informed the Humans testily, "herd Nolish Goats. Or anything else. Lanivarians evolved from hunters. And before you suggest I, a civilized being and curator of this Library, go out in the dark to hunt what aren't elk at all?" *Appealing as the notion was.* "Let me remind you a group of large animals will leave a track through snow even a Human could spot. Blindfolded."

"I'm sure Mal's going to suggest you stay right here, Esen, with the others," Joncee said.

The words dropped into a sudden hush, sending uncomfortable ripples outward. *Alien. Them.* A hint of *monsters.*

Joncee wasn't in any sense against us—he just wanted all the strange tucked safely away. I angled an ear, hearing Paul draw a breath to object.

I jumped in first. "That's my intention, Joncee. Mal. After all," I showed a hint of fang, "we've over a hundred esteemed foreign scholars trapped *here* until you resolve matters. Not a group the Botharan planetary government wants upset. Imagine the ramifications to trade alone."

Joncee hadn't. Hadn't thought offworld, being concerned with fugitives near the homes of friends and family. *That was our job.* I could almost read the words in his face. Fair enough.

Paul saw it too. "They're reasonable people who understand the circumstances—those we've been cleared to explain," he said, putting it back on the constable.

Who finally sat, joining us. "Then let's get on with it." Mal took out his trusty notebook. "The Woolies can spin themselves. I'm sending out searchers."

"I'll be one," Joncee volunteered. "There's more standing by."

Mal nodded. "First, we need to know what—who—we're after." He looked my way. "I've images and some physiological details from the collection, thanks to Lionel. Anything else you can tell me about the Sacrissee? Will they seek shelter? Come back here?"

Paul gave me his *be forthcoming* look.

The worryingly vague one.

Sometimes—rarely—he wanted me to spill Every Fact, which I loved to do but would take a few days. Other times, I was to reveal the Key Thing, but regarding the Sacrissee, I couldn't, not here. Paul knew the Emboldened were atypical of the species; he didn't know how much. I was certain he wouldn't want me to tell everyone, as I'd then have to explain how. *Snorted their boots?*

Paul added a slow blink. *Ah.* He wanted only the Pertinent-to-the-Moment Bits. Those searching knew the landscape—Mal himself had grown up on the farm next to Rudy's and Paul's. The fugitives scampering across that landscape, however, were alien.

"Sacrissee move with greater confidence in low light," I said, picking what might help Human hunters. "They'll have no difficulty tonight." The snow cover, with a clearing sky and two moons? Almost bright enough for a Lishcyn. *Well, no.* "As for the temperature—even stripped, they'd feel the cold no more than a Human dressed appropriately."

Evan shivered; I trusted he'd learned that lesson.

"Even if they're moving with the herd, the Sacrissee will seek a hiding place before dawn. I—these are generalizations," I cautioned.

"Better than ignorance," Mal avowed, seeming grateful. "If that's it?" At my nod, he stood. Paul, Joncee, and the others did the same. Evan hid a yawn.

When I stayed sitting, the Humans stopped. "Esen?" Paul asked quietly.

"They shouldn't have left the *IN* of the Library, even if attacked here," I said at last. "For them to flee *OUT* was highly irrational." By species' norms? Almost insane.

Yet so was leaving Sacriss System.

Dissolving the bodies, well, that wasn't. Sacrissee recycled their corpses.

Still. Maybe we shouldn't think of them as Sacrissee. The Emboldened had had a rational—for them—and compelling reason to come here. A reason not yet fulfilled.

"I've changed my mind." I looked up at Paul. "I don't think they'll take shelter. They've a purpose. They'll keep moving toward it."

Mal nodded. "We've kept it quiet that ships aren't moving. That was my initial assumption: they'd head for the landing field—for a way offworld."

The wrong one. The Emboldened wouldn't try to leave Botharis without their answer—without finding a home for their kind. That was their imperative. Something I couldn't explain to the constable until I knew more about them.

Paul knew I held something back. He let it go, but his lips tightened in their *you'd better be right, Es* line.

I slanted my ears in a *trust me.*

Joncee harrumphed. Once sure he had our attention, he lifted a big hand and held it palm up. "Sorry to say, I've more news and you won't

like it. Art and Lenan, and I'm betting Ruth had a hand in it, went behind me and the rest of the Preservation Committee to register a complaint with the county about this business of straying aliens. County
bumped it to the provincial board, and now?" His hand turned, a blunt
thumb threatening the ceiling. "It's gone to Grandine."

"They take months to respond," Lionel said.

I sincerely hoped so. From Paul's tight lips, he did, too.

Joncee heaved a sigh. "Not this time. I've been notified a representative from the planetary gov arrives tomorrow, on a fact-finding mission. We're all—*all*—" with a look at me, for some reason, "—to
extend our fullest cooperation."

My ears went flat. Paul just shook his head, but Lionel stood at attention, eyes bright with resolve. "Our documents are in order," he
stated, ready to battle bureaucracy for the Library.

I yawned, deliberately showing teeth.

"A problem for tomorrow," Paul said, reading my hint. "Unless you
need us, Mal?"

The constable rubbed a hand over his face, then glared at Joncee,
who lifted his shoulders and let them drop. "I need you," Mal told us,
"to take care of the people here."

"If you find the Sacrissee—" I began.

"You'll be the first to know." The constable's expression softened.
"No need for everyone to lose sleep tonight. Go."

Elements

PAUL and Esen had gone to meet with their staff, staying to help the scholars, while what sounded like the remaining adult population of the nearby village and farms headed out to hunt Sacrissee through the night.

When they'd asked how to help, Evan and Lionel had been given a task of their own. To rest. The morning wouldn't be any easier, according to Paul, who'd promised he and the still bright-eyed Lanivarian would join them shortly to do the same.

Lionel led the way to the farmhouse, wielding a hand light that shone a reassuring distance along what was a wide path, free of snow— or freed of it, by the even piles alongside. Luggage in hand, Evan kept a half step behind, uncertain of the company he kept.

When he'd first met Lionel, having had his share of supervisors already in his career, he'd formed an immediate and favorable impression of the former Survey officer. That this was a person to respect, who'd do the dangerous, difficult work without asking others to do it for him, who'd drive others but be right there to help.

It hadn't hurt that Lionel'd shared with him stories about Paul's start as a First Contact Specialist under his command.

But on the Survey Ship *Mistral,* Evan had researched more of Paul's past and learned how Lionel Kearn once had slandered Paul, accusing him publicly of being in league with the mysterious ship-destroying monster called Death, and misused Survey resources in his pursuit. A pursuit forcing Paul to fake his own death and hide, abandoning his life and Lesley. He'd even tarnished poor Esen's name.

To his shame, Evan had been so consumed by his own outrage he'd accused poor Esolesy Ki of being the monster, ready to arrest those he'd considered friends—even though Lionel had recanted his story and worked to clear Paul's name. *What had he been thinking?*

That he didn't understand.

They'd forgiven him.

As they'd forgiven Lionel. Embraced him. Made him Library Administrator, treating him as a confidant as well as friend, even though every misfortune that had happened to Paul and his alien friends could be blamed on the person walking him to their farmhouse.

What had he missed?

Evan's every instinct told him there was more to it. Something he couldn't see and hadn't found to make sense of Lionel Kearn, Esen, Esolesy Ki—above all, something to explain how Paul could forgive Lionel for ruining his life.

He stopped in his tracks.

Lionel halted and turned, dipping the light. "Evan?"

"I know about all of it," he heard himself say, and couldn't stop. "You, Paul, the Esen Monster. What I don't understand—I'm sorry, but how could they forgive you?"

"Because they're better than I was."

"And you—" Evan felt on a precipice. "You can forgive yourself?"

Shadows deepened eye sockets and hollowed cheeks, stealing the life from Lionel's face. Evan realized he'd gone too far, probed a wound beyond his comprehension, but it was too late.

"Never," Lionel told him, the word colder than the night. He resumed walking to the farmhouse.

Evan Gooseberry followed, two steps behind, and felt like a child.

Evan had been inside the primitive wood and stone building everyone called the farmhouse before. He'd concluded the "farm" part of the word must be because most of what was outside was allowed in, from mud and straw to the startling nuisances called mousels. He remained unsure why the fragile structure hadn't collapsed around them during Lambo's molt, and had no idea why Paul would want to live in it.

Or Esolesy Ki, elegant and civilized in her silks and fashionable tusk inlays.

As for Esen? Evan harbored a suspicion the Lanivarian might like having mousels in chomping range, not that he'd ever ask. Some things he didn't want to know.

He'd not imagined the building could be transformed.

Lionel paused courteously before the steps, having no trouble reading stunned Evan's reaction. "Lovely, isn't it?"

Evan nodded. Snow brought out sturdy graceful lines he'd missed before, emphasizing the strength of the roofline. The white fluffy stuff draped playfully along sills and railings, bringing to life the great branches of the tree leaning close, and, most wonderful of all? Soft light spilled outward from every window and door in warm welcome.

Did he deserve one? Facts alone don't tell people's stories, Great Gran would say, yet he'd jumped to conclusions about Kearn's past and present with nothing more. Refused to trust Paul and Esen, as if his feelings were more important than theirs.

Worse, with his own kind he'd abandoned his training as a diplomat, Evan realized, now mortified to his core. They'd come to a peaceful, positive resolution. How dare he, an outsider, question or disturb it?

"Administrator Kearn." Evan gazed at his companion, unaware his contrite expression was one his coworkers enviously described as "wistful puppy" behind his back. "What I said back there—it was completely out of line. I don't know what came over me. Your past—it's none of my business. Please accept my apology."

"None required, Polit Gooseberry. What came over you was concern for your friends. Frankly, I think better of you for it." A considering look, then a nod. "Speaking of those friends, of Paul, Esen, and Esolesy, may I offer you a word of advice—something I wished I'd been given long ago?"

Evan's seniors didn't, as a rule, ask permission before doing so. Or Great Gran. Evan stamped cold feet and snuck a longing look at the door, but he knew the only right answer. "Yes, sir." The "sir" was involuntary, and he winced inwardly. "Administrator."

A little cough. "I'd appreciate Lionel." A feigned shudder. "The title makes me feel like I've a report to write."

And, Evan thought with another tinge of remorse, his formality punished someone already punishing himself. The offer, after his blunder, was more than generous. Moved, he offered his gloved hand. "Lionel. Thank you."

Lionel took it. Held it, peering into his face. "My advice, Evan. It's easy to trust if you understand the situation. When it comes to our friends, to Paul, Esen, and Esolesy Ki?" His grip tightened. "Trust them even if you don't. Especially then."

A chill sank into Evan's bones that had nothing to do with the temperature. Was this because of his question? Had it exposed some inner flaw in his capacity for friendship? Surely, he'd proved he trusted the three—and Paul's Bess, though she was a child. They'd been through so much together—done so much to help others—he'd come to care for them, deeply.

To know them. *Unless he didn't at all.*

What a ridiculous notion.

"I will," Evan told Lionel as their hands separated, then looked up at the waiting lights, with their homely promise. The sandwich he'd shared with Esen felt a distant memory. "Will there be supper?" he asked—with some doubt. His past experience didn't suggest Paul or his friends spent much time cooking. Or any.

Lionel chuckled. "Could be something to reheat. Eggs, unless Esen's been nibbling. We'll take a look."

Evan told his stomach to be patient.

Outside the door was a mat of rough fibers. A stick with dried grass tied at one end stood against the wall, an unlikely weapon against snow. Though the path had been mostly cleared, Lionel wiped his boots on the mat and Evan imitated the action. A mechanical knob, old and with no apparent locking mechanism or alarm, allowed Lionel to open the door. He held it for Evan. "Coats on hooks, boots on the rack," he explained, coming inside and stripping off his outerwear.

Inside was warm and toasty, allaying one of Evan's remaining but unspoken fears, that the farmhouse wouldn't be heated. And that wonderful aroma—

He hopped, hurrying to put on his slippers. "Smells like supper waiting for us after all."

"Does, doesn't it." Lionel sniffed. "Odd."

Evan glanced at him. "Why?"

The other gave a small start, as if he'd forgotten Evan's presence. "No reason. Paul must have put a casserole in the oven. Most thoughtful." But Lionel didn't look appreciative; he looked disturbed.

Why the aroma of incredibly appetizing food would disturb him—whatever "a casserole" was besides delicious—Evan couldn't guess. Did Lionel think Paul at fault, leaving food to cook itself during a crisis? "Maybe someone else did it," he suggested.

Half of Lionel's face was in shadow, hiding its expression. "No one else is allowed in the farmhouse."

Digesting that in silence, Evan followed Lionel down the hall through the center of the house. The circular rugs he remembered were gone, replaced by protective sheets over the wood floor. He wanted to ask if those were for the snow, and if repairs to the farmhouse were complete, and if Paul had returned to his bedroom—none of which were important right now because Lionel was, well, he was sneaking toward the kitchen.

Sneaking being how you moved when you placed each foot with care to be silent and taking a look into open doorways before hurrying past them, and sneaking was most assuredly not how Evan Gooseberry expected to walk through the farmhouse. Not again.

But he didn't need to be told to copy Lionel's caution, and be careful where he stepped. He'd seen those who moved liked this—Paul Ragem surprisingly among them. Had taken training from his friends in embassy security to be, if not skilled, at least not the liability he'd been once.

The cooking smell was joined by others. None unpleasant. Fresh cut wood. Plant smells. There were, come to think of it, pots with plants before every window in sight, as if some of the Garden had moved indoors for the winter. They passed the open door into the former parlor, with its boxes of dried vegetation and sand meant for a non-Human sleeper, Evan noticing a stack of puffy sleeping pads on a flat platform.

Was this where he and Lionel were to sleep? With Esen?

Of course it was, he told himself, putting his luggage inside the door. Paul's room upstairs was much smaller—tiny even. Hopefully, the repairs included dusting. There'd been cobwebs last time—not that he should be thinking about where Paul slept at all—

Lionel reached the opening to the kitchen and stopped, pressed against one wall. After a quick look inside, he pulled back and signaled Evan close with a bent finger. "There's someone in the kitchen," he whispered.

Someone who knew how to cook, according to Evan's growling stomach. Was still doing so, by the chink of dish to counter, a more harmless and inviting sound hard to imagine—until he remembered Lionel's comment. *No one else allowed.* "Who could it be?" he whispered back.

Shaking his head, Lionel gestured they should retreat. He pulled out his com link after their first steps, fingering the device.

A cheerful voice rang down the hall. "Oh, do hurry up. It's getting cold."

Ending the mystery. Evan grinned with relief. "It's just Lesley," he said, no longer whispering.

Lionel caught his arm. Still a whisper, now harsh and urgent. "Who's 'Lesley'?"

"Paul's—" Evan closed his mouth. *He'd been wrong.* Lionel Kearn, in person, had interviewed everyone on Botharis in Paul Ragem's life, from his teachers to his family to—he wouldn't—couldn't—have missed the person Paul loved.

Who wasn't Lesley.

"She's someone I met this morning," Evan said instead, then hesitated. "Esen said Skalet had seen her home. Lesley lives in the village." So saying, he regained some of his confidence. While he'd no idea how many, or few, inhabited the Hamlet of Hillsview, surely Lionel wouldn't know them all. "She must have decided to help here instead."

"We've had our share of new faces tonight." The hall wasn't well lit, so Evan still couldn't read Lionel's face, but he didn't sound convinced.

It must have been his imagination because the other tucked away his com link and gestured toward the light at the end of the hall. "Come, Evan," Lionel said briskly. "Introduce me to your new friend."

23: Office Night; Lobby Night

NEITHER of us would find it easy to sleep tonight, not while the Emboldened traipsed the countryside, pursued by groggy but determined Botharans. Who wouldn't, Paul assured me, offer the three harm.

We couldn't say the same about the Emboldened, especially if they were cornered, but Mal had had that glint in his eye that meant he hadn't wanted advice on how to do his job. A job he'd been doing very well, so after asking to be notified, Paul and I went to look after everyone else.

Evan—already half-asleep—had gone with Lionel to make themselves comfortable in our farmhouse. I'd offered Esolesy's grass boxes, but Paul mentioned stuffed pads, which were this me's and new—not that I minded sharing, but they were *new*—and quilts, which we owned in extraordinary abundance and I'd gladly share, generations of Ragems having left them in our house, so he might have let them sleep on piles of those. But no.

I politely didn't keep grumbling as we headed for the Lobby to check on those still in the Library.

Suddenly, I found myself in Paul's office. It smelled like Sacrissee. With overtones of various Humans, including the one hustling me inside before we were spotted, closing the door so quickly I had to pull in my tail and yelped at him.

"Sorry. Lights, full." My friend stood looking at me. "What didn't you want to say in front of Mal and Joncee?"

"You might want to sit down," I advised.

Paul ran a hand through his hair, something I secretly believed he did to remind himself what I was. Or how relatively young, which, while true, I did not consider flattering in the least. "The condensed, quick-as-possible version, Es," he urged. "The staff are waiting. We need answers."

"I've one," I promised. "The Emboldened appear to be a kind of Sacrissee, but they aren't. Not only. They're something else, too. Modoran."

Intelligent. Predatory. Prone to flashes of temper and possessed of the tooth and claw to make interpersonal dispute bloody if not fatal. If my Lanivarian-self was canid, Modorans tended, especially to Human eyes, to inspire thoughts of the feline. Ersh preferred to compare them to wolverines. She'd been magnificent in the form.

I was more—kitten. *Highly embarrassing.* I'd have to wait another few centuries for a better translation of relative age.

Paul let out a low whistle. "They're chimeras."

The ancient Human word for an organism created by blending two—or more—distinct species. Chimeras posed a challenge for mine. No, not challenge—potential disaster. My tail slipped between my legs, ever-expressive of dread.

"I don't dare be one. I can't predict what one I'd be." I looked at Paul sorrowfully. "I can't help."

His eyes flashed. "You help in every possible way, Old Blob. Whatever the Emboldened have done to themselves—or had done to them—don't try that form. Promise me."

I nodded, my tail relaxing.

"What we need," he aimed a thumb at the now-opaqued window, "is to find them before they harm anyone else or leave this world."

"They won't go without their answer. Their new home. That's their purpose." At his look, I lowered my ears. "If I'd told you in front of Joncee and Mal, they'd have wanted to know what the Emboldened asked the Library—which is confidential—and want to know why they need a new home—which I can't very well explain without talking about boots and hair and—"

Paul raised a hand in defeat. "Fine. You were thinking the same thing I was. I should have known."

I was? As I'd no idea what my clever friend had thought, I kept my expression set to alert and eager.

"Esen-alit-Quar." His eyes narrowed. "Don't tell me you weren't planning to go outside and—" an eloquent, if perplexing finger flutter, "—become what can find our missing guests."

Oh, that. "So—I should?" I asked, that seeming the correct response. When he smiled, I knew it was.

Then I thought of the snow outside, the potential of the most appropriate form, and bounced with anticipation. "You could come too. We could romp! Or not," I added in a mature and serious tone as Paul's eyebrow rose ever-so-slightly. "I'll find them myself. Without romping."

His eyes softened and he rubbed under my ear. "Romp a little. Just promise to be careful. The Emboldened might be in trouble, but they haven't hesitated to defend themselves."

If I hadn't been so excited by the idea of a good romp—this me adding *CHASE* joy to the mix—and arguably overtired, I might have remembered that for a pure Modoran, self-defense involved poison glands at the base of retractable claws. A poison that caused such overwhelming pain in other species—or prey—the victim spasmed and tore off their own skin before death.

Before I could have my fun—*likely not the interpretation Paul wanted me to make, but I couldn't help it*—my friend and I joined those gathered in the admin hall, close to the Lobby but far enough we shouldn't be overheard by the aural equipment possessed by our current group of scholars.

The plan was to brief our suffering staff with what we *could* tell them, constrained to a cautionary what we *should*—so I let Paul do the talking.

"The trains will be running tomorrow. You're sure?" Ally asked. She, Carwyn, and the rest of our staff encircled Paul, their postures a balance between exhaustion and cautious relief. It had been a very long day for all but Zel and Travis Doctson; the pair who worked evening maintenance had just arrived.

They still looked stunned by what they'd seen as they crossed the Lobby, so I didn't tell them about the Iftsen accommodation. Or the damaged Garden gate. Or—they'd find out. Duggs had left a list.

"They should," Paul replied. "The medship will be here soon. Once they've done their examination, they told Mal the procedure will be to process our guests as quickly as possible and get them home. That means trains by afternoon. Outbound only." Relief spread at this. *Here.* Those waiting in orbit to come down or en route from Hixtar Station wouldn't be happy.

Paul made a face. "I hate to ask—"

"Too slow, Director." Henri poked him in the chest with a finger. "We've organized shifts for the overnight. Those with family needs have them covered. Tuggles' nephew's to send supper up from the pub for staff and Ally's ordered a truck of consumables for our clients from the market. Don't fuss, Es," she warned, wriggling the same finger in front of my snout.

I went cross-eyed trying to follow it. "Wasn't fussing," I muttered, somewhat daunted.

"Good. We've the latest *Commonwealth Dining Guide for the Non-Human* from the collection. You're sure the Chow will serve us all breakfast." Breakfast being the one safe-so-far meal offering of the Chow. Lionel was of the opinion Lambo fed us well at the start so we'd leave him alone the rest of the day. *Not that we did.*

Every eye locked on me.

"I said so, didn't I?" *Not that the Carasian had responded other than to sulk.*

"I'll confirm with Lambo." Paul bumped me gently with his shoulder. "Esen will stay during the food distribution to negotiate as necessary." By negotiation, he meant keep our usually mannerly scholars from abusing the staff or one another during what might become a scrum over edibles. Most would have consumed whatever e-rations they'd brought by now.

At least they'd brought them, thanks to the caution I'd put on page two of our brochure about the Library's lack of approved interstellar food service.

"Happy to help." After all, I hadn't contributed other than to clean the accommodation—twice—and was, come to think of it, hungry. *There could be chips.* I angled an ear, catching Paul's exhale as he prepared to broach the less happy topics. I bumped his shoulder in encouragement.

Carwyn raised her hand. "Director, any special instructions for the Sacrissee?"

Everyone waited with interest for the answer, meaning everyone knew who'd been moved into the basement, if not the result. A Human trait. The more unusual the subject, the faster rumor spread.

As for Carwyn recognizing the species? Maybe in other workplaces with a plenitude of alien visitors the staff became jaded, uncaring who was what, but we'd hired the intelligent and curious of a world once boringly Human. In the first month they printed up flash cards to test each other on how quickly they could identify who came through the doors. By the second, there were competitive checklists underway similar to those used by bird enthusiasts, and I'd started to fret.

When I'd fretted at Paul, he'd chuckled. We were, he'd assured me, painlessly educating a significant slice of the local population about the wider universe. Botharis would never be so alone again.

Presumably everyone's checklist now included Sacrissee.

Just not murder. The constable had been clear who needed to know at this stage, and who didn't. None of our staff, beyond Duggs and Lambo, had been told.

Secrets and truth. Trust and "appropriate timing." The tangles of needful deceit caused me sufficient grief within my own family. I found myself drowning when it came to our expanded one.

But I wasn't alone in it, and Paul Ragem never faltered. Wherever we'd lived, his steady composure and awareness of others made him a point of stability for those around him—including me. And today I'd complained about sharing his attention. *Not the best Esen.*

"Thank you, Carwyn. Both basement levels remain off limits. We put the Sacrissee there because they are afraid," Paul told our staff, his voice and expression solemn. "The constable is looking into why and will take care of them."

The truth. *The parts they needed.* A distinction I noted for future reference.

"There'll be a triple time bonus in your next pay," Paul announced, rousing a chorus of tired cheers. "What you've done—are doing—is show true Botharan kindness to strangers very far from home. We couldn't be more proud of you."

Words. It was how he said them, I decided, proud of my friend, that made backs straighten and heads come up, eyes gleam.

To finish, Paul went to each person, taking their hand and thanking them personally. Not to be outdone in courtesy, and because I, too, was grateful, I followed to do the same, trusting our staff not to squeeze what wasn't a hand like theirs.

I finished with Henri. She bent forward to whisper an encouraging, "I'll put aside some chips," laughing when I licked her chin.

I'd have liked to lick Paul's, too, but the milling group was now between us. Catching my eye, he held up his com link, mouthing "Lionel."

While not the finest example of interspecies' communication I'd experienced, I guessed this meant Lionel and Evan were waiting for him at the farmhouse, so I waved farewell to Paul.

Who touched finger to nose, then pointed at me.

That one I knew.

Be careful.

I grinned at him, tongue hanging loose.

I was always careful.

Elements

LIONEL curled his hands around a mug full of an aromatic tea he dared not drink, watching a stranger take over Paul and Esen's kitchen. That wasn't all Evan's Lesley had taken. He recognized the fabric she'd tied into a skirt as one of Esolesy's prized caftans and the shirt?

Was Paul's.

The result clung to the curves of what was one of—no, was the most stunningly unique Human female he'd seen outside of a work of art. To cook, she'd tied her wealth of white hair into a smooth knot at her neck and rolled up Paul's sleeves, but the warmth of stovetop and exertion simply added color to her high cheekbones and a glisten of sweat to flawless skin.

"Here you are." Lesley slipped a full plate in front of Evan, her every move graceful.

Every move terrifying. Lionel wanted to flinch each time she picked up a knife. Whoever this Lesley was, she wasn't Botharan. Wasn't Kraal.

Perhaps wasn't sane. She'd taken Evan's hands as if they were old friends. Greeted him the same way, without waiting for an introduction. Swept them to the long kitchen table set for over a dozen, with every type of utensil made into a glittering tower at each, and insisted on pouring them her "special" tea.

She hadn't made supper; she'd made everything possible. The stove-top was jammed with pots bubbling away, and the oven door barely closed over more. Steam billowed into the rafters and condensed on the windows, soaking the bottoms of curtains.

The counter was covered in a litter of ornately carved fruits and vegetables, their peels and seeds patterning the floor. She'd even made a decorative arch over the sink out of hardened noodles, festooned with flowers made from eggshell, and Lionel had a real fear there was nothing left in the cupboards.

"This is for you, Lionel." A bowl appeared in front of him, and this time he couldn't help but start.

Then lean forward. "This is—" he looked up at her, jaw dropping in surprise. "This is my favorite soup—how did you know?"

Lesley smiled. Just a smile, but for an instant, Lionel felt crushed beneath it, as if something immensely old and powerful had noticed his existence. A wink dispelled the feeling. "Lucky guess. Will Paul be here soon?"

Evan's fork stopped midair. "Should we wait?" he asked. He put the fork down. "We should wait." He looked toward the door as if willing Paul to appear.

The younger Human felt it too, Lionel realized. That they'd stepped not into a kitchen, but into some bizarre fantasy of every kitchen there'd ever been and never been, at the mercy of its spoon-wielding queen.

"It'll get cold if you do," she said, almost scolding.

The instant before he'd been eating like someone starved, albeit politely. Now Evan picked up the utensil and brought the bite to his mouth with visible reluctance, meeting Lionel's eyes with worry in his own.

He forced a reassuring nod. "Tell me, Lesley. How did you come to be here?"

She held a finger to her lips before turning to the stove.

Evan shook his head.

However she'd come, Paul had replied to his signal and was on his way.

The com link seemed to burn in his pocket, so close and yet—to test her vigilance, Lionel coughed once.

Lesley spun around. "Drink your tea," she insisted. "It'll help everything."

"Thank you." He lifted the mug, pretending to take a sip.

Unfortunately, Lionel hadn't used the code for "danger"—hadn't foreseen a serious threat in someone cooking, unless it was Lambo—for that reason choosing the less alarming "be prepared" they used day-to-day in the Library to warn one another of a tricky problem. All he could do was trust Paul interpreted the code as something wrong at the farmhouse.

And hope Skalet eavesdropped and came too.

24: Lobby Night

HENRI continued to smile cheerfully, not that every being in the line appreciated the baring of teeth for good cheer, but we'd been unable to stop her. "Please assure the scholar this pie is theta-class rated, Esen."

I filled my cheeks to the utmost, the scholar in question a Dwelley and of a lineage more amphibian than mammal. Puffing before dialogue was only polite—

Carwyn thrust a full tray of greens under my arm, depositing it on the countertop. "The vegetarian option."

Behind the goggles, I could see the Dwelley's huge pupils dilate, a sign of distinct excitement.

Ally leaned over me. "Carwyn, we were saving those for the Anatae!"

"No one told me—hey!"

The Dwelley, in no need of translation, snatched the contents of the entire tray against its glistening bosoms and waddled away, munching happily.

The next in line, who was the last, moved up to the Assessment Counter and regarded me dolefully, that being the default expression of an Anata with an empty revis. "I don't suppose there's anything left."

"Of course there is. Wait right here."

"Wait?" Wide supple nose flaps turned pink with conflicted

emotion. "If I wait, I'll miss the party." Clutching its revis, the scholar turned and toddled off.

"Want a pie?" Henri asked me.

I shook my head, full of chips, and looked after the scholar. "What party?"

"I'll take one, please." The Oieta's Soft Companion, Myrtle Rice, walked up with a pleased smile. "I was afraid I'd taken too long settling Fem Splashlovely. She says you've a wonderful aquatic zone."

We did. I'd tested it myself as Esippet Darnelli Swashbuckly, but endorsements were always welcome. "Thank you. If Fem Splashlovely would care to leave an official comment?" I ventured, ears up. "It'd be most helpful." We needed a new brochure anyway.

Myrtle's face fell. "I'm sorry. I don't think I should ask her—she's upset about being stranded here overnight. At least she has a place to sleep. Sorry—" she added hastily. "I appreciate the tent, but it's like a respirator sales convention in there." A wave toward the Lobby. "I don't think anyone's going to rest."

How tantalizing!

"We've some cots in one of the offices," Henri offered. "If you don't mind sharing."

The Oieta's Soft Companion smiled with relief. "Thank you. That would be perfect."

Henri lifted the counter's gate. "Carwyn?"

"This way, Fem Rice."

As the Human came through, I nipped by to go out.

"Esen!"

I gave Henri my best cheery face. "Just going to check on things," I explained.

"And I'm a tree."

Which she wasn't, so I tilted my head to await an explanation.

She leaned on the counter. "You. Party. Not the best idea when Paul's waiting for you at the farmhouse, after a day like this."

I'd argue a party would be the best and only way to end a day like this, but didn't, having Virtue and a Mission on my side. "Paul's asked me to do something for him first. This is me, doing that. After I check on things," I finished triumphantly, backing a few steps in case she tried to grab me. "Like the party."

Henri threw up her hands. "Go on, then. Don't say I didn't warn you."
I could have used a warning, but that would be later.

Free to go, I went through the now-empty hall from the Assessment
Counter to enter the Lobby itself.

Skalet hadn't been wrong about the sous tents. Impolite and risking
a planetary incident, yes, and probably had given the Sacrissees' enemies passage down to Botharis, but what I saw as I walked through the
result was, well, charming.

The tents were no longer tents, mind you. They'd started that way,
as those were the instructions given our staff, and the tents themselves
were tough and self-erecting with a tug or two.

Then our guests had taken over. I'd feared chaos.

I should have known better. Most of those using the tents for their
comfort weren't Human, few were humanoid, and they weren't outside
anyway. Our guests were also, as random groups of unrelated beings
went, highly intelligent and resourceful folks who knew what worked
for them.

Some reclined atop the tents, collapsing them into what looked to be
comfortable beds. Though with the shelled, it was more a case of something to stop them rolling whilst asleep.

Others had shredded the supposedly uncuttable Kraal material, glu-
ing the result with mucus against the walls.

Maintenance wouldn't be happy about that.

An undetermined number had worked together to fill the center of
the Lobby with a massive stack of tents curled into tunnels or folded
into triangles. By the sounds coming out of the maze, there was indeed
a vigorous party underway somewhere inside. Every so often a limb or
tentacle or pseudopod would appear, wave gaily, then vanish.

Hopefully, no one was being consumed as part of the joy. We'd need
to count them again tomorrow and be ready with the appropriate con-
dolences.

I sniffed, detecting a smoky smell that might be cooking or some
other activity. Skalet had said the tents came with internal fire suppres-
sants. *A claim that might be tested.*

I spotted more tents along the upper walkway. What had been tents. They'd been turned inside out, whatever tech and conveniences the Kraal had installed now dangling outside. Which made excellent perches for several others and in fact there was a—

I'd a Mission. I paused to sigh wistfully. The party would be over before I returned and Humans were diligent creatures. Much as I longed to check out each and every not-a-tent in the Lobby for myself, the instant everyone left, staff would dismantle this glorious mayhem.

Maybe they'd take a day off first to let me explore.

Time for me to get to work.

Makings

OOLA crouches in the last safe patch of darkness, stares with her glowing yellow eyes at the strangest *OUT* imaginable. At a city built of ranks of starships, aliens and groundcars crawling like insects between them, nothing normal, nothing familiar. Nothing of the *IN.*

Neither is she.

The once-fearful thought brings her strength. A mammoth machine rolls slowly by, a ship in its grasp, and she dares bolt into its shadow. Dares move with it.

The *howl,* her hope, comes from ahead, within this *OUT.*

Oola crouches behind a metal box stinking of alien, the instinct to hide all that makes sense in a world gone mad.

She's sought sanctuary. Her own kind. Fled here down Rattisila's streets. Streets that should have been safe; pursued down them; fought for her life in them—

She trusted the *howls* so like her own led to a safe *IN.* The proper *IN.* A place for her.

Instead, she finds this. This isn't any of those things.

This is a starship, doors open to the night and unguarded, without the lights marking the ramps of every other ship.

This is a trap.

Every so often, a *HOWL* comes from the dark mouth of the ship. Oola is young and untaught—should be *IN* with her kin-group and safe still and nowhere near this place—but she knows the sound doesn't come from someone like her.

Knows it isn't real.

She would run, but others lurk nearby, in hiding but not so well as she, not so well at all. They wait for her to bolt and reveal herself.

Let them. Oola feels her new claws emerge.

They are only Human.

25: Field Midnight

WORKING together at the All Species' Library of Linguistics and Culture must have improved Paul's appreciation for my abilities and good sense immensely. Or he'd seen no other option.

Whichever the case, having been asked, and so very nicely, by my dear and first friend to cycle as required—with romp as necessary—I left the Library feeling wonderfully liberated. Not a feeling to take seriously, I knew.

But while it lasted, I planned to enjoy it.

Any scent trail to follow would start where the invaders' tunnel ended. There was the not-so-minor problem of Teri Terworth, guarding the hole for no good reason I could see except to make my job harder.

Had I planned to rely on scent, that is.

There were other forms.

Esen-alit-Quar the Lanivarian loped into a snow-dusted row of coniferous shrubs, put her clothing in a neat pile, com link on top, and cycled. Two shrubs disappeared—

And a very different me emerged.

Translucent was I, and gleaming, with firm boneless limbs on either side of an equally firm body. There were those who referred to this fine and noble form as a Karras Slug.

No slug was I. The resemblance was less valid than between a

Human and a plant with two stems. This me paused for several respiratory exchanges to be insulted.

But a task had I, and further indignation must wait.

This me moved over the hard wet, expending precious bodily fluids to pass without growing stuck and freezing in place. Not that this me would suffer, but freezing would induce an untimely torpor.

No face had I, unlike those who exposed their orifices and flapped loose skin. This me expressed myself with surface chromophores and able-to-glow cartilage beneath a clear thickened integument. The images I could portray were succinct yet more brilliantly eloquent than any mere tremors through air. This me paused for several respiratory exchanges to be smug.

But a task had I, and the ideal me to complete it.

Senses had I, refined and potent. Pits along my sides and limbs to detect electromagnetism. The fluids coursing over my body dissolved tastes. Disks at my dorsal and ventral ends responded with exquisite sensitivity to infrared, the better to find what was warm inside. For this me was a predator, when the opportunity presented itself.

As tonight.

Not that I was to engulf and digest the Sacrissee, I reminded this me, somewhat alarmed by the strength of its drive to do just that and newly reminded of Ersh's favorite lesson: biology was the trap in any form.

Plus Paul would not be happy with me.

The hunt alone would have to do. This me paused for several respiratory exchanges to, well, pout.

This me resumed moving over the hard wet, each condense and expand of my body sliding me forward with a silent quickness prey wouldn't expect. Then there was this me's ability to launch from ambush. This me paused for several respiratory exchanges to anticipate.

But a task I had, and anticipation wasn't success.

This me resumed, crossing the taste of Human, Human with canid helper, Humans without. I saw their warm shapes in the distance, poking streams of high frequency radiation into what, to them, was dark. They wouldn't see me. Air had stopped moving, so this me cared nothing for the orifices of the canid.

At last I crossed the taste of Elk—the Botharan version—and curved back. This me spent several respiratory exchanges savoring the taste— *Rhonda might not miss one*—then discovered the other taste trying to hide in the midst.

This me wasn't fooled. This me grew excited, and I had to tamp down the urge to glow and summon nonexistent hunting partners. This me paused for several respiratory exchanges to be lonely.

You couldn't lose patience with a Karras, the part of me about to remembered. *They needed to emote or wouldn't move at all.*

This me resumed the hunt.

Elements

HE'D had nightmares like this, where people he knew and trusted turned out to be hollow, each beloved face a mirage swept away by some terrible truth.

This wasn't a dream, Evan Gooseberry told himself, much as he'd prefer it to be. Lesley wasn't Lesley.

Some of her was. The beauty, the movement, the glimpses of innocent joy. Those he held onto when the rest came out. The near-frenetic movements, the compulsive cooking, the way he'd catch her looking at him and at Lionel. Not with curiosity or interest.

More as if she enjoyed an exhibit, on display just for her. Her tiny, possessive smile after such looks drew warnings from every part of him and he was grateful beyond words for Lionel Kearn.

Who sat across the table from him, giving him encouraging nods between Lesley's bursts of discomfiting hospitality, at every moment exuding calm and confidence. A seasoned First Contact Specialist, able to handle anything or any who, and Evan copied the other's posture, tried for what calm he could, and did as Lionel, refusing to drink her tea.

Which wasn't as hard as he'd thought, given the practice he'd had refusing Uncle Stan's cider, also referred to as "special" in that knows-what's-best voice. Great Gran had warned him early on to avoid the stuff, though she drank it in quantity, growing quite cheerful after a few cups.

Thinking of his silly but always caring family helped Evan lower his shoulders, presently trying to climb to his ears, and take a deeper breath.

"Look at you," Lesley said fondly, and for a horrified instant Evan thought she'd pinch his cheek like his uncle. Feeling her pat the top of his head wasn't much better. All at once she leaned forward, twisting to study his face. Their breath mingled. Evan held his.

"I must do a bust. Oh, did you hear me?" She straightened. "I rhymed!" Lesley laughed.

To his astonishment, hers was the sweetest, most contagious laugh Evan had ever heard. He smiled before he knew he would, watching Lionel do the same. When the laugh continued, both chuckled out loud.

"What'd I miss?" Paul Ragem asked, coming into his kitchen. Gray eyes swept the room, touched Evan and Lionel, then came to rest on Lesley. "Why, hello."

Lionel coughed. "This is—" Her quick frown silenced him.

The frown vanished behind a smile that would melt candles. "Paul. Oh, to finally meet you in the flesh." She came around the table to offer her hand, only to envelop Paul in her arms, planting a kiss on his cheek. Releasing him, she blushed, bringing her hands together at her waist. "Excuse me. It's just—Esen's shared so much about you. I feel—I'm Lesley." Her head tilted. "Would you like supper? I've made tea."

Paul took it all in stride. "Yes, thank you. Lesley." He said her name slowly, as if testing it, then smiled. "It—everything smells delicious. But first—" He gave an apologetic shrug. "I'm afraid Esen forgot to tell me to expect you."

"Ah. I understand. She's waiting for the appropriate time. I could have told her there's no such thing, only the time you have. As for me?" Lesley collected a long wooden spoon and waved it like a wand. "I've time again, thanks to our Esen. She found me—but I'll leave all that to her." She sighed happily. "It's good to be home again, Paul. To be together."

Evan's misgivings came flooding back. That this Lesley was some kind of predator. That she meant to do Paul harm in some way. He half rose from his stool to do—

Having no idea what, he sank back down. Lionel nodded in grave approval.

All the while, Paul's expression had taken on a disconcerting focus, as if he comprehended more than anyone else. "You're going to live here?" Almost nonchalant. "Esen said so?"

Lesley laughed. "I have been living here. For—for—" Her face clouded, then cleared. "I've been in the greenhouse. This is much nicer. I was right to come."

Paul's lips mouthed the word "greenhouse" silently, then looked to Lionel.

Who appeared as confused as Evan and shook his head.

"Now, sit and I'll bring your supper." She paused, looking beyond Paul to the opening into the hallway, then at the door leading outside. "I thought the rest would be coming—no, how foolish of me." Her eyes refocused on him. "They're on Picco's Moon."

Paul Ragem froze, blood draining from his face, eyes round.
SMASH!

A start. A shudder. Then, like a curtain coming down, Paul's face became normal—but it wasn't normal, Evan realized, this was a mask, even his grimace at Lionel.

Who held up the broken handle of his mug. "Sorry about that."

"Don't bother cleaning up," Lesley said cheerfully. "Esen will look after it."

And Evan Gooseberry knew he'd witnessed a rescue, even if he'd no idea from what.

After putting a plate of food in front of Paul, Lesley walked to the far end of the long table and sat. She didn't speak or look at any of them as she unbound her hair, pulling it forward to veil her face. Her final movement before becoming utterly still was to rest her folded hands on the wooden top and steeple her fingers, head bent as if staring down at their tips.

As if surprised to have hands at all.

After watching her for a few moments, Paul methodically turned off the stovetop and oven, leaving the pots as they were. With a nod, he left

Lionel with Lesley. With another, he collected Evan and together, they left the kitchen.

Evan waited until Paul turned on the light and stepped into Esen's bedroom with him before hurriedly closing the door. "What's going on? Who is she? You know, don't you."

Paul let out a long breath. The look on his face when he looked up jolted Evan's heart. The mask was gone, revealing a dark, terrible dread. "Someone from Esen's past," he said heavily. "Someone I thought—we'd thought—had died."

"Like you." Evan's hand shot up to cover his mouth, but the words were out.

"It seems so," the other agreed.

"Is Lesley—is she dangerous? When I first met her—" At Paul's sharp look, Evan winced. "We met this morning in the greenhouse." He felt his face grow hot. "It was all rather surreal, looking back. She was—naked. And beautiful. She knew my name—knew yours—and I thought—I assumed she was the love you told me about, the one you'd left here. That Lesley was—" He made himself say it. "—waiting for you."

"In the greenhouse." For a wonder, this lightened Paul's expression. "In winter." His lips quirked to the side. "Evan."

"It seemed plausible then," he defended. *If not now.* "I came back to bring her clothes—" Evan frowned, struggled to remember. "It was only this afternoon—I hit my head on a tree," he admitted. *That hadn't been all, had it?* "There was a ShimShree. I mean, I followed its track in the snow. That was—that was before Esen found me. I think," he qualified, feeling a few socks in his brain. "I'm sure Esen told me Skalet took Lesley home—to the village. I don't know why she'd come here instead. Or be naked." He rubbed his eyes and yawned. "I'm sorry. I'm not making much sense."

"Skalet's in this?" Paul shook his head. "You've made more sense than you know," he said, abruptly grim. "Let's get you some quilts—" He opened a closet stuffed from bottom to top with colorful blankets and began pulling them out with more force than necessary, spilling them on the floor.

Which wasn't like Paul, and Evan blurted, "Don't be angry with Esen." At the warning frown, he raised his hands but didn't, wouldn't, stop. "Please don't be. She was only helping Lesley—who needs help. I'm no medtech or psych, Paul, but Lesley's personality, what she says, how she acts? I think she's broken."

Paul grew very still, the frown turning into a look of intense concentration.

Wisely, Evan let him be. He picked up quilts, then stood with his arms full, too exhausted to know what to do with them.

"The pads are new," Paul roused to tell him, indicating the puffy stack. "We don't have extra pillows. Esolesy puts them under the grass."

Evan stifled another yawn. "I could sleep on the bare floor. This will be wonderful. Shall I make a bed for Lionel too?"

"Please. I'll send him right in. Good night, Evan." A wry grin. "Quite the start to your vacation."

"It's been adventurous," Evan said. He grew serious. "Esen?"

Paul ran a hand through his hair, leaving it sticking up. Evan resisted the impulse to smooth it.

"Esen," his friend echoed, but with reassuring exasperation. "There's nothing she won't try to fix. I just wish—" His voice trailed away as he looked at Evan.

"Wish she'd tell you first?" he suggested.

Paul pretended to shudder. "Not always, believe me. Now," briskly. "Get some sleep, my friend. With any luck, tomorrow we'll start resolving problems. Who knows?" With a mischievous grin. "Might get skates on you yet."

"'Skates'?" *Was he to worry?*

The other laughed and drew him into a quick warm embrace. "I'm never angry with Esen," he whispered while they were close. "Don't tell her I said so."

Then Paul was gone, leaving on a small glow light near the door. Evan stood a moment, relishing the trust as much as the display of affection.

There were other flat raised platforms, but Evan pulled two of the pads to the floor, laying quilts on each. He chose the bed farthest from the door so Lionel didn't have to walk over him, then dropped on top of it, unable to make the effort to remove his slippers, let alone any clothes.

Being flat was nice. Feeling the room spin gently around was nice. Evan closed his eyes.

Opened them.

How could he sleep with Lesley in the house?

By remembering Paul was here, too, and Lionel. Esen would be coming home any moment. He wasn't alone.

Though he really should call Great Gran—

And with that, the young diplomat closed his eyes again, oblivion waiting.

26: Forest Midnight; Cave Midnight

THERE were Humans *with* the Sacrissee.

They weren't the Humans chasing the Sacrissee. These Humans led them and possibly were complicit in the theft of Rhonda's herd, if so, implying collusion and pre-planning. This me paused for several respiratory cycles to be astonished.

Then resumed the hunt, there being an enlarged trail of tastes to follow.

This me veered after Elk for some time before caring Human and Sacrissee were no longer part of the trail. This me paused for several respiratory cycles to be embarrassed.

I reversed to slide back along my own trail, saving bodily fluids, then crossed the taste of Humans and Sacrissee. This me altered direction to pursue.

The fields around the Library and the Hamlet of Hillsview were behind me. Another sort of plant culture appeared on every side. The tall mixed forest coating the hills wasn't complete wilderness, its fringes harvested for wood and sources of syrup, mushrooms, and other things found only where trees grew, but the result was dense enough to encourage all manner of tasty warm creatures.

I'd had chips. I wasn't hungry. WASN'T!

This me was and paused for several respiratory exchanges to sulk.

A task had I. This me resumed movement. I lifted my limbs to sense the quickest path through the plants. Bending around those too large to slide over was tiring and slowed my progress; slowing expended more fluids to keep me from sticking and freezing, but I was a Karras on the hunt! This me paused for several respiratory exchanges to be relentless.

Though slowed, those I followed stood high, not long—*a precarious body choice*—and thus were slowed themselves and constrained to larger openings in the forest. After the second hill and valley, this me could "see" them at last. Six warm, delicious shapes.

Five.

This me suspected snow on my dorsal disk and spun around to aim my other set of receptors at them.

Five shapes. This me paused—

Three.

None.

PREY MUST NOT ESCAPE!

This me did not pause for any respiratory exchanges. This me moved with great haste—after spinning around to my former orientation—though had this me not been in a desperate-for-a-Karras charge up a treed hill, the not-Karras me might have reasoned what had happened, but no.

Full-on instinct, that bane of ephemeral life, took hold.

This me barely managed to grip and stop before splattering, warned by limb sensors of something solid ahead. Having stopped, rational thought resumed. The solid was an abrupt rise of rock, its surface coated in runnels of ice. A cliff. This me paused for several respiratory exchanges to be grateful not to be splattered.

This me could taste the prey—*those I wanted to find*. I slid around the clearing, hoping to discern directionality.

While my form kept busy, the rest of me solved the mystery. Despite the solid appearance of the rock face, there must be a cave with an entrance nearby.

Suggesting what sort of Humans I was tasting. Kraal, according to Skalet, maintained extensive maps of the local cave systems, better ones than the Botharans. Their preferred hiding place for weapons; such investment in future invasions had become a habit.

Were they hiding the Sacrissee? Why?

One way to find out.

This me moved close to the cliff, then flexed in the middle to raise my first four limbs. Finding a break in the ice curtain, I shunted more fluid onto the surface of my dorsal disk for protection and to improve the contact, then touched the rock with it.

This me emitted a healthy pulse of electromagnetism. The pits on my limbs collected the echoes; my nervous system interpreted them. Solid rock.

This me shifted over to repeat the actions. Solid rock.

It took three more shifts before the echoes gave back something more interesting: a large hollow space.

This me wanted to pause for several respiratory exchanges to rejoice, but the rest of me knew, if there were Kraal, I'd just set off their alarms and possibly given them a headache. I turned about to glide quickly into the cover of nearby trees.

This me, and the rest of me, paused for several respiratory exchanges to regret. I'd such a wonderful plan for my hoped-for, encouraged-by-Paul, romp. I'd pounce at least once, a Karras able to grab its ventral disk, swell internally, then release to fling itself through the air in a limb-waving wriggling uncontrolled flight of, my record to date, over thirty-six body lengths. It would have been amazing.

And not going to happen tonight.

Time for another me.

My choices weren't as limited as they might seem. Being small, nimble, with excellent night sight were traits of several sentient species, especially if I included those gone extinct. I had, however, learned some valuable lessons while living with Paul.

Don't be something afraid of caves.

Even more importantly—

Don't be something easily distracted.

Then there was the part about a form with some cleverness, able to communicate, and ideally one that wouldn't elicit an instant and painful defensive reaction in those I met.

Leaving me with Bess.

I emerged from the forest and searched for the entrance to the cave as a small, slight, Human child apparently ten years of age. A naked shivery child, but I expected to find more Humans before freezing any of me.

More exactly, have them find me, I thought cheerfully a moment later, when a portion of the cliff swung open like a door.

Elements

PICCO'S Moon.

He'd been there, on Ersh's mountain. Been witness to the violent exchange of flesh as Esen and Skalet shared memories. Held the Human Skalet as she'd bled—

Now Lionel sat a table's length away from a being who named the place not as the home of the crystalline Tumblers or their gemmed excretions—and those who gladly collected them—but as her own.

As her kind's.

Lesley was a Web-being.

How was this possible?

If it was, he reasoned coolly, forcing panic down, Lesley would be her name in Human form. Esen being the child Bess, that made Lesley much, much older.

Lesley lifted her head. She looked around the room, a hand holding back the curtain of her hair. Spotting him, she hesitated with a puzzled expression, then gave a brilliant smile. "Lionel Kearn. You're here."

From a being with perfect memory, hesitation was troubling. "I'm here," Lionel confirmed. "Paul will be right back. Evan's gone to bed."

"Evan, Evan. Evan the sweet." Lesley giggled and tipped her head. "Evan with a secret. Want to know what it is, Lionel?"

"I don't—"

"Evan isn't Human."

Lionel blinked. "I beg your pardon?"

"He wore Esen's hat and gloves. Gave them to me and—well." An eloquent tongue tasted her full upper lip. "Evan's mostly Human, if it makes you happier. You don't look happy anymore, Lionel. Why is that?"

He needed Paul here. Esen. Skalet. Anyone else to deflect the now-rapt attention of this alarming creature. Lacking those, Lionel forced a smile. "I'd love more tea."

"I can do that for you, Lionel." She rose like a dancer, was dancing, he realized, as she went to the stovetop. "It's cold," she said, displeased. "Why is it cold?"

"My apologies, Lesley." Paul entered the kitchen, filling it with his presence, and Lionel shuddered with relief. "I thought you were finished. It's getting late."

"Lionel wants more tea." She lifted the kettle. Swung it aimlessly. Her eyes fastened on Paul. "It's too late for tea?"

"It is." Paul went to her and gently took the kettle, putting it aside. "But I'd like to talk with you for a moment, Lesley, if you don't mind."

Her fingers walked along his chest, paused, then curled. "I don't mind." She sat, Paul taking the seat at the head of the table, next to her.

Lionel moved to sit across from Lesley, defying the meaningful glance Paul gave him. He'd information the other needed, now. Proof what she was. "Lesley, tell Paul how you tasted Evan's hat," he prompted.

"And his gloves. Don't forget those, Lionel," she said brightly. "That's how I know Evan isn't fully Human. Isn't that a delicious secret?"

"What it is," Paul said, almost a scold, "is Evan's business and none of ours."

Lesley's eyes filled with tears. "It was just some fun. I meant no harm." The tears spilled down her cheeks and her lip trembled. "Will he forgive me, Paul?" She started to rise. "Where is Evan? I must beg him to forgive me—"

Paul caught her hand. She drifted down again, her eyes locked on his, pleading, and he released his grip. Something changed in his face then, a new understanding, and his voice became inexpressibly gentle. "You've done nothing wrong, Lesley. Lionel and I understand how you know about Evan, but he won't. We mustn't share what you've learned about him with anyone outside the Web. Do you understand why?"

Her tears vanished. "Because Evan doesn't know what we are. We're a secret from him. The greatest secret." Lesley clapped her hands. "You're very clever, Paul."

"If I were," he said ruefully, "I'd have listened when Esen told me she'd something important to tell me, about what she brought from Dokeci-Na. That was you, wasn't it." With the start of an amazed smile. "Riosolesy-ki. And here you're Lesley, this lovely Human."

She blushed as beautifully as she did everything else.

Paul took a deep breath. "But Esen knew you—knows you best—as Lesy."

"See? You are clever," the ancient Web-being told him. "How interesting, hearing my name from one of you."

"Enjoying yourself, Lesy?"

At Skalet's voice—at its tone, Lionel thought, harsh enough to make him stiffen—Lesley cringed, her hand gripping Paul's wrist.

No, it wasn't that—

"What have you done?" Lionel heard himself say, when he could see it, and knew she'd not thank him for his concern.

—like him, Lesley reacted to the ruin of Skalet's face.

"What was needful. What have you?" With a scathing look to Lesley.

"Made us a most enjoyable supper," Paul informed her, appearing unaffected. Lesley responded by shifting closer; she didn't let go of his wrist.

Seen together, both as Human females, the resemblance between the two was striking. Lesley older, face and body almost untouched by age or trauma; Skalet much younger, perhaps half Lesley's relative age or less, her face weathered skin over elegant bone, that skin further marked by the hideous cut; her body the same, scarred skin over bone and corded muscle.

No, Lionel decided. There was no real resemblance. Skalet had lived her long years. Fought for them. Achieved with them.

Skalet turned deliberately to meet his stare, and Lionel knew he'd looked too long and deeply. This once, he refused to hide his admiration. Let her see his pride.

This once, she gave a tiny nod. *Acceptance.* Then dismissed him, turning to Paul. "Where's the Youngest?"

"Esen's outside." He glanced at the chrono on the wall, eyebrows drawing together. "I did—" he added thoughtfully, "—tell her she could romp."

Skalet looked disgusted. Lesley smiled and patted Paul's arm. "Esen loves to romp. I do too. Esen and I—Esen and you—" She stopped smiling and stared up at Skalet. "Esen shared for us. How could she do that?"

"Because she's the Senior Assimilator of our Web."

Lesley burst out laughing. "Of course she isn't. Ersh is."

For the first time, Lionel saw Skalet at a loss. She gestured—a strangely helpless, desperate gesture—to Paul.

Who'd already understood this about Lesley. Who'd understood the instant she'd mentioned gathering on Picco's Moon that whatever Esen had brought home with her wasn't whole or complete. That, whether out of mercy or her own unimaginable grief, Esen hadn't shared with her web-kin the loss of Ersh and her Web, and now certainly wasn't the time to reveal it.

Lionel felt sweat break out on his forehead.

"Esen's a blob of many talents," Paul Ragem said easily, though Lesley's hand remained on his wrist and his was the nearest living mass to a Web-being who could lose form-integrity and cycle without warning. Who would, how could she not, if she learned the whole terrible truth. "Another time I'll tell you about her cooking."

"Esen cook?" Lesley chuckled. "I don't believe it. She uses the replicator unless one of us is home."

"She's learning. There've been some successes. Some—" He held his nose and Lesley looked delighted.

It had to be Esen, Lionel realized. Living with Esen. Paul understood these incredible beings in a way no one else could. Cared about them.

Had made one of them care for him.

And wasn't that the point? Paul Ragem would be remembered—be loved—by the dear little Blob. What he'd been teaching Esen about Humans, about friendship and living with other species, was already part of her and part of her Web.

That love kept Paul safe now, because she'd shared it with Lesy.

"Skalet? You came with news?" Paul leaned forward. "Skalet."

She started, dragging her eyes from Lesley. "Yes." Her voice steadied. "Yes, I do. Two ships have entered the system, both out of Sacriss VII— Not now, Lesy!"

Lesley had stood, whipping off Paul's shirt. She looked disappointed. "But I love that form."

Skalet's frustrated grunt made all of it inexplicably normal. *How far they'd come*, Lionel thought. "Clothe yourself and let me finish." She waited until Lesley pulled the shirt over her shoulders and sat before continuing. "One ship's Kraal, moving without stealth. The *Tesseer Ra*. They state they have Sacrissee on board—officials of importance."

"You believe them?"

"I've confirmed their last port of call. They have not been forthcoming about why a diplomatic mission would land here as opposed to the capital's shipcity."

"And the other's our medship?"

"About that." Her fingertip touched the table. Made a circle. Stabbed the heart of it. "There is no inbound Commonwealth vessel," Skalet said at last. "The constable has been fooled into communicating with the *Trium Pa*, for reasons my affiliates on board are working to discover."

Confirming she'd been betrayed—meaning there was a small war going on over their heads.

"How long—"

Paul silenced Lionel's question with a look. "They implied a contagion. Demanded information and ordered the trains stopped. Hampered search efforts."

"Ploys to control the situation. I've yet to learn Captain Haben-ru's intent."

"Do so. I expect you to handle this."

Skalet bowed her head to Paul, eyes bright as she straightened. "My response is ongoing. In the meantime, maintaining the ruse is vital. Do not trust com links."

"We haven't been, not since the basement. Leave the rest with me." Grim and definite. "And this other ship?"

Not another Kraal, Lionel pleaded to himself. They'd more than enough.

"It's come from Sacriss VII with the *Tesseer Ra*. An unnamed private vessel registered to Molancor Genomics, a Commonwealth medtech company." Her chin rose. "You aren't surprised."

Paul nodded. "Esen's learned the Emboldened are chimeras, a blend of Sacrissee and Modoran. That expertise had to come from somewhere."

Lesley, subdued till now, looked up. "I won't be that," she stated firmly, a handful of hair ready.

"Of course not." Skalet scowled. "I've no further information on them yet. Molancor has significant data protection."

"Ask Evan."

Her scowl became chilling. "He's a diplomat, Lesy, not a comptech."

"Evan's a chimera too." Lesley slid a look at Paul. "You said I could tell those of my Web."

"I did," with a smile. She wiggled her shoulders as if pleased.

Skalet looked repulsed. "A remote connection at best."

"We'll see." Paul rose to his feet, Lionel doing the same. "I'll find Mal immediately. As for Evan? I'll let him sleep. If we've time for that?"

"If not, I'll inform you both. By tomorrow, even the Botharans will know what's in their system." A slow, wicked smile stretched her lips. "While you'll be busy entertaining."

"'Entertaining?'" Lionel repeated.

"The representative from Grandine. Who must be truly dedicated, to come despite knowing you've had three trains-worth of non-Humans crowded in the Lobby since yesterday. Unless that's why. A moment when the Library can't possibly show to advantage. I expect you'll handle it." Giving Paul back his words. "Unless—" An eyebrow rose. "Would you like the representative intercepted? It can be arranged."

"You're enjoying this," Paul accused mildly.

Skalet held up her finger and thumb, a hairbreadth apart.

"Tomorrow for that, too," he declared. "Lesley, please make yourself comfortable in my room until we make other arrangements. Skalet will show you the way. I'm sure you know it," with a raised brow of his own.

"Of course."

"Good night, then." But as Lesley rose to leave, Paul reached for her hands and bowed over them like someone from a story, then looked into her face with a gentle smile. "Family is important. I'm glad you're here, Lesley."

She regarded him for a long moment then smiled in return. "As am I. I see why Esen loves you, Paul Ragem. This night, I do think I'll dream about—"

Skalet whimpered. The involuntary sound held such pain Lionel flinched and would have reached for her without thought of the consequence.

A whispered, "Lionel, no," saved him.

Then Paul, without leaving Lesley, shifted his full attention to Skalet who, after that one outcry, stood shivering, her eyes fixed on what only she could see. "Skalet. S'kal-ru!" he called, the name ringing, as if summoning her from a distance. "'May our enemies hear our footsteps and find no peaceful rest.'"

She gasped and blinked, then glared at him. "You quote N'kar-ro at me?" With fury.

"Did I get it right?" he asked.

"You did not. 'May my enemies hear my—'" Skalet stopped. "Foolish Human. You'll overstep one day."

Paul grinned. "And you'll be there to tell me."

Skalet growled in her throat, then snapped, "Come, Lesley."

Once the pair were climbing the new staircase in the pantry, Lionel put a hand on the table to support himself, weak at the knees. "What was that about?"

"Best guess?" Paul responded slowly. "Esen's told me Web-beings sleep as their form requires, but don't dream. I've the sense she doesn't understand—or trust—the concept."

"But Lesley said—" Lionel paused and looked toward the pantry. "She's different, isn't she."

"I think so. And I think—I think it's time you went to bed, too, my friend. We'll need you sharp tomorrow, with those documents."

Not what he'd started to say, but Lionel didn't press; just as he'd watched Skalet leave, unable to offer help. He shook his head in mock despair. "With regrets, Director Ragem, I believe I feel ill. Yes. Ill. I'll probably need to stay in bed tomorrow. Maybe the rest of the week. Better yet, I'll take a vacation, like our Evan."

"And miss all the fun?" Paul said, with a smile that held no doubt of him. "Sleep. I'm going to meet Mal at the Chow, then come back." A nod to the cluttered kitchen.

"Let me help—"

Paul shrugged. "I won't sleep till she's home."

Lionel's gaze shifted to the curtained window. Beyond that was the dark and the cold and strangers who'd killed— "Esen's not romping, is she."

Paul took his shoulder and gave him a gentle but firm push toward the hall. "Good night, Lionel."

27: Cave Night

THERE were two female Kraal and one male. They dressed as Botharan farmworkers—not a serious attempt at disguise since they'd belts and weapons over top and, by how they moved, armor beneath. I did think the local winter face masks a clever cover for their affiliation tattoos. Outside. Inside the cave, sitting around the heatbox, sweat was beading along their eyebrows and I waited for the first to rip off the things.

The cave seemed natural, with an uneven floor and sloped ceiling. The outer wall was streaked with damp, as if the icy fingers outside tried to find a way in, but the door through which I'd entered was all but imperceptible once closed. *Not natural.* A modern grav sled sat in a puddle of snow melt, whatever cargo it carried still wrapped against the elements.

Dusty unmarked crates were piled against a wall, most likely packed with what the constable should find and render harmless. A Kraal weapons cache of unknown age? By now, the components could be unstable. As soon as I was done with the living occupants of the cave, I'd make sure Mal knew where to find it and was forewarned to take precautions.

I named the older Kraal female Shirt, as she'd given me one of hers to wear. The younger was Socks, for I'd hers, and the male was Vest for the same reason. They'd accepted—for now—my woeful tale of falling through ice then getting lost and had ignored me after supplying the clothes.

Too busy staring at their companions.

The Emboldened Sacrissee had removed their cloaks. They stayed together close to the grav sled, away from the Kraal but in range of the heatbox. Acklan Seh kept filling and emptying his nasal sac, producing an unsettling rumble. Saxel Sah was in the center, as the leader should be. Maston Sah had an open wound on one arm, and kept her hand clenched around it.

As for staring, their huge yellow eyes did it much more effectively.

They, too, ignored me. *The challenge of youth.* Though in this instance, the benefit. I kept myself as small as possible, content to have my companions explain what was going on. Which they would. Eventually. Once they started talking.

Ephemerals always did.

I busied myself guessing. Skalet, when it came to the deplorable capabilities of her favored culture, was never wrong. She'd said Kraal had made the attempt to either kidnap or kill the Emboldened in the Library, so the corpse puddles? Kraal they'd been.

These Kraal, however, had helped the Emboldened evade the constable's search teams.

Which didn't preclude kidnapping or killing, as moving a target to a secure location first was an acceptable tactic, if less potent a statement, but it did appear the Emboldened hadn't wanted to be found by more reasonable Humans. Why?

I hated thinking like her. But I must. I couldn't think like the other species in the cave. The *yet* was like a sly little voice from behind my shoulder, like a demon from one of Lesy's fun scary stories.

I sighed inwardly. Poor Lesy, stuck in the greenhouse, full of Skalet and now me. She needed somewhere nice to live; pleasant, happy things to occupy her. While I waited for revelations, I pondered how to sneak a hidden set of rooms within our planned—

"We followed the captain's orders," Shirt said, apparently tired of staring. "It's all there. Check for yourselves."

The three Emboldened sprang into motion, patting the wet cover with "huffft, hufffts" of anticipation before the male undid its fastenings. The two females rolled the cover up and put it aside, to reveal six shiny canisters, each about the size of this me, identical down to the blinking displays on their sides.

Commercial cryounits. They'd each an interstellar transit label. From here, I could read the name *"Stellar Trumpet"* and make out something about mushrooms. Why Human smugglers so often defaulted to "mushrooms" was beyond me. It wasn't as if fungi were hard to grow. *Or even, to this me, that appetizing.*

The Emboldened studied the displays.

"What's in them?" Vest whispered to Socks.

Not mushrooms. A guess I kept to myself.

"Not our business," Shirt snapped.

Hearing this, Saxel swiveled her head around. "But it is. This is our future," she informed the Kraal proudly. "The future of this beautiful world. Our sanctuary."

"Once you take it for us," Saxton added, nasal bulb adding that menacing *howl.* "That is the arrangement."

It was? What about their request to the Library? As for claiming sanctuary—which I took very personally—to borrow Lionel's bedroom was one thing. To take an entire planet, let alone ours, when they'd asked us to find them a welcoming new home?

Greedy, that's what they were. And rude. Excessive—

"The captain leads our force down tomorrow, Hom," Shirt told him.

A Kraal invasion force?

The voice in my head was getting annoyingly shrill. *It had good reason.* Hard to credit Skalet hadn't seen this coming, but she had been distracted lately. Unless she did know but elected to wait for more *appropriate timing.* Which I'd accepted from Ersh—and maybe did a bit myself—but was not acceptable from our resident Kraal warning system. *There'd be words.*

"Good." Maston prowled around the canisters, tail lashing with emotion. "The others would cull our kind. Left us sterile, to favor this lineage instead." Her nasal bulb filled, producing that low *howl.* "No longer. These shall be our legacy, not theirs. Superior. We will create the greatest *IN* of all!"

"Within the great Kraal Confederacy," Saxel added quickly, as if finally realizing they weren't the only beings involved. "Under the direct protection of your captain and noble House."

A shame she knew better than name it.

"That's the arrangement," Shirt acknowledged, but being Human helped me catch the scorn in her eyes before she ducked her head. Whatever these Kraal were doing, it wasn't preparing Botharis as a new home for the Emboldened and their barrels of unborn. I felt a rush of pity, but my being Human wouldn't help or stop anyone; until I'd opportunity and living mass, I couldn't be anything else—*other than a Quebit and thus even less use.*

Saxel strode forward with a fierce, demanding *HOWL*, suggesting I wasn't the only one to read Shirt's expression. The three Kraal jumped up and gave way, accepting her display of authority. I crouched where I was, projecting *nothing to see here.*

To my surprise, Saxel's tail tip brushed my cheek as she passed me. *Not ignored, then.* In full Sacrissee, the gesture was tender, an offer of care. Not that they'd much of it. Providing a safe *IN* and a selection of nipples—if you could beat out other sibs, aunts, and whomever else was thirsty—qualified as parental devotion for the species.

Modorans, Ersh-memory told me, kept their litters close until their young were almost full grown, that generation helping guard and teach the next. They were demonstrative, affectionate parents, permitting no harm to their offspring. Well, except for Ansky, who'd left her litter on the doorstep of the male she considered most likely to be the father.

If the Emboldened's Modoran genes held those species' tendencies, and if they were expressed in the chimeras? *Bess might have protectors.*

"You are servants," Saxel told the Kraal with her own scorn. She held up a white disk. I couldn't be certain without being closer, but it looked alarmingly like an old-style locator-key—the sort used to find and access a high value prize. Or target—Kraal games often included a playful element of assassination. They'd been popular before these Kraal's time, shared only with those of impeccable affiliation. Not, in Skalet-memory, with non-Kraal. "We're the ones who risked all to come to this world. Now we have provided this fine *IN* and the supplies your captain wanted. Found for you this place, forgotten and lost by your House and its allies until now." She gestured around the cave.

It wasn't that impressive. A thought I'd remember later.

"Leaders do not talk through servants," Saxel continued. "Give me a com link to your captain. I will confirm our plans." She thrust out her hand, thumbs and fingers spread.

Shirt gave a short grudging nod, and Vest passed a Kraal military translight com to the Emboldened.

Finally, some information!

I may have looked too expectant. The next thing I knew, Socks had me by the arm. Without a word, she dragged me to my feet, then away from the little gathering, dropping me near the crates.

As a child would, I huddled in seeming misery. As a child wouldn't, I wished for my Lanivarian ears. Lacking those, I set other, loftier goals. No Kraal invasion. No Emboldened colony here or on Minas XII, especially not one started with frozen embryos who'd probably been kidnapped from Sacrissee before being stolen again.

Growing determined, I toyed with the fastening of the vest, that also being what children did.

Only to stop myself and carefully remove my fingers, remembering whose garment it was. Explosives were likely. Poison. Pins. Really, who were these Kraal that they'd dress a lost child in something dangerous?

Humans who didn't intend to return that lost child and risk exposing their presence or weapons cache. I'd be taken offworld to live in a sous family. Work as a servant. Taught a trade, perhaps.

I could almost hear Skalet laughing at me. These Kraal? They'd tricked the Emboldened, maybe even into committing murder, and by the presence of the grav cart, had robbed the *Stellar Trumpet,* most certainly after killing its crew. These Kraal were the reason Mal and the Commonwealth medship feared a plague, why the Library was stuffed with anxious scholars overnight—*partying, but anxious*—and our staff couldn't go home.

And stolen Rhonda's Elk herd, who might not find their way home, risking the village cheese supply. *I'd priorities.*

In sum? These were not good people. Lowering my head, I glowered through my hair at Shirt, Vest, and Socks, who paid me no attention, being busy glowering at the Emboldened clustered around their com, talking to their captain.

Bess had been doomed the instant I'd approached the cliff. They'd attempt to dispose of this me once they'd no witnesses.

I should have stayed Karras and stunned them silly.

There wasn't much to do in a cave. Particularly in a cave with those who didn't want you there and were pretending you weren't. You could, and I did, compose Urgian limericks featuring unlikely, if hilarious events involving my companions and itching powder. As I couldn't laugh aloud, the entertainment value was minimal. *Though I'd tell them to Paul later.*

So it was a relief when the Kraal dimmed their light, two taking turns in sleep sacks, except now I was lying on cold, hard rock.

Lying on rock meant less entertaining thoughts, the sort I'd managed to avoid, insisted on filling my head. First and foremost, Paul.

Who'd not be happy, right now. He might even be angry with me and I'd deserve it, having been sent to find the Emboldened—*which I had*—not be embroiled in whatever scheme they'd hatched.

Which I had.

Before being angry, and even if angry, my dearest friend would be worried. Paul was awake and worrying at this exact moment, I knew beyond any doubt, it well past time for me to report. Had things gone better—or at least remotely closer to plan—I'd already be home with a hot cup of spurl, about to try out my puffy new sleeping pads—

Which Evan had and Lionel. Leaving one for me. Wholly inadequate, as I'd intended to pile them all on my sleeping platform, then to snuggle between—

Instead, I'd rock and Paul worrying.

I didn't shift to ease shoulder or hip, determined not to let those sleeping around me know I wasn't. Sleeping. I cracked open an eyelid. Vest wasn't sleeping either, the Kraal on guard by the cave door, nor was Maston, the Emboldened's eyes glowing in the dark.

A trait I found remarkable, given it belonged to neither Sacrissee nor Modoran, proving once again you couldn't treat an evolved life-form like an ingredient in a recipe. As Ersh would say, expect the unexpected in biology. Surprise was the rule—unless you were a Web-being.

Well, there was me, but with Ansky gone, another such surprise seemed highly unlikely.

Ersh-memory surged up and through me, not that I wanted it . . .

. . . to find Ersh/myself in the kitchen, our web-kin gathered to share food as ephemerals did.

Ansky, deplorably pregnant again, this time as a Modoran. Two rows of pink engorged teats poked through her fur, teats she played like an instrument, tapping one after the other.

Skalet slammed a pot on the table. "Stop that!"

"Why?" A sly tilt of her head. "It's pleasurable. You should try it sometime. Pleasure."

"There's no pleasure in the risks you take," Mixs told her. "Intimate acts. Disgusting fluids. Being trapped like this and useless." Antennae stabbed at Ansky's swollen abdomen.

"A rare, brief consequence," Ansky replied equanimously. "Of use, being my gift to the rest of you. I say again, Skalet, you should try it for yourself. Have a little fun."

"Oh, you'd be so round, Skalet!" Lesy's tentacle tips turned pink, beak chittering as her Dokeci-self giggled uncontrollably. "You'd—you'd—waddle. You'd leak—"

"Stop your nonsense," Skalet ordered furiously.

Lesy wrinkled and turned black, wrapping her arms over her eyes.

Ersh/I chimed dissent; all fell silent. "Lesy. Don't be upset. Skalet didn't mean it."

Skalet, who most certainly did and was still enraged, made a visible effort to compose herself. "I shouldn't have shouted at you."

An arm lowered to let an accusing eye peek out. "You scared me."

"I know. I'm sorry." The rest, even Ansky, came forward, hands and antennae touching Lesy in tender reassurance. Only Skalet remained distant.

Did Skalet, the Youngest, suspect? Ersh/I wondered.

Could she grasp that Lesy *fantasized*?

That Lesy, alone of all her Web, could envision the unreal, the *hadn't happened* so powerfully she often believed it over the truth in her own flesh?

Ersh/I barely could.

All Ersh/I could do was protect the others from her . . .

. . . I was in the cave, lying on rock, surrounded by beings whose life spans were less than a flicker within Ersh's, perhaps a blink within Lesy's, and, while a somewhat greater length compared to my own thus far, still would be dust long before I'd matured enough to be other than this child.

Relative age was so annoying.

Ersh-memory lingered at the back of my mouth, drawing with it the far more recent flavor of Lesy . . .

Urgent needs. Lazy contemplation. Images not from memory or experience but creations of the self. So many bring joy.

Others bring dread . . .

I whimpered, myself again and full of grief. Poor Lesy. Surely the universe was difficult enough to bear at times without—

"You're cold," said the Emboldened lying next to me. He pulled me against him, curling his body around mine.

While unexpected—and at first quite alarming—the rush of warmth soothed this me.

Accepting my lot, I closed my eyes and went to sleep.

Elements

EVAN woke with the lazy languor of a solid sleep, free of odd dreams and chirping socks, resting on a comfortable bed with a not-a-blanket on top.

Curiosity cracked open one eye and sent his fingers exploring.

A quilt. Stiffer than the blankets he used at home, with threads worked through layers of fabric, but warm. Lionel must have put one over him last night, because he distinctly didn't remember doing so himself.

Evan opened both eyes and stretched, lifting his head. Lionel's bed was gone. Light streamed in along the edges of the curtain. They'd let him sleep into the morning.

Or Lesley had eaten everyone, saving him for lunch.

By day's light, he could grin at such fantastic notions and feel guilt for his dark thoughts of the night before. Lesley was a person, not a monster. And an excellent cook. If she was back in the kitchen, there could be breakfast waiting.

Evan went to throw his feet over the side of the bed only to discover he was already on the floor. He chuckled—

—then stopped as the rest of him woke up. The rest remembered yesterday.

The murdered Sacrissee. Who hadn't been murdered, but who might have been murderers—they'd been rough with him at the start, not that it mattered—

Everyone would be up and about very serious business indeed, while he was staring at the ceiling, with its faintly alarming little cracks in the plaster and cobwebs in the corners.

Evan rolled to his knees and got up. His clothes were wrinkled and sweat-stained, as was he, but those were things he could fix. After putting his pad with the others, and the quilt on top of that, as Lionel had done, he opened his luggage.

He couldn't help wondering if anyone else had, despite the "Diplomatic Privilege" stickers. If Skalet had brought his luggage, he'd be sure; Evan didn't think personal belongings or privacy rated high in the Kraal's regard. Joncee Pershing seemed the sort to care.

Evan checked the contents. They appeared untouched. As they would if Skalet had searched it, leaving him suspicious again. He shook his head, refusing to worry. His things were here and he was grateful.

Clutching toiletries and a clean set of clothes, he went into the hall, then tiptoed straight to the accommodation Paul had shown him. It was through a door before the kitchen, and he hadn't been wrong, last night.

The farmhouse accommodation was splendid. The floor, walls, and ceiling were tiled in muted soothing colors. There was a generous shower stall with controls for everything from water spray to sand. A soaking tub waited behind a curtain, with a collection of bubble baths and fragrant oils on a shelf. As well as the usual biological accommodation in the corner, there was another.

After a curious inspection, Evan stepped back out. Definitely set for non-Human use.

The shower it was.

Awake, scrubbed, and dressed. Hair shaped into its proper smooth round—having developed a flat spot overnight. Teeth gleaming. Evan smoothed the front of his new sweater, a light green knit he'd bought on Dokeci-Na and worried would be too warm. Now he wore it over an undershirt and under a jacket and felt ready to embrace the wintry world.

He pulled aside the curtain. The clouds were gone and the wind too, leaving behind a glittering wonderland of white beneath that incredible sky. When Evan turned away from the window, beams of sunlight shot everywhere, illuminating a very odd room indeed.

It wasn't so much the sloped floor or bedding, though there was a wide variety of boxes and elevated platforms as well as a hammock folded and waiting against a wall.

It was the abundance of wardrobes. Big ones, small ones. Thin ones, wide ones. No two the same, all wood in differing styles.

What could be in them?

Evan knew he shouldn't look. Closed doors were a signal to keep out. He respected his friends' privacy. Curiosity wasn't any sort of justification.

That said, he'd never been in a room full of non-Human stuff—personal stuff—before. The accommodation alone had been an education.

How many more surprises waited behind these wooden doors?

He'd take a peek inside one. Just one.

In the end, Evan looked in them all.

"You're quiet."

Evan looked up from his bowl. "Sorry, Lesley. Thank you for this." The kitchen was sparkling clean, countertops bare. So far, Lesley had confined her cooking to a large pot of oatmeal, adding honey and spices and fruit until the concoction was a divine, if gooey, mass she'd plopped in front of him. "It's very good."

"Something's not good." She sat across from him. "You're quiet."

"So are you." She hadn't spoken, till now. Her clothing today was subdued, too, a brown sweater with a black jacket, over a pair of black pants, but she'd added some artfully twisted salad greens to one lapel and swept her hair to one side. She wore shoes, somewhat to his surprise.

"I'm being inconspicuous," she responded with a wise little smile. "I promised Skalet when she gave me her clothes. While the officious person is here, at least. You're being quiet."

Accused a third time, Evan sighed and sat back. "I did something wrong. I went in to Esen and Esolesy Ki's wardrobes—looked at their clothes."

Lesley regarded him quizzically. "What's wrong with that?"

"I didn't ask permission—"

"I never do."

"I should have. Trust me. And now?" He shook his head. "I'm confused and I've questions. Questions I can't ask because I shouldn't have looked in the first place!"

"You're not quiet now." With satisfaction. "Go ahead. Ask me. I'm in charge of all wardrobes, you know. Everyone's. I'm the only one who fully appreciates fashion. And I take care of things." A flutter of long delicate fingers encompassed the sparkling kitchen.

Considering the state of it when he'd gone to bed, Lesley must have worked most of the night.

Evan sighed again. "All right. But please don't tell Esen or Esolesy Ki until I can. I'd be embarrassed if they found out from someone else. I'll confess—"

"I'm sure you will." She looked amused. "You're silly and sweet, Evan Gooseberry. Tell me what confused you."

"There's—there were clothes they can't wear. Clothes for species other than Lanivarian or Lishcyn."

Her amusement deepened. "Don't you play dress up, Evan?"

"Pardon?"

"You aren't so long past the age of wearing your elders' clothing. Of pretending to be what you're not." She pulled her hair into a crown. "A queen." Grabbed his spoon and waved it through the air. "A starship pilot." Drew her hair completely over her face and uttered a deep hum. "A Heezle!"

Evan felt vaguely insulted. "You're telling me those extra clothes are for play?"

Her face reappeared. "Play is the best."

He could almost hear his first therapist, urging him to play. Offering toys shaped like his fears—*FEARS!*

—hadn't worked. An attempt worth making, his later therapists had said, because some children responded. Some, like him, did not. That was all.

"My cousins and I would pretend to be space pirates," he said. A peace offering, because Lesley seemed to expect an answer. "We'd draw scars on our cheeks."

Instead of being impressed, she laid a hand over her cheek, her eyes wide and troubled in another of her mercurial changes.

"What is it?"

"Nothing." She drew her fingers slowly down her cheek, as if checking for scars. "Some of us are more prone to drama than others. Like Esen, playing with clothes."

Should he tell her of the clothes that disturbed him most? He'd almost missed the little wardrobe in a corner. The one full of clothing for a Human child. A little girl. But Paul and Esen had told him Bess didn't live here—

"Now you're quiet again. Tsk." Lesley held out her hand. Reluctantly, Evan rested his on top. She'd a warm hand, not as delicate as it looked, callused by some work. Her fingers wrapped around his, thumb caressing. "Beware what you think you know, Evan," she told him. "It's never all the story. Sometimes," that full glorious smile, "it's not even the best part. Come. I'll make eggs. You will pose for me."

"'Pose?'"

"I'm a famous artist. I will make your sweet face famous, Evan Gooseberry." Having made this announcement, Lesley flowed to her feet. "First, I do eggs."

He hadn't posed for an artist other than to hold still while Trili sketched his nose. She'd been, it turned out, sketching everyone's nose then turning each into a clever caricature for a who's who game they'd played at the last embassy party. Lesley's request was far more significant. A portrait by a famous artist.

Which, Evan decided with contentment settling through his bones, explained everything about Lesley, from her name to dancing naked in the snow. Great Gran had impressed on him that artists were free spirits, to be allowed to explore their creativity in whatever medium or lifestyle called to their muse. An explanation she used for the occasional Gooseberry recorded in The Lore, including her own uncle, who'd arrived at some sudden life choice and willfully disappeared from the lineage, a departure marked with a neat black box around the date.

If Lesley turned his face into a work of art, Great Gran Gooseberry would be thrilled. She might even commission it. Evan pulled out his holocube, dismayed when he saw the queue of waiting messages.

Rather than open any, he found his new favorite image of Great Gran, taken at the tiller of her sailboat. Her hair was a brilliant rainbow around her head, her joyful smile like the sun itself.

The boat was heeled over almost into the waves and how it stayed up—her friend risking life and limb to let go of a rope to snap the image—was a marvel.

"Eggs are ready," Lesley sang out, coming toward him with a huge black pan. "Who's that pretty one?"

"My Great Gran," he told her, enlarging the image between them. "I can't wait to tell her I'm posing for your art, Lesley. She'll be very pleased. I could call her—"

"Later. You inspire me now, Evan."

Obediently, he put away the device.

"Don't move." Lesley tipped the pan upside down, depositing a steamy fluffy mound of cooked eggs on the table. Humming to herself, looking up at Evan with great concentration, she set to work sculpting the mound with a spoon and knife.

"What are you—"

"Stop!" Almost a shout. "Don't move a muscle, Evan," she warned more gently. "I must work quickly, while we have the light. Keep yourself busy. Tell me about this 'Great Gran.'"

If he wasn't to move a muscle, how was he to answer? Evan made a helpless little sound in his throat.

Lesley laughed. "You can move your mouth. I've finished that." She pointed the knife midway up the mound.

She had? Evan swallowed. "Great Gran raised me from a baby. She's a wonderful—"

"So she knows what you are."

He blinked.

"Stop! I haven't done your eyes."

"Sorry." He held his eyelids wide open. "Yes. Of course she does. Great Gran knows everything about me."

Lesley absently scooped some egg up on a finger and transferred it to her mouth as she studied Evan's face. "Do you?"

"I—I think so, yes. I had a very happy and active childhood. Well—once I got better," Evan replied, going into more detail than he'd planned because Lesley kept watching him in that unnerving way, her finger still in her mouth. "As a small child I couldn't go outside. Some medical issues lingering after my birth. Our birth. I'd a twin. Great Gran told me when I was old enough. She didn't—I don't remember her. Why am I telling you all this?"

Lesley's finger came out with a loud "pop!" She smiled. "Because it's what you are, Evan. You're brave with people. You give them your heart when you could keep it safe. I like that most about you," she said simply. "Your courage."

A generous slant on his tendency to share too much, too quickly—and, as Trili told him many times, to believe the very best about everyone until proven otherwise. And even then. Evan felt humble and wonderful at the same time. "Thank you, Lesley."

"Oh, you like it?" she asked with delight, gesturing grandly to the egg mound.

Evan tried his utmost to see anything but egg—egg now cold and congealing—but failed. "I'm not sure what I'm supposed to see," he admitted.

"That's because we need pepper." Lesley rushed to the counter, returning with a peppermill as long as her arm. She wielded it over the egg mound with vigor, producing a rain of small black flecks.

Evan tried not to sneeze.

The pepper clung to valleys and outlined slopes until suddenly? While he'd never thought to see himself in eggs—there he was. "How remarkable!" He stood up and looked from all sides; she'd even captured the shape of his hair—not flattened either. "This is art, Lesley," Evan said, thoroughly impressed. "I don't know how you did it. And so quickly."

"I do my best work when I don't think about it for long." Lesley cut off his egg-nose with her spoon, plopping the mass into her mouth. She handed a second spoon to Evan. "Come on. It's not going to last, and I used all the eggs. Eat up your face, young sir! Start with an ear."

Dubiously, Evan did as he was told, delighted to find his "ear" was tasty and still warm inside.

"Well done!" Lesley tapped his spoon with hers. "Beat you to the other one," she crowed, and he hurried to dig out the other ear, filling his mouth with it.

She laughed her wonderful laugh and Evan felt a warm glow of joy.

Then he felt a *SPLOT* as a soggy mass of egg landed on his forehead. Lesley readied another handful.

He leapt up to grab his own to throw—

SPLOT! Egg stuck, then fell from his fine new sweater. "Gotcha!" she shouted, ducking below the table as he threw. A gleeful, "Missed me!"

Evan grinned and grabbed two handfuls, running around the table. "Here I come!"

Playing after all.

28: Cave Morning

I'D slept, much to my own surprise. Without dreams, which was not. Web-beings didn't dream. According to Ersh, in answer to yet another of my persistent questions, it was because we didn't sleep either. Not in our true form.

In others, depending on the species, sleep was required. I'd found it alarming at first, despite Ersh's insistence the process of regularly falling comatose and senseless was normal and essential. Ingestion, respiration, the exit of metabolic wastes—all had their pleasant, if quaint sides to them—but sleeping?

I mistrusted it. Not that I could help myself. If whatever form I was in, once I'd learned to hold one, needed sleep, I'd pass out eventually, waking some time later with a disconnect in memory as if sleep had erased me. While I grew to accept the necessity, and even enjoy the initial stage of relaxing in a comfortable safe spot?

Waking on the hard cave floor brought back all my initial dislike.

I opened my eyes cautiously.

There was more light than I remembered, possibly what woke this me. The Kraal had erected bar-shaped illuminators on the stands in order to examine their treasure. They'd moved the crates into the center of the floor and removed their lids. Now they sat, backs to me, going through the contents with Kraalish glee.

And caution, wary of traps. These Kraal, I decided, were thieves and unentitled to their find. Our friend Rudy would agree.

I could use Rudy Lefebvre about now, Paul's cousin not only tough and good in a fight—enjoying a battle against odds, or bar scrum, more than most—but he'd patrol experience to give him an edge with the criminally inclined. I supposed three armed Kraal might be a stretch, even for him, but he'd surely bring help.

I could use some.

Until then, it was Bess to the rescue. I sat up, rubbing my eyes in my best *harmless me* fashion as I looked around for the Emboldened.

They'd gone with the grav sled and its canisters, moved to the wall opposite to the Kraal. I'd slept through that? *A thoroughly treacherous ephemeral habit.*

When no one reacted to my sitting up, I answered the call of another ephemeral need, following the fragrance into the farthest corner. They'd provided that essential to troop movements and successful cave sharing: a collapsible digester.

Which only worked if you aimed, explaining the smell, though given the height of the drying urine stream, I wasn't sure the Humans were to blame.

We were all lucky the chimeras hadn't retained Sacrissee arm glands. Tartt? *There was a pungent aroma for you.* Eyes would water—

"Come here, Small One," Saxel called. "There's food and water."

The Kraal didn't twitch at this squandering of limited resources, implying I wasn't to be murdered this morning.

Oh, good.

Or they anticipated a change in the situation, soon.

Might not be.

Elements

LIONEL was unable to resist another glance over his shoulder at the peaceful farmhouse. A peaceful farmhouse containing a strange Web-being and unsuspecting young diplomat, and if he had to pick a recipe for disaster this was it, so like the one that had locked Paul Ragem in a Kraosian dungeon with Esen-alit-Quar. *Lesley wasn't the dear little Blob.*

"Are you sure we should leave them? What if she—" He couldn't say the word. "Is Evan safe?"

Paul didn't slow or look around. "From what Esen's told me of Lesy, she's harmless. And far more likely to obey Web rules, so Evan's ignorance of her true nature protects him." His strides lengthened, each step crunching in the overnight drifted snow. "My concern's Esen at the moment."

There'd been no word. Lionel hadn't had to ask, finding his friend in the kitchen, seeing the toll of a sleepless night on his face. After they'd shared a quick breakfast, Paul had showered and dressed for the day, reappearing to start work as if nothing was wrong.

When everything felt out of place. He'd a concern of his own. *Skalet.* "We need to keep the situation on the *Trium Pa* stable," Lionel said, not for the first time. "You're sure Mal's going to cooperate?" The constable couldn't have been happy: first to be tricked by Kraal, then to be asked to back Skalet's play when they'd no idea what it was.

"He will for now, but Mal has to make a full report when the government rep arrives. Just before, he'll pretend to discover the medship's signal's been faked."

"That's too soon." Lionel stopped, tried to keep his voice steady, but this—*this was betrayal!* "The Library isn't safe, Paul. We've seen it. The Kraal can reach her here. She's not invulnerable." The words echoed across the snow and Lionel took a deep breath to calm himself. *Be reasonable.* "Skalet's made us her allies. She's fighting for her identity—her future. We must support her."

"And we do that by keeping out of her way." A sidelong look. "Trust me, Lionel. Evan's safer than you'll be if you mix yourself in one of Skalet's plots."

What good was being safe? "I can handle myself," Lionel countered stiffly. "We owe her our best efforts. If you won't help Skalet, I will."

Paul's answer was a sigh that made a cloud in the crisp early morning air, one both walked through without another word.

"Last time we saw Esen? Henri?" Ally turned to her coworker, who jerked a thumb toward the Lobby.

"She went to the party. I warned her not to get distracted—"

Paul was gone. Lionel shrugged apologetically and hurried after him. The Lobby was—*unbelievable.*

His first reaction was despair at the mess, for without Duggs, however were they to get the building back in operation? Let alone the security risk—but as Lionel looked closer, he had to smile.

"They're happy," Paul said in a low, wondering voice, seeing it too.

Scholars were perched in the openings of an enormous megalith comprised of folded tents, consuming beverages and breakfasts. Others strolled without regard for the floor's guiding paths, in small mixed groups deep in conversation. The giant open space seemed more a thriving eclectic university campus than crowded waiting room.

"I take it Lambo opened the Chow," Lionel commented.

Paul grunted an agreement, busy walking around the ungainly structure, peering into openings. "She'd love this."

"Oh, yes. Think she's inside?" A Web-being could get stuck in a form; *there'd been the incident with the Rands.*

His friend straightened, running a hand through his hair. "I'd like to say yes," he admitted quietly, "but I sent Esen after the Emboldened last night."

Lionel grabbed Paul's arm. "What?" *And he'd been worried about Skalet?*

A somber look. "I knew she could find them."

"Of course, but—" Lionel withdrew his hand. "Forgive me." If anyone protected Esen and kept her interests closest to heart, it was and always had been Paul. "I shouldn't forget how capable she is."

"She has her moments." Paul stared up at the collection of modified tents inhabiting the raised walkway. Lionel didn't think he saw them. "I'd expected she'd be done by now." More briskly, looking at Lionel, "It's possible they sought an *IN* for the night."

"Even probable," Lionel agreed. "Ally said Mal's waiting for us— what is it?"

Paul's gaze had locked on something past his shoulder. "We're out of time."

Lionel turned.

Three figures were entering the Lobby from the side hall. Joncee Pershing, in his "up for reelection" suit he'd also pull from the closet to officiate at weddings, with two unfamiliar Botharans.

The government representative had arrived.

Hours early. Too early, and what that meant for Skalet was beyond his aid now. Lionel had to believe she'd be aware. Adjust her plans.

What such haste meant for the Library was another problem entirely, and Lionel resisted the urge to check his pocket for the datacrystal with their documents. It was there, though permissions and agreements suddenly seemed the flimsiest of protections if the Preservation Committee had found an ally at this level.

The taller female carried a cup of something hot, implying a successful stop at the Chow, while the shorter towed an elevated vid recorder, gaining the immediate interest of nearby scholars. Both wore a type of business attire not seen on this side of the ocean; the one with the cup in a crisp blue suit over a red sweater, the other brown over yellow.

Spotting them, Pershing waved, heading their way. As they neared, Lionel caught his breath. The one in blue and red wasn't a stranger. He glanced at Paul. "Is that—?"

"Yes." The shock on the other's face vanished, smoothed away as if by a tide. "It's Nia. She's done well for herself. I knew she would."

For Paul Ragem knew Niala Mavis very well, indeed; she was the love he'd left on Botharis, whose heart he'd broken by pretending to be dead. *If she'd come to shut down the Library?* Lionel's heart ached for his friend. "I don't know what to say," he whispered. "I'm sorry."

"Don't be. I hadn't worked up the courage to find her. My mistake." Paul's regretful little shrug didn't fool Lionel for an instant. *Just as well Esen wasn't here.* "Shall we greet our new guests?"

When he thought back to the day he'd met Niala Mavis, what Lionel remembered most were her hands. She'd long fingers—there'd been a piano in the room; he'd assumed she played. As she sat, listening to his poison about Paul Ragem and his ship-destroying alien monster, those fingers had gripped one another until they'd gone bone-white, her hands quivering as if trying to escape her lap. She'd given no other sign of distress. Had answered his questions with greater courtesy than he'd deserved.

When Lionel'd returned to this world fifty years later, desperate to set the record straight and exonerate his friend, Nia had refused any contact. As had Sam Ragem, but Lionel knew Paul's uncle never believed his beloved starstruck nephew guilty of anything but causing his family grief.

Lionel had no idea what Niala Mavis believed. Other than she'd waited, like Paul, keeping her distance until this moment.

She knew them. Lionel caught the flash of recognition in her eyes as they walked up to her, but that was all.

Joncee didn't smile. "Director Paul Ragem, Administrator Kearn, this is Special Envoy Niala Mavis, straight from Grandine." The reeve leaned close. "Now remember what I told you—about the jobs the Library provides. It's our single biggest employer outside farming. Major impact on our economy. I can provide figures."

"Please send them to my office, Reeve Pershing." Niala had a low, soft voice. "Thank you for your time." She waited until Joncee caught the hint.

"I'll leave you to it, Envoy Mavis. Director." Joncee shot Paul a warning look the envoy couldn't possibly miss. A message of support.

Once the reeve had left, she turned to them. "Director," she greeted with a nod. "Administrator Kearn." Without. "My assistant, Onlee Natson."

"A recording of a special envoy's activities is required by law." The assistant, having blurted this out, kept a stranglehold on the tether as she gave a wide-eyed stare at a passing Urgian, then flinched as an Anata hurried up to Paul.

Whose eyes hadn't left Niala Mavis. "The All Species' Library of Linguistics and Culture welcomes an official record," Paul said.

"Even of this?" The envoy gestured with her cup at the cluttered Lobby.

"Oh, especially of this. Excuse me a moment." Paul turned to the Anata. "What can I do for you, Hom Bunkabo Del?"

A digging claw snapped open to gesticulate. "In return for what to us seems a minor offering of newly accepted verb declensions, we received an excellent and helpful response to our question, concerning the true name and thus origin of a smut decimating our grain crops. Now we will know who to blame and more importantly where to seek reparations and treatment." The claw snapped shut with distinct satisfaction. "As for my personal well-being? My revis is replete, thank you, Director. I wished to convey my gratitude to your staff. An excellent night under trying circumstances." The scholar peered up at the hovering recorder. "If your local government would allow a shipcity," Bunkabo Del proclaimed, voice sharply louder, "we wouldn't have had to impose on these fine beings. Did you get that?" To Onlee.

Though clearly discomfited to be addressed by the non-Human, she managed a nod. Lionel bit his lip to hold in a smile. *Henri's work, at a guess.*

"I'll pass along your thanks," Paul said gravely. "We hope to have the situation resolved as soon as possible."

The Anata waved nostril flaps with satisfaction and moved away.

And the next scholar stepped up, for as if Paul's attention had been a signal, a line quickly formed, of varying species. Each expressed satisfaction with the Library and its staff, while decrying the lamentable lack of government support for crucial infrastructure. Lionel's favorite was the group of Urgians who'd composed pointed limericks about the deplorable lack of a space station, although they mispronounced the name of the planet.

Throughout it all, Special Envoy Niala Mavis waited with remarkable patience. Onlee eventually stopped twitching as aliens shouted into her recorder, even pulling it lower to accommodate an Ervickian.

Paul thanked each, but the instant there was a gap in the eager line, he held up a hand to deter the rest. "Please save your comments, honored guests. They're greatly appreciated, but the Special Envoy should continue her work." He turned to her. "My apologies," he said very quietly.

They were of a height, of a shared ancestry described in bone and proportion, as well as thick black hair—hers shorter with its waves tamed. Paul's eyes were gray, hers blue, but for a heartbeat or less, the same intense curiosity filled both, as if they searched across time.

Until she frowned, ending the moment. Her gaze turned cold. "No more stunts, Director Ragem. These people are right to complain. Why are they still stranded here? I was told there's nothing wrong with your trains—"

Every being in range stopped moving, then burst out in loud and no longer happy variations of "What? Did you hear that? Who said that? Is that true? There's a train? Get off my tail!" and so forth.

"A discussion for my office, please," Lionel interrupted, before matters got worse. *Though hadn't they?* "With Constable Lefebvre present."

"You," she said, and there it was, the heat under the ice. The fury.

Lionel didn't back down or look away. Didn't dare, with the number of fervently interested ears and other organs aimed their way. *If she wanted to see aliens stampede for the doors, she'd only to wait here a moment.* "My office," he repeated firmly, doing this for Paul and all they'd built.

Without waiting for an answer, Lionel turned to lead the way.

29: Cave Day

THE Emboldened took turns napping and guarding, someone always within tail touch of the canisters. The Kraal, having organized the weapons they'd found in order of size—*as far as I could tell*—kept themselves occupied throwing knives at each other. The idea being to catch the one thrown at you and return it. They were disturbingly good at it.

They didn't look to be preparing for an invasion anytime soon.

While pleased not to see troops pouring through the door, something had changed while I'd been comatose on the floor and I faced one of the difficulties of appearing to be a ten-year-old Human child. *I couldn't ask.* Well, I could, but the limited range of questions that could legitimately come from this me—without raising suspicion or angering the adult Kraal—was a serious obstacle.

As far as I could tell, the plan for the day was to wait. Wait inside the cave. Wait without knowing what might be happening outside the cave, which for me became harder and harder as time passed.

As it should, I abruptly realized. No Human child waited with this much patience. Young Ycl, yes, but they had to hide from cannibalistic parents, so selection favored those who didn't mind sticking under a rock for days.

Being Bess? I stood and walked over to the Kraal, stopping when a knife embedded itself in the floor in front of my feet.

"What do you want, child?"

As Bess, I'd a range of appealing expressions, some of which Rudy called unfair. Usually before he gave in and fed me whatever Paul had suggested I not have, took me where Paul had suggested I not go, or—the point was, this me had some power over adults.

Maybe not these adults, but it was worth a try. I set my lower lip to a tiny quivering pout. "I want to go home. When can I go home?"

Socks retrieved her knife, giving me a grim look. "What were you doing out in the first place, huh?"

They'd asked me this before and while a child might falter and make a mistake, I'd perfect memory at my disposal, as well as Correa's stories of her misadventures as a child—it was a wonder the Human had survived to adulthood—and launched into my version once more.

"I was playing with my cousins and I fell through the ice and Aran and Sindy pulled me out but my clothes were all wet and if you stay in wet clothes outside in winter you could die!" Having said this in one breath, I gasped another and kept going with a will. "Sindy's aunt fell in the water in winter because she wanted to save her dog and the dog was fine but Sindy's aunt froze to death because she didn't take off her wet clothes. I did." Another pause for breath let me gauge Socks' patience and the distance between us. "Aran and Sindy told me to run in circles to keep warm while they went for help and I did. I ran really fast but I forgot to run in circles and I got lost and—" Seeing the Kraal make a fist, I gave a heart-wrenching little sob and threw myself at her, wrapping my arms as far around her armored middle as I could. "YOU SAVED ME!"

Such was the power of this small me, the Kraal actually—if awkwardly—patted me on the back. I looked up at her with my eyes as wide as they could go. "Do you know where my house is? Can you take me home?"

Trapped by child, she looked toward the others. "We passed that cabin—"

"No," Shirt said, then smiled a dreadful smile at me. "There's a terrible storm outside and we mustn't open the door until tomorrow, when it's all over. You understand, don't you, Bess. It's not safe for anyone to go out in storms, especially children."

Socks pulled away.

The weather forecast for the rest of the week called for clear, cold, and sunny, but I nodded. "Storms are dangerous," I said, careful to make it sound fearful when what I felt was smug. The Kraal couldn't sneak around without being seen. Botharis might lack fashionable clothing stores, but even the Hamlet of Hillsview constabulary could mount an aerial search. While the Kraal were trapped, there was hope yet. "We stay inside in storms," I agreed.

Tomorrow, was it?

Or tonight.

I'd a new plan. To wait in the cave with everyone else and see what happened.

It wasn't as if I'd an option.

Elements

THE display from the farmhouse kitchen was distracting. Worse than distracting, mystifying, for Lesy and the Human had gone from throwing food at one another to wiping egg from each other's faces—if not from clothes and hair—to this: sitting quietly at the table, viewing images of strangers from his device. As if, in Human terms, they were friends trading personal histories.

A new and pointless diversion of Lesy's.

Skalet turned to other displays, the one with the kitchen burning into her back, whispering nonsense, adding confusion. She should be—was—grateful to Evan Gooseberry for bringing their web-kin back to her senses, however dubious those were. Lesy was as she'd been before.

She closed her eyes. That was it. There was the danger. Lesy as she'd been.

Unsustainable.

The realization chilled her blood. Esen hadn't shared the past with their sister; hadn't shared the pain they'd both learned to endure. She must—but what then? Lesy had been—was—the vulnerable one, to be spoken to gently, to be kept from anything unpleasant or distressing, protected because Ersh knew she was weaker than the rest.

Esen remembered. Esen knew. She'd been the best of them at keeping Lesy amused and happy. Esen, who cleaned up Lesy's many and varied messes without complaint. Who played her incessant games—

including the appalling hide-and-sneak up on her Elders. Who'd been Lesy's companion on trips away from Picco's Moon before any of the rest were given such responsibility for the Youngest.

Looking back, remembering within the context of now, who'd been the responsible one of that pairing? Ersh's wisdom, surely, to see what Esen was capable of from the beginning.

Skalet opened her eyes and turned to stare once more at the Human and Web-being. What would Esen see? A new hope for Lesy—some manufactured friendship with a Human barely old enough to walk on his own, let alone comprehend what they were?

All she saw were lies.

A symbol arrived, covering the display. It spread to every display, pulsing and urgent. A request for connection.

House Virul.

Skalet turned off the kitchen display. Shut down the feeds from inside the Library as well before seating herself in front of a featureless wall, for the request was that rarity between strange Kraal: face-to-face.

One hand stroked the air; the other tapped a code against the fabric over her thigh. *Connection confirmed.*

A figure formed, seated before a wall of equal plainness. Male. Old, for Kraal, with all that implied. His affiliation tattoos were a maze impossible to read with one glance. This face—its history—would take study. *Intriguing.*

Blue eyes. The missing ear. *Who* she faced became clear, and Skalet found herself poised on the keen edge between danger and destiny. *At last.* "Courier Virul-ru," she identified.

"Courier S'kal-ru. I've anticipated our meeting for many years. I see you are done with House Bract."

She allowed herself a tight smile. "I will be shortly. To what do I owe this honor?"

Virul-ru touched a finely done, easily missed tattoo against his left nostril. An affiliation to House Oalak, an ancient and tenuous connection a lesser Kraal might have thought abandoned. Not so Skalet, who well understood the deeper workings of this elegant society. The oldest affiliations were brought forward in times of change—renewed as being of greater and proven reliability. *Admirable.*

Does yours hold? his gesture asked. A perilous question.

She didn't hesitate, touching the same area on her face. *Affirmation.* "Our accomplishments have at times interwoven." Not always at odds. *Not yet.*

"To mutual advantage and the betterment of the Confederacy," Virul-ru replied, settling the issue. This was a meeting to forge a deeper alliance.

To lower her guard would insult them both. Instead, Skalet allowed herself a gracious nod. "I live to serve."

"As do I. I would share an image."

Another would be flattered. Virul-ru had bypassed easier, safer strategies, going straight to *Show the Throat,* an offer of affiliation given surety by exposing a dangerous, exploitable weakness. There could be no doubt of House Virul's desire for her allegiance.

Or that her life was forfeit, should she view the image then refuse.

"Do so."

The image appeared to float between them, offset so as not to obscure their view of one another. Rendered in the cooler end of the spectrum, it showed a lifeless starship adrift against a backdrop of stars. The image was framed in what might be script or an abstract decoration. Whichever, the style was not in web-memory.

This wasn't Veya Ragem's *Sidereal Pathfinder.*

Nor, as in that other image, were the stars in this background unidentifiable. This ship—a Kraal cruiser, Tyrant class—floated between Botharis and the leading edge of the Kraal Confederacy.

"There are more like this," Virul-ru stated. "Someone or something draws a line in the sky, S'kal-ru, where there was none before."

Skalet saw much more than the image. Saw conspiracy and fools. Virul was a Great House, Bract a Noble one, thus lesser as well as newer. Bract wouldn't have been privy to a secret of this magnitude, but they could well have sniffed a new interest in Botharis by their betters. Sought to act first and seize their own advantage via Arzul the ambitious.

Petty squabbles when the Confederacy—perhaps all in this part of space—faced an unknown threat.

She bowed her head the slightest amount, acknowledging no path forward but this. No glory but what was offered here and now.

Time to show her own throat, and seize it all.

"I would share an image, Virul-ru."

Opportunity.

Skalet hung the heavy distance rifle by its strap across her back and tucked three Library datacrystals inside her armor, information the deadlier weapon. Ignored her cold weather gear in favor of a persona-shield, having no guarantee who waited in the scoutship behind the Ragem barn. The distort-hood hung loose down her back.

Let them read her face.

Cieter-ro had claimed the *Trium Pa* on her behalf, diminishing Bract and putting Arzul on notice of her extreme displeasure. Unless her ambitious underling saw greater glory elsewhere and a trap waited. If so, she'd be pleased to turn it on its designers.

Regardless, she'd a home for Haden-ru's skin on her wall. Then?

Well, then things would become *interesting.*

About to close the room entirely, activating its security measures to forbid anyone entry, Skalet paused, then keyed in an ident. Lionel Kearn would have access, should he dare her door. Would find the images she left floating in air and understand the implication. Veya Ragem's ship. Now Veya Ragem's world. There were no coincidences.

Precautionary. Not, in any sense, a farewell message or gift. Lionel was not a friend. A capable ally close to Esen's Web. Of such value. That was all.

It was time once more to secure S'kal-ru's future—her destiny—within the Great Houses of the Kraal Confederacy.

And, above all, discover what used dead starships to mark its territory and why.

30: Cave Day

SOME forms, like the ShimShree, had internal biorhythms so robust, it was said they could tell the time at home while traveling in space. Which wasn't as useful as you might think, given space travel avoided time throughout much of its duration or no one would be able to travel anywhere.

That said, I'd no internal clock worth mentioning as Bess, but I could count. Count seconds to myself, add those to minutes, and sum the lot into hours, then—

The game grew boring after three hours, twenty-two minutes, and four seconds, meaning it was time to nudge my hosts into more information.

The Kraal, having tossed knives then engaged in vigorous exercise, pretended to sleep. I'd have suspected it was to avoid interacting with this me—Bess full of traits able to annoy adults, not that I'd dare with these—but it was the Emboldened they wished to avoid.

Sacrissee in such a cozy safe *IN* would have sought to separate from each other as much as physically possible, turned to reduce the chance of eye contact, and basically operate as if alone. Unless in rut, but that didn't appear likely.

Modorans, on the other hand, would comfort one another with mutual grooming and communal naps, between bouts of wild impatience at being confined. *They'd pace.*

By my observation, having rested and now become bored, the chimeric Emboldened exhibited the worst traits of both, not the best. The three would cuddle together with touching tenderness, then one or more of them would explode out of the group with that grim *howl* of theirs and begin pacing violently, slamming tails into the rock walls and generally being a hazard to anyone in range.

Such as me. After the fifth such eruption of reckless manners in a cave, I moved as far from the Emboldened—and Kraal—as possible, taking shelter behind a stack of opened and emptied weapons' crates.

It being impossible not to think about what might be happening outside, I spent some time listing the best possible outcomes. Lesy safe in the composter. Or a pot. The party in the Lobby ongoing—without fire damage. Duggs back in the Library and not mad about the party. *This was fun.*

Mal would find the trail of these Kraal and follow it to the cave. Paul would stay safely behind with Lionel and Evan—Skalet would help Mal—

My imagination sputtered at this point. Her inability to be a team player wasn't my web-kin's fault, but it was predictably inconvenient.

I hugged my legs to my chest and rested my chin on a knee.

More realistically? There'd be an alien riot in the Lobby, Lambo refusing to open even for Paul. Kraal would land in my Garden at S'kal-ru's order, burning my poor shrubs, then take over despite Lionel's protests. Evan would decide he didn't want to be friends with anyone who couldn't keep a Library open and go home without playing in the snow, while Mal would quit and retire for real to the southern isles with Duggs—both wearing flowered shorts.

The last might not be realistic, as I'd no idea if the two liked one another, let alone owned matching shorts.

I tensed at a soft sound from behind me and turned my head cautiously in case one of the Kraal had thought of a new game.

It was Saxel Sah. She was moving stealthily along the wall, one hand on it, the other aiming the locator-key at the rock. Her tail looped over her shoulder and she stepped past me as though I were invisible.

Or she didn't consider me of any importance to whatever she was doing. *Age-prejudice.*

While I'd no idea what she could be hunting, the fact she was? This cave had another secret.

I was bored enough to be excited at the thought. Hidden treasure! *Later, I'd remember that feeling.*

Elements

WITH an abruptness Evan now considered a sign of her free creative spirit and not an insult, Lesley had stood and walked away in the midst of their chat about his family, leaving him in the kitchen. Evan had tidied the eggs—and himself, changing sweaters.

Not quite sure what to do next—other than keep out of the way, for Paul, Lionel, and Esen had their hands and paws full with the crowd in the Library, Mal and Skalet with the murder investigation, and if he could help, they knew where to reach him—he'd thought more about family and called Great Gran.

By the time Evan finished describing his adventure in art and eggs, Great Gran was laughing so hard tears poured from her eyes. "I like your new friend," she said once calm again.

"I do too."

"Is this Lesley interested in—" Be-ringing fingers wriggled suggestively.

"She's older than you are," Evan protested.

"So?" Ample eyebrows joined the dance. "I'm not dead, you know."

When he sputtered, she relented, gazing at him fondly. "Evan, it does my heart good to see you look so happy."

"I'm sorry I didn't come home this time," he told her with a rush of remorse.

The smile he loved. "Nonsense. I gave you the trip to use as you wished. You'll come and visit when that's the right thing to do." Her smile turned mischievous. "And, oh, the party we'll have then. You know everyone wants to hear about your work."

"No, they don't," he dared answer. "Everyone wants to see if I'm keeping sane. It's my cousins' favorite pastime."

Her smile disappeared. "Evan—"

"I don't mind," he told her, surprised to find it was true. "I'm doing the work I love. I'm good at it, Great Gran, and proud of what I've accomplished."

"I'm proud of you too. So, tell me the rest of your vacation plans. You've four more days there on Botharis?"

"I do. You should see—wait, I can show you."

Evan jumped up and went to the kitchen door, holding the holocube steady. He opened the door, letting in an unexpected pile of snow. Reaching over it, he aimed the intake so Great Gran could see the magnificent snowy landscape, watching her face expectantly. "See the snow. Isn't it beautiful?"

"It is. I remember—who's that?"

Evan looked in time to see the black vessel rise over the barn and accelerate to a dot high in the sky. Snow slid off the barn roof as if startled.

"I'll have to go, Great Gran," he said, thumbing off the connection.

Black, with weapons? Landing behind the barn? It must be a Kraal ship, but friend or foe—that was the real question.

Paul would know the answer.

On his way to the Library, Evan solved one minor mystery. A machine cleared snow from the path, a machine that blew it to either side in high fluffy arcs, and under other circumstances he'd have stopped to ask the operator if he could try it.

Things being as they were, with strange spacecraft and murder, he fought his way through the thickened layer alongside the path to bypass the machine and operator, if not the oncoming plume of flying snow. Evan covered his face with an arm and held his breath.

In the nick of time, the operator turned off the machine before it engulfed Evan in snow, pulling down a mask to reveal Correa Faster's grinning face. "I'd have shifted over, Evan," the maintenance worker assured him.

"Next time!" He milled his arms to keep upright. "Have you see Paul or Lionel? Skalet? Esen?"

She shook her hooded head at each name. "But a mucky-muck from Grandine's arrived," Correa offered. "Good guess they're busy with her."

Grandine was the planetary capital. "A government official?" Evan hazarded.

A nod and frown. "Nothing but trouble when that lot pays attention to us, that's what I know. You tell her I said so."

Evan would rather not directly address a senior member of a foreign government, thank you, let alone one of his own, and couldn't imagine expressing any such sentiment.

Fortunately, Correa didn't expect a commitment. "Bye!" Swerving around him, she set her machine at the snow as if it were a loathsome bureaucrat, sending it flying.

Evan lumbered back onto the cleared path and brushed snow from his pants, then pressed on with new determination. If there was anyone here who understood how to productively tiptoe the often frayed edge between Human governance and the alien?

It was a Commonwealth diplomat.

Evan's skills met their first serious test at the entrance to the admin corridor. He wasn't the only one looking for someone in authority. It appeared every scholar had decided now was the time to Make a Personal Statement.

And if he'd thought they'd been touchy about being passed in the Assessment queue? That was nothing to the ire expressed as he sidled past being after being, working his way to the front of this new line with a continuous: "Excuse me. Pardon me. Sorry, didn't see that—oops. Here you go. Excuse me. Pardon. Important business. Coming through—oh, thank goodness—"

This last as Henri grabbed his arm and dragged him with her. "Take a number!" she shouted to the outraged scholars, then closed and locked the door.

"There were numbers?" Evan asked in some embarrassment.

"No, but it'll keep them thinking for a while." She grimaced. "So much for interstellar peace and harmony. We were doing just fine out there till the rep showed up with her big mouth. Now everyone knows there was never a problem with the trains." Henri wiped her brow with the back of her hand. "It'll be hairy till we get the landing field back and can start moving people out—including staff."

"'Never a—'" Evan stared down at her. "But what about the risk of contagion—the threat of a quarantine—the Commonwealth medship—"

"Oh. Sorry, Evan. You haven't heard. They aren't telling us much, but word is?" A finger stabbed upward. "All a hoax. No medship; just fake messages. Folks aren't happy Mal was fooled—and he looks ready to skin someone's hide, let me tell you—but it happens to the best." She shrugged. "You know the saying. Kraal can steal your toenails before you know your boots are missing."

At a loss how to respond to that, Evan didn't try. Something wasn't right—something *more* wasn't. "I need to talk to Paul or Mal. It's urgent."

A nod down the empty hall. "They're in Lionel's office. Make sure you tell that government rep what it's like out here now. And tell her she'd be more use mopping the floor! You tell her I said so."

Evan sighed. "Yes, Henri."

"Another thing." Fingers caught his sleeve. "Have you seen Esen? Paul's asking."

"No. Is something wrong?" he asked, seeing Henri's blue eyes fill with worry. *Had Esen been on the Kraal ship?* "I'll help look." Not that he'd any idea how to start.

"Couldn't begin to know where," she told him, echoing his thought, then gave him a little push. "Go help Paul finish up in there. He'll know how to find her."

"I will." About to leave, something she'd said clicked. "What did you mean, 'get the landing field back?' Why can't ships land?"

"Priority clearance's gone to two inbound ships, from Sacriss, if you believe it." Her round friendly face went hard. "Word is, one's Kraal. Guarantee you no other ships will come close while that beast's finsdown." Henri shrugged again. "Do what you can to help, Evan. We'll need all we can get."

"I promise."

The administrator's office door was closed. Having been told to enter by Correa and now Henri—who were Library staff—Evan paused to straighten his jacket before opening the door and walking inside.

This not being the first or only time he'd walked in cold on a meeting of his superiors—who typically forgot having sent for him until he showed up then found a use for him after all—Evan arranged his face in a professional *here to assist* and didn't flinch at the surprised looks sent his way.

The sharp "Who are you?" came from the head of the table. The newcomer.

Thus acknowledged, Evan faced that person and gave a bow precisely the depth to convey *desire to help with the confidence to do so*, very aware of the recorder hovering near ceiling height in one corner. As he straightened, he assessed the official's bearing, clothing, expression, and came to a quick conclusion. Henri was right. *She was trouble.* "I am Polit Evan Gooseberry, assigned to the Commonwealth Embassy on Dokeci-Na. My intergovernmental clearance level—"

"Is irrelevant." She shot a searing look at Paul. "The Commonwealth has no business here."

"Special Envoy Niala Mavis, I suggest we welcome Evan to this meeting." Paul gave him a smile. "He's a close associate, with full access to the Library."

"Who's witnessed most of the events we've described to you," the constable contributed. Lionel nodded, cementing his support.

"Very well. Onlee?" At her command, the second stranger rose and went to stand near the recorder and behind the envoy.

Before he sat, Evan bowed again. "I'm not here representing the Commonwealth, Envoy. I'm on vacation."

The corner of the envoy's mouth deepened. "You've terrible timing."

Don't contradict—but don't be diminished. Evan risked a smile. "Or the best, if I can be of service. Thank you," he said to Onlee as he took her seat, receiving a gratified look from the assistant. Superiors never paid attention.

Seated next to him, Lionel leaned over as if to speak, then shook his head.

Skalet, the other senior on staff, was conspicuously absent, giving Evan a more reasonable hypothesis as to who had taken off from Paul and Esen's backyard. Anyway, the Lanivarian detested space travel. Not points to volunteer.

Before they could restart a discussion he might not follow, Evan looked around the table. "The scholars are in an uproar." For Henri. For himself, "Is it true? The crew of the *Stellar Trumpet* weren't sick—the medship was a fake?"

"Yes," Mal said grimly. "We—I've been a pawn of the *Trium Pa*."

"We were all fooled. Would still be, but Skalet brought us the information," offered Lionel.

"At her request," Paul added, "we've pretended to believe their ruse as long as possible."

"Didn't matter. The Kraal were done," Mal said, opening his notebook and flipping to a page. "Seems their endgame was to get access to the *Stellar Trumpet*."

By the quick exchange of looks, this was news to the rest too.

"You were told to wait for my orders, Constable Lefebvre." The envoy's tone developed an edge. "I've full authority over any and all investigations and actions pertaining to the current situation."

"I know, but you weren't here yet. With respect, Envoy Mavis, we'd bodies to recover. They weren't getting any fresher."

Paul stirred. "Why are you here, exactly? I can see the Hamlet of Hillsview Preservation Committee having a provincial regulator check on us. Not a special envoy."

Her eyes were a cold blue. "The current situation came to our attention. Plague. Aliens on the loose. I assure you these things get noticed, Director."

"But you did send a request for information through the committee." Lionel spread his hands. "We agreed to full disclosure, Envoy Mavis. That goes both ways."

"The purported traffic coming through this *Library* of yours needs to be tracked and confirmed by a third party." A thin smile. "Or did you think we'd authorize construction of a shipcity and orbital station on your word?" This at Paul.

Who, to Evan's surprise, became positively gleeful. "The proposal's gone that high?"

"It'll go no higher," she warned, "if this business of missing Sacrissee and dead Kraal isn't resolved."

"It will be." If anything, Paul looked even happier.

Lionel didn't. "Envoy Mavis," he said, sounding ready to jump off a cliff, "you still haven't said why *you're* here."

A cliff it was, Evan thought, beginning to see how Lionel Kearn had dealt with his superiors in Survey.

Her hand rose, two fingers making a scissor cut in the air. Her assistant pulled down the tether and deactivated the recorder. In Evan's experience, never a good sign.

Mal closed his notebook and sat back, face inscrutable. "Like that, is it?"

"Worse," she said. The envoy's gaze went around the table, touching each face, stopping at Evan's. "What I'm about to say goes no further than this room. Polit Gooseberry, if you can't keep a secret from your government, leave now."

Evan didn't move.

"Very well. I'm here at the request of the Kraal Confederacy. They've asked for a negotiator from our government to hear some new proposition they have in mind for Botharis. The *Tesseer Ra* carries my counterpart, able to speak for the highest levels of what passes for theirs." Envoy Mavis put her hands flat on the table. She'd long fingers and strong knuckles. "Most of you know we've had such requests before from the Kraal. Those were nothing but preludes to invasion."

Paul had that *listening to more* look. "Something's different this time."

"You're right." She nodded. "The subterfuge is new. The pretense of escorting a Sacrissee delegation to the Library. Landing here. We believe this proposition is something that won't meet with favor from the lesser Houses. As those have been the ones using Botharis as a game piece?" Her hands pressed down, fingers going white, but her expression remained calm, even aloof. "I'm to ensure we won't be their latest battleground."

"They couldn't pick better for the job," Mal told her. His demeanor had changed since the recorder went off. He *knew* her, Evan realized. "But hells, Nia. Couldn't Grandine at least send some security? No offense, Onlee."

"Oh, I asked the same question," the assistant replied.

Envoy Mavis shook her head. "The Kraal want this meeting kept secret, Mal. So do we." She gave a humorless chuckle. "Officially? I am here at the request of the Hamlet of Hillsview Preservation Committee."

"What do you need from us?" Lionel asked quietly.

The envoy eased her grip on the table. "A meeting place. Neutral. Secure."

Paul nodded. "I'll arrange it. What else?"

Her look at Paul held some emotion Evan couldn't read. "Curator Esen-alit-Quar. I'm not here to deal with the Sacrissee, but they'll be a factor. Mal's told me she's your expert on the species."

"She's working on the situation," Paul replied evenly. "Until she's back, Evan's more than qualified."

Never volunteer. Evan tried to catch Paul's eye.

Too late. "Evan was accepted into the *IN* of the individuals here," Lionel confirmed. "An excellent choice."

"I'll need a briefing." Envoy Mavis looked to Evan. "If you would?"

And now he'd a task. "I'll do my best, Envoy," he replied, giving it the right touch of enthusiasm with a qualifying *I'm only a junior.*

"Let's finish this," the envoy said, opening her two fingers. Onlee reactivated the recording and the envoy, without so much as a blink, impressed Evan by picking up the conversation precisely where she'd left it. "I'm here to find out what happened. Go on, Constable. I'm sure your people did more than collect bodies from that ship."

"They took a look." Mal opened his notebook. "A grav sled's gone from the *Trumpet*'s loading bay and her cargo manifest's light by six cryo-canisters of mushrooms." He tapped the page. "If the Kraal took them, they contained something more valuable."

Paul and Lionel exchanged looks. "Whatever it is, my guess is the Kraal weren't the first to steal it," the former stated. "Good odds Molancor's here with the Sacrissee to recover their property."

"Molancor Genomics?" Finding himself the center of attention,

Evan had to keep going. "I know of the company. They've outlets on most Commonwealth worlds. Molancor specializes in helping babies born with significant medical issues." He pressed a hand to his chest. "Like me. My Great—my family told me I might not have survived without their care. What do they have to do with—" He gestured around the room.

Paul answered. "The Sacrissee who came to us, Evan, whom you met? Esen collected hair samples from their clothes and sent them for analysis. It indicated 41% of their genetic makeup was Modoran. They're chimeras. Makes me wonder if Molancor Genomics has that technology."

"Such a risk, politically as well as to the patients." Special Envoy Mavis dipped her head like a curious bird, a lock of black hair falling across her forehead. "I've met Modorans. From what I've heard of Sacrissee, they're very different. Why that blend?"

"We don't know yet. Evan? Your thoughts?"

"Unlike Sacrissee, these individuals appear aggressive. Demanding. They called themselves the Emboldened and were, I can attest. Extraordinarily bold among strangers. Willing to move in the open." Forgetting he was the junior in the room, Evan followed the trail, certain he was close to the truth. "The mere fact they could leave Sacriss System suggests that could be the ultimate goal. The Sacrissee could want to move past their species' dependence on the *IN*. It's hampered them in the past. They call interstellar space the Vast *OUT* and are forced to rely on treaties with other species for trade and protection. Including the Kraal."

"Again, the Kraal." The envoy leaned back, her eyes hooded. "You've your own. Where's your head of security? Skalet—odd name for one of them."

"For use while outside the Confederacy," Lionel said quickly. "A not uncommon need for privacy."

"Hmm."

"Skalet's investigating matters," Evan dared say. Dared assume, because if Skalet wasn't learning the motivations of the Kraal on the *Trium Pa*, she was dead. He'd heard enough of the Confederacy to be sure of that. They'd only one penalty for treason—and thousands of ways to implement it.

Lionel tensed slightly beside him. If they hadn't been sitting close, he'd have missed it. Understanding, Evan continued quietly. "Skalet is exceptionally competent."

"She's exceptionally good at avoiding meetings too. Don't give me that look, Lionel," Mal retorted. "I've no problem with your Kraal working here. Only the company she keeps."

"We weren't thrilled to have the *Trium Pa* linger in our space." But the envoy seemed grimly amused. "What's the local expression, Director Ragem? Better the Kraal you know—?"

"—than those who come hunting them," Paul finished. "The *Tesseer Ra* doesn't seem to be our hunter," he continued, plainly speaking now for the recorder. "The Library received a communication a short time ago from the government of Sacriss System stating the Kraal are on a diplomatic mission, bringing officials here with a request for the Library. No doubt their request concerns the Emboldened and these canisters."

"Neither of which we have," Mal pointed out.

"What we do have," Paul said, "is a building full of innocents, caught in the middle. We have to get them to safety. Envoy Mavis?"

A frown. "There's nothing—"

He leaned forward. "Nia. Please." Their eyes locked.

After a long moment, she nodded. "Very well. Onlee, arrange for air transports to convey the Library's guests to suitable accommodations in—" An eyebrow lifted.

"The capital?" Paul responded quickly. "Once there, their ships can land at Grandine's field."

"Make it happen, Onlee."

"Yes, Envoy."

"Thank you." Paul exhaled with relief. "Send us the bill."

Her lips twisted. "You can be sure of that."

Evan and the others stood when the special envoy rose to her feet. She turned to go, then spun back to face Paul. "Don't think this Library of yours makes a difference," she told him, a hard edge to her voice.

"Understood. Thank you." Paul offered his hand.

"No difference at all," she repeated, staring down at it.

He let his hand drop and nodded, watching her walk out the door, her assistant taking the tether to drag the recorder with them. Evan sensed an undercurrent of emotion; he couldn't tell which until he looked at Paul and saw the regret filling his eyes.

It couldn't be.

The door closed.

It was. This wasn't how the story was supposed to go, Evan thought with all the despair of his young and, yes, romantic heart. Paul was to be happy. Have Esen at his side and his lost love restored. If anyone deserved a second chance—

It was then Paul smiled at him, a sweet, sad smile that said he knew everything Evan thought and felt, thanked him for it, and asked for acceptance.

Not of this. Evan looked away.

"Well." Mal tucked his notebook into a pocket, then rubbed a hand over his face. "Kraal everywhere you look, except ours."

"I think I know where she might be—or where she's gone." Evan pulled out his holocube and keyed the image to display where they could all see it. "This was an hour ago."

"That's the *Septos Ank.* Skalet's gone to the *Trium Pa.*" Lionel turned on Paul in sudden fury. "You sent her into a trap!"

"I told her to handle it," Paul replied quietly. "She will."

A rebuke. Lionel's face hardened, but he gave a short nod.

"What about Esen?" Evan asked.

Paul shook his head, then went out the door.

"She's not answering her com," Mal said, then gave Evan a keen look. "Don't worry. My people are watching for her too. Can't see Es missing the chance to meet our new visitors."

"In the meanwhile, Evan," Lionel said gruffly. "I can use your help. Time to tell our guests they get a free trip to the capital."

Evan nodded, numb. Henri was wrong. Paul didn't know how to find Esen either.

Where was she?

31: Cave Day

S AXEL Sah didn't want the Kraal to see what she was up to—I
thought this charmingly naive of her and the other Emboldened,
given that Kraal were raised on subterfuge and these Kraal had nothing
to do but spy on those sharing their cave.

Since I had nothing else to do either, I eased myself after her as she
continued to search the wall, hoping she'd ignore me.

Yellow eyes glanced down, proving my optimism unfounded.
"Would you like to play a game, little one?" she whispered, and
crouched in front of me.

This close, the pattern of pulsing blood vessels on her nasal bulb
resembled an aerial view of a river system. River systems would be
easier for searchers to spot than our trail here, my having come to the
regrettable realization earlier today that my Karras self would have
done an excellent job of erasing any footprints beneath not only with
my wide sliding cylindrical body, but the mucus I'd smeared so abundantly with it.

Oh, dear.

"Here." Saxel held out the white disk.

I'd wanted to see the thing, not touch it, but had no choice but take
it. I needed two hands, being Bess. "What's the game?" I asked.

Not that I couldn't guess. Use an innocent child to do your dirty work. Another tactic crossing species' boundaries and, given our companions, dangerous.

She leaned closer. "This is the key to a secret door. A special door. Those who gave it to me were tricky. They told me how to find this cave, but not where to look inside. You might know better. You're their kind."

I must have frowned.

"Human," she explained, as if the multiple trillions of the species presently drawing breath had anything more in common than a briefly shared evolutionary path on the same planet.

Admittedly, more than a Sacrissee—original or chimera—could say. "I'll try," I said, then stared into her eyes. "You promise to protect me from them. They are *not* my kind."

Saxel didn't pat me on the head, the gesture of no meaning to her species, but I thought from her expression she understood. "I will. Now hurry. Play the game!"

She stood and wandered away, catching and keeping the attention of two of the Kraal.

I sighed, then tilted the "key" back and forth. There wouldn't, by Skalet-memory, be a matching keyhole. What I needed to do was bring the locator close enough to the hidden "special" door's control panel for it to activate.

Which could be on the ceiling. Less likely. Kraal and this me did share a mean maximum height and arm reach, not that I was there yet, and some convenience would have been put into the design.

Just nothing obvious. I sighed again. Saxel, who'd come to a stop near her companions, waved at me as if we were old friends. The Kraal, their attention alerted, stared at me.

I waved at them too.

Tucking the Kraal locator-key into one of the pockets of my Kraal vest, while keeping my fingers in contact, I began to aimlessly roam around the cave. As it wasn't my first time doing so—in fact, it was my seventeenth, not that I'd been counting—the Kraal stopped staring at me and went back to whatever they'd been doing.

At least I'd something to do too.

Makings

OOLA watches from hiding as another like her follows the false *howl* and enters the starship. Sees Human figures leap from the shadows to enter behind. Springing their trap.

She will not allow it again.

Though it isn't instinct, isn't natural, when she sees the next approach, Oola gives a tiny *howl* of her own to draw them into her shadow. Her *IN*.

She finds comfort in being two, no longer alone. The other is younger and male. Has the pale blue writing on the back of his hand. AULE-TB356994. Shuddering with fear and confusion, he can't form words, can't tell her his real name.

Aule she thinks of him as she pulls him close and grooms his face.

When the next is drawn toward the trap, Aule *howls* with her to bring the other to their tiny *IN*.

And when the Humans find them—

They fight together.

32: Cave Day

A hand clamped over my arm, plucking me from a promising crevice. "What are you up to?" Shirt demanded.

"Looking for bats," I told her. "My Da says there are always bats in caves and I've seen one, you know, right up close and it was soft and fluffy and—"

"Bats bite and carry disease," the Kraal informed me, giving me a shake. "Do not find bats."

Her grip hurt, so it wasn't hard to make my lower lip tremble and my eyes fill with tears. Though I was tempted to correct her on behalf of the harmless and helpful Botharan species, I settled for a sullen, "I promise."

"Good. Now go sit with your soft furry friends." She shoved me toward the Emboldened.

I managed not to fall, but the Emboldened rose as one, tails lashing with displeasure. "I'm fine," I told them, preferring not to start a disagreement with those armed to the teeth. My "furry friends" didn't have the sense of a Bess, giving me the added burden of being responsible for my seeming elders.

"Sit here," Acklan offered as they sat again, patting the rock beside him.

Saxel held out her hand. Aware of the Kraal's attention, I took it in mine as if that was what she wanted, sliding onto her knee and curling into her body. A body stiffened with offense at the contact, so I didn't delay putting the locator-key into her other, hidden hand. She relaxed at once.

Then dumped me on the floor, making the Kraal laugh.

"I've checked a third of the cave," I whispered, curving my lips in a smile as if the rock wasn't hard and my feelings weren't a little hurt. *There'd been no need for dumping.* "I can't look where they're sitting," in case they thought that a good plan.

"Why not give them the locator-key?" Maston proposed quietly. "It was the arrangement."

Not a good plan! Before I could object—straining credulity even with the non-Human—Acklan spoke up. "Yes. These are House Arzul. They show us their faces in trust."

It seemed unkind to tell them the more likely reason the Kraal had shed their too-warm masks was because they didn't care if the Emboldened saw their affiliations. Meaning I wasn't the only witness the Kraal didn't intend to leave alive to speak. *Not that they'd believe this me.*

Maston moved uneasily. "Those who came to us were not Arzul."

"Yet were of our *IN*." Acklan's tail moved restlessly. "Did they not tell us our shipment was secured? Did they not take our place so we could leave to hunt without interference?"

"They were of our *IN*," Saxel agreed, to a chorus of pleased "huffft, hufffts."

I was horrified. Skalet wouldn't be. What a Kraal after true glory sought most from life was death—specifically a meaningful, remembered death—and while I'd argued to Ersh the end result would select against selfless bravery and commitment to the chain of command? The Kraal had thought of that. Those heading into battle situations banked germ tissue, knowing the greater their perceived glory, the more in demand their ultimate contribution to the Kraal gene pool would be.

Acklan's unpleasant revelation explained what I knew had troubled Mal and Paul—and probably Lionel, if not Evan the innocent. Three armed Kraal assassins versus three surprised and unarmed beings? Bone-tipped tails and poisoned claws against personal body armor and shields?

In Skalet-terms, the more credible scenario was that House Bract, acting through the *Trium Pa*'s captain, had ordered the three to sacrifice themselves. We would have believed the Emboldened dead and not looked beyond the Kraal for why, had Paul not had me sniff out the truth.

One I would not be surprised my web-kin guessed for herself.

Three dead, along with the crew of the *Trumpet* and quite possibly soon the Emboldened and their stolen embryos, to find this "forgotten" cave and a few crates of old weapons. Even by Kraal standards, where was the glory?

Saxel's nasal bulb inflated, then gave that low shuddering *howl*. "We trust those of our *IN,* no one else." Her yellow eyes found me, something cold in their depths. "No more talking."

While I could argue that was the single worst way to keep a Human child quiet, not being one gave me a useful depth of understanding. I closed my mouth and sat still.

It was going to be a long afternoon.

Elements

THE All Species' Library of Linguistics and Culture was empty. Lionel walked the echoing corridors with Evan, trying not to shiver with apprehension, but this could be real. This could be the future and not just the aftermath of a flood of grateful scholars evacuated from their semi-imprisonment, not to mention an exhausted staff grateful to go home.

The Library could stay empty, its dream dead, and he didn't know how to stop it. Not when the one person with power looked at Paul Ragem with such hate.

And at him. Niala Mavis didn't spare him. He supposed he—

"Rather peaceful, don't you think?" Evan asked, free of Lionel's worries. "For a change."

"It's not supposed to be," he replied, unable to keep frustration from his voice.

"I know. But they'll be back—maybe not these scholars," Evan qualified, "but Carwyn said there's a backlog of ships waiting to land. Surely, that's good news."

"Once we clear the field, my friend, which means resolving whatever problems the *Tesseer Ra* and Molancor brought with them as well as whatever's going on with the Emboldened and Kraal already here." *And hope S'kal-ru prevailed.*

"Plus find Esen," Evan added to the list, no longer smiling.

"Indeed." He lightened his tone. "Esen's fine, you'll see. Mal's people have her by now, or she's home with Lesley." *Gather your wits,* he warned himself.

Paul's head appeared in the entrance to the Chow. "There you are," with forced cheer.

Lionel wasn't fooled. "She wasn't in the Lobby." Evan had helped him look into the various tent-iterations in the Lobby and walkway. "Though there are—" He paused, searching for the right word to describe what the scholars had left for maintenance.

"Remnants?" Evan supplied helpfully.

"So many remnants." He made a face. "We'd best quadruple the pay for maintenance this week."

"Noted." Paul beckoned them inside. "Lambo, a quick bite, if you please."

"I don't," came a disgusted rumble. "I should be closed and on holiday, like everyone else. Except you," with a thoughtful click. "You don't take holidays. It isn't healthy."

"Maybe not," Paul agreed, "but we're still in the midst of a crisis, even if it's smaller."

Eyestalks converged. "You haven't found Esen."

"We will."

Paul smiled at Evan.

"Have you news from Skalet?" Lionel did his best to make the question seem ordinary. "A change in the *Trium Pa*'s orbit?" And wasn't that his other fear, that she'd leave?

"No to both."

"Here is food." the Carasian rumbled, dropping three small wrapped objects on the counter. "Kraal are the problem. Kraal are the solution."

Paul took his and lifted it in thanks. "Kraal have been Botharis' particular problem far too long. But why now?"

A claw snap. "Duggs said because you made this place."

"For their use too."

"And Esen said that." The giant grumbled to himself. "You should find her."

"Damn right," Paul said under his breath. Louder. "In the meantime, Evan? Special Envoy Mavis is ready for her briefing on the Sacrissee."

"Are you sure I should do it?" Evan swallowed. "The envoy wasn't pleased I crashed her meeting."

"She got over it." Paul slid down the wall, making himself comfortable on the floor. "She was more upset I was there." Lionel saw him give Evan a sad little smile. "Lionel knows too. About Nia. The love I wasted." He took a bite as if nothing was wrong.

He didn't fool anyone. "Isn't there something you could do?" Evan turned to Lionel, his green eyes pleading.

"No, Evan." Paul waved his free hand. "This isn't about Lionel, or my past. This is about clinging to a dream when reality is—when reality is what it is. Now. Eat up, both of you. Nia needs us to help her save the world—or at least keep the Sacrissee busy while she does. Evan, I'd like you to call your Great Gran."

"About Molancor."

A bright, quick mind came with that soft heart and good nature. Despite the emotions in the room, his own worry close to pain, Lionel found he could smile after all. "Yes, Evan. We've people trying to get information," he explained, "but it's not going to happen before their ship lands. Anything you and your family might know could help."

"Finish food then talk," Lambo ordered. "Don't waste my extraordinary efforts when I should be on a holiday."

Lionel unwrapped one end of his "extraordinary effort" to find a piece of something pale and possibly meatish—or fish, by the smell—encased in limp cooked leaves. He scowled at the Carasian. "You can do better than this."

Every eyestalk scowled back. "You should have come for breakfast."

Evan, on the floor beside Paul, looked up. "It's tasty."

"Don't humor him," Lionel grumbled, still glaring.

"Lionel wants to be angry." The eyestalks tilted into smug. "Good."

"I don't—" He subsided, because Lambo wasn't wrong.

Paul rolled up his wrapper and stood. "We don't need anger or fear," he said firmly. "We need to trust our friends to do their best, and do ours. Lambo—I'm promoting you to the Library's acting head of security. While Lionel and I take care of some business, I want you to stay with Polit Gooseberry and keep order."

Lionel looked up. "What—"

The Carasian leapt over the counter, landing with a crash as though every pot in the Ragem kitchen had hit the tiles. "I will take heads!" he roared, snapping his great claws in the air.

Evan bolted for the door, coming to a halt when Paul chuckled. "That's the spirit."

"You're sure about this?" Lionel whispered to his friend.

"Of course he's sure. And very smart," Lambo rumbled. "For someone who can be smart, Administrator Kearn, you are stupid."

"As head of security—" Paul continued, ignoring them both, "—I expect you to ensure our communications are not overheard by the Kraal—or anyone else, for that matter."

Ah. Lionel suddenly understood. Paul knew the Carasian continued to do his own research. He didn't know the topic had shifted—that secret still kept by Esen, Skalet, and himself—but the level of subterfuge required to bypass Library security meant Lambo should have the capability and knowledge. The best they had without Skalet here.

Eyestalks whirled, then a handling claw thrust out. "Give me your holocube, Evan Gooseberry."

Evan drew it back to his chest.

"Go ahead, Evan," Paul ordered. "Lambo won't go into your personal data or damage it."

Then he looked straight at Lionel. "You'll need your coat."

He was no expert, but to Lionel's nose the Ragem barn smelled like a barn should, with the exception of no recent livestock. From inside, the huge structure was unsettlingly airy, with gaps between immense wooden planks letting in air and sunlight.

And snow. He stepped over the next fingerlike drift. "You could seal this up," he commented.

Paul half smiled. "Barns have to breathe, Lionel. So long as the roof's snug?" He gestured grandly to the crisscrossing maze of timbers overhead, each gripping the other in a centuries-proven mutual solidity. The roof they supported was, as far as Lionel could see, free of holes.

Given a beer or four, Duggs would go on for hours, extolling her mostly profane admiration not only for the original builders and those who hadn't meddled with what worked since, but also the Botharan trees they'd had at their disposal. There remained forests of the giants, but modern Botharans valued them more now as wilderness habitat.

Duggs didn't feel they'd miss a couple.

"We're going to miss her. Duggs," Lionel clarified.

"She'd every right to be angry." Paul led the way into the large boxed-in area used, Lionel'd been told, by earlier generations as a nursery for the Botharan equivalent to sows with new piglets. His friend rested a hand on a well-gnawed strip of wood and gave Lionel a somber look. "But it wasn't the tents—wasn't only that. Duggs has known we weren't fully honest with her. About the Library." He patted the wood. "About this. Offworlders doing special projects—plans with gaps in them. It was a matter of time before she'd had enough."

"You couldn't tell her about Esen," Lionel protested.

"No. But if she'd stayed?" A pained shrug. "We could be safer without her, Lionel, much as I hate to admit it."

Because if anyone might have discovered the truth, it was Duggs.

"Come on." After a survey of their surroundings that appeared habit, Paul knocked on the wood.

The floor opened, revealing a set of rough wooden stairs.

"Now can you tell me where we're going?" Lionel asked.

Paul, already on the second step, turned to look up at him. He didn't smile. "We're testing a relationship."

The stairs led back in time, the flight ending in a tidy cold cellar. Neatly labeled jars filled shelves of wood worn from generations of such use. Sacks of vegetables were stacked on the floor. There was even a floor-to-ceiling rack for wine bottles, mostly empty, but with a few laid on their sides, and Lionel began to frown. "I don't see—"

"That's the idea. This way and quickly." Paul walked through the wine rack and vanished.

"How—" Lionel could touch the bottles. Pick one up. The entire rack felt solid. Paul stepped out again, but he still couldn't see the moment or the door. "I really need you to explain this," he said wonderingly. "This—this isn't Human."

A grin. "It's not. This is Smootian flicker-tech. They use it to build settlements inside ice caps before anyone else notices their presence. It isn't something they often share. Esen and I made some friends."

Of course they had.

"This protects the Library collection. There are other ways in; this is Esen's favorite." Paul moved his hand quickly, passing it through a bottle, then slowed and tapped it with a finger. "Empty, by the way. The entry flickers open—temporarily deconstructs the rack and bottles—when triggered by movement at a preset speed. There's a persona-lock as well. I can pass, and any Esen. Skalet. I think you can too."

Lionel frowned. "You 'think'?"

"Give it a try. If you're not authorized, you'll feel as if you've walked into the rack. Put an arm over your face—just in case."

"You think Skalet authorized me." Lionel looked at the rack, seeing her lean scarred face, her cool analytical gaze. "You're testing our relationship. But why would she?"

"If she did—if you can pass through—you'll know."

An actual test of her trust. The desire for it, for proof he mattered in some way to such a remarkable being, made Lionel tremble inside. "If I can't—that would change everything, Paul. I won't be—I couldn't work with her, not after that. Not the same way."

"I understand." With compassion. "But if she's left us a message, it's through there."

Making fear a betrayal, if he let it decide for him.

So be it.

Arms down, Lionel walked forward as if the rack wasn't there.

He found himself standing in an ordinary lift, like any in the Library other than having doors with persona-locks on either side. Paul appeared through the wall right after him and clapped him on a shoulder. "Now we know."

"We do," Lionel agreed, more numb than relieved. "What now?"

Paul activated the lift. "That," he pointed to one door, "will open into the collection. The other to Skalet's private quarters. Her access only, until now."

The lift traveled deeper than the two basement levels of the Library building. It still stopped before Lionel was in any sense ready. "There could be poison," he warned.

"I'm sure that's the least of it." Paul indicated the ominous waiting panel. "One way to find out."

"It's revenge, isn't it." Lionel told his friend. "For what I made you do in specialist training. You finally found the means."

A chuckle. "Look at it this way, Lionel. Skalet's many things. Inefficient isn't one of them."

"So if she wanted me dead, I already would be? Charming thought." But it was, oddly, reassuring. He took a slow breath, glanced once at Paul, then put his hand on the lock.

Lights played over his face. He felt a vibration underfoot, as if something else measured his mass or some other characteristic. Then, Skalet's voice: "You aren't alone, Lionel. If you are being coerced, you will both be dead in 1.5 seconds. 1.4—"

"I am not coerced," Lionel said, interrupting the ghastly countdown. "I'm with Director Paul Ragem and authorize entry for us both."

Lights played over Paul's face. "Confirmed," the voice said. "Are you sure, Lionel?"

It was as if she stood there, waiting for his answer, judging him by it. There could be only one reason. They'd kept a secret from Paul, and there must be something in her quarters that would reveal it.

Skalet trusted him with the choice. *Would Paul trust him again, if he made the wrong one?*

It was time. "I'm sure. Let us both enter."

33: Cave Day

I'D counted another two hours, two minutes, and forty-two seconds before anything notable happened in the cave. While the number itself had a pleasing symmetry—had I been a Quebit—the notable thing was a communication received by the Kraal.

And their reaction, for after conferring briefly, the trio jumped to their feet in startling unison and began to arm themselves.

Sensibly alarmed, the Emboldened rose too, giving their *howls.* "Are we under attack?" Saxel Sah demanded.

"Give us weapons!" The other female lashed her tail against the wall, cracking rock and making the request slightly redundant.

As suited this me, I shrank into a corner to watch.

Shirt sent Vest across the cave. He approached with his hands open and wide, stopping out of tail reach. "We've received a report," he told the Emboldened. "A Kraal cruiser, the *Tesseer Ra,* has landed, claiming to carry Sacrissee officials. The *Tesseer Ra* is of House Virul, which sits in opposition to the rightful expansion of House Arzul to this world." He touched the back of his hands to his cheeks. "Are these Sacrissee affiliates of yours? Is this expected?"

"It is predictable. They would cull us from existence. They are our enemies." Saxel's tail stroked a canister. "And yours. Last night your captain assured me our plans were underway. Has that changed? Does this one ship scare House Arzul? Is it mightier than your *Trium Pa?*"

The other two Kraal came up during this, the anger in their faces enough to make this me wish to be even smaller. *Possibly a Quebit.* Fortunately, their displeasure focused on the Emboldened. "We take precautions. Captain's dropped early with our forces. Due to proximity of the *Tesseer Ra,*" Shirt gritted out, "we're to go dark. No outgoing communication until our reinforcements arrive."

"Surely they will not move *OUT* during the day—they will be exposed and expose us!" From Acklan, showing I wasn't the only one to have checked the weather beforehand. "We must defend ourselves."

A chorus of *howls!* From my lower vantage point, I could see claw-tips beginning to show. Kraal hands moved closer to weapons.

Not good. I prepared to be a distraction.

"We could split up," Socks said, looking at Shirt. "Move the assets to that cabin—"

I didn't need Skalet-memory to translate that into *be rid of the witnesses sooner than later.*

I could explode—

"We do not go *OUT!*" Saxel's tail struck the floor. "This *IN* is our side of the arrangement." She lashed out again and held up the locator-key. "You are servants who are uninformed and unimportant. Your task is to protect us. To protect this."

"We've got the cave and weapons—"

Shirt thrust up her hand to silence the other Kraal. "Then inform us," she said, her face set and hard.

The Emboldened put their faces together to "huffft, hufffts." When they drew apart, Saxel lifted the locator-key like a talisman. "This opens a second door, one inside this cave. A door to a legendary treasure hidden here long ago by House Noitci. This treasure means glory for House Arzul and House Bract, and will ensure our joined future on this world."

Why would Kraal give the means to find their treasure on Botharis to a Sacrissee, not another Kraal? Admittedly, Kraal weren't welcome on the planet, but non-Humans were even more conspicuous. We'd enough paperwork bringing them through on our trains.

Unless Noitci had had no choice. If that House lacked trusted affiliation in the Sacriss System through which to pass the locator-key to either Arzul or Bract, a simple, commonplace transaction would be a safe alternative.

From there it made sense. Who better to find this cave, appallingly close to our Library, than that most ordinary of arrivals: aliens come with a question? As for the timing, Arzul and Bract would have their own reasons for urgency, but I thought the Emboldened hadn't lied. Their desperation provided the Kraal with opportunity.

Still, what did Noitci gain by elevating two other houses? What sort of treasure was it? *Skalet would know.*

I saw doubt in Shirt's face before greed erased it. "We must find the keyhole. Give me the locator-key."

Claws came out. "First, you will swear a blood oath to protect us and our future."

Saxel knew her Kraal after all.

Elements

EVAN stared moodily at the door through which Paul and Lionel had left, wishing—wishing he could fix things. Not that people were things to be fixed, nor were their relationships any of his business, but it wasn't fair—that Paul had longed all these years for Nia and she, well, she hadn't longed for Paul.

Not like he did. Evan allowed himself a small, heartfelt sigh.

"It's ready."

"What? Oh. Thank you." He took his poor little holocube from between those sharp clawtips gingerly, wary of the white block and wires now affixed to the device. "Is all this part of it now?" He certainly hoped not. It'd never fit in his pocket, for one thing.

A clatter suspiciously like a laugh. "You will return my equipment, Evan Gooseberry, once you obtain the information the director needs."

"I'll call Great Gran now," he said. "She's probably expecting it. I hung up on her this morning."

"Good. Hurry. I need to inspect the meeting room." A claw snap. "As the new head of security, I must be vigilant!"

Evan hoped Paul knew what he was doing, giving Lambo the job. *Not his decision.* One plus. The giant creature didn't need weapons to be intimidating. The mere notion of Lambo with a blaster made him queasy. "Calling," he said, and focused on the cube. It appeared to work normally.

There. "Great Gran."

"Evan! How lovely. Who was that?"

"Oh, the ship? Someone from the Library. Great Gran, I don't have—"

"Why is there a Carasian looking over your shoulder? And such a handsome one, too. Hello."

Evan turned his head and almost hit a gleaming black eyestalk with his nose.

"Hello, Female Antecedent of Evan Gooseberry," boomed the Carasian. "I am Lambo Reomattatii, Head of Security. Yes, I am very handsome."

"Security? Evan, why do you need security?" Great Gran looked alarmed. "Is something wrong?"

"No, Great Gran. Lambo and I are setting up a diplomatic meeting. It's standard procedure." Evan wished he could elbow the Carasian away, but he'd only bruise himself. "I need to ask you about Molancor Genomics."

To his consternation, her alarm deepened. "Whatever for?"

"The company's sending a delegation to our meeting. I was hoping for a bit of background. So I say the right things. You told me they did some procedures—to help me as a baby?"

"Now you listen to me, Evan. You don't mention that. Not to any of them."

Evan felt, more than heard, the Carasian's interested rumble. "But—"

She leaned into the vid until all he could see were her huge troubled eyes. "Molancor likes keeping tabs on its patients. I didn't hold with that. I don't. They did what they did. Saved you, and your fathers and I were grateful, but I told them that you were a Gooseberry, in my care, and they'd better back off. They weren't agreeable, so I took them to court. Don't come to their attention again, Evan. Promise me."

He didn't like any of this, but— "I promise, Great Gran, but this isn't anything to do with me. We think Molancor might be involved in the production of chimeras. That's when two—"

"I know what it is. There's no 'might' about anything Molancor can or would do. You stay clear of them," more sharply than he could ever remember her speaking to him.

As if she noticed, too, her voice suddenly gentled. "Trust me, dearest boy. Put all this aside until you can come home and we have our conversation. It's overdue, Evan, and I'm sorry. But until then," firmly, "our family matters aren't to be discussed over coms or with—no offense, Hom Reomattatii, but some things are private."

The link went dead. "She hung up first," Evan said numbly. "Great Gran never hangs up first."

"Her information was useful. A confirmation of suspicion, plus a new tactic to learn more." A triumphant snap of a claw. "If this company maintains contact with patients, they may prove the easier source of data."

Evan didn't listen, his mind whirling. *Have a conversation—*about what? Great Gran gleefully told his friends and, yes, even strangers about him on coms—if he forgot and answered when not alone. In embarrassing, if flattering detail.

What sort of family matter would she consider private? *What had Molancor* done *to him and his twin?* The question made him tremble, brought up echoes of distant, buried *FEAR—*

A claw nudged Evan in the back. "We must go and prepare the meeting room." Eyestalks whirled. "Which room is it?"

Evan snapped to attention. Gooseberry secrets could wait and must. "It's not a room," he told Lambo. "We're meeting on a train."

The train had been Paul's idea, a way to meet on neutral ground while avoiding the alien *remnants* filling the Lobby with the unmistakable aroma of overcrowded, undercleaned space station. Had Botharis had a space station, it would have been the ideal place to gather, safely above the planet. When Evan suggested building one would be a good idea, Envoy Mavis had stared at him, then shaken her head in seeming disgust.

The train it would be. Trains, because one sat waiting at the landing field station, Goff Cameron sent to prepare and operate it. A second train was warming up outside the Library's main entrance, and the two would meet midway, in the hills. The passenger cars would be coupled— a detail Evan trusted wasn't part of his job—with the meeting held in the car from the Library.

The Library's passenger cars were designed for use by an assortment of body forms and enviro-suits, with seating and stanchions able to slide along tracks in the floor and ceiling to offer support in different configurations.

Previous users, however, hadn't damaged the furnishings.

"Two snoops," Lambo announced with satisfaction, dangling the crushed devices in question from a claw. He'd clambered through the car and over the roof with deplorable glee, leaving scrapes, a bent stanchion, and dented chairbacks, to Evan's dismay. "Kraal tech."

Evan winced. "Can you tell if they were Skalet's?"

"Do you think so?" the Carasian asked cheerfully, as if unaware of catastrophe. "Could be. The chassis are weathered. They've been in place for months. Perhaps since the train was operational."

"I don't suppose you could put them back—forget I asked," as Lambo squeezed the devices into pancakes.

The original car design hadn't had provision for a meeting, but Evan and Lambo—mostly Lambo—had wrestled in three collapsible tables from a Library storeroom and set them up, clipping their ends together.

Tables Lambo, for reasons only clear to the mind within those pulsating plates, immediately tested to learn if they'd hold his weight. The answer being no, they'd two tables, the third in shattered pieces tossed outside the train car.

"It'll do," Evan declared, satisfied.

Human needs considered, it was time to prepare for the Sacrissee. After tilting a bench seat on its hinge, Evan set the car windows for opaque, leaving thin strips like peepholes open to the view. There wasn't much to be done about a floor meant to be hosed regularly, but Evan, finding the car chilly once he removed his coat, raised the ambient temperature a few degrees.

Embassy security liked it when guests didn't wear coats.

"How's this?"

Evan looked up to find the Carasian had wedged himself between vertical hand—or whatever—holds and the ceiling, great claws hanging free almost to the floor as if ready to sever body parts. "Terrifying," he admitted.

"Indeed," the Special Envoy said as she entered the car. "We want a productive meeting, Lambo, not to have our guests refuse to enter the car." Amused.

Amused suited Niala Mavis. Evan tried a tentative smile. "How's the rest?"

She took her time, walking around the joined tables. "The windows?"

"The Sacrissee will be more at ease if they don't feel exposed to the *OUT*—that's what they call outside. The Kraal will want to see their surroundings, hence the slits."

A nod. "Good. Will we be able to offer refreshments, or does the train shake too much?"

Evan took offense on behalf of the Library. "The trains are wonderfully smooth. What service would you like?"

"Serpitay for the Kraal. What's the equivalent for Sacrissee?"

Finally a question straight to his expertise. "Vegetable juice. Root vegetables, room temperature."

Lambo dropped with a thud that rocked the train car, pointing with a handling claw to a sealed jug. "I brought that."

"Thank you. Lambo, as acting head of security, I'd appreciate your advice to my assistant about where to position her recorder. Onlee's in the next car."

A proud snap, and Lambo edged sideways past the tables, squeezing through the connecting doors with a scraping sound.

"Polit Gooseberry?" The envoy took one of the Human-suited seats and gestured to the next.

The briefing. He eased down, assuming his *ready to inform* expression with a slight undertone of *doesn't know everything* caution. The rules were not to volunteer and not to speak before your senior, which Evan found increasingly difficult when all she did was look at him. Finally, he swallowed and ventured a courteous, "How may I assist you, Special Envoy Mavis?"

"Nia, please." She'd a generous mouth. Now it curved in a real smile. "You're my first interstellar diplomat, Evan. I admit, I'm impressed."

"I thought you were annoyed." Evan felt his face grow hot and added hurriedly, "I'm sorry. I shouldn't have said that."

Her smile grew. "No, you're right. I apologize for being rude to you.

This entire situation?" A sweep of fingers through the air. "It's not enough to prevent another Kraal bloodbath. We—the Botharan government—have an opportunity to show the rest of the universe we aren't ignorant or unwelcoming."

Evan raised his eyebrows. "You approve of the Library?" *Not what he'd expected.*

"How could I not? The All Species' Library of Linguistics and Culture has been a breath of fresh air on a world still figuring itself out. We're young, Evan, by Commonwealth standards. By most standards. Young and without much to offer." She leaned forward, eyes intent. "Unfortunately, the Library's a single building, in a rural, remote area. Most Botharans don't know it exists and wouldn't understand if they did."

"You do. I'm glad," he dared tell her.

If wary. This was a career politician, a highly ranked and accomplished one, the sort whose skills included making you believe anything she wanted. The sort who wouldn't necessarily lie—

Just never tell the whole truth. At the thought, Evan sat straighter, unconsciously shifting his demeanor to what Trili called his ambassador-to-be look. "What do you want from today, Nia?"

She sat back, reassessing. "A tomorrow," she said finally. "I'd settle for that, with Kraal boots on the ground. Our history together isn't a good one, Polit. I can't say I like how this new chapter has started."

He did some reassessing of his own. "Then use the assets at your disposal. If anyone can get you that tomorrow—and with the Kraal—I guarantee it's Esen-alit-Quar and Paul."

A finger traced a mark on the table. "'Guarantee.' Strong word."

"I stand by it," Evan replied. "They saved the Mareepavlovax on Dokeci-Na because they understood the motivations and key factors before anyone else. Did the same on Urgia Prime, and if your world wants to be on the interspecies' stage? Paul, Esen, and their Library are your greatest resource."

"He still inspires—" Her cheeks gained color, as if she'd said more than she meant. "I'll take your recommendation, Evan. I do believe in the Library," this softer. "Even today, under the strain, I see how important it is. The promise here. Esen—have you heard if she'll join us?"

"I'm sure she'll be here soon." *If not*, Evan thought, *they'd lose Paul to the search.*

"Very well." Nia sat back. "You'll be with me, Evan, but whatever you can tell me in advance will help." She tapped the table. "First, the Sacrissee. Common pitfalls." Another tap. "Second, these chimeras—how to address that topic if it comes up. Third—"

The pair set to work, Evan grateful to concentrate on anything but the question that wouldn't leave him alone. The one whimpering at the back of his mind like a *FEAR* he'd yet to face.

What had Molancor done to him?

It had a shadow, one he couldn't bear to examine because if he did, nothing would be the same again.

What was he?

34: Cave Day

THE search proved several things to me, most previously known from Ersh-memory or suspected, but it was gratifying to have evidence of my own.

Treasure hunting lowered the effective intelligence of participants, regardless of species.

Treasure hunting diminished the tolerance of the participants for one another, regardless of species.

And, a personal favorite, treasure hunting made me disappear.

Having some concern Saxel would try to enlist me again, I'd initially tried not catch her eye. I needn't have worried. The Kraal and Emboldened worked out an interesting compromise, neither ready to trust the other, taking turns to hunt in pairs with the locator-key. Saxel with Shirt, Acklan with Socks, and Maston with Vest.

While each pair went through the cave in what I'm sure they believed a systematic approach to keyhole hunting, the other two pairs watched them as if they might find the treasure and vanish with it if not watched.

I could have jumped up and down and shouted and they wouldn't have noticed. Had I known how to open the cave door to escape, I might have managed that, too.

Not that I didn't take full advantage of their fixation on the unfindable. I helped myself to more rations and water, then borrowed a Kraal belt to snug the shirt and vest around my thin middle. Folding one of the Kraal sleep sacks, I made myself comfortable.

Maston and Vest were the more vigorous searchers, tossing aside whatever was in their way. Maston occasionally lost her temper and would slam the locator-key against the rock as if that might help it work. Her partner would swear at her and try to take it. She'd hit him with her tail and they'd move on to the next spot.

On the surface, Socks and Acklan were more cooperative. Socks used her knife to etch lines into the rock, marking out a nice grid pattern. Acklan would pass the locator-key from corner to corner and side to side within each indicated block. When the result proved negative, Socks would put an X in the block.

Acklan would slam the X with her tail tip, rock would flake off, and the nice grid develop gaps. Socks would redraw the line, swearing under her breath, and it went on like this until I couldn't stop yawning.

Shirt and Saxel, as befitted leaders, spent their turn trying to outsmart each other and arguing over which patch of wall to investigate first. That went on until Saxel tossed the locator-key to Maston and that pair took over.

I didn't intend to help them. Helping them, I reasoned, wasn't helping this me, who was safer ignored. That said, I was used to helping—granted, helping people who deserved help, but helping was of itself a reward. According to Paul, and he was almost always right about everything.

The problem was those searching thought they were being thorough, but they weren't. There were at least two small portions of the wall each pair missed every time. One was inset sufficiently to be in shadow even when a Kraal waved a hand light. The other jutted out like a fist. I'd no idea why they unthinkingly avoided it, unless it appeared nothing more than a loose bit of rock.

If I were inclined to gamble, I'd put my credits on the inset spot. It had that classic keyhole look from a storyvid—*always interesting*—but more importantly, it had been behind stacked crates.

If I were going to hide something, I'd hide something else in front of it. A tactic I thought Skalet would favor—if she'd thought of it first. Thinking of my web-kin, I felt an unusual longing for her Kraal-self to walk into the cave. Rudy was formidable, but S'kal-ru the Courier would have my captors begging to die for her. *Literally.*

Such flawed personal ambition made the Kraal what they were—and would end them eventually—but for now, I was confident Shirt, Socks, and Vest would fall to their knees before my web-kin. Who was, no doubt, too busy cowing more important Kraal—ideally the captain of the *Trium Pa*—to bother helping me.

I didn't like being in the midst of Kraal plots and counterplots.

Most of all, I didn't like being in a cave with something so many of them wanted to find. Especially as Bess. Paul wasn't going to be pleased. If he'd any hint of the trouble I was in, he'd be frantic, and if Kraal were dangerous?

They'd learn what my friend would do.

Which wasn't going to happen. Paul wasn't going to put himself at risk to save me, when I'd put myself in the cave and at risk in the first place. I really needed a plan.

All at once, I came up with one.

I began taking stealthy looks at the fist spot on the wall. Socks had had to etch around it to make her grid. In fact, the way it was constantly being missed made the spot so obvious, it might just be the one.

Proving something else about treasure hunting. If you sneak looks at something often enough, other treasure hunters pay attention.

Elements

LIONEL Kearn's skin crawled, his mouth gone painfully dry. Skalet's permission was no substitute for her presence. She belonged here, in this most private of sanctuaries. No one else. White everywhere, but the black of weapons arranged on one wall. A ornate knife embedded in another. Clean and stark. Elegant.

Unspoiled, until they'd walked in.

She'd known they would. Paired images floated in the air between them, left to greet them. The time for secrets was over.

Unable to read Paul's expression through the wrecks of starships and patterns of stars, worried about his reaction, Lionel finished his explanation. "It's why Janet Chase—Victory Johnsson—went after your father, then came to Botharis. She had this and—" Lionel coughed and went on, "It came to Esen. Someone had found the *Sidereal Pathfinder* and sent this image."

"Mother's ship."

The voice was unreadable, too, as if Paul Ragem held everything close, let nothing out, and Lionel couldn't blame him. "We were looking for answers—"

"'We'?"

Fraught that word, but Lionel had made his decision. *The truth.* "Skalet and myself. I enlisted Lambo to help. The Carasian's a drive engineer and was already—"

"Esen."

There it was. "And Esen." Lionel didn't bother trying to explain, to soften it. Paul knew Esen's motivations—her heart, that so-Human term—better than anyone. "They didn't recognize the frame around the image. It's not in their shared memories."

"A new-to-her species. Gods. It'd be like fudge." At last Paul moved, but only to shake his head. "I knew Esen was hiding something. I'd hoped it was Lesy, but—I knew it was more." A silence Lionel didn't interrupt.

Then, firm and clear. "And now we've a Kraal wreck near Botharis. If the starfield rendering is reliable?"

"I believe it is. Our analysis of the *Pathfinder* image found no tampering or overlay. The ships could have been moved to their specific locations." Lionel shrugged. "That seems unlikely, but until we know more, we can't exclude the possibility."

"Shown within similar frames . . . presumably to convey the same message." Stars reflected in sober gray eyes. "You've a working hypothesis?"

"When it was only the *Pathfinder,* lost in unexplored space, the most plausible scenario was a reaction to trespass. We'd gone where we weren't welcome. Now?" Lionel put a hand beneath what remained of the Kraal ship. "This feels like a conversation. Dreadfully one-sided, so far." He looked at his friend. "Paul, we can't ignore the connection with your mother. Her ship. Now her home world."

"We do today." Spoken as a command. "The *Tesseer Ra* sent this— and they sent it to S'kal-ru the Courier, not our head of security. If it's a request for information, we have to trust she's careful what she provides. But asking for a Botharan negotiator with authority? That's deal-making. The Kraal won't reveal this image to Nia. We can't do it for them."

Lionel nodded. "To protect Skalet."

"And Botharis. This image? It's proof of weakness. Houses have fallen for less and we can't destabilize the Kraal who might—just might—be here to propose peace." A show of teeth to make Esen proud. "Unless we need them to fall."

He'd been so proud of Skalet's trust. Was relieved to keep Paul's, but

Lionel frowned. "She let us in here for a reason. Now you say there's nothing we can do."

"Nothing we dare do, not before having more answers. Have other such images been received? If so, by whom? Did the frame-makers find these ships as derelicts, or act against them?" Paul eased his tone. "We pretend we didn't see these." He swept his hand through the Kraal image, dispelling it. Hesitated before doing the same to his mother's ship. "I could wish you'd told me sooner."

"I'm sorry. Esen—she didn't want more rumors about Veya to hurt you. Neither did I."

"Poor Old Blob," Paul said, his expression softening. "That's why she was so emotional when I showed her Starfield the Very Strange Pony."

"The what?" Lionel felt he could be forgiven a smidge of confusion.

"The toy Mother left for me to find—the secret message she'd sent with Stefan? Esen was with me when I found it. When I learned Mother never believed I'd died and that she trusted me to come home when I could. If not for the accident," Paul let his grief show, "she'd have been here to welcome me."

"About that." Lionel steeled himself. "Paul, we're no longer sure it was an accident. Lambo discovered the rest of the *Pathfinder*'s crew had vanished. I—the circumstances are suspicious."

A brief silence, then, "You've been digging into Survey records? Lionel, we both know they'd love another shot at you. What were you thinking?"

"That Veya Ragem can no longer defend herself." The look on Paul's face made Lionel blush. "I've covered my tracks. Not saying I've accomplished anything yet, but I won't give up."

"You never do. Nor does a certain Blob." All at once the warmth vanished, replaced by resolve. "About Esen—I'd another reason for coming here with you, Lionel. Thank you for opening the door."

Paul went to Skalet's wall of weapons, the large, blatant kind rightly illegal on Botharis and throughout the Commonwealth. Lionel watched his friend unhook a belt of what looked like grenades, then take a bag of tiny balls of unknown, but doubtless lethal, nature, and understood.

"You're going after her."

Paul fastened the belt around his waist. "I should have gone sooner."
He donned his winter coat, tucking the tiny balls into various pockets.

Not preparing for a hunt. This was— "You think Kraal have Esen."

A sober look. "Don't you?"

It fit. Kraal on the planet, in orbit, more coming. Esen wouldn't risk others, a trait making her vulnerable to those who would, and she'd stay in an untenable situation to protect the Emboldened. Take chances—

Lionel reached for a needler. "I'm coming with you. We'll get Mal—"

A hand caught his wrist, stopping the motion. "I need you here, Lionel. Mal running the search." The hand shifted to his shoulder, Paul's gaze searching Lionel's face. Then, the ghost of a smile. "Mind the Library. Keep in touch. If we're not back in time?" Almost wistful. "Help Nia save the world. I always knew she'd do great things."

"I will." Lionel shook his head. "But, Paul—where will you look?"

"Everywhere. Anywhere." A pause, the hand dropping. Paul stepped back, seeming already to leave. "As long as it takes. You know that."

He did. "Find her," Lionel said huskily. "And anything more I can do—just ask."

Paul actually chuckled. "You'll have to lock Skalet's door. Only you have that key."

35: Cave Day

MY companions in the cave put remarkable effort into the fist-sized bump on the wall, considering the source of their inspiration had been this me—a Human child they'd yet to take seriously, and probably wouldn't again. The bump was now so much pulverized stone on the floor—and dust in the air—but had there been a door hidden behind it, it would have been found.

Leaving the inset shadow on the other wall at which I didn't sneak looks. Besides, my plan wasn't done. It might even work—

Their brief and unproductive collaboration over, Kraal and Emboldened were at opposite ends of the cave, glaring accusingly at one another. They were tired, they were angry and frustrated, and, best of all?

At any moment, they'd discover their share of the food and water was gone. Along with some personal belongings purely to be annoying. As Skalet had taught me—*I'd listened sometimes*—the best way to defeat an enemy is to help them defeat themselves.

My ultimate goal? That they wouldn't kill one another before someone thought to open the cave door and toss their opponent outside, allowing a small me—possibly a very small Quebit—to nip out too.

I should have remembered the success rate of my plans.

Sure enough, Vest jumped to his feet. "Where's the water?"

The Emboldened looked at one another, then Maston shouted, "Where's ours?"

And, if they didn't think of me, at any moment—

—the cave door opened.

Too soon!

Then, *utterly ruining my plan,* new Kraal burst in through the opening, a flood of black armor and too-ready weapons.

The Emboldened *HOWLED!*

Someone fired—

I knew the sounds of war regrettably well, thanks to Skalet-memory. The angry buzz of blasters. The scrape of metal against bone. The screams choked on blood. Heavy thuds and bangs and—

I'd no idea who battled in the cave and wasn't immediately interested in finding out, preoccupied with getting small and fragile me out of harm's way. Head down, I scurried forward on hands and knees, an awkward motion for an adult Human, but as Bess I was adept.

A body landed in front of me, eyes staring up, a sizzling hole where his—her chest had been.

Socks.

Avoiding the hole, I climbed over her corpse. Though sorely tempted by the not-entirely-dead mass in reach—*a bigger, stronger me high on my list*—I wasn't about to cycle into web-flesh until I knew what was happening.

A projectile slammed into the wall, peppering me with rock shards. As I wasn't the target—a strange Kraal leapt up and shot back—I ignored the cuts and kept scurrying.

A two-thumbed hand wrapped around my arm, pulling me behind the grav sled with its cargo. The canisters were designed to survive starship collisions; mere close-range blaster fire wouldn't bother them. Yellow eyes looked down, surveying me for damage. I gave a nod, the Human gesture become ubiquitous. "Take shelter!" Saxel Sah urged, pushing the locator-key into my hands. "Find the *IN.*" She pushed me away. "Hurry."

I turned around. "I know where it is. Come with—"

The Emboldened weren't listening. They shoved at each other, white froth spilling over their lips, in a battle frenzy as fixed and hopeless as any Ganthor herd.

Acklan Seh *HOWLED!*

Together, they leapt over the canisters at the attacking Kraal.

I couldn't help and wouldn't watch. Keeping low, I scurried along the wall, chased by a horrid chorus of buzzes, thuds, and screams. How I wasn't hit owed more to the preoccupation of the rest with larger, more dangerous targets. *It wouldn't last.*

I reached the wall where the crates had been. Dared rise to my feet to shove the locator-key into the tiny shadow I'd guessed might be the right one, rewarded when the wall lifted away in front of me.

I found myself going down a hallway.

As the battle raged behind, no longer in anyone's sight line, I risked staying on my feet to move more quickly. Mixs-memory identified rapid-set cement and metal arches. The cement on the walls and floors had cracks—*not new*—but the arches were rust free. Watertight. *Sealed,* whispered another thought, *and waiting.*

There were lights, the dim sort that distorted my shadow as I kept going. The floor began to climb, rising within the hill, and I stepped over blast door seals, by the look never used.

This wasn't a treasure vault.

I'd no idea how long I had to explore, so I broke into a run. The hall bent, continuing its climb within the hill, and there was only one thing Kraal built like this—

I had to be sure.

The hall ended and I was. Ahead of me was a massive open column, ringed by multileveled railed gangways. Off those were doors to control rooms and fine wood-paneled living quarters and who knew what else that didn't matter.

What did, what the battle in the cave was for, filled the column, sullen black except for the spill of ornate gilt curlicues down its sides, as if a golden waterfall had frozen on contact. Old tech. Dirty tech. Abandoned generations ago in a rare moment of mutual self-preservation by the greater Houses of the Kraal.

It was called, with typical Kraal hubris, a Peacemaker.

Arguably the thing made peace, if you didn't want to live on the planet's surface after its use. Like the ugly multitude of such weapons in Ersh-memory, the strategy of its deployment, according to Skalet, was to hold the threat of extinction over a captive population in the blithe assumption the threat would be believed and the population accept their overlords. Why the Kraal who'd hidden it here hadn't tried to subdue the Botharans with it, I'd no way to know.

Of course, the Botharans were stubborn enough to have let them try.

I hoped for a better reason. For someone those years ago to have lifted their hand from a control, sealed the bunker and hidden its location, refusing to be part of this. Refusing to let anyone else.

Skalet would be amused.

The past was behind. It was now urgent I know who fought in the cave—even more urgent, to know who was winning.

And if they wanted the weapon for its still-valuable components, or its threat.

I retraced my steps a little quicker, being downhill, wishing I'd a plan more effective than "don't get blasted." Skalet's lessons hadn't covered a Human child trying to stop armed troops. *Though had it occurred to her, there'd have been one.*

As Bess, I'd allies if the Emboldened survived their own thirst for violence. If they had, before I counted on them, they'd need to answer some questions.

Beginning with had they known what "treasure" Arzul had told them would help conquer Botharis? Let alone the business of them escaping Kraal, only to meet up and stay with Kraal later the same day—who weren't, of course, the same individuals, but lacking everyone's affiliations I'd yet to be clear which Kraal were which.

Point being, there were entirely too many Kraal on Botharis and Duggs might have been right after all.

Silence rolled up the hall to engulf me, silence and wispy trails of smoke. Remembering one lesson of use, I dropped to my stomach and used my elbows to ease forward. My left arm and leg complained; I paused to check. A bruise or three, and one rock fragment had torn my borrowed shirt and left a shallow scrape across my forearm, but nothing to slow this me.

I crawled over the wide lower edge of a final seal—a detail I hadn't noticed in my panicked flight from the battle. The outer door itself, a huge slab of metal, hung overhead as if ready to drop and chop me in two.

Closing it would be a priority.

Close it and lose the key.

I sighed to myself. Wrong. Paul would want me to close it and give him the key so he could give that to a responsible someone in the Botharan planetary government on the valid assumption that once they learned what sat below their beautiful forest, not far from the Library train tracks, the Botharans would prefer to remove the Peacemaker from their world entirely.

With care. Keys were useful; but being a Kraal missile, there'd be layers of code, possibly with biometrics tied to affiliations those long dead expected to be still in force—Humans being even more optimistic than I was—and traps.

There were always traps.

Silence in the cave. I eased out to let one eye see, impatiently brushing aside the thin lock of hair that fell into my face at the worst moments. Not that I'd do as Skalet, who'd seared the follicles from her scalp, adding baldness to her form-memory. *She'd a tendency to extremes.*

In any form, I'd a tendency, when faced with unpleasantness, to procrastinate before dealing with it. As a delaying tactic, I liked to think of my internal dialogue as preparing myself for the worst.

Ersh had called it my silly dithering. Paul occasionally called it fussing, but being in every sense kinder, would point out the value of stopping to think before acting.

Smoke, acrid and smelling more than this me liked of cooked flesh, settled around my head and it was move, or cough and betray my position. I rose to my feet, put my back to the wall, and sidestepped into the cave.

To find myself alone.

Bodies were slumped where they'd died. I didn't need Skalet-memory to paint a picture of what had happened. Shirt, Vest, and Socks had died with glory, in Kraal terms, taking the five intruders down with them. No, four. What I'd thought were two bodies turned out to be halves of the same one.

I found the Emboldened in a sad heap in front of their precious canisters. Those, while scorched, were intact and so my responsibility.

Being the living.

There wasn't much time. More Kraal would be coming, none likely to appreciate my presence. My search for a control or slot to close the inner door failed and I wasn't willing to touch the frame with my bare hands. So be it.

Next, I removed the distort-hoods from those with intact heads, taking a good look at each face.

Finding one in Skalet-memory. Haben-ru, captain of the *Trium Pa*. She seemed smaller, dead. Less adversary and more victim, though Skalet would disagree.

The tattoos of the rest would give my web-kin what she'd need to track the complete net of affiliations, though Bract was clearly visible on each.

If these were the reinforcements Shirt was expecting, why kill one another? Was it a consequence of my having whipped the Emboldened and Kraal into a fury—the first shot a mistake, the rest inevitable?

I hoped not, but the other answer, that those in the cave were expendable and meant to die, didn't make me feel any better.

I stripped off my donated vest, shirt, and socks, tossing them aside rather than take with me what could be traced, then turned my attention to the Emboldened.

Who hadn't been after sanctuary. Hadn't needed to ask the Library their question, only to have a way to reach these hills. Had come believing they and the Kraal could take this world from those already here.

We had to learn who'd fed them that dangerous notion. It'd be the same ones who believed it for themselves. I did know we hadn't failed them, not that Paul would take comfort from it.

Having rid myself of pockets, I tucked the locator-key under a canister, then gave the grav sled a pat.

"Time to go."

Elements

L AMBO produced a long white cloth to cover the joined tables, refusing to say where he'd obtained it. Onlee, having parked her recorder into a "discreet" corner, high on a metal shelf—not that anyone could miss the thing with its ominous lens—unpacked a case containing, of all things, an ornate ceremonial serpitay set.

"Surprised?" Nia smiled at Evan as she helped arrange the tray. "Don't be. Among the legacies of past Kraal rule are vineyards throughout the Lowesland. We'd export the wine back to them if we were on better terms. Ever tried it? It's a little like port. Has a good kick."

"I haven't. As a junior at this meeting, I wouldn't be required, would I?"

"No. If those off the *Tesseer Ra* bring a bottle of their own, I'll drink from it, they'll taste ours."

"But—" Evan thought better of his protest. "They won't poison you—they need you to represent Botharis. You'll be safe to drink."

"While they can't be so sure." Her smile turned bitter. "Meaning they'd win the first test—to brave our hospitality. It's always a game."

A detail to record. The academy didn't teach new diplomats about this distant branch of humanity; what Evan knew he'd picked up on his own, like this. "With Kraal at the table," he responded, "the Sacrissee may participate in the ceremony but won't drink where they can be seen by those not of their *IN*. They'll pretend." He mimed bringing his cupped hands to his mouth. "Don't be surprised if they dump their cups on the floor, then ask for refills."

"Wore boots," Nia replied, lifting her foot.

Evan found himself liking her. As he'd planned to actively detest Niala Mavis for Paul's sake, the feeling felt awkward even if he couldn't help it. Nia was smart, brave, and doing what she could to make things better. She wasn't like most of his seniors, either, talking with him as if they'd the same rank.

Though that was probably because Special Envoy Mavis didn't know what a "polit" was in the Commonwealth and had no grasp how junior Evan was. Granted, he did have an excellent security rating, but that was mostly because he'd seen and done what his seniors insisted he be officially cleared to have seen and done, however long after the fact. *Governments*, Evan Gooseberry thought, *probably worked much the same way throughout the universe.*

Lionel entered the train car, nodding appreciatively. "Ready to depart, Special Envoy?"

He'd entered the car alone, sliding the door closed behind him, and Evan winced at the ice in Nia's: "Where's your director?"

"Ah yes. Director Ragem and Curator Esen-alit-Quar will join us on the way," said with such bland confidence, Evan almost believed it. "We've a tight window. Shall I tell Kelly to start the train?"

Evan could almost feel Lambo's amused, many-eyed look his way. How was he supposed to know Kelly Kiser was the most experienced train operator on Botharis and someone able to—according to the admiring Carasian—field strip an engine with her eyes closed? All he'd heard was Rhonda couldn't do the job because her Elk were missing and had sent her younger cousin. *It hadn't inspired confidence.*

Nia didn't budge. "Exactly where and how will they join us? I was told there were no stops between here and the landing field."

"That's quite true." Lionel consulted the chrono on his wrist. "Kelly?"

"When you tell me what's going on." Nia slammed her hand on the table, rattling the glasses. "I told Paul no more stunts!"

Lionel rested his own hand on the table. "And I tell you, Special

Envoy Mavis," low and certain, "we must start the train. Paul and Esen will be here because they have to be."

Evan felt his heart thudding in his chest, understanding what must be happening. "He's gone after her. Paul. He's stopped waiting."

A frown, but Lionel didn't deny it. "We have people in jeopardy," he confirmed. "We have an unresolved instability in orbit, and the only thing under your control, Special Envoy, is to get to that meeting on time."

"Do it," she ordered, lips tight.

Evan decided he liked her even more.

36: Forest Afternoon

THE best thing about a forest, to a Web-being, was the astonishing wealth of living mass waiting to be assimilated. Not that I was greedy.

In fact, I was very particular.

As Bess, I'd activated the grav sled and towed it out of the cave—the attackers having cooperatively left the hidden door open so I didn't have to find it or decipher how it worked. Or encounter a trap, so all in all, I was grateful.

Now to cover my tracks and, hopefully, slow anyone trying to enter the cave.

The sun was still up, if sinking to the west, adding some urgency to my task. There'd be searchers out and I couldn't count on them being from Mal.

I cycled and flowed over a large tree. Flowed *into* the tree, at its base, turning it into more of me before I quickly flowed out again.

The tree, now missing an Esen-sized portion of its trunk, fell over as if surprised, striking the ice-coated cliff with a huge crash I detected as a pleasing vibration against myself. Maybe no one with ears would be listening.

My plans often included such wishful thinking.

Leaving the excess mass to moisten the snow, I went after another tree. Then another. By the time I was done I probably wouldn't need to cycle again for a decade, was slightly dazed by the desire to sleep the rest of winter, but my task was complete. The open cave door could no longer be seen. The expansive clearing where there'd been trees was, admittedly, obvious, but all in all?

I was satisfied. Even if other Kraal knew the cave was there, they'd need heavy equipment or explosives to get to it, the use of either being noticed.

As a bonus, I hadn't crushed the grav sled, which I'd forgotten about by the fourth tree and really should have moved farther away before I'd started, trees tending to fall in unpredictable directions. And bounce. It had been close. Aromatic needles covered the canisters, along with cones and an old stinger nest.

I cycled back to my Lanivarian self, glad to be that me again, and began brushing those off.

"To think all these years I've been using an ax."

I turned to find Duggs Pouncey propped against what remained of a tree, shaking her head.

"Thought I'd caught some new Kraal machine taking down the trees till you were you, Esen." Duggs offered me a sip from the flask she'd pulled from a pocket. When I shook my head, she took a long drink, then fixed me with her keen eyes. "What are you, anyway?"

"In so much trouble," I replied sadly, unable to decide if Paul or Skalet would be angrier.

She laughed.

"You seem to be taking this," I put a hand to my furred chest, "unusually well." I sniffed. "How much have you had to drink?" Had it been sufficient to make her doubt her senses tomorrow?

A Web-being could hope.

Duggs grinned at me and lifted the flask. "Tea." She walked over to the grav sled, the wide webbing beneath her boots keeping her above the snow. "This something we need to get under cover?" As if we discussed a proposed change to the Library blueprints.

"I'm sorry," I said, trying to keep up. "You saw me. You saw—the other me."

"Yeah, yeah. The bright blue blobbie you. Eats tree trunks. Nifty trick." Her gaze went to the pile of splintered wood, branches, and associated debris against the cliff. "You trying to mark the spot or keep someone out?"

Blobbie me? "Out," I said stiffly. "There are weapons in there." Along with corpses and a planet-ending missile.

"Damn. Another Kraal cave?" She spat. "Mal thought he had them all."

"Hidden door," I told her, and gave in to the moment. "The canisters contain Sacrissee embryos. I need your help to get them to safety."

"My cabin's through there." A nod at the still-standing trees. "Spotted what looked to be a Kraal aircar flying this way, low to the ground. Followed it. Then you started waking the neighborhood."

"That was a terrible idea." *And I'd thought Evan impulsive?* "Why didn't you call Mal?"

Her cheeks colored. "I've a bit of a rep, when it comes to Kraal sightings. Thought I'd best be sure this round. C'mon. My place isn't far. What, Esen-alit-Quar?" She pointed a gloved finger at my snout. "Thought I lived in the village?"

Duggs arrived in the morning and left at the day's end, reappearing whenever we'd an emergency, and to my vast shame, I'd never wondered till now where she spent the rest of her life.

I brought my ears forward and risked a tongue-lolling grin. "I thought you lived with your tools."

Earning another laugh. "Not wrong." She sobered. "I've an aircar and coms. Unless you want to stay out here?"

"Wait." The cold was seeping into my bones, but I wasn't ready, quite, to accept what was happening. "Duggs. Aren't you afraid?"

"Of you?"

I wasn't sure if I was insulted or reassured by her incredulous response. "I am—what I am is a secret."

"That I get." The finger again, this time tapping my nose gently. Her face lost the dour lines I'd begun taking as Duggs-usual, becoming relaxed, almost unguarded. "Knew there was one. It was in the design, you see. All those daft closets—other things—" A lopsided grin. "Didn't like being on the outside, Esen. Never have. That's why I resigned, fun as Iftsen accommodations can be."

"They aren't that fun," I complained, then couldn't help it. I licked her finger. "Please, don't leave us, Duggs."

Her keen eyes studied me. I put my ears at their most innocent and waited. All at once, a look of vast satisfaction crossed her face. "Damn. She's one too, isn't she? That Kraal *family* of yours with the poker up her ass."

Oh dear. I whined deep in my throat, then managed a defensive, "Skalet has excellent posture."

"Any more?"

Having my tail between my legs was warmer anyway. "Lesley," I heard myself confess. "You haven't met her yet. She's living in the greenhouse while she—recovers. She hasn't broken anything. Just some pots," I added hurriedly. "The window was my fault."

"What window—don't answer that." Duggs pinched her nose, staring at me. "Lionel's in on it. He'd have to be. Why in all the hells would you pick Botharis? I love the place, but it's so Human the building codes might as well be pre-contact."

"It's Paul's home."

A glower. "Sentimental fluff ball."

I'd been called worse. Granted, I was as fluffed as my thin pelt allowed. "He needs his family." I pointed to the grav sled. "These do too. Before more Kraal come." And before this me froze.

"Hop on," Duggs ordered, in a tone very like Paul's when I wasn't to ask more questions.

So I did.

Awkwardly straddling two of the frigid metal canisters, each with an interior colder than the outside, I gave her a mournful look.

"Don't be such a puppy," Duggs told me. She peeled off her outer coat and laid it over the other canisters. "Get on."

"I am not a puppy," I protested haughtily, stepping on the garment.

"Sure." She tucked the edges around me. "Stay put."

Her coat was bulky and still warm.

Best of all, it smelled like a friend. I curled into a contented ball as Duggs began towing the sled and closed my eyes.

I'd figure out how to explain all this to Paul later.

Makings

THEY'D been three.

They are two, now. Oola, who'd been alone and won't be again, supports the other as they flee from shadow to shadow.

The Humans are less. They accomplished that. Aule had.

The other—a female, larger—pants with pain. She is badly hurt. Oola knows those *IN* would reject the other to save themselves.

She is not like them.

She will not be them.

Footsteps behind. Shouts of anger. The Humans had been less. They are more again and follow a blood trail.

"Leave me," says the other.

"I will not." Oola *HOWLS* her defiance.

HOWL!

An answer—from ahead. Away from the ships and the Humans.

Oola's been tricked once. She will not be again. She stops, looks for another way.

The other sags, a weight she cannot lift and will not abandon.

She sinks down with the other and *HOWLS*.

37: Cabin Afternoon

THE setting of Duggs Pouncey's cabin was, to my Lanivarian-self, perfection. No other buildings in sight. No damp muddy patches I could see; granted there might be a pond or stream under the snow, but it was up a hill. Surrounded by a wilderness teeming with mousels and other treats, not that a civilized being such as myself would abandon my responsibilities to romp outside, but—

"If you're not gonna eat that—"

I pulled my attention from the entrancing view out the window in time to see the Human steal another piece of bacon from my plate. "I was!"

Duggs tucked it between her teeth and bit. "Too late," she said around the mouthful.

Showing my far more impressive set, I gathered my plate of delicious refried pub chips and bacon closer and resumed eating, happier than I'd been in a while. I'd been comfortable around Duggs before she knew what I was.

That she was comfortable around me now was a gift to treasure, as was this moment's peace before everything started again. Duggs had used her com, cautiously, to let Paul know I was here. He was coming. As for the rest? *Lesy and caves and Kraal missiles could wait.*

I'd bacon.

I snapped up the next strip, content with my lot.

We sat to our meal on stools pulled up to a workbench. It might have started as a table, but to make room for her guest, me, Duggs had to roll up blueprints and remove a toolbox, then brush sawdust to the floor with the side of her hand. She'd looked at the sawdust, then me, shaking her head.

Despite its location, the building was brand-new. So new, wires hung from the ceiling and there were notations on the unpainted walls with arrows to indicate where light fixtures and interior walls would be. Tape marked out rooms on the floor. She'd installed an excellent accommodation—Human-centric, but this was her house—but slept in a hammock. The kitchen was a portable cooktop and food storage unit in a corner.

She'd chuckled at my joke about living with her tools because she did. My tail drifted back and forth. Finished, I licked bacon grease from my fingers and gazed around with curiosity. Duggs was a stickler for projects getting done, on time and properly. This partial building didn't seem like her. "Why haven't you finished this?"

Duggs leaned back. "And when have I had time, Esen-alit-Quar, creator of the most outrageous design challenges of my career?"

My ears bent.

She laughed at me. "I only sleep here. I'd rather be on the job." The remarkable Human stood, picking up her dishes. I did the same, looking around for a sink.

"Gimme yours. I've a box out back. Figure if it's frozen, nothing's gonna rot." Duggs headed to the back door.

What a sensible plan! I'd have to see if Paul would let me implement it in our kitchen.

Thinking of Paul, I padded behind Duggs. "You're sure he said to stay here? Indoors?"

Our breakfast dishes disappeared with a clatter. Duggs closed the door. "He was pretty clear." She grinned. "And how I was to pull your tail for him."

I flattened my ears. "Paul did not say that." Though I curled my tail out of reach. My dearest friend wouldn't have been happy to receive Duggs' call with its cryptic "Esen's here," but we'd little choice. With Kraal in the area?

Duggs had agreed with me. We'd keep information off coms as much as we could, though I'd have liked to tell Paul about the thousands of embryos I'd rescued. The canisters were presently concealed in the cavernous rear section of Duggs' aircar; her tools and construction supplies moved to the snow under a tarp. We'd both looked for tracers but hadn't found any. A risk we had to take.

As for the grav sled? Duggs set it skimming out over open fields, presumably until its battery died and it sank into the snow, hopefully not terrorizing Rhonda's missing elk.

"Sorry to drag you into this," I told her earnestly.

"Most fun I've had in months. C'mon. Let's take a look at that device you found."

The locator-key was in the pocket of the plaid woolly shirt she'd lent me. I eyed her warily. "Being amused by danger is not the best Human characteristic."

"No. No, it's not." Duggs nodded as if to herself, her face growing serious. "I need to tell you something, Esen. Something few know about me." She brought cups of hot tea to the workbench; sat with hers between her hands. "I'm Botharan and so were my parents, but my mother's family were sous Kraal, settled in southern Lowesland by House Noitci. Yes," grimly at whatever showed on my face, "she was born in one of those damn tents.

"What they don't put in history tapes? When invasions fail, the sous are expendable, abandoned by their House. My guess is they're usually slaughtered by the locals. Not what happened here." She stared into her cup. "Botharans understood the sous Kraal weren't combatants. They were offered land to work. Given jobs. Treated like their own. My grandparents were good people." Her eyes lifted, there was something dreadful in them.

I didn't want to know. As a friend, I couldn't not. "What happened?"

"Noitci learned some of their people hadn't died as they should. They sent a cleanup squad to erase the stain on their honor. I was away at school—" The cup shuddered on the wood. She picked it up absently. "—I found them. What was left. Helped with idents as best I could. Thought I'd take up forensics afterward, but it turned out I was better at building than solving crime."

I growled. "Mal shouldn't have called you."

A shrug. "I owed him a few beers; wondered how he'd collect. I'm telling you this, Es, so you know I understand what we're up against. There are good and decent Kraal. I'm descended from some. But the noble Houses?" A spit to the side. "They give that for us. The

Confederacy won't last. It can't sustain itself. But while it does, we're a game to them, our worlds a way to keep score. I don't want their attention on mine."

Echoing Ersh's assessment of that doomed branch of humanity.

A scowl. "Your Skalet's another player. Going against Bract on her own? Won't end well."

The truth, if not how Duggs meant. "Skalet's never without resources," I said mildly. I pulled out the locator-key and set it between us. "Whatever you think of her," I said then, because Duggs deserved it and so did my web-kin, "she guards Botharis from all Kraal." I wrinkled my snout. "And blames me for the necessity every day."

"That why she can't know I know? She'd blame you for that too?"

"No," I said very quietly. "It's so you stay alive. First and foremost, Skalet guards our secret. I forced her to accept Paul and Lionel. She won't accept anyone else."

Duggs smacked her hand on the wood and hooted with laughter. Once done, she wiped an eye, only to chuckle at me. "You look like you bit a pickle."

I flipped my ears and wriggled my nose. *I certainly did not.* "I don't understand your reaction," I complained.

"We've hated each other's guts from day one, Esen. I'll be glad not to change."

I frowned.

"Don't worry about it," Duggs advised, still inexplicably cheerful. "You'll tell Paul—"

"I must."

"And Big Scaly. She has to know."

My frown drew furrows over my snout. "Who?"

Duggs' mouth opened into an oh of delight. "Is she you too? Esolesy Ki! It all makes sense. You live together—"

I rested my chin on the table in abject surrender.

"—you're never seen together. That's gotta be awkward."

"You've no idea," I muttered.

She leaned an arm on the table, resting her cheek on it so I gazed into her one eye and a nostril. "Sorry, Es." A sincere eye, if the nostril didn't tell me much. Tea on her breath and the remains of an excellent shared supper. "You're just so interesting."

A being after my own heart. Which wasn't helpful at this moment. I lifted my head, doing my utmost to look boring. "For the safety of my sisters, I can't answer every question," I warned her. "But I can answer a few—not now," as she raised her head and drew a breath. "Now," I said, feeling the mature one. "We should learn what we can about this device before Paul gets here."

Duggs nodded, though her eyes twinkled, and I knew beyond doubt her brilliant mind was filling up with questions.

I'd rely on Paul for the trickier ones.

The locator-key was small, round, and—as seemed the rule for Kraal tech—carved with elegant abstract designs. It might have been a little sculpture, meant to stop paper blowing in the wind. A thing I'd learned existed at my first interview with the Hamlet of Hillsview Preservation Committee, as they'd stuck a carved rock on top of my application, though in their case I was reasonably sure the idea had been to prevent my application from getting away without Due and Thorough Attention.

Kraal, as befitted a paranoid society, didn't allow anything remotely identifiable or unique in their artwork. They just liked it fancy.

Duggs produced a small scanner and ran it over the device. I tensed, ready for a puff of poison or gas. She wrinkled her nose at me. "Don't fuss. It's one-use only. Daresay that's all the trap they need. Activate it too far from the sweet spot, and it'll run out of juice before taking you there."

"The Emboldened—the Sacrissee who came to the Library—they had this," I clarified for her. "They were told where to start looking. That it was close." I could hear Skalet's favorite lesson: *worry about coincidence, Youngest. It hides the truth.*

She spun the device. "This is old. Older than anything I've got from my grandmother. What's in this cave still of value?"

About to answer, I angled my ears. "There's an aircar approaching. Paul's here!"

"Or someone else." Duggs looked grim. "Let's make sure who before we open the door." She closed the blinds over the window, pushed the locator-key back in my hands and me toward the rear of the room, then went to stand beside the front door.

After picking up a hammer.

Skalet would approve.

Elements

THE new captain of the *Trium Pa* surged to his feet, vacating the command chair. Staggered, but caught himself. Blood streamed down the side of his face, obscuring the Bract tattoo as he saluted with the rest of the bridge crew. "The ship is yours, Eminence."

Gratifying. "My confidence was not misplaced, Cieter-ro." Skalet flicked fingers dismissively. "As you were. Status?"

"There were two drops while affiliations were being confirmed, Your Eminence. Suecop-ro, report."

The display split, one half showing the comp officer as she rose and saluted. There were bruises on her neck and her armor smoldered, but her head was high with pride. "Your Glory. Haben-ru fled in disgrace, taking her adherents to the surface. Our captain would not allow them to be shot down." With a barely hidden sneer at Cieter-ro.

Who appeared unconcerned. "Correct, Your Eminence. I take full responsibility for their escape."

"I am impressed. You chose not to fire into the atmosphere and cause an incident. The Botharans will apprehend our fugitives, adding to Haben-ru's shame. *Impeccable,* Captain."

The comp officer flushed but didn't hesitate. "My apologies, Captain. I was at fault."

"You will learn, Suecop-ro."

Her image vanished. No need to say what all here knew. A second insubordination would be the comp officer's last. *Clarity.* Skalet felt the perfection of it. Relished the potential.

Now for the next vital step toward her own. "Break orbit, Captain. Move the *Trium Pa* to the coordinates supplied by the captain of the *Tesseer Ra* and hold."

"At once, Your Glory!" Cieter-ro's eyes gleamed with pride. He and his crew would gain affiliation with a Great House should Skalet's play succeed, an improvement in their status none could have imagined in their lifetimes. "We are yours!"

Skalet ended the link.

"Just so," she murmured, putting the back of her hand to the still-warm tattoo beside her left eye. She turned to the Kraal officer waiting at attention. "Report."

"Your Eminence. A single train car and engine have pulled up to the station. It will convey our delegation to a point halfway along the track where the Botharans, in their train, will host the meeting. Virul-ru has accepted those terms."

Skalet had no doubt who'd made those arrangements. *Clever Paul.* Had he less compassion, he'd have made a superior Kraal.

"Coordinate with the *Trium Pa* to get a track on the pods dropped earlier. If I were Haben-ru?" Skalet smiled. "I'd stop that meeting."

38: Cabin Afternoon; Aircar Afternoon

IT had been Paul landing in front of Duggs Pouncey's cabin in the woods. Paul, who came in through the door in a rush of cold air and snow to grab my head between his hands and shake it.

Being upset. Thoroughly, deeply upset, and having been the cause—*again*—I tried to keep my ears up while explaining, though it was hard to talk while my head was in motion without biting my tongue and I wasn't sure he listened. "I didn't mean to be gone all night. And today. I couldn't help it. I was stuck in a cave with the Emboldened. There were Kraal and then there were more Kraal with blasters—"

He stopped shaking my head. "Blasters? Idiot beast!"

"You are listening," I exclaimed, which perhaps wasn't the key point so I kept going, trying to erase the stark look on his dear face. "It's all right. They killed each other but we saved the embryos. Duggs and me."

His mouth moved without sound.

"They're in her aircar. They came from Sacriss on the *Stellar Trumpet*—"

"Gods. Let the man breathe, Es," Duggs interrupted. She'd put away her hammer. "Get your gear off, Paul. I'll get something to put in our tea. I know I need it."

Paul let out a long breath then rested his forehead on mine. "You weren't hurt?" he whispered.

"Not a scratch," I assured him. "Duggs made me supper." I blew bacon breath at him. "She put our dirty dishes outside to freeze."

"Uh-uh." He straightened with a gleam in his eye I was glad to see. "Nice try. We've a sink." Paul took off his gloves and hat, removed his coat, and put it on a hook by the door. He wore a Kraal grenade belt, and it wasn't empty. I managed not to whine. When he bent to undo his high winter boots, he said quietly. "The Emboldened?"

"They're dead again," I told him. "For real."

"We haven't much time, but—" He looked at me. "Duggs? I'll take that drink."

"We haven't much time," Paul repeated a moment later. He didn't sit at the workbench, rather leaned a hip against the windowsill, a hand cradling the mug Duggs had passed him after a deep swallow and respectful second look. "Here's the short of it. We've two ships on the landing field, both from Sacriss VII. One's registered to Molancor Genomics. No doubt they've come for the Emboldened, the embryos, or both."

I pushed my head through my sweater—Paul having brought me clothes, if not the boots still under a bush—to ask. "Our scholars? Their ships?"

"All fine," with a nod to say he shared my priorities. "The planetary government sent a special envoy. She's arranged for everyone to be evacuated to Grandine and for their ships to land here."

Duggs lifted her cup. "So no plague. Told you." This to me.

Paul nodded. "What we had—have—is potentially more dangerous. A crisis of affiliation on the *Trium Pa,* our Kraal who wouldn't leave. A faction created the pretense of a Commonwealth medship to cover up poisoning the *Trumpet*'s crew and stealing the canisters. Our assumption is they also dropped the Kraal hunters who infiltrated the Library and died trying to kill the Emboldened."

"They were Bract and supposed to die," I corrected. "So the Emboldened could leave the Library without being followed. And maybe," for this only now occurred to me, "Haben-ru feared we might bring the Emboldened over to our side. We'd been helping them."

Paul's eyebrow rose. "Go on."

"Arzul Kraal met the Emboldened outside the Library. I followed them—" I angled an ear at Duggs, "—into a cave. When other Kraal came, I escaped." He looked tempted to grab my head again, so I pulled out of range. "Then Duggs found me," I finished brightly.

After a look to say he knew I'd left out most of it, Paul took another swallow. "Duggs, I hate to drag you further into this after you've said you're leaving."

"I'm not," she replied. She'd taken a stool and sat with her arms crossed on the table, listening to Paul. "Esen talked me into staying. How can I help?"

"That's excellent news." He sent me a grateful look, one that turned to guarded when I lowered my ears halfway. "You can fill me in on the details later."

Duggs snorted. "Sure won't be me doing it."

Going to be like that, was it? I showed her a fang. She toasted me with her mug.

"Something I should know?" Even exhausted, Paul had no trouble switching into that intimidating what-have-you-done tone.

It wasn't all about me. I raised my ears. "I know what Haben-ru and the *Trium Pa* were after. I found a Peacemaker in the cave. It's not far from here. The Emboldened were given a locator-key. It opened the bunker door as well. Show him, Duggs."

She tossed him the disk, then turned to glare at me. "A bloody missile?"

"I was about to tell you," I said defensively. "The Emboldened believed the Kraal—their allies, not the ones who attacked, who might have been their allies—" I stopped to regroup. "Kraal promised to invade Botharis then share it with the Emboldened for their new home."

"They fell for that?"

"They'd run out of hope," Paul told Duggs. "Did you hear when this invasion would take place?"

"The cave Kraal said their troops had dropped, but only Haben-ru and three others came to the cave."

Duggs let out a string of colorful words; I added two to memory.

Paul held up the disk between thumb and forefinger. "This takes a ground force out of the equation. Let's assume someone on Sacriss VII had or obtained it—there are more weapons and artifact dealers there than in the Confederacy. To be of any use, this had to be brought to Botharis and taken within range. To use non-Kraal was clever. Or a last resort." He frowned, pocketing the disk. "I trust you closed the door, Es?"

I knew he'd want me to do that. "I did my best," I told him.

"That you did," Duggs said and laughed. "Damnedest thing I ever saw."

Paul's eyes flicked to me, a question in their depths.

"And I brought you the key," I reminded him proudly, rather than answer it.

"More, later." He stood. "Now, why we're short of time. Sacrissee officials, and Molancor, are on their way to meet with the special envoy. Evan and Lionel are with her to help with them—to delay, if they can, till we can get there. But the main issue? There's a high-ranking Kraal negotiator in the mix. Something big's in the wind." He gave me the look that meant we were in serious trouble. Though occasionally it meant we had to stop trouble from getting serious.

Not happy with either option, I panted to dump heat.

"Duggs, your aircar has cables? Mag grapples?"

"Of course."

"Good." Paul had the distinct look and energy of someone with A Plan.

Normally, from him, I considered that a Good Thing, but something about his look made the hair rise on my back. "Why do we need cables and grapples?"

"We're going to land on a train."

I'd seen this before. Insanity was, among Humans, contagious. Not the illness, but the willful lack of sense brought on by a truly impossible idea, and I wasn't going to be part of it.

"You'll be fine," Paul said encouragingly, reading my ears. "Won't she, Duggs?"

"Unless we crash and burn," Duggs replied with reprehensible cheer.

"Let's not."

I ran my paws over the rear seat, looking up with alarm. "Duggs— there aren't any belts!"

"Took'm out. Got in the way."

Rather than cite safety regulations and be ignored, I hopped into the front seat and squeezed between the two of them, squirming my way under Paul's arm. "Careful of the grenades, Fangface," he warned. "Oh, and these." He held up a handful of small balls.

Duggs let out a whistle. "Those Kraal anti-personnel bombs?"

"I do believe so." Paul tucked the dreadful things back in his pocket.

We were all going to die.

"No one's going to die," he assured me as the big aircar broke out of the snow, rising with a tight turn that brought us through a treetop, branches sliding over the transparent hood.

Duggs shouted "Whoo—OOP!"

I buried my snout in Paul's armpit.

I'd been safer in the cave.

When we didn't crash immediately, curiosity brought my snout up again. That, and the smell of Paul's coat. As Esolesy, I considered it my duty as his friend and partner to advocate for Paul to acquire a new wardrobe. Classic, yes, but following the more reliable trends; he was, after all, a fine specimen for a Human.

As Esen, I'd have appreciated Paul not wearing his favorite coat all the time, constant use turning the garment into a confusing time capsule of his wanderings and encounters.

Now there was a tang of Skalet, who'd clearly fondled the weapons he'd acquired.

And then Lesley—

It was at this point I returned my snout to his coat, using a paw to push it open so I could follow the faint and hopefully implausible trace to his shirt.

Lesy, as Lesley, had touched Paul's shirt. Within the past day.

Right over the pendant! I snorted and inhaled to be sure—

"Stop that." Paul pushed me away. "You're making a wet spot. Now what are you doing?"

I didn't bother to answer, as it was perfectly clear what I was doing. *Had Lesy gone in his closet or—* I wanted to see his face, which required squirming onto his lap and twisting—

Duggs grabbed my leg. "Damn it, Es. Do you want us to crash?"

"You took out the seatbelt," I growled back. "This vehicle is unsafe!"

"Don't blobbies bounce?"

"Don't call me a blobbie!"

Being mostly in Paul's lap I felt his every muscle tense. Which made his lap much less comfortable, and I whined.

Then his hand latched onto the scruff of my neck and I whined louder.

"Wasn't her fault," Duggs said kindly. "I saw her eating trees."

The hand in my scruff tightened and I felt Paul's breath in my ear. Which tickled, but this didn't seem the moment to twitch. "She knows?" he whispered.

Amazing, really, how much incredulous horror he could pack into one brief whisper. Ersh would have been impressed. Had I not been busy trying to figure out the least upsetting yet factual answer to Paul's question, while in his lap and him holding me by the scruff, I'd have been impressed too.

I settled for "Mummrf."

Duggs gave me a hearty pat on the rump. "Don't fuss," she ordered; I wasn't sure which of us she meant. "Knew there was something up at the Library. Just glad to find out it was only Es and her sisters."

Oh dear.

Paul's hand opened. To my surprise, it descended again, but this time to rub behind my ear. Which didn't prepare me at all to hear him say casually, "Skalet and Lesley."

"*You* know?" I half shouted, twisting frantically with my own incredulous horror.

"Gonna make us crash—" Duggs commented.

Paul wrapped his arms around me. "Calm down. It's all right."

"It is?" I asked, greatly dubious.

"Yes," with that tender note to his voice meaning it was, after all. "Lesley introduced herself last night. She made supper."

That couldn't be good. I had to know. "How's the kitchen?"

"Interesting. I cleaned up."

This time. Paul had no idea how much Lesy liked making messes. Or he'd started to and didn't mind, which was its own entirely new and wonderful thought. Even if we were flying far too close to the ground and dodging trees—

"There was a pot she didn't use. I think you know the one I mean. With a blaster hidden in it? You can tell me about it later."

—I whined again. "Is this because Duggs is about to crash?"

"Am not. WHOOO-OO!" The aircar made a sickening swerve left and down. "Might not," Duggs qualified happily.

I felt words warm against my skin. "Idiot beast."

They lightened my heart. "I'm gone one day," I complained.

His embrace tightened, as if saying that was a day too many. *I couldn't disagree.*

Though now I wondered if I'd any secrets left from this amazing Human.

And if Lesy, as Lesley, had detected mine, the preserved Esen-bit in the pendant under Paul's shirt. Being Human, she might not. Being Elder, she probably had. Another worry to add to my list.

Elements

L EAVING its other two cars behind, the engine pushed theirs from the Library platform, smooth and slow at first to test the link, then picking up speed. Lionel stood where he could watch the oversized Survey emergency survival shelter recede into the distance, cognizant of the journey that had put the dream called the All Species' Library of Linguistics and Culture in it and on this world.

He remembered listening to a very young Paul Ragem talk of his vision for a place like this. Remembered being in awe of a mind able to soak up languages like a sponge. Hadn't appreciated Paul's heart, then, how it encompassed everything that lived and thought. Being younger himself and cynical.

The snow-covered structure passed from view, marked only by an assortment of tree-shaped tops that shouldn't be here, let alone grow, but did. Like Esen herself. Their friendship had been inevitable, Lionel thought, looking back through the years. Paul the dreamer, the explorer.

Esen the personification of everything Paul loved.

He had to find her.

The last vestige of Esen's Garden disappeared behind the first hill and Lionel turned away, refusing to doubt.

A row of eyestalks regarded him. "I have received a report from my esteemed counterpart in security, Merri Higbee. The other train has left Port Village Station."

Merri was one of Mal's deputized constables at the landing field, and normally a mobile medtech aiding livestock. As for "Port Village Station?"

Someone was getting grandiose ideas. And why wouldn't they, seeing who came off these latest ships? Well-dressed diplomats, likely with escorts. Even the dreaded return of Kraal on Botharan soil signaled a major shift from the routine of passenger transports and their preoccupied, sometimes gullible scholars. The wider universe had arrived. *Opportunity.*

Potential disaster. How often they arrived looking the same.

"Thank you, Lambo."

A claw twitched as if the great being longed to salute but knew better.

Lionel eased along the table to where the special envoy sat with her assistant and Evan. The three looked up as he joined them. "We're on schedule, Envoy Mavis," he reported. "We should meet the other train in 30 minutes. Barring elk."

Nia's forehead creased. "Elk?"

"Rhonda's herd's still on the loose. Kelly's keeping an eye out for them, in case any wander on the tracks."

Onlee burst into a laugh, then looked contrite. "Sorry. It's just— wandering livestock, when we're worried about this?" She indicated the table, with its cloth and waiting trays.

"We can't be late. Won't be." This with a sharp look at him.

Lionel accepted the responsibility. "As I said, Envoy Mavis, Kelly's alerted."

"Sit with us, then. Lionel." She didn't quite smile. "Nia, here and now."

"Nia." He inclined his head, then took one of the seats arranged for Human posteriors. "Is there anything else I can help you with?"

She looked very young, suddenly. "What do you know of House Virul? The other Great Houses?"

Lionel settled back. "They've been an interest of mine over the years," he admitted. "I'm most familiar with Bryll and Noitci. It may be useful to know the root of their affiliations is derived from . . ."

As he continued, he felt as if Skalet stood behind him.

Nodding approval.

39: Aircar Afternoon

"WE'VE got company."

"I see them. Es."

"I'm going." Paul gave me a boost, and I climbed into the back. Where there were no seatbelts—but giving Duggs room to move in a crisis was probably the safety feature of greater use.

Besides, being in the back meant I, who hadn't seen "them" could look out the side.

Duggs had turned the aircar to follow the train tracks. She and Paul were of the belief this wouldn't attract undue attention from any watching Kraal, as local Botharans routinely flew the route as if we'd made the mark on the landscape just for them.

Until this moment, I'd been preoccupied with another concern: the *landing on a moving train* portion of Paul's plan, due to take place once we intercepted the train in question, an event taking place all too soon.

I put my snout to the hood and peered out.

"Edge of the woods," Paul directed in a grim voice.

Not on this side. I scrambled to the other, finally spotting what had my Human companions worried. A pair of black figures, barely visible against the line of tree trunks.

"It's an ambush," I said, or rather squeaked. "Why is there an ambush?"

"Because they're Kraal," Duggs snapped. "What are we going to do about it?" The aircar began to slow.

Because Paul had bombs in his pockets and around his waist. I gripped the front seat, putting my head between them. "We do not end eph—we don't kill," I told Duggs.

To my relief, Paul nodded. "Stick to the plan."

Duggs muttered Very Bad Words, but the aircar accelerated.

Paul had told us how the meeting would work, how a second train was on its way from the landing field with the Kraal and Sacrissee. "Can we warn the other train?" I asked.

"We can't trust coms."

There was mass below. "If you stop—"

Paul took hold of my ear, gently. "We stay together. This thing go any faster?"

"Not recommended." Duggs grinned suddenly. "Let's see why not!"

We were going to die.

Well, at least it'd be together.

Elements

THE tap-tap-tap came during Lionel's description of the fall of House Bryll, and at first Evan thought someone was fidgeting. Not that he was, caught up in a story of epic bloodshed and betrayal—even if it had happened generations ago—but Lionel was very thorough and had been talking for a while now.

Tap-taptap-tap.

Lionel stopped. Nia frowned. Both slowly looked up.

"WE'RE UNDER ATTACK!!" Lambo's shout was so loud, Evan's first reaction was to cover his ears. His second was to duck under the table, but as no one else was, he dropped his hands and gripped the edge.

"I SHALL DEFEND US!" the Carasian bellowed as he climbed to the ceiling, hammering the metal with his great claws, the grip of his handling claws bending the shelving.

Tap-taptap-tap.

"Lambo—stop!" Lionel was smiling. "It's Paul."

The giant paused, eyestalks bent. "Are you sure?" A claw moved stealthily into strike position.

"Yes. Yes. We have to open the hatch." Lionel climbed on the table.

"Clear it," Nia ordered, climbing up with him.

Evan hurried to help Onlee remove the trays, putting them on the floor. The bottle and glasses rattled against each other, the car having developed a most alarming shudder. *Like Great Gran's yacht*, he thought suddenly. "Pack coats around them," he said, grabbing his from the hook to tuck around the fragile objects.

Meanwhile, Lionel and Nia flipped the latches on a panel in the center of the ceiling. Lambo seized it in the tips of an outstretched claw as it came loose and dropped.

A slender dappled snout appeared in the opening. It was Esen, ears pinned back by wind, jaw hanging in a grin.

"We didn't die!"

40: Train Afternoon

IF Duggs had bothered to tell us she'd regularly landed her outsized construction aircar on moving vehicles, platforms, and once on a ship at sea during a hurricane, I might not have left little holes in the upholstery of its front seat. Then again, she'd enjoyed watching me fret.

I was beginning to suspect our relationship moving forward would be full of such interactions and resolved to learn everything about her colorful life in preparation.

A magnet at the end of a rope had attached us to the train, grapples had matched our speed and direction, then Duggs pushed a button and we'd lowered to touch without a bump. Having done so, no one inside appeared to notice, so Paul had to climb out onto the roof of the moving car to tap a code with Duggs' hammer.

Being answered by heavy thuds from inside.

Which wasn't a relaxing moment even if Duggs had supplied Paul with magnet grips, the wind whipping along the top of the car. A car that began to shimmy with the imbalance of us on top, so she'd suggested he hurry it up.

When the hatch opened, they sent me through first as the least useful pair of hands. I couldn't help my relieved "We didn't die!"

But then it was to work, and quickly.

I dropped into the car, helped by Lionel and a strange Botharan female in a business suit who had to be the special envoy and made a good first impression by not grabbing my tail.

"The Emboldened are dead. We have the embryos." I pointed up needlessly, the first canister already coming through the hatch.

"OUT OF THE WAY!"

I jumped down with the others as Lambo landed on top of the table, claws ready to receive the canister. Which he did, the table cracking beneath him but holding. "TAKE IT!"

The wind overhead wasn't that noisy, but I supposed Lambo needed to express his joy somehow.

Evan and another stranger took hold of the canister. He managed to give me one of his brilliant smiles and I let my tail drift sideways. Once.

Having an urgent message to convey. "Lionel—there are Kraal waiting in ambush ahead of you. Train-to-train communications are—" primitive, being Botharan tech, "—secure. Warn the other train, and stop this one. Duggs will go for Mal."

With the grenades and bombs, Paul adamant Skalet wasn't getting them back. What I wanted to know was how he'd got them in the first place. *My web-kin didn't share.*

Lionel ran for the door to the engine. Lambo passed down the third canister and reached for the fourth. It was a wonder more Carasians didn't work in freight—

"Where's Paul?" With concern.

"Up there with Duggs." I sniffed her as discreetly as possible. She had the smell of someone who'd traveled over saltwater, and maybe walked outside during the trip. Also of peaches and hand-washing. "You're from Grandine."

"Yes. I'm—"

"LAST ONE!"

"—Special Envoy Niala Mavis. Please call me Nia. And you're Esen-alit-Quar?"

She could have gone with *only Lanivarian in the system,* and I appreciated the courtesy. "I am. You can call me Esen. Paul's told me about your mission." I lowered my ears in sympathy. "We have—"

The train came to a stop just as the table collapsed under the combination of Carasian, the final canister, and Paul—who'd dropped down unaware of the weakened state of the furniture. Next came a final jolt as Duggs disconnected her aircar and lifted away.

We'd done it.

Almost.

I looked at Nia. "We need to talk."

Kelly came forward into the car to let us know the other train had halted. "The Kraal want to deal with their own. Goff says they've the gear, all right."

I watched Paul, Nia, and Lionel do that Human thing where they held a meeting with their eyes and reached a consensus in under a second. *It was most mysterious.*

"Tell them we expect prisoners," she said. Kelly nodded and left.

"I should be there," Lambo rumbled in disappointment.

Paul rapped his knuckles on a claw. "The special envoy is a target too."

The giant cheered. "I WILL PROTECT YOU!"

Nia winced. "Protect me quietly, please."

"I will be stealthy," in an almost-whisper. Promise made, Lambo crunched over the ruined table, heading for the vulnerable leading end of the train car. Unfortunately, a lower handling claw snagged the white cloth, dragging broken table bits with him until he stopped to try and shake it off, looking rather desperate.

Evan helped remove it. Eyestalks whirled gratefully, then Lambo continued through the car at greater speed. Nia's assistant, Onlee, made a valiant grab for a mass of coats on the floor—no, for the tray of breakables under the coats. She managed to rescue a bottle before a spongy foot came down, producing the unmistakable *smash* of glass. An eyestalk bent, but Lambo gave no other indication he'd noticed the carnage, continuing on to his post.

"You made him head of security," Lionel commented.

"I feel safe," Paul said, though how he kept from smiling I couldn't guess.

We hadn't suffered a Kraal attack—yet—but the train car looked as if we had. The Library Lobby being in no better shape, I had to hope the meeting could be moved to the other car. Assuming they weren't attacked in the next few minutes. *Safety seemed in short supply.*

Having helped put the canisters in a tidy row on the engine end of the car—a move seemingly to prevent the Sacrissee from retrieving their own embryos, but I didn't point this out—dear Evan busied himself removing table wreckage from the chairs. Those, being metal and bolted to the floor, had survived with only a few dents, proving the value of the design, if not the comfort.

Nia's assistant Onlee stood to one side, holding the bottle. I'd the feeling she wanted to open it.

"Thank you, Evan." Nia took his hand. "I truly hope you don't plan a report on this to your Commonwealth."

He looked charmingly flustered. I was mildly offended, but Paul clapped his shoulder, affecting a rescue. "I vouch for our diplomat."

No longer being Bess, I knew I must be mistaken when Nia's expression as she looked at Paul appeared to fill with bitterness and distaste. Neither could be right. I'd excellent hearing and there'd been worry in her voice when she'd asked after him.

I fell back on my usual working principle that Humans, especially in groups, were confusing. Although I could be angry at Skalet and worry about her at the same time.

As now. As Paul and Nia sat to exchange needful information and, by their body language, possibly argue over definitions, I edged close to Lionel. "The captain of the *Trium Pa* is dead," I whispered.

He started and gave me a worried look I understood completely.

"It wasn't Skalet. Haben-ru left the ship to look for—maybe you should join that." That being a conversation now including hand gestures.

"Is she safe?"

In no sense, but I knew what he meant. "We won't know until she decides we should. She's always been like that," I added.

"And you—you're all right?"

"I was stuck in a cave with Kraal." I put my snout near his ear to whisper, "As Bess."

Lionel's eyes widened, then he patted my arm. "Poor you."

I tipped my ears to show my appreciation. In my experience, sincere sympathy for the consequences of my occasionally hasty choices was hard to come by—*and not always deserved, but this time it was.* "It's what I found that—"

Nia surged from her seat. "What?!"

"And Paul's just told her."

To the credit of the person selected by the Botharan Government to represent the entire planet this afternoon, after that one understandable outburst, Nia composed herself. Outwardly, at least. I could smell a tinge of stress-sweat, but no one else had my nose and I certainly wasn't going to bring it up.

Besides, the other Humans in the car smelled worse.

Also not something to mention.

"This missile. Is it still functional?"

This to me, so I dipped my ears to indicate indecision. "What I saw appeared intact. The doors and automatic lighting worked. I didn't go into the control room to check. There was a battle underway." I tried for nonchalance; it came out with a hint of whine and I heard Paul take a quick little breath.

Evan gasped aloud and he lifted his hand in apology. "You could have been killed," he said earnestly.

"I hid," I assured him.

"Wisely so," Lionel told me. "What I can add? The Peacemaker was designed for extended storage. I think we must assume this one remains an active threat."

"Against this world." Nia gave me a tight smile. "You've done Botharis a great service, Esen. If I'd gone into negotiations with the Kraal without this information, I might have believed their lies."

"They aren't the same Kraal," Paul objected. "Nia—you know that."

"What I know is the Confederacy's arrived on our doorstep at the exact moment we've discovered the weapon they left on our world—a weapon for one purpose. To annihilate those who oppose them. That's not bargaining. They're here with an ultimatum, and I won't bow to it." She turned to Evan. "Polit Gooseberry, I wish to open negotiations with the Commonwealth to bring Botharis under its protection. Can you do that?"

Evan licked his lips, glanced at me, then nodded. "I'll need a translight com."

The Commonwealth was an ocean compared to the palm-sized puddle that was the Confederacy's handful of systems and allies. A noxious poisonous puddle, granted, but in no way was this a fair fight. And a fight it would be, because a toehold on Botharis threatened to complete an arc putting the Commonwealth in the path of any Kraal expansion.

Paul knew it too. "Nia—"

"What, Paul? Wait? Hear them out? Listen to every side while this world burns, the world you abandoned until it suited you to come back?" Her voice was cool and even. She might have been listing the ingredients in fudge or describing the weather, and the effect was so disturbing the hair rose between my shoulders and I held back a snarl.

I must have wrinkled my snout because she turned on me next. "I want peace, Esen. But it's never been something the Kraal gave us. It's been what we've had to take."

Paul ran that hand through his hair, but he wasn't exasperated with me. "Nia, I'm agreeing with you. If they've come with an ultimatum, we need one to counter it. The only choice, the right one, is dangling Commonwealth entry."

"As if I want your approval. Or need it."

"Just listen, please. Set up the offer through Evan. Have them stand by for you to sign it—but hear the Kraal before you do." Paul looked at me. "In case we're wrong."

"It's why we built the Library," I said, knowing what he wanted. "To prevent fatal mistakes. The Sacrissee are part of the Kraal agenda, a part we don't yet understand, and the most dangerous thing right now—more than a missile—is that ignorance. You need to ask the right question."

Nia's gaze shifted to the canisters. When it came back to me, I saw the glimmer of fierce resolve. "What are they both afraid of?"

Elements

THE train eased into motion and up to speed. Kelly remained on alert for stray elk, though she could be forgiven for worrying more about stray blasterfire.

The sun wouldn't set for another hour, but it was low, this time of year, and already behind the hills. Shadows stretched across the snow and turned the forests into impenetrable walls. They were minutes from a meeting that would reshape this world and these forests, its people and their lives, regardless of outcome.

Still, the time crawled. Lionel glanced over at Evan, holding a similar watch at the opposite window. The young diplomat looked serious and focused. As he should be, having started the process of absorbing little independent Botharis into the galaxy-spanning Commonwealth.

Bureaucratic dithering and layers of authorizations should have bought them breathing space, but dear, helpful Evan had known exactly whom to contact and what to say. Special Envoy Niala Mavis found herself in the unenviable position of being a word and thumbprint away from making planetary history. Not that the vast majority of the Commonwealth would notice.

The Kraal would. Those in the Commonwealth aware of the Kraal would, too, and there'd be a space station in the night sky, with patrol ships and Survey presence and very likely observation stations on both moons to keep watch over the neighborhood.

Necessary evils? If there was a bright side, the artisans in the village would have a new market for their goods. He'd probably not be able to afford a second pot.

Lionel pretended to look out the window again, watching the reflection of the car interior. Nia sat poring through her notes, reading some aloud to Onlee who sat with her recorder on her lap like a forlorn pet and the bottle of serpitay she'd rescued between her feet.

Paul sat on a portion of cleared floor, legs outspread and head against the wall; his eyes were closed—not asleep, but catching what rest he could. Able to rest because Esen was curled next to him, her eyes drinking in his face, and Lionel felt something in his own heart restored.

Nia moved, then, as if to ease her neck. Saw Paul and Esen. Watched them for a long moment. Did her face soften?

It might have been the reflection, distorting the image.

Or, Lionel admitted to himself, *his own wish for peace.*

Lambo snapped a claw, making a sound like a bell. "The other train is in view. I am ready!" With that, he crouched, great claws open in menace and aimed at the door. "NONE SHALL PASS!"

"Thank you, Lambo, but they're supposed to," Nia reminded him. "Remember what we discussed. You need to be behind us."

Eyestalks drooped in disappointment, the Carasian rattled and clanked back through the train car, a passage this time free of table bits and cloth. Or glass. They'd cleared the car by tossing debris out the door; Lionel'd have to send maintenance along the tracks before the regular service resumed. *If it did.*

Lambo paused hopefully in front of the canisters. "I could—"

"All the way back, please," Nia insisted.

"Kelly says we should brace ourselves," Lionel warned the others. "There'll be a slight bump as we connect, to be sure the hookup is solid."

"Onlee?"

"The recorder's secure. I've this." The assistant held up the bottle. "I hope they brought glasses."

Nia glanced at Evan.

He raised the translight com. "Ready to send at your command, Special Envoy Mavis."

Evan was right to be formal, to be sure they acted in every possible way to ensure her authority was unquestioned.

Lionel couldn't help but look for Esen.

The scoundrel grinned at him, her lovely tail sweeping from side to side.

"Optimist," he accused. *Though in times like these, optimism became necessity.*

The bump came, less than he'd anticipated. Both operators knew their work and were wary of setting off whatever the Kraal had brought with them.

Paul opened their door and stood to one side.

Cold air entered, ice dust forming.

Then the other door opened.

And Skalet walked through.

41: Train Sunset

I appreciated a dramatic entrance as much as the next being, but this, I told my web-kin with a fang, was too much.

Of course she smiled at me, more than pleased with herself and my reaction. This was Skalet the Smug. Skalet the— I narrowed my eyes. I knew that look. She'd accomplished something difficult and important.

I only hoped it was to the benefit of those who lived on this world, because behind Skalet were those who didn't.

"Special Envoy Mavis," my web-kin greeted with a flawless bow. "I am Courier S'kal-ru. May I have the honor of introducing your guests?"

Nia's bow was the precise degree higher, acknowledging Skalet as an emissary of noble, but lower rank. "Please do so."

Two Kraal entered first, taking positions beside the open door. They weren't introduced, though I supposed being in full armor with massive rifles carried across their chests was sufficient. Lambo rumbled and snapped a claw, receiving assessing looks.

Next came a diminutive male.

Like Skalet, his face was bared. His affiliation tattoos were so dense his skin appeared a mottled black and red, his blue eyes shockingly bright in the midst. His right ear was missing and he walked with a black cane, no doubt a weapon, but wore no obvious armor, only a black suit, the fabric stiff with muted silver threads. A slender case hung from a strap across a shoulder.

Perhaps a weapon. Perhaps something better.

"Courier Virul-ru," Skalet introduced, touching the backs of her hands to her cheeks, wounded and whole.

Was that a note of respect in her voice? She'd acquired a new tattoo, curled beside her eye. If real, she had been busy.

The guards at the door saluted as well, but in sequence to ensure one had hand to trigger at all times.

I took a closer look at Virul's courier. He exuded a sense of weight, as if he were more dense than normal Humans—*unlikely*. Suddenly, I realized where I'd felt this before. Or rather from whom.

Ersh.

A Human of unusual power, then. Who wielded it by his own will, no others. Incredibly dangerous, yes, but Skalet-memory claimed his office—and hers—was governed by a constraint uncommon in Kraal society. Couriers were granted extraordinary authority for the simple reason they alone acted to hold the Confederacy together.

Most of the time. They'd been known to prune it.

"Welcome to Botharis." Nia bowed, long and low, proving she recognized what the Kraal had sent.

The rest of us weren't to be introduced, which was fine by me. Unless our contribution was required, not being brought to Virul-ru's personal attention and doubtless excellent memory was healthy.

I lifted my snout, catching the scent of what—who—waited to enter next. *Sacrissee.*

They were magnificent. As a first impression went, that was as far from the Sacrissee of old as it was possible to go. Not that I hadn't seen fine specimens—including Lesley's lovely rendering—but in general the species tended toward attractive, shy, and prone to smear tartt.

They didn't look much like the Emboldened either. The two officials who entered the car were as tall as Skalet, with a confident upright bearing. Yes, they'd horns and bright yellow eyes, but these faces were wider, the bodies more slender and graceful, and their fingers were elongated. Their hides differed too. Where Sacrissee were uniformly light and dappled and the Emboldened almost black, the male official's coat was light brown, with white flashes up the sides of his head. The female was reddish, darkening to bronze on her head and limbs.

Colors held in Ersh-memory, before the Sacrissee had decided to venture into space and culled those different from the majority, as if diversity were some contagion they feared to carry offworld.

I could be judgmental. But from our perspective, reducing variation in a species not only diminished its robustness, it meant one or more of us became conspicuous. Forget my youth. As a Sacrissee, Mixs had been white with faint reddish stripes on her upper shoulders; after the cull, she couldn't risk being seen. Ersh had told her to be patient. *Had she seen this coming?*

They wore long open vests, white and worked with red and black symbols that looked very much like affiliation tattoos, if stylized.

Nia gave me a look and the tiniest nod, recognizing them too.

The Sacrissee noticed the windows, covered but for slits, and gave low approving "huffft huffts" to one another.

"Welcome to this *IN*," Nia greeted, not missing the moment.

An ordinary Human male followed the Sacrissee, dressed in a medical smock as if carrying a satchel marked with the Commonwealth symbol for medtech weren't enough. Thickened eyelids and bright red hair hinted Hinesburg II, one of the older Human worlds; the broad nostrils at—since his smock had "Molancor Genomics" printed on the breast, there was little point guessing. His gaze found me, lingered on Lambo, then locked on the canisters.

He actually licked his lips.

Far from me to fault someone for loving their work, even if public lip-licking seemed obsessive in anyone not a Hurn, but given the tech's focus on the non-Human, I decided this was not someone to invite home. I saw Evan's fingers curl into fists as if he'd come to the same conclusion—or had his own immediate dislike of this stranger. *Uncharacteristic.*

Nia checked beyond the seven now in the car, seeing no more to come. She looked at Virul-ru. "There were to be prisoners," she said mildly.

Skalet lifted her hand. The two guards deactivated their distort-hoods, revealing shallow cuts beside their left eyes. Battlefield "tat-toos." They'd earned a new affiliation. House Virul.

"As you see, we do not always war with each other," Virul-ru replied. His voice was reed-thin but strong. He lifted his cane slightly. "Shall we be seated, Special Envoy?"

"Of course."

It took a moment. I detected Evan's handiwork in the tilted bench for the Sacrissee—who noticed too and huffft'd in appreciation, but de-clined, preferring to stand with their backs to the Kraal guards. Which made me wonder if they'd a reason for that other than to maintain a *ready-to-run* posture. Their tails looked normal, but without a closer look—or snort in their boots—

Which wasn't going to happen. Though if they spat, I could find saliva on the floor. *Around such fond hopes did my life revolve.*

Virul-ru sat facing Nia. Skalet went to stand behind and to the right of the courier, the position of greatest reliability. I lowered my ears at her. She smiled again.

We were going to talk about so many things after this.

Lionel copied Skalet's move, going to stand behind and to the right of Nia. Paul had eased back to sit on a nearby bench beside Evan and Onlee, a seating arrangement that kept the three out of the way should Lambo need to leave that end of the car, while letting the Carasian loom menacingly over the canisters.

We hadn't discussed where the sole Lanivarian in the room was supposed to be. I'd the feeling *somewhere inconspicuous* covered the options preferred by everyone else.

Instead, I set my ears to paying attention and calmly took the seat beside Nia—just in time remembering to move my tail out of the way, to face my web-kin and Virul-ru.

"Curator Esen-alit-Quar," Nia introduced me, having no choice. "Our—expert."

I kept my lips over my fangs and gave a little bow, aware of Paul's quickly hidden dismay. *It wasn't as if we'd had time for a plan,* I con-soled myself.

"I'd like to check on our embryos." The Molancor tech patted his satchel.

"'Embryos?'" Lionel gave a dismissive little cough. "These are mushrooms. Administrator Kearn, at your service," he introduced himself to Virul-ru and the Sacrissee with a small bow. "The shipping label and manifest are quite clear."

"Those canisters contain our stolen children," the female Sacrissee objected. Her nasal bulb inflated, delicate blood vessels blue within its skin. "We insist—" Yellow eyes slid to Virul-ru and the bulb deflated, the *howl* almost imperceptible even to this me's ears, but very familiar. "We respectfully request the scientist be allowed to confirm this and, if so, to take our children in his care."

Virul-ru nodded. "They are the future."

Nothing a courier of his stature said was irrelevant. Nia knew it, too. "Lambo, please permit— Who are you?"

The tech had started moving. Now he stopped and, by the look on his face, suddenly realized he might not want to be the center of attention in this gathering. "Nesel Gabbert, Senior Researcher for Molancor Sacriss, your—honor—Envoy."

I kept my ears up. "Then I'm sure you're aware Botharis is a signatory of the Machin Protocol, Hom Gabbert, as is the Commonwealth."

He didn't like it. He'd like what I said next even less, and I displayed a cheery fang to show him how little I cared for his good opinion.

"Why have you added Modoran to the Sacrissee?"

Elements

PAUL tensed beside him and Evan sympathized. But he agreed with Esen. Someone had to speak not only for the embryos, but the Emboldened themselves.

And challenge Molancor—

Predictably, Gabbert's response was a flat, "I am not allowed to breach client confidentiality."

"Come now," Esen said, still looking cheerful. "I've spoken with the Emboldened—a brave and daring group, if I may say—and analyzed their genome. And just look at you." With a lift of her snout to the grimly motionless Sacrissee. "You're not typical at all. Handsome, but I see some new—and old—looks." Her cheer dropped away. "You're modifying yourselves. Why?"

"To survive," the female Sacrissee replied.

The terrifying older Kraal stirred. "Curator. Special Envoy. If we are to have such urgent honesty today, permit me to save time. S'kal-ru. The images."

"Your Glory." She held out her hand, palm up and supporting a compact vidprojector. A series of images appeared, floating between Virul-ru and Nia. Lambo gave an interested rumble.

Paul leaned forward, eyes intent, but all Evan could see were ships. Each image held a broken, lifeless wreck drifting alone in space. He'd no idea what the connection could be, unless they were—

"Sacrissee," Lionel identified. He pointed to one. "Interplanetary freighter." To another. "Passenger transport." His hand dropped. "I wasn't aware you'd suffered so many losses."

"Not all at once. The first went missing over fifty years ago. The rest, over the years between." Virul-ru put a second hand on his cane. "None have been recovered."

"But these images—" Nia frowned.

"Were sent, one at a time, to Sacriss VII." Skalet made an adjustment. The images became smaller, aligned in a row, and around each was now a frame. To Evan, it looked disturbingly like Great Gran's Gooseberry wall. *A collection.* The Kraal enlarged one to show a frame's detail. Abstract markings. Similar, possibly identical to the frames around the rest.

Who would collect images of dead starships? And who would frame and send them like this?

The male Sacrissee spoke, his voice so low and deep Evan felt it in his bones. "The Vast *OUT* has once again become a hunting ground. When this happened in our distant past, Sacrissee culled the weak and vulnerable, to make the *IN* stronger and resilient. To our shame, we no longer possess what would make the *IN* strong enough. We looked beyond."

Virul-ru's fingers tapped his cane. "It is our shame to have failed those within our affiliation by treaty. We support our allies in their efforts, even as we search for their hunters."

"And have you found anything?" Lionel closed his mouth, then bowed. "Forgive the question."

"I ask it too," Nia said firmly. "A threat to space traffic threatens us all."

"Bringing me to our proposition, Special Envoy Mavis." Handing his cane to Skalet, the courier put his slender case across his knees. "A new relationship between us."

"We're not Inhaven 413." Nia's look was a summons. Evan stood, coming forward to hand her the translight com, careful of Esen's paws as he withdrew. "Botharis will not be a Kraal protectorate, Virul-ru. I am prepared to accept entry into the Commonwealth." Nia's finger hovered over the waiting pad.

Esen reached out to touch her hand. "Wait."

42: Train Sunset

I might not be able to read each and every nuance of Human expression, but Skalet wasn't being subtle. The slight lift to her eyebrow, that deepening at the corner of her mouth? Amusement at Nia's conclusion; respect for her resolve.

Meaning the Kraal had something else in mind. "Hear him out," I told Nia, removing my hand.

She gave me a look I'd no trouble reading either, having seen it from Paul. *You'd better be right.* I flicked my ears in a *so do I,* not that I knew if she could read them.

Paul could. Lionel and Evan.

Disconcertingly, Virul-ru bowed to me. "My thanks, Curator." His hands rested on the case. "I speak for the Kraal Confederacy, with full authority to propose and commit to our unconditional and permanent withdrawal from Botharis and its system."

Nia pushed the translight com at Lionel, who took it. Both looked alarmingly numb, so I spoke before Virul-ru changed his mind, using a phrase from Skalet-memory. "What surety is offered?"

His eyes shone. "This." He opened the case. "We will find and remove all contingencies."

The elegant black velvet lining made the four disks inside look like priceless artifacts. There was an empty fifth slot and I knew what belonged in it.

They weren't artifacts at all. They were locator-keys, and if I had to guess? "Contingencies" meant there was more than one Peacemaker hidden on the planet.

I truly didn't like this culture.

Paul rose to his feet, the Kraal guards shifting to focus on him. Gabbart used the distraction to crouch and hurry to the canisters, going to his knees in front of them as if in worship. The more likely object was the Carasian looming like a great god over him, but Lambo's all-eyed attention was locked on Skalet.

"I am Paul Ragem. Special Envoy?" He came forward, the Emboldened's locator-key in his hand.

Skalet actually looked impressed. I showed her a fang. "This is proof you don't speak for all in the Confederacy," I told Virul-ru. "I was with the Sacrissee—the Emboldened. They were promised this planet for their new home by Houses Arzul and Bract. This was the means."

Nia took the locator-key from Paul, lifting it between finger and thumb. Her blue eyes were ice-cold. "Is House Virul playing one of its games?"

But I was looking at the Sacrissee and saw their look of disgust, a look the Emboldened didn't deserve. "They'd lost hope," I said, unable to stop myself. "They claimed you were culling their kind and had to flee for their lives."

A *howl*. "True Sacrissee accept the cull for the good of the *IN!*"

I rose to my feet, fangs showing. "They were your people."

"Our way is none of yours, but I will answer." The female's tail lashed. "We kill no one. Waste no one. How can we, when we don't know what we need to become or how? Gabbert, explain."

The Molancor scientist straightened from his crouch. "It's true. We wouldn't be part of anything wrong. I can open our records—"

I laid my ears flat. "This isn't about you."

He swallowed. "A minute percentage of chimeras exhibit extreme aggression. They're a danger to others and to themselves. We—the Sacrissee made a home for them on Sacriss III. We catch them and—" he subsided.

Anyone would, seeing the loathing on Paul's face. "It's a lifeless rock."

"A challenge," the male Sacrissee protested.

"A testing ground," I said to that, ears still flat and a snarl beneath the words. "To see if those extreme traits help them survive where you can't. No wonder the Emboldened fled."

"They were afraid." The female Sacrissee held out her hands, palm up. "We're all afraid. The Vast *OUT* looks back at us, hunts us, and even the smallest *IN* no longer holds safety. We want a future." She stiffened, the tail lashing again. "We have our people's permission. We do not ask yours."

I wanted to bite them, but Paul looked sad, all of a sudden, then gave a slow accepting nod. *Being better than me.* "Who takes them to Sacriss III?"

The Sacrissee looked at one another, then at Virul-ru.

The courier's lips stretched in a smile that made my tail want to disappear. "House Bract has—had the contract."

"And this." Nia held up the locator-key. "Your House has a hole in it."

"Not for long," Skalet vowed, and for some reason looked at Lionel.

Who abruptly drew himself up like a soldier on parade, ready to salute, and how a Human saw what took me another heartbeat to grasp about my own web-kin was a mystery for another time.

She was leaving. To chase the puzzle I'd put in front of her, of missing ships and strange markings, yes, but this was every bit as much about finding her place again amongst the most powerful of the Kraal and leaving me.

Leaving Lesy.

Had she guessed I hadn't shared about Ersh and the others? Known I must and couldn't bear to be part of it?

Whatever her reasons, she'd be back, being part of our Web.

It might not be in Lionel's lifetime.

Elements

S HE was leaving. To serve House Virul and this wizened little Kraal before him, and if Lionel could say a word to stop her—

He wouldn't. Skalet—S'kal-ru—deserved whatever glory lay ahead. She'd rise through the ranks of the Great Houses once more, working from the shadows. *Impressive.* Would follow the new clues they had, of the Sacrissee receiving images as well as the Kraal—who wouldn't admit their weakness. Who didn't dare. *Paul had been right.*

She'd left him her sanctum. Might contact him there—

Or not.

Lionel, to himself and quietly, suspected this—what Skalet chose to do—was the unstated goal of Esen's Web: to aim the course of ephemeral species toward survival with a nudge in this generation, a poke to that one.

If Skalet could help the Kraal survive themselves, how petty was his wish to be—what, her friend?

And inappropriate.

He'd a duty to this world, the Library, and these people. Still—

Because she looked at him, *allowed it,* Lionel took one last lingering look of his own, memorizing her stern, cool expression, the eager light in her eyes, the graceful lines of her face and hands. He closed his eyes, hearing his heart thud in his chest.

Then opened them to look at Virul-ru, who'd begun to speak.

43: Train Night

"**O**UR proposal stands, Special Envoy Mavis. The Kraal Confederacy will revoke any and all interest in your system and world forever, a commitment that will be enforced, with blood if necessary, upon every House by those I represent."

Nia held up the locator-key. "And this?"

He let her see his disgust. "An honorless weapon from the past. House Virul has vowed to eradicate every last vestige. We are grateful to do so here." His eyes narrowed. "That's not what you want."

"If you're going," Nia told him, "what I want is for you to be gone. Anything left on Botharis is ours to deal with."

Skalet looked amused. "You could blow yourselves up."

"You could make a 'mistake' and do the same." Nia pointed to the case. "That comes with locations and every code necessary. No tricks."

"Biometrics?" I showed fangs.

"There are none." Even so, Virul-ru leaned back slightly, as if he thought I was volunteering to bite. *His skin was probably coated in poison.* "Peacemakers were built to outlive their makers."

Nia considered this, then looked to me.

"It's your planet," I told her. "Though a question remains. I think it's the right one."

Her eyes gleamed. "Indeed." She turned to Virul-ru. "We have an impartial witness to all of this—the Commonwealth, in the person of

Polit Evan Gooseberry. I have, as I'm sure you do, a recording. It seems our guests from Sacriss have what they came for. Hom Gabbert?"

"The embryos are in excellent shape." Gabbert left his hand possessively on the canisters. *They hadn't wanted the Emboldened anyway.*

"We even have an excellent serpitay—and vegetable juice—with which to toast this epic moment in our histories." She let the hint, no more, of a smile touch her lips. "If no glasses. I am inclined to accept your proposition, Courier Virul-ru, but I have, as Esen says, one question left. Why?"

"I act for the good of the Kraal Confederacy. In this instance, I act for its continued survival." He brought his cane down once on the floor. "That, Special Envoy, is my answer."

Botharis was no threat to the Kraal. Of no value, other than as a field for games of hierarchy and glory, and I saw then the larger picture. The one Skalet must.

The Sacrissee weren't the only ones to receive warning images of dead ships. Survey kept theirs hidden, the Sacrissee reinvented themselves in a species-appropriate if dire attempt to survive, and the Kraal?

Must have received images as well. They consolidated their resources. Pulled together. Retreated from what they must believe a superior foe and if I'd a guess? The same offer was being made right now to Inhaven Ag-Colony 413 and every other non-Kraal world in the Confederacy.

What did they know we didn't? I had to trust Skalet would find out.

Nia rose to her feet. "On behalf of the Planetary Government of Botharis, and all its citizens, I, Special Envoy Niala Mavis, do accept the proposition made this day by Courier Virul-ru on behalf of the Kraal Confederacy to leave our system and never come back."

She threw the words down like a gauntlet. Virul-ru rose to his feet and smiled, then offered her the case with a bow. "Our surety and bond. The codes are beneath the cloth."

I stood and took the thing, holding it so Nia could put the locator-key I'd brought into the final slot with the rest.

Kept holding it as Onlee came up with her bottle and Evan with a container of juice. The Sacrissee refused to drink, meaning I'd no access to spit, but the old courier tipped the bottle back and drank without hesitation, handing it to Nia who did the same.

The Kraal who had been Bract or Arzul but were now Virul and who knew what else carried the canisters of unborn Sacrissee chimeras into their car, the Molancor scientist hovering like a mother, the Sacrissee uttering their soft "huffft, hufffts" as they followed.

I watched them go, hearing Ersh's voice. *Biology's messy, Youngest. But it's all they have. You can't stop life trying to survive.* It didn't help.

Evan watched, too, his face grimmer than I expected, and I thought the Commonwealth might receive a tip to pay close attention to the work of Molancor Sacriss.

Virul-ru and Nia signed and pressed their thumbs to paired copies of the simple document the courier had brought. It was paper, traditional for Kraal and on Botharis, and some might have found it ironic their one congruence was now used to separate them.

I found it implausible, but then I'd Ersh-memory and Skalet's. The Great Houses of the Kraal plotted over generations, schemes twisting and turning, goals hidden even from those given the responsibility of setting the path. I'd believe they'd decided to mix their precious bloodlines with Ervickians before I believed they'd leave Botharis alone.

The Kraal left, Skalet with them, and not a glance back or a smile did my web-kin offer. Fair enough. She played a game now and took care not to draw us in with her. If I hadn't thought the Cosmic Gods were laughing, I'd have considered this an act of charity.

The train cars unhooked, ours heading back to the Library, the other on its way to the landing field and ships. Lambo appeared asleep.

Nia went to stand at the door, looking out into the growing dark and receding lights of the train car. Perhaps checking for elk.

Paul went to her. I tilted my ears, reasoning if he didn't want me to hear, he shouldn't talk where I could.

"Congratulations."

"I'm not sure they're deserved." Her voice was low and shaky. "Did that just happen? Did the Kraal just give us everything we want and walk away? Or was I a fool."

"You'd the opportunity," Paul said gently. "You'd no choice but take it."

"With help. Esen's. Everyone's. Yours." Almost too quiet for my ears. "Funny, isn't it. All this time, I've wanted you to stay dead."

This wasn't good. Not good at all. My tail tried to creep between my legs.

Paul stood beside a person who could say such a terrible thing, and all he did was nod, as if Nia was being entirely sensible.

"But you're not," she said next, a little louder and with an emotion I wished I could grasp. "And it matters, the work you do here. Your Library is important."

"We think so."

"Those ships." She let out a long breath, fogging the window, then faced Paul. "I've a question for the Library. I've no new information to offer."

"You don't need it, Nia." His head lifted. "You want to know what's going on. Who sent those images and why."

"I think we have to know—all of us. Don't you?"

"I do." Paul turned his head to look right at me.

He knew about his mother's ship—and that I'd been listening, but that wasn't the important bit. He knew! *I spend one night in a cave and have no secrets left.* Other than the stashes of fudge I'd hidden as Esolesy Ki, and for all I knew he'd found those too.

While I'd looked forward to not having secrets from my best, first friend, I'd envisioned more a careful sharing, with each revelation coming out in a way that made me seem—if still at fault, at least with excellent-at-the-time reasons.

But no. While I'd been gone, Paul had learned everything I'd kept hidden and now I'd have to wait and see if he planned to scold me for all of them at once, or if this was going to be a drawn out sequence of daily or weekly scoldings. There'd be intervals of not-scolding because he was too kind to berate me constantly even when I'd deserved it.

Then there was Duggs—

I sighed. Twice.

"Hello, Esen. Glad you're back and safe." Evan looked worn around the edges; understandable, given the circumstances. "Quite the day."

"We'll play in the snow tomorrow," I promised.

"'Play.'" He shook his head. "Sorry, Es. I can't. I'm leaving tonight.

Onlee says I can travel with them to Grandine. Catch a flight from there. I'm going home."

My heart sank. "What's wrong? Is it—was it Lesley? Did she do something?" *Try to eat you being high on my list.*

"What?" He seemed genuinely surprised by the question. "Oh, no. She's very nice. Talented too. I wish we'd had more time—but I have to see Great Gran."

I licked his chin. "Then I promise not to have an emergency next time you come." I considered a moment. "Or if we do, you can stay with Duggs. She has a nice cabin in the woods. Well, it's not nice yet, but it will be—"

He wasn't listening. He was staring beyond me at Paul and Nia, something wistful in his eyes.

All at once, I wondered if Paul had a secret of his own. Not that he'd had time for one, but still.

Maybe we could trade.

Makings

THEY come to them, for Oola will not leave the other and the other cannot run.

They come slowly, tails curled in the aspect of peace and calm.

And they have eyes as yellow as a flower, and their fur is in strange new colors, and they *howl* softly.

Oola *HOWLS* back, raising her deadly hands, claws out and glistening with poison. Stands over the other. Refuses to leave.

They crouch and make a circle around her and the other as if creating an *IN* with their bodies, then stop.

Oola hisses a warning.

"Be not afraid," one says.

She is not and *HOWLS.*

"Come. We will care for you both," says another.

Lies! Oola slashes her hands through the air.

"You are what we want to be. You will save the *IN*."

She laughs and *HOWLS* and slashes her hands in the air and dares shout back. "You lie! I am *WRONG!*"

Then those around her and the other grip hands with one another, as would a kingroup before settling to sleep around the young ones and the helpless, as her kin once did, but no longer—

"You are not wrong, child of ours. You are the future."

And when they *howl,* everyone together, it becomes the sound of comfort and belonging, the sound itself an *IN* so safe Oola answers instinct.

She lowers herself beside the other and submits, willing to be saved.

Closes her eyes, alone no more.

44: Farmhouse Night

ALONE at last. Lionel hadn't been in the mood for sleep or company. He'd stayed with Nia to brief Mal on the Kraal "surety" and to arrange something more secure than a velvet-lined case for what could lead anyone to five planet-destroying missiles.

Home at last. And it smelled like supper.

I stopped inside our farmhouse doorway, in no mood to clean up after Lesy even if having to clean up after her meant she was herself again.

Though after almost five hundred years of cleaning up, you'd think I'd be used to it.

Paul sniffed. "Lesley's in the kitchen."

He sounded equally reluctant to find out what she'd done to it, so I licked his ear. "Maybe it's sandwiches."

"It doesn't smell like sandwiches." He looked at me with some dismay. "Will she cook all the time?"

"Oh, no." Neither of us were ready for the big messes. *We'd talk about art supplies tomorrow.* "She makes good sandwiches," I said thoughtfully, being hungry, and edged toward the kitchen. *How bad could it be?*

"Wait." Paul had his serious, *be truthful* look a bit earlier than I'd expected.

"We're standing in a puddle," I pointed out.

He lowered his voice. "Before we see Lesy—are you going to tell her? About Death. About what happened?"

I flattened my ears, but he was of our Web and deserved to know. "Yes." When Paul kept looking at me, standing in the puddle, I added a grudging, "Soon."

"Good." He gave a relieved smile and took a step into the hall. "We might as well eat— What's all this? Have you been shopping?"

"Been in a cave," I reminded him, coming to see what had caught his attention. A tall shipping crate stood in a shadow by the door. "Is it a present?" I hurried to it, exhaustion forgotten as my inner Lishcyn came to the forefront; such crates could contain silk. I read the label. "It's not a present."

"Then why's your tail wagging, Fangface?" Paul asked, coming to read over my shoulder. *"Lesley Delacora, Resident Artiste of the All Species' Library of Linguistics and Culture. Esen—"*

"Well, she is an artist." With access to Ersh's bottomless funds and a taste for beautiful things, details I thought Paul should discover for himself. "And what a clever cover story." I should have guessed the web-kin known for her ability to make a niche within cultures would do so in ours. *If not this fast.*

"She's given herself a job." He looked at the ceiling. "And my bedroom."

"She may want the entire house," I advised him. "We'll have to get Duggs building sooner than we thought."

"About Duggs—"

Oh, no. We were not starting this in the hallway, while hungry.

"First one there gets the sandwich!" I dropped to all fours, happy to cheat.

There weren't sandwiches. There was a covered dish on the stovetop, a stack of plates keeping warm beside it. Otherwise, the kitchen was utterly normal. No, cleaner than normal. I looked around twice to be sure.

Paul lifted the lid and smiled. "I see you shared the recipe for Auntie Ruth's Macaroni."

"How'd she make it without a mess?" I protested. The last time I tried to make Paul's favorite comfort food, *which I may have shared,* I'd boiled-over starch coating, well, everything. Including me. "It's not fair."

He raised an eyebrow. "That's your first thought?"

Starch was hard to wash off. I flipped an ear.

He chuckled, then we served ourselves and sat to eat, Paul pouring glasses of wine.

Except we didn't. Eat or drink. Or talk. We'd lit a candle and dimmed the lights and sat looking at each other across the table, as if our nightly routine had somehow gotten stuck.

Or as if it couldn't start, without the truth first.

"I put the blaster in the pot," I said at last. "Janet Chase brought it to the kitchen to kill me with, but Skalet had poisoned her so she couldn't. Before she died, Chase showed me why she'd come to Botharis."

Shadows flickered across Paul's face. "Mother's ship. The *Pathfinder.* Lionel showed me. Like the Sacrissee—and Kraal. They received a similar image, of a ship in Botharan space." He touched his glass. Turned it. "I understand you wanted to protect her memory for me, Es, but it wasn't necessary." With a hint of warmth.

"I know that now." I poked at my supper, then said very very quietly. "I didn't want you to come home and find—I hid the blaster and image, then I ate her corpse. I did *not*—" I emphasized, looking up at him, "—assimilate a single molecule."

"I'm glad," he said seriously, then the corner of his mouth quirked. "Might not have been my first concern. You know. Blaster? You?"

"I can't be killed like that," I reminded him haughtily.

A sober, "I remember."

He'd watched me absorb the energy of similar weapons in my greenhouse on Minas XII, when Skalet had sent Kraal to flush us out of hiding. Remembering, I found a bright spot. "Joel could still visit."

Paul shook his head. "Sorry, Old Blob. I sent him a message to turn around—travel's hard on him right now." He turned serious. "And I'm not so sure space travel is safe for anyone, anymore."

"Skalet's hunting whatever it is," I assured him, and myself. "If the Kraal know anything, she'll find out."

He lifted his glass to me. "You caught that." Paul took a sip, then tilted the glass as if watching the light play through it, but I thought he saw something else. "Lesley found out Evan's not entirely Human."

Because of my lack of hat and mitts. "Does he know? Is that why he went home?"

"We didn't tell him, but the whole business with Molancor bothered him. When we parted, he looked like someone after answers. Then, of course, there was Nia."

Usually, I could follow my friend's leaps. Sometimes. *On occasion, Humans being tricky.* This time, I floundered. "Because Nia's helping Evan get home?" That couldn't be it. "Because she made him promise not to tell? Because he won't." Paul sat back, waiting for me to give up and ask. Knowing that game, I stared down my snout at him. "Because she's fertile and he wants to tell Great Gran about her?" Evan having told me a fair amount about his relative's ambitions for him.

"Stop." A quiet chuckle. "You're not even close. Evan knows who Nia is. Who she was."

"I know who she is too." I raised my ears encouragingly. "Who was she?"

"When my stint on the *Rigus* was over, Nia and I were to sign a life contract. Marry."

His secret. I knew what a Human life contract was.

Just as I knew what this was—a moment of grief for what might have been. *I just didn't know what it meant for us.*

"But you met me," I said, as cautiously as I'd step on ice. *Not that this me would.*

Paul took a deeper drink of wine. "That I did."

Ah. "Evan. You told him because he was falling in love with you." Then Evan, being his romantic self, had jumped to conclusions about Lesy's Human-self, explaining those confusing Paul-cares-for-Lesley comments.

Much as I could sympathize with our lovelorn young diplomat, Paul was my concern, and hadn't Nia the once-loved told him—*where I could hear*—that she'd wanted him to stay dead?

It didn't bode well for a reconciliation. *And I'd thought his family a problem.*

I leaned forward to take a tiny sniff. "Are you all right?"

"No. Not yet," he admitted, a finger touch on my snout. His gray eyes glistened. "Humans cling to emotions. To hopes. Longer than we should sometimes. You've noticed, I'm sure."

Not the time for a list. I nodded instead.

"I didn't tell you about Nia because I couldn't. I was afraid if I did I'd have to accept she was gone too. It was my way of holding on to her. To what we felt for one another. It wasn't rational." With the same slightly impatient edge he'd use when scolding me.

Paul wasn't to scold himself. "And when we came to Botharis," I told him, "you didn't tell me about Nia because you knew I'd try to find some way to—to—" I left it there and touched his nose. "For you."

"You'd want to fix it." A gentle smile. "Not everything can be fixed, Old Blob. Not everything should be. At least now I know Nia's well and she's done well. My disappearing—my being dead, then coming back? It hurt her and she's mad at me. As she should be. But she's bigger than that. Stronger. We can work together for the Library and this world, and that's enough. It has to be." He pointed a finger at me. "And you're to leave her alone. Promise."

My ears might have been at their most innocent, which always made Paul suspicious. "I promise." I found I'd an appetite after all, and put a forkful of noodles and cheese in my mouth.

"Duggs."

I sputtered and covered my mouth, winding up with noodles and cheese stuck to my paw. "Not fair," I grumbled, licking it clean.

Paul grinned. "Served you right."

"She wasn't afraid of me," I said wonderingly. "Not of anything about me."

"I think Duggs was more worried we'd Kraal in a secret basement, not that I know why."

"I do. Her grandparents were sous, abandoned in Lowesland. They were murdered by House Noitci."

We sat in a different silence for a moment, mourning those lost. Including the Emboldened, who, like the sous, had wanted a new life and died for it.

"So, Old Blob. Do we pack?" Paul asked.

I squinted at him, not sure he was serious. "Because of Duggs?" I wrinkled my snout. "She called me a blobbie!"

He laughed. "Then we'll stay."

I watched something less happy cross his face. "What is it?"

"Duggs has shown she can handle what you are. Lionel—he'll be fine. He understands. But Evan. Esen, he plans to come back. To stay our friend."

"Of course he does. He is."

Paul leaned forward, eyes filled with sorrow. "For that to happen, he can't know."

Because I was all he feared. Because I was a lie and Evan needed truth. Needed certainty.

My heart felt heavy, but I lifted my glass. "To the friends who can't."

He clicked it with his. "To the friends who can't."

We finished our meal, and most of the wine. I blew out the candle while Paul put the empty gooey dish into the sink to soak. We'd our routine back and I yawned, content again.

Paul rubbed my head. "You've three of those nice puffy new pads. Who gets the extra?"

"I am not sharing again!" I protested.

But I would. Always.

I waited for Paul's breathing to shift into a deep, well-earned sleep before getting up. I climbed the stairs to the loft where people thought he slept, then touched the control to lower the secret stair to where he had, until Lesy.

She was sitting in his lounge chair, as Lesley, wrapped in blankets and looking out over the Garden. "Youngest."

I padded over, sitting at her feet to enjoy the view. The moons' light flowed over the snow, blue-tinged and soft, turning mysterious everything known and familiar by day. Dark figures came in view, cautiously skirting the bio-eliminator field that isolated the Garden. Rhonda's elk. "We'll get you home tomorrow," I promised them.

"Don't," my Elder said, her voice soft. Mysterious. *A talent.*

"You want them to stay free? I thought you liked cheese."

"Esen."

"Sorry." I grew serious and looked up. "'Don't' what?"

"You and Skalet taste of loss. I don't want to know why. Don't share it. Let me keep us together, on Picco's Moon. Let me know the others are still there, on Ersh's mountain. See them there. See Ersh."

"But—it's not true," I said, trying to understand.

"Why does it have to be?" Her hand found my head, tenderly rubbed under an ear. "Seeing them like that makes me smile, Youngest. That's all I ask of life. To smile. Will you let me?"

It didn't feel like a reprieve. It felt like Ersh, leaning over my shoulder, chiming a solemn request to keep Lesy happy no matter what. It felt—

—as if I were the Senior Assimilator for the Web of Esen, and one of my own had asked for mercy.

I leaned into the caress. "I'll take you to meet Ally Orman tomorrow. She works in the Response Room. There's art."

"Art?" She laughed her wonderful laugh. "Tell me more, Youngest."

So I did.

Elements

IT wasn't *FEAR*.

Wasn't anxiety. Though he'd requested an indefinite leave of absence and that's what Trili would suspect, knowing him. That Evan had been upset by what happened, and what might have happened, on Botharis. They'd be patient, his friends. Even his superiors.

And be wrong.

Determination was what made his heart pound in his chest. What had his brain on fire until he couldn't sleep. The determination to know the truth, for how could he be with his friends, do his work, if he himself was a lie?

Evan Gooseberry pulled up his knees and balanced his notebook—a new one—on top. The journey to Great Gran would take two days and he'd use every minute to prepare. To think of every possible question.

He wrote . . . *What am I?*

Below that . . . *What really happened to my twin?*

Below that . . .

Evan paused, feeling the tug of another, equally imperative curiosity. He'd inquired about SeneShimlee before he left. According to Carwyn, who kept a list, there'd never been a ShimShree at the Library.

Where there were wardrobes, full of clothes for others who'd never been.

Evan flipped the page, staring at the blank white sheet.

Then wrote . . .

Esen, Esolesy Ki, Bess.

Out There

SPINS the orb does like a planet or moon. White, the orb is, with a black hole at its heart. A hole edged in striated gray, leading into *comprehension*.

Hangs the orb does suspended in space, surrounded by stars and nebulae.

Or is the orb held by thread?

Clings the orb does, to what it had been, to what it had been made for.

To see.

All the while, Veya Ragem wonders—

Why does her eye float beyond her reach?

Main Characters

Web-beings (in order of arrival in known space)
  Ersh
  Lesy
  Ansky
  Mixs
  Skalet
  Esen-alit-Quar, Esen in a hurry, Es between friends
  Death *Author's Note: Esen wishes you to know the stranger was named by those attacked. A Web-being not of Ersh's Web.*

The Trusted Few (who know of Esen, her abilities, and the Web)
  Author's Note: Don't blame me. Esen wants their loyalties made abundantly clear for you.
  Paul Antoni Ragem—Human; former First Contact Specialist, Survey, Esen's first and best friend; went by the alias Paul Cameron while pretending to be dead for fifty years to protect Esen's secret

Joel Largas—Human; owner of Largas Freight on Minas XII; father of Char Largas; grandfather to Paul's twins with her, Tomas and Luara Largas.

Lionel Kearn—Human; Paul's boss while in Survey, former First Contact Specialist; led the hunt for the so-called Esen Monster (Death) while Paul was pretending to be dead to—you know the rest. Now in Paul's Group and dedicated to protecting Esen's secret

Rudy Lefebvre—Botharan Human; Paul's cousin; former patrol; searched for the truth while Paul was pretending to be dead, etc., now captain of the *Largas Pride* and in the Group, etc.

Staff of the All Species' Library of Linguistics and Culture

(those named in this book, in order of responsibility)

Administrator: Lionel Kearn

Director: Paul Ragem

Curator/Head Gardener—Esen-alit-Quar (Esen as Lanivarian)

Assistant Curator/Gardener—Esolesy Ki (Esen as Lishcyn) *Author's Note: Esen hopes you've noticed this means she does twice the work. Oh. Now Paul points out she's only one of these at a time and leaves the conclusion to you. Also, the staff wish to add that while they adore Esolesy, she's more a big softie than boss.*

Assessment Counter—Henri Steves (Botharan)

Response Room—Ally Orman (Botharan)

The Anytime Chow Inc. Food Dispenser Operator—Lambo Reomattatii (Carasian)

Head Contractor/Maintenance Supervisor—Duggs Pouncey, Botharan who built the Library and remains on staff and in charge of maintenance/repair. *Author's Note: Esen's convinced Duggs stayed to make sure no one—especially Skalet—messes with her work. Paul agrees.*

Head of Security—Skalet (who remains in her Kraal form but doesn't use S'kal-ru on Botharis among non-Kraal). *Author's Note: Skalet is in no doubt that Duggs remained in order to make her life more difficult.*

Greeter/Coordinator of Intersystem Passage—Carwyn Sellkirk (Botharan)

Greeter—Quin Spivey (Botharan)

Greeter—Envall Ragem (Botharan)
Maintenance Personnel (exterior)—Correa Faster (Botharan)
Maintenance Personnel (night shift)—Zel Doctson (Botharan)
Maintenance Personnel (night shift)—Travis Doctson (Botharan)
Train Operator—Rhonda Bozak (Botharan); also maintains herd of
    Botharan Elk used to produce cheese for village
Train Operator—Goff Cameron
Train Operator—Kelly Kiser

Botharan Authorities

*Author's Note: Esen would like to point out that considering the
small population of the planet and their stubborn nature, Botharis has a well-functioning democratic system despite the way
each level of government ignores the others.*

Assistant to Special Envoy Mavis—Onlee Naston
Constable Malcolm (Mal) Lefebvre—was a Commonwealth patrol-
    ler; now retired to care for the Hamlet of Hillsview; Rudy's uncle
Preservation Committee Member, Hamlet of Hillsview—Art Firkser;
    author of historical romances; publisher of the *Hamlet Times*
Preservation Committee Member, Hamlet of Hillsview—Lenan
    Ragem; architect
Preservation Committee Member, Hamlet of Hillsview—Ruth
    Vaccaro; retired schoolteacher
Reeve Joncee Pershing—elected head of the Hamlet of Hillsview
    Council; also runs the post office and claims office; volunteer
    firefighter
Special Envoy Niala Mavis—currently assigned to negotiate with
    non-Botharans on behalf of the planetary government in Grandine;
    was once involved with Paul Ragem
Deputy Constable—Merri Higbee; normally mobile livestock
    medtech
Deputy Constable—Teri Terworth *Author's Note: Esen says to keep
    an eye on any relative of Jan Terworth, close or not. Now Paul
    adds: she's overreacting and Teri's a very nice person. To which
    Esen adds: Jan is not, and she'll stay cautious, thank you.*
Deputy Constable—Tuggles Cameron; Paul's cousin; raises scruffs
    (Botharan pet canid)

Paul's Family

(those mentioned in Web Shifter's Library series, in alphabetical order)

Char Largas—Paul's temp contract partner, mother of their twins, Tomas and Luara

Delly Ragem—Paul's grandmother on his mother's side, now a sofa in Sam's attic

Envall Ragem—distant cousin, works at Library

Jan Terworth—cousin

Kevin Ragem—cousin

Luara Largas—daughter of Paul Cameron and Char Largas, sister of Tomas

Rudy Lefebvre—cousin

Sam Ragem—Paul's uncle on his mother's side

Stefan Gahanni—Paul's contracted father; drive machinist; lives on Senigal III

Teri Terworth—distant cousin

Tomas Largas—son of Paul Cameron and Char Largas, brother of Luara

Tuggles Cameron; Paul's cousin; raises scruffs (Botharan pet canid)

Veya Ragem—Paul's mother, starship navigator: died on the *Smoke-bat* 18 years before Paul stopped pretending to be dead. *Author's Note: Esen reminds us Human relationships are complicated.*

People of Importance to Evan Gooseberry

(those mentioned in Web Shifter's Library series, in alphabetical order) *Author's Note: Evan adds those from his first adventure* with Paul and Bess as set out in the e-novella "The Only Thing To Fear".*

Bess*—Human; the "Esen" Evan meets and befriends on Urgia Prime *Author's Note: Esen wants to remind everyone this seemed an excellent choice of form when she picked it.*

Aka M'Lean—Human; Senior Political Officer, Commonwealth Embassy on Dokeci-Na and Evan's boss

Ekwueme-ki—Dokeci; Leader of the Mariota Valley Project on Dokeci-Na

Evan Gooseberry—Human; Political Officer, Commonwealth Embassy on Dokeci-Na; one of the few accredited Gooseberrys of his generation. *Author's Note: His Great Gran wishes everyone to know Evan is the most eligible and sweetest Gooseberry. Interested parties should get in touch with her directly.*

Gooseberry—the only Human surname with an unbroken legal line of descent from fabled Earth, as set out in The Gooseberry Lore.

Great Gran Gooseberry—Human; keeper of The Gooseberry Lore and responsible for assessing the legal status of claimants to being real Gooseberrys; raised Evan

Hymna Burtles—Human; manager for Burtles-Mautil Intersystems Holdings on the Mariota Valley Project on Dokeci-Na

Justin Gooseberry—Human; Evan's cousin, eldest son of his Aunt Melan

Lisam Horner—Human; security at the Commonwealth Embassy on Dokeci-Na; friend of Evan's

Lucius Whelan—Human; acquaintance of Great Gran; friend of Justin Gooseberry

Lynelle Owell—Human; security at the Commonwealth Embassy on Dokeci-Na; friend of Evan's

Melan Gooseberry—Human; Evan's aunt

Ne-sa Kamaara—Human; Commander of the security detail of the Survey Ship *Mistral*

Ny Wimmerly*—Human; Ambassador at the Commonwealth Embassy on Urgia Prime

Petara Clendon—Human; Captain of the Survey Ship *Mistral*

Petham Erilton—Human; Admin Staff at the Commonwealth Embassy on Dokeci-Na

Pink Popeakan*—Popeakan; nickname Humans give Prela on Urgia Prime

Pre-!~!-la Acci-!~!-ari*—Popeakan; also known as Prela or the Pink Popeakan; Evan encounters this individual on Urgia Prime

Prela—Popeakan; Esen's nickname for Pre-!~!-la Acci-!~!-ari; she and Evan encounter this individual on Urgia Prime

Sammy Litten—Human/Modified; xenopathologist at the Commonwealth Embassy on Dokeci-Na

Sedemny Gooseberry—recorded as having "died by carpet" in The Lore

Sendojii-ki—Dokeci; artist particularly famous in capital of Dokeci-Na

Simone Arygle Feen*—Human; Senior Political Officer at the Commonwealth Embassy on Urgia Prime; Evan's first boss

Snead—Human; Comm Officer on the Survey Ship *Mistral*

Stan Gooseberry—Evan's uncle; known for his cider

Teganersha-ki—Dokeci; historical figure: the infamous leader who united Dokeci-Na and established their moral system as well as plumbing; in reality: Ersh's name in this form. *Author's Note: Esen has her doubts Ersh would appreciate Evan carrying her image—a small bust—with him for inspiration, but she has yet to figure out how to tell him.*

Terry Koyak*—Human; Evan's coworker and friend at the Commonwealth Embassy on Urgia Prime

Trili Bersin—Human; Political Officer at the Commonwealth Embassy on Dokeci-Na; Evan's closest friend there.

Warford—Human; Senior Medtech on the Survey Ship *Mistral*

Wenn Gable Gooseberry—Evan's cousin; called a "Putrid Gripe" by Great Gran for tormenting Evan, when a child, about his phobias

Others Who Appear

Author's Note: Esen wishes several didn't, but admits every past has its trouble spots. Paul has moved the Kraal to their own category for clarity.

Acklan Seh—Sacrissee chimera; Emboldened

Aran—a name used in her story by Bess (Esen)

AULE-TB356994 (Aule)—Sacrissee; male who escapes Molancor Sacriss

Bob*—Human; alias Diale gives his Sweat Provider and colleague

Bunkabo Del—Anatae; scholar visiting the Library

Celiavliet Del—Anatae; who refused to leave the Library *Author's Note: Esen firmly intends not to let another being hide in her Garden. Firmly. Family doesn't count.*

Cureceo-ki—Dokeci; curator of the museum on Dokeci-Na about to host a show of Lesy's artwork

Diale—Hurn; security tech specialist from Minas XII; worked with Paul to set up the Library; has history with Cameron & Ki, Paul and Esolesy's company

Elfien—Vlovax

Janet Chase—Human; was captain of the *Vegas Lass* while Paul was pretending to be dead, but turned out to be a criminal; alias used by Victory Johnsson; murdered by Skalet

Jumpy Lyn—Ervickian; henchbeing of Chase; murdered by Skalet

Lance Largas—Human; crew on the *Largas Regal*

Lesley Delacora—Lesy's Human-self

Maston Sah—Sacrissee chimera; Emboldened

Myrtle Rice—Human; Soft Companion to Oieta Fem Splashlovely

Nesel Gabbert—Human; Senior Researcher Molancor Sacriss, a division of Molancor Genomics

OOLA-TB333401 (Oola)—Sacrissee; female who escapes Molancor Sacriss

Osmaku Del—Anata; "head of off-world inquiry" who led delegation to the Library

Palrander Todd—Human; henchbeing of Chase; murdered by Skalet

Pearl—Vlovax

Pearlesen—Esen's name as a Mareepavlovax

Rampo Tasceillato the Wise—Carasian; philosopher quoted by Lionel Kearn

Riosolesy-ki—"Dokeci"; Lesy's name in this form

Saxel Sah—Sacrissee chimera; Emboldened

SeneShimlee—"ShimShree"; Esen's name in this form

Ses-ki—"Dokeci"; Esen's name in this form

Sindy—a name used in her story by Bess (Esen)

Siokaletay-ki—"Dokeci"; Skalet's name in this form

Sly Nides—Human; henchbeing of Chase

Splashlovely—Oieta visiting the Library; Soft Companion Myrtle Rice

Tallo—Iedemad; Library client and entrepreneur

Thielex—Lexen; Library client and musical prodigy

Tory—Human; alias of Victory Johnsson

Vanekaelfien—Mareepavlovax

Victory Johnsson—Human; birthname of Janet Chase/Tory

The Kraal Confederacy

Cieter-ro—Kraal; Captain of the scout class ship *Septos Ank,* attached to the *Trium Pa*; affiliated with S'kal-ru

Dal-ru—Commander of spy outpost; House Bryll; from Skalet-memory of Battle for Arendi Prime

Haden-ru—Captain of the *Trium Pa*; House Arzul

House Arzul—affiliated with Bract

House Bract—Noble house and S'kal-ru's first real affiliation, via the Bryll Courier involved in Battle for Arendi Prime

House Bryll—Noble house; in Skalet-memory betrayed during Battle for Arendi Prime to House Bract by S'kal-ru and House Bryll's Courier

House Conell—lesser but ancient house, but one to which Cieter-ro and S'Kal-ru are both affiliated

House Noitci—affiliated with House Bryll and House Bract; once invaded Botharis

House Oalak—an ancient affiliate of House Virul

House Ordin—affiliate with House Bryll and thus House Bract and House Noitci

House Virul—as one of the Great Houses, claims responsibility for guiding the future of the confederacy

Maven-ro—Lieutenant at spy outpost; House Bryll; from Skalet-memory of Battle for Arendi Prime

N'Kar-ro—ancient Kraal philosopher

S'kal-ru—Skalet's name as a Kraal; highest rank: Courier *Author's note: Esen says there's no point listing affiliations as her web-kin's stuck her nose in the business of every House, including those now extinguished—and some of those were Skalet's fault.*

Shirt—Kraal in cave; House Arzul; Esen's name for her

Socks—Kraal in cave; House Arzul; Esen's name for her

Sous—Kraal noncombatants; by custom, safe from attack

Suecop-ro—comp officer on *Trium Pa*

Vest—Kraal in cave; House Arzul; Esen's name for him

Virul-ru—Courier for House Virul and the Inner Circle of Great Houses; sent to negotiate with Botharis

Ephemeral Species

Author's Note: Esen would like you to know this is far, far, far from a complete list. Her universe is a large and lively place. Also, that as a Web-being, she and her kind are not ephemeral, being semi-immortal and originally from space.

Acepan—species extinct before Humans arrived in this part of space, multi-legged and not fond of the cold.

Anata, Anatae—herbivorous species who have yet to live down mistaking performers dressed as edibles for edibles during a Festival of Funchess

Articans—inhabitants of Artos *Author's Note: appear Human but have significantly different biology*; xenophobic religious fanatics who view the boneless as sin; responsible for the death of Ansky

Botharan—a Human from Botharis. For example: Paul Ragem. *Author's Note: In Esen's opinion, the finest of his species. She admits to prejudice.*

Carasian—species with hard carapace/shell, claws, multiple eyes, and significant sexual dimorphism. For Example: Lambo

Cin—one of two communal species (see also Rands); in their case, varied cognitions are present in a roughly humanoid body.

Author's Note: Esen points out Ersh forbade taking this form, citing "one personality is enough."

Crougk—largest land-based sentient species, horse-like *Author's Note: While Paul disputes this, Esen remains convinced.*

D'Dsellan—insectoid; a Panacian from the homeworld, D'Dsel, or living there. Mixs' preferred form under the name Sec-ag Mixs C'Cklet.

Dokeci—species with five arms/three eyes; pendulous abdomen drags with age; Ansky's preferred form for cooking; Lesy's preferred form for art, as Riosolesy-ki. Esen as a Dokeci is called Ses-ki, being too young to be taken seriously.

Dwelley—species more amphibian than mammal; cheeks puff in polite conversation

Efue—species about which the Anatae come to the Library, there being confusion about certain substances and good taste

Elves—what the Dokeci call the aliens they find and transplant from the moon around S'Remmer Prime (see also Mareepavlovax)

Engullan—species with a cinnamon tang; bright yellow makes them wince

Ervickian—species with two brains, two mouths, and pliable morals; most are con artists or petty thieves

Feneden—species new to Esen until Ersh memory informed her this is a species Ersh preyed upon; locate themselves using polarized light

Ganthor—species vaguely like warthogs; tough, with a herd instinct; often mercenaries; need implants to use comspeak; otherwise use olfaction/physical gestures/clickspeech

Grigari—species known for their music; black-and-white stripes, 2 pairs of feet, 3 tails (one prehensile), long-fingered hands; mane collects sensory input; Ersh considered them "show-offs"

Heezle—species resembling pillars of ooze; no interspecies hang-ups; bats eye covers to assess interest in mating and inattention means "come hither"

Human—humanoid species, bipedal; wide variety of shapes and sizes; prone to curiosity. They are loosely organized with a Commonwealth, although at the far reaches a new Trade Pact is forming. For example: Paul Ragem. Esen as a Human is called Bess.

Hurn—species enamored of Human sweat, ring of lip-smacking mouths around the neck; For example: Diale, security expert on Minas XII.

Iberili—species that hibernate for 300 years at a time *Author's Note: Esen has no intention of wasting that much time asleep, even if Ersh found it restful.*

Iedemad—sluglike species that must wear osmo-suits to tolerate anything but a water-saturated environment

Iftsen—theta-class species, but live in such a chemically "rich" environment they use non-oxy facilities; known for "party" habit; several subspecies (See also Mobera)

Jarsh—extinct species with memorable voice; Esen sings to Paul to show him what the Web remembers

Jylnics—aquatic species; tentacles; move with reckless speed; one made advances on Paul

Karras—species that hunts by detecting electromagnetism and infrared (body heat); also known as Karras Slug *Author's Note: Esen would like some appreciation for her patience while in this form, as it stops to emote between every major action even when she's in a hurry.*

Ket—species, humanoid but extremely sensitive hands; work as masseuses and always have a hoobit. Esen as a Ket went by Nimal-Ket, the name on her acquired hoobit.

Kraal—Humans belonging to the Kraal Confederacy; strict hierarchy organized by affiliation to Houses; do not interbreed with non-Kraal Humans and may go extinct or become a subspecies. Skalet's preferred form, in which she is known as the Courier S'kal-ru.

Lanivarian—canid-like species known for its loathing of space travel; Esen's birth-form. As a Lanivarian, her name is Esen-alit-Quar.

Lexen—species who employ respiratory tubes in their music

Lishcyn—species with scales, five stomachs liable to react violently, and poor night vision; their homeworld is a Dokeci protectorate; as Paul's business partner and friend, Esen remained Lishcyn while he was pretending to be dead, under the name Esolesy Ki.

Lycorein—aquatic species resembling a very large otter

Machinii—species infamous for killing their own children in a failed attempt to modify them into what could survive a climate disaster; led to the Machin Protocol, an agreement not to impose genetic modification on a population without informed consent. *Author's Note: Esen says that despite Ersh's admonishment that "biology is all they have," she wishes ephemerals would take better care of the whole package.*

Mareepavlovax—species the Dokeci discovered and called Elves; also known in Web memory as Ancient Farers, Final Scourge, and Last Reapers (See also Vlovax.)

Mobera, Moberan—subspecies of Iftsen (there are several); frilled face

Modoran—species, feline, dirty (except under UV) white fur, aggressive and large, needs implant to speak

Nabreda, Nabredan—subspecies of Iftsen (there are several); protruding forehead

Nideron—species that inflates a nostril hood in disdain; aggressive toward weakness; 7-digit hands

Nimmeries—aquatic species; thrum when impatient; engaged in border dispute with Oietae

Octarian—species with multiple chins, pouch, auditory tentacles

Odarian—species with trunk (sputters in conversation by exhaling moist air) and elbow pouch

Oieta, Oietae—aquatic species; filter feeders (shrimp-esque); color changes with emotion; size of a Human. Esen's name as an Oieta is Esippet Darnelly Swashbuckly.

Ompu—species Ansky watched go extinct

Panacian—general name for insectoid species living in the Panacian system and elsewhere. (See also D'Dsellan.)

Petani—species; associated with ShimShree offworld as translators and transport

Popeakan—arachnoid species known to be reclusive and to work within groups: to interact with other species requires the Offer; twelve jointed limbs, 3 eyes. For example, Prela.

Poptians—species who deals in gems on Picco's Moon; gloved tentacles; green faceted eyes

Prumbins—species that grows larger with age; vertically pupiled eyes; not aquatic

Quebits—species that resemble little canister servos with extruded flower-like appendages; work as janitors/repair crew on starships; known for their intense focus on minutiae *Author's Note: Esen will not travel as a Quebit again. Unless she has to, and if so, she expects something to fix.*

Queeb—species with tentacles and six eyes, forked tongue

Rands—one of two communal species (see also Cin) who travel/live in clusters of less than 20

Refinne—massive aquatic species; lives in deep water and is blinded by light

Rrhysers—species that are standard tripeds, thump chest plates, broad nostrils, infamous for their temper and will let offspring play anywhere

Sacrissee—species deer-esque; evolved from solitary, shy herbivores; architecture is designed to provide peepholes and prevent interaction

Screed—species with knees at height of Human waist

Seitsiets—species who generate internal hydrogen while asleep, so need weights or will float away

ShimShree—species adapted to below freezing temperatures; build structures using spew; associated with Petani; Esen's name in the form is SeneShimlee

Skenkrans—spacefaring species with leathery wings (not skyfolk)

Skyfolk—non-spacefaring species with wings; gliders; doleful and solitary

Smoot—species who illegally homesteaded the waters under the south polar cap of Urgia Prime

Snoprian—humanoid species, similar to Humans except for their voices and vestigial feathers

Tly—Humans who live in system of the same name

Tumbler—crystalline species native to Picco's Moon; excretions considered rare gemstones; Ersh's preferred form and Tumblers called her Ershia the Immutable.

Urgian—species with no calcified skeleton, four arms; hosts of the Festival of Funchess *Author's Note: Esen experienced her first with Evan in "The Only Thing to Fear"*; known for poetry/dance

Vlovax—small creature that rises from the ground to complete a Mareepavlovax (see Elves); named Devil Dart by the Dokeci

Wz'ip—species like stone; graphite filaments and exterior vents; what Esen sometimes becomes to sulk *Author's Note: Esen points out she doesn't sulk. She mopes. Cutely.*

Ycl—amorphous coalition of cells; obligate predator of "living flesh," so their world has been declared off limits to anyone tasty

For more information, visit the *All Species' Library of Linguistics and Culture* on Botharis. A fact for the collection, delivered in person, will be required in exchange. Please refer to the Library's guidelines before planning your trip. Pamphlets are available on Hixtar Station.